Praise for **Miss Bugle Saw God In The Cabbages**

"Entertaining and witty – Enid Blyton for Bitches"
19

"A witty evocation of friendship, class and testing boundaries"
Times Educational Supplement

"Genuinely moving, offbeat, funny novel about two generations of women
from childhood to motherhood"
Scotland on Sunday

"A brilliant recreation of the social manners and class divisions
of the 1950s"
The Bookseller

"A gentle, compulsive read that'll make you feel glowy"
Minx

Sara Yeomans was born in Gloucester in 1943 and lived the first twenty years of her life in Gloucestershire. She graduated from Sussex University in 1964. She has taught English, worked as an A.S.M., scriptwriter, director and puppeteer. After the birth of her third daughter in 1982, she stayed at home to be a full-time mother and a freelance journalist. In 1989 she became assistant editor of Devon Life. She now teaches part-time at Exeter College and writes for the other part of the time, except when she is driving her youngest daughter to and from discos in outer Devon, sawing logs for the fire and hatching tortoise eggs in the airing cupboard.

Also by Sara Yeomans

Travels with a Pram and
Hot Flush and the Toy Boy
(The Women's Press, 1994.)

Miss Bugle Saw God in the Cabbages

Sara Yeomans

PIATKUS

First published in Great Britain in 1998 by
Judy Piatkus (Publishers) Ltd of
5 Windmill Street, London W1P 1HF

This edition published 1999

The moral right of the author has been asserted

A catalogue record for this book is available from the British Library

ISBN 0 7499 3078 0

Set in 11/12pt Times by
Action Typesetting Ltd, Gloucester

Printed & bound in Great Britain by
Mackays of Chatham PLC, Chatham, Kent

I would like to thank Dawn Perkins for her skill, patience and generosity in preparing this manuscript.

To my mother, with lots of love

Part One

Chapter One

'Heel-toe, heel-toe, gallop gallop gallop gallop; heel-toe, heel-toe, gallop gallop gallop gallop; right-hand star and new top couple, gallop gallop gallop gallop; left-hand star and new top couple, gallop gallop gallop gallop ...'

Miss Laetitia Willow, known (secretly) to 4A as 'Tit', bounced down the country-dancing lines of Tarminster High School for Girls and they bounced down behind her. 'Swing your partner, swing the next man, swing your partner, swing the lady ...'

Tall girls (men) swung small girls (ladies) by elbows and crossed hands and Miss Willow glanced at her watch. Seven minutes to the bell. She wound the dancers down and switched off the gramophone. 'Right, girls,' her voice echoed round the wall bars, 'you've just got time to shower.'

Groaning, 4A shed its gym knickers and Aertex shirts, wrapped towels round its heads and filed into the showers. Twenty-eight adolescent bodies shivered and squealed as the water squirted onto them.

'It's cold, Miss Willow,' someone complained.

'No running,' said Miss Willow, marking the Period Register off on her clipboard. 'Judith Littlewick, you had a period last week. And the week before. Get into the showers.'

'I'm already dressed,' muttered Judith Littlewick.

'Do as you're told.'

Slowly, pouting her best Bardot pout, Judith Littlewick began to strip. Her bust was round and pert and insolent and

3

the envy of 4A, whose bosoms ranged from pancake flat to drooping. She stared at Miss Willow and Miss Willow turned away, defeated, as the break bell rang. Raising a triumphant eyebrow, Judith dressed herself again and sauntered out of the gym. The rest of 4A stuffed damp towels around the tank of the musty towel room and formed a line.

'You may go,' said Miss Willow and they went, single-file along the left-hand side of the corridor, past the glittering eye of Miss Bugle, the Headmistress.

The rain, which had saved them from rounders and athletics and kept them in the Hall for Country Dancing, still beat against the classroom windows. Some girls perched on radiators, others stood in the space in front of the teacher's desk. Somebody started a beat and 4A's feet and hips and hands took up the rhythm, fingers snapping, feet tapping, hands slapping against thighs and elbows and doing the hitch-hike jive as Ann Dangerfield climbed onto the desk. Judith Littlewick slipped off a radiator and joined the dancers on the floor.

'One, two, three o'clock, four o'clock rock; five, six, seven o'clock, eight o'clock rock; nine, ten 'leven o'clock, twelve o'clock rock; We're gonna rock around the clock tonight ...'

Ann Dangerfield was singing from the desk, raging on an imaginary guitar while the other girls danced on the classroom floor, spinning, rocking, beating out the rhythm. All around them, the rest of 4A hand-jived and sang, 'We're gonna rock until the broad daylight ...' The bell rang. It was the end of break and time for R.I. with Miss Bugle.

Miss Bugle, an alarming spinster of uncertain years and an unpredictable sense of humour, was hot on Religious Instruction and Personal Hygiene. She laced her theological discourses with detailed instructions about washing thoroughly under the arms and round the corners every morning once one had reached the age of thirteen.

'Life,' said Miss Bugle, on this wet Wednesday morning, as she fixed 4A with her glittering stare, 'life is like a barrel of apples. You can have two hundred good apples in the barrel, but it only takes one bad one to turn the whole lot rotten.' She

4

paused dramatically and hitched up her left shoulder strap. No one dared to laugh.

'I first met God,' continued Miss Bugle with a sideways smile, 'in a row of cabbages when I was fourteen. The same age as you are now.' 4A held its breath. 'I know what you are thinking,' said Miss Bugle, spiking Judith Littlewick with her brilliant eye. Judith pouted and gazed at her Bible. 'You are thinking, "The poor old trout's finally flipped. Gone round the bend. Lost her marbles."' She grinned and hitched her shoulder strap again. 'But I say it again and I mean it. I first saw God in a row of cabbages when I was fourteen.' Judith Littlewick was writing something on a scrap of paper. 'I'm glad to see that you are taking notes, Judith,' said Miss Bugle, raising her right eyebrow quizzically. She paused long enough to frighten the note-writer, then turned to the blackboard and drew a row of improbable cabbages and a stick figure lying on its front with its nose pointed towards them. While her back was turned, Judith passed the note to Ann Dangerfield. It said; *I first met God when Clive Carpenter French-kissed me Down the Dance last week*. Ann giggled silently and stuffed the note into her pencil-case as Miss Bugle turned back to face the class.

'Those cabbages made me realise something,' she said. 'God isn't someone sitting on a cloud, wearing a long white nightie, looking down on you and me, marking us off in a register when we go to church, giving us gold stars for being good and black marks for being bad and counting them up when we die to see if we'll go to Heaven or Hell.' She stared at them in the silence; she had got them now. 'God,' she said 'is around us and within us, above us and below us, in everything that lives and has its being and is wonderful. Wonder full. Full of wonder. *Like cabbages*.'

The class was astonished. The silence went on and there was a sense that a bolt of lightning might be hurled at 4A at any minute. Then Susie Perkins put up her hand. 'Don't you believe in a real God then, Miss Bugle?' She asked the question quietly, in case He might be listening.

Miss Bugle pinned her to her seat with the brightness of her eye. 'Oh yes, I do!' she cried.

'I don't,' said Philippa Foster bravely and Miss Bugle

skipped with glee. 'I love it when we have an atheist in the class,' she squealed.

Jean Scrivener was shocked. 'But how can an atheist go to Heaven?' she asked.

'I don't know,' replied Miss Bugle to the dismay of 4A, who genuinely wanted an answer. 'There are things we can never know for sure while we are here, caught in this phase, this halfway house of our existence. All I am certain of is that I caught a glimpse of understanding when I saw those cabbages.'

But cabbages were not enough for the questing minds of 4A. Somebody had to know about life after death; somebody had to know what God looked like and how He operated; and if the Headmistress of Tarminster High School for Girls didn't know, what hope was there for anybody else?

The discussion caught fire. If there was a God, why did He let wars and earthquakes and murders and miscarriages and hare-lips happen? If there wasn't a God, what was the point of anything? If there wasn't a God, what happened to you after you died? If there was God, why had He invented death?

Miss Bugle grinned, eyes sparkling as she frolicked round the desks. 'I can't answer those questions,' she told them, and again they felt shock and disappointment and uncertainty. 'But I *do* believe in God.' The safety net was slung across the universe again. 'For a flicker of a moment, when I was fourteen, I understood. There is a magic in all living, growing things, a quiver and a spark, a gift of life no man or woman can create.' For a flicker of a moment, 4A thought it too understood, and then the bell rang and the moment passed.

'Before you pack up, girls,' Miss Bugle said, 'I want to remind you all of the importance of Personal Hygiene. You are all young women now. Your bodies are changing. It is perfectly natural for them to produce fluids and perspiration. It is, therefore, essential that you take the utmost care when you wash each morning. Good morning, 4A.'

4A rose to its feet. 'Good morning, Miss Bugle.'

With a final hoik of her left shoulder strap, Miss Bugle strode out of the classroom.

After school, before she caught the Swain's Chard bus back home, Ann Dangerfield went into Woolworths with Jenny Cornwood and Philippa Foster and bought a roll-on deodorant.

Chapter Two

Joan Dangerfield yawned, poured herself another cup of tea and took it back to bed. Eight o'clock. The Greenwich pips and the news. A Royal Birthday and the National Anthem. Joan sat up straight in bed and toasted the birthday Royal in tea. Then she propped herself back against the pillows and planned her morning. She must change the sheets and clear the breakfast things before Mrs Cornwood arrived to do the real housework of the week. Her husband's bedclothes lay untidily on the twin bed on the other side of the little table, sheets and blankets thrown carelessly back and his eiderdown tangled up with his pyjamas on the floor.

Joan sighed, drank another mouthful of tea and swirled the leaves round in the slops. Three times anti-clockwise and empty the slops into the saucer. A flight of tea leaves exploded like fireworks and when she looked out of the window, two magpies were balancing on the garden fence. *Two for joy*. Joan Dangerfield smiled, yawned again, then went to run her morning bath.

'Da-de-da-de-da-de-da-de-da-de-da-de-daaaaaa ... Well, I told you I'd be back again this morning, da-de-da-de-da-de-da-de-dadada,' sang Pete Murray to the signature tune of *Housewives' Choice* as Joan turned on the Light Programme and plunged her hands into the washing-up bowl. She gazed contentedly out of the kitchen window at the June flowers and the mown lawn and the five magpies wobbling on the poplar tree at the end of the garden. *Five for a letter*.

The postman was trudging up the lane that ran between the gardens. Joan heard the letter drop onto the hall floor and went to pick it up. Only a circular. Perhaps she should put up a notice like the one Lady Hennessey had on the Tradesmen's Entrance at the Manor: *No Hawkers, No Circulars*. It would look very grand, thought Joan, to have *No Hawkers, No Circulars* up on the wall beside her front door. But it might frighten away the tramp who came every spring and autumn and exchanged handwritten poems for bread and cheese and cups of tea with the housewives of Swain's Chard.

Humming along with *Younger Than Springtime*, she filled the kettle for another cup of tea but changed her mind when she saw Mrs Cornwood advancing up the lane. It would not be a good idea to start the morning with tea; they'd get nothing done that way. She would have to wait until eleven o'clock.

'We'll do the bedrooms and the bathroom first today, Mrs Cornwood,' said Mrs Dangerfield.

'Right you are,' said Phyllis, slipping off her cardigan and donning a flowery pinny. She always smelled of Lifebuoy soap and Gumption, thought Joan, who always smelled of Johnson's Baby Powder.

Up the stairs they went, armed with the Hoover Junior, a bucket, cloths, a broom and dusters.

'I'll get on with Annie's room,' said Phyllis, looking with disapproval at the half-open drawers and the bundle of dirty washing in one corner. 'I'd never let our Jenny leave her room in such a state,' she muttered, loudly enough to make sure that Joan could hear. Joan ignored her and switched on the Hoover Junior.

Hidden on top of Ann's wardrobe, Phyllis found the new roll-on deodorant from Woolworths. 'I say, she's growing up, isn't she?' Phyllis leapt out onto the landing and waved the roll-on at Joan. 'Deodorants and that. It'll be bras and high heels and mascara next.'

Joan went rigid. Any suggestion of the advance of womanhood in her younger daughter came as a personal threat to her; deodorants, like brassières, mascara and high heels, were things that Nice Girls were not interested in until they were at least sixteen.

'Funny,' said Phyllis innocently, examining the lilac-coloured bottle, 'our Jennifer's not at all interested in that sort of thing yet,' and she replaced the deodorant on top of the wardrobe.

Joan drove the Hoover angrily along the landing. 'There'll be plenty of time for that later,' she said whenever Ann broached the subject of a bra. So Ann had sneaked into the Lingerie Section of Woolworths after school one day when she was supposed to be at Choir Practice, and spent the week's dinner money on a 32A white lacy number which she kept in a brown paper bag in the bottom of her duffel bag.

Now Joan finished the landing and carried the Hoover downstairs in silence. She would deal with the deodorant when Ann came home from school.

'But everybody uses it,' said Ann. Her mother was holding the offending bottle between her forefinger and thumb and dangling it above the waste-paper basket.

'Who is everybody?' Joan asked.

'Everybody – Judith Littlewick, Susie Perkins, Jean Scrivener ... everybody. And Miss Bugle's always going on about washing under your arms and Personal Hygiene.'

'Going on?' repeated Joan. 'What sort of English is that? I'm quite sure that what Miss Bugle means is that you must wash yourself properly. If you wash yourself thoroughly and give yourself a dusting of talc, there is absolutely no need for this sort of thing. It's so ... *common.*'

With perfect timing, she dropped the lilac bottle into Ann's waste-paper basket and swept out of the room, leaving her daughter to consider what she had said. Ann narrowed her eyes, chewed on an imaginary piece of gum and practised looking common in the mirror. Honestly, she thought, anybody'd think she'd left a packet of French letters on top of the wardrobe. She wondered what a packet of French letters looked like.

Chapter Three

'That woman makes me wild,' said Phyllis Cornwood to her husband Arthur when he came home from his second delivery round.

Arthur smiled. 'What now?'

'Oh, she just thinks she's so grand and fine. Her daughters wouldn't even sweat, they're so posh.'

'Hang on,' said Arthur, 'you've lost me.'

So she told him about the deodorant on the wardrobe and how she had waved it under Joan's nose and Arthur laughed so much that Phyllis began to laugh too and then she had to go out of the house and up the hill to clear her head.

She climbed the hill above Swain's Chard as she did at least twice a week when the irritations of cleaning for the village threatened to disturb her peace. The woods rose above her and she climbed on until she had left them behind and came out onto the bare hillside where the gash of the old quarry bit into the landscape. She climbed on and on, following a steep white path up to the final pitch.

On top of the hill at last, she leaned against the wind and looked out over three counties. Hundreds of feet below her, on the plain, Tarminster Cathedral and the river shone in the afternoon sun and a great purple run of hills stretched from east to west fifty miles beyond it. The wind blew through Phyllis' brain and she turned her face towards it to let the sun and the space and the place soak into her.

Miss Cameron sailed into the classroom, an aura of mystery and literature about her. It was whispered in the school that she was a Woman with a Past, a woman who had once turned men's heads in the streets because of her extraordinary beauty; a woman who had known actors and artists, who had been wooed by Ambassadors and Heads of State. It was even rumoured in the Upper Sixth that she might be the illegitimate grand-daughter of somebody Thomas Hardy didn't marry.

'Open your Wordsworths and turn to page one hundred and twenty-three,' Miss Cameron began to read.

> 'The sounding cataract
> Haunted me like a passion: the tall rock,
> The mountain and the deep and gloomy wood,
> Their colours and their forms, were then to me
> an appetite ...'

Her dark contralto voice filled the room with falling waters, cliffs and massive trees, and the girls felt shivers run up and down their spines.

'And I have felt,' continued Miss Cameron conversationally, so that for a moment they thought she was speaking personally,

> 'A presence that disturbs me with the joy
> Of elevated thoughts; a sense sublime
> Of something far more deeply interfused,
> Whose dwelling is the light of setting suns,
> And the round ocean and the living air,
> And the blue sky and in the mind of man.'

She paused to let the words soak into them. On the hill above Swain's Chard and Tarminster, the living air and the blue sky soaked into Phyllis Cornwood.

'Wordsworth was a pantheist,' said Miss Cameron. Phyllis lifted her face again to the wind and the sun. 'Wordsworth saw God in every natural thing about him. He believed in the power and the necessity of natural beauty to impel and inspire the human spirit. Wisdom and Spirit of the Universe.'

'I see cabbages on the horizon,' somebody whispered and 4A began to laugh.

'Have I said anything amusing?' Miss Cameron enquired. They assured her that she had not and she continued. 'John

11

Keats – Romantic poet, like Wordsworth, and boxer, unlike Wordsworth – wrote: "Beauty is truth, truth beauty, – that is all Ye know on earth, and all ye need to know." Write it down, girls.' She repeated the lines and waited. 'Now think about it.' She gave them half a minute to think about it. 'The message is the same. It is beauty that feeds and sustains the human spirit. But Keats was writing that about a man-made beauty – an urn. A Grecian urn.'

'What's a Grecian urn?' whispered Susie Perkins to Jean Scrivener.

'Thirty bob a week,' said Miss Cameron, quick as a flash. '"Beauty is truth, truth beauty, that is all Ye know on earth, and all ye need to know." Remember it, girls. Remember it all your lives.'

'They are batty. Utterly loopy. All of them,' said Ann Dangerfield after the lesson.

'Sex-starved, poor old things,' said Judith Littlewick. 'All their fiancés got killed in the war and it sent them round the bend.' They giggled.

Philippa said, 'There's the Bugle seeing God in a cabbage, Cleopatra Cameron looking for Him in some old Greek pot and Tit Willow bouncing about in pursuit of the Dashing White Sergeant.' They collapsed in laughter again.

'Thank God we won't be spinsters,' said Judith. 'It must be awful, having to go out and earn your own living all your life ... I mean, I'm glad I'm not a man. I'd hate all that responsibility of finding a serious job and keeping a wife and family.'

Judith had worked out her Life Plan long ago. She would leave school after 'O' levels and go to Tarminster Tech to do shorthand and typing. She would then get a job as a secretary to a solicitor or a businessman who would fall madly in love with her, marry her and set her up for the rest of her life. In the meantime, she would rock 'n' roll.

Now she was taking two tiny clothes-pegs out of her blazer pocket and clipping them onto her lapel. 'Seven,' she said.

Ann looked at her in awe and did some quick mental arithmetic. 'Seven? Are you sure?'

'Last night,' said Judith smugly, 'after Youth Club. Clive Carpenter.'

Ann was shocked and impressed. The wearing of clothes-pegs on the blazer lapels was a secret code for the sexual steps the wearer had taken. One was a kiss, two was a French kiss, and so on up to ten, which meant you had Done It. Gone The Whole Way. The furthest that anyone else in 4A had gone was four.

The small bird-like figure of Miss Goodenough fluttered past them. She was Miss Bugle's sidekick and she taught Latin and a bit of R.I. She smiled nervously as she passed the girls. 'What pretty clothes-pegs, Judith,' she said, 'although I'm not sure that they are strictly uniform, you know.'

Without a quiver, Judith said, 'But they're there to remind me of the Seven Deadly Sins, Miss Goodenough.'

The teacher was enchanted. 'Ah, I see – of course. Each colour represents a different sin. What a clever idea, dear.'

And off she scampered, leaving Judith, Ann and Philippa hurting and breathless with laughter.

Chapter Four

Philippa Foster was large and square and pale and plain. When she was thirteen, her mother Madge had, in a desperate attempt to fluff her up a bit, given her a home perm over the kitchen sink. All that had happened was that Philippa's pale fawn hair had stuck out in surprised spikes around her pale fawn face.

The only remarkable things about Philippa Foster were her eyes, which were dark navy blue (like school knickers, she said), her sense of humour and her kindness, which was legendary. All her school reports focused on her kindness. *History: Philippa tries hard but has difficulty in memorising dates. She is always very kind. P.E.: Philippa tries hard but lacks co-ordination. She is kind. Music: Philippa tries hard but lacks natural musicality. She is a very kind person.*

'You've got to be kind,' said Philippa Foster to her reflection in the bathroom mirror, 'when you look like me and you lack co-ordination and musicality.'

But inside her large square body and behind her pale, plain face, Philippa knew that she was really somebody else. She was dark and wild and fiery and flamboyant with the spirit and soul of a gypsy. It was simply an unfortunate mistake that this spirit and soul had got put inside the wrong body so that only a bit of it could get out through the navy-blue eyes. Inside herself, Philippa knew that she was really Sophia Roncetti, a part-Italian, part-Red Indian dancer and film star who moved with grace and musicality and glorious co-ordination.

Madge Foster and Joan Dangerfield sat beneath adjacent hair-

14

dryers in Sharon's Salon. 'I see young Ann's beginning to develop,' shouted Madge above the roar of the dryers. She and Joan were best friends and deadly rivals on the Swain's Chard cocktail-party and amateur-dramatic circuits. Joan, swathed in a hairnet and clamped by curlers, pretended not to hear. 'Such a pretty girl,' continued Madge in a voice that implied, 'You'll have trouble with her.'

Sharon, shampooing a third head at the other end of her salon, smiled into the mirror. It was funny how her ladies never realised that every word they spoke above the hot storm noises of their dryers could be heard by everyone else. Unless, of course, everyone else too was inside one of the great silver helmets.

'It'll be boys before you know where you are,' teased Madge.

No fear of that with Philippa, thought Joan savagely, baring her teeth at Madge in the mirror. 'Nonsense,' she laughed airily, 'Ann's only a child.' She practised an expression in the mirror and then asked, 'Is Philippa still growing? She must be the biggest girl in the class now.'

Fifteen all, thought Sharon, and she went to switch them off and comb them out.

'I can't believe the summer holidays are nearly here,' sighed Joan, as pink and blotchy from the heat they left the salon and crossed the street for tea at the Chalet Suisse. They found a corner table. 'Six weeks of holidays and then back to "O" levels. Oh, by the way, how are Philippa's elocution lessons going? So good for her self-confidence and co-ordination.'

'Marvellous,' said Madge. 'Simply marvellous. Letty Willow thinks she's got a distinct talent.'

Distinct talent, thought Joan. The words echoed in her memory. People had said that about her once. She tilted her tea cup, drank until it was almost empty and then absentmindedly swilled the slops round the bottom of the cup three times.

Madge laughed. 'Go on – empty it, I dare you.'

Joan looked around. There was nobody else in the Chalet Suisse and so she tipped the cup upside down, emptying the slops into the saucer. There she was again, drawn in tea leaves – the dancer.

'What have you got?' enquired Madge.

'Nothing. Just a mess of tea leaves.'

The dancer was often there. She was Joan herself, of course. Joan Jackson as she had been then, aged sixteen, high-kicking her way down the stage in the second line of the chorus in the Tarminster Operatic and Dramatic Society's production of *Desert Song*, glittering with sequins, glorious with make-up and with the best legs in Tarminster.

'You were wonderful,' people had said to her afterwards. 'Absolutely wonderful. You've got distinct talent,' and she had kicked and tapped and glittered her way into a daydream of a career as a dancer. 'Don't be silly, dear, of course you don't want to be a chorus girl! Good gracious me, whatever next,' her family had said. Silly Joan, always so impractical, always such a dreamer. So they had sent her to Miss Fawcett's Secretarial College for Shorthand and Typing to knock some sense into her.

Then John had come along – dear, kind, reliable John with his rather small feet and his Ladies' Outfitters business inherited through three generations. And no, of course she did not want to be a dancer. What she wanted was to be married to a nice man like John Dangerfield and live in a nice house in Swain's Chard. And they were right. She had been happy. She *was* happy.

But sometimes, in the mornings, after John had gone to the shop, after she had had her bath and before she got dressed, if Pete Murray played the right tunes on *Housewives' Choice*, Joan would remember the steps and dance them again. Alone on the landing she would dance in her petticoat and the ridiculously, impossibly high-heeled shoes that she kept at the back of the wardrobe and would never wear outside. And if the music went on being right, she would high-kick her way down the stairs until the record ended and the postman shoved a bill through the letter-box. Then she would put the shoes away in the back of the wardrobe again and get dressed in her house-working clothes and wait for Mrs Cornwood to arrive so that they could get on with the serious business of vacuuming the house and cleaning the bath.

And at least twice a week, after they had finished cleaning and Mrs Cornwood had gone home, whatever the weather was doing, Joan would don a headscarf and her outdoor shoes and climb the hill above Swain's Chard. She would stand at the top for half an hour or more, looking across the river and the plain, feeling the wind and the rain and the sun on her face. She never wondered why she did it or realised that it was as necessary to her as eating and drinking and sleeping.

Chapter Five

Joan stood at the top of the hill and gazed back down the slopes towards the woods and Swain's Chard. Henry, the Dangerfield Labrador, lolloped about, chasing smells and pouncing on shadows. A girl on a pony appeared from behind the shoulder of a lower hill, followed by two more girls pushing bicycles. The rider pressed the pony into a canter and then a gallop, and Joan sighed as Jennifer Cornwood thundered towards her, easy and careless and bareback. The bike-pushers came closer and turned into Ann and Philippa.

'Don't talk so soft, our Jennifer,' Phyllis had said, wiping floury hands crossly down her apron as she stirred dumplings into the Friday stew. 'Buy a pony indeed. Our sort don't buy ponies. Leave that nonsense to the posh people.' I knew this would happen, she said to herself. I knew this would happen if she went to the High School. And then, the very thought that her daughter had passed the eleven-plus and won her way into the High School had softened her heart with pride, making her smile into the stew. But wanting to buy a pony ... ridiculous.

All through the 1A year, when they were eleven and twelve, Ann Dangerfield, Jenny Cornwood and Philippa Foster had daydreamed their dinner hours away with talk of ponies and hunting and gymkhanas, of snaffles and curbs, of saddles and girths, dandy brushes, curry combs, withers and fetlocks and hoofs. 'We could save up,' they said. They did, secretly, in biscuit tins under their beds, and they fed the dream on advertisements in the *Horses and Ponies For Sale* column of the Friday night *Tarminster Echo*.

'It mightn't be such a bad idea,' Joan had said to John one

Friday evening in the summer of the 3A year, after *The Archers* had ended with Christine sailing triumphantly over the final jump at the Borchester Show, da-de-diddley-dum-de-dum. 'Having a pony would give her something to get her teeth into.' John had looked startled. 'I don't mean literally,' Joan had said impatiently. 'I mean a hobby – an interest. Stop her thinking about Other Things.' John had looked puzzled. 'Boys,' muttered Joan. She dished up the Friday-night fish and played with the idea in her mind. It would be a bit like *The Archers*, she thought, having a pony in the family.

'She's got to learn the meaning of money,' Norman Foster had said to his wife. 'Philippa can't just say she wants a pony and expect it to fall into her lap. Ponies don't grow on trees, you know.'

None of the parents knew about the secret biscuit tins underneath the beds.

Joan and Madge discussed the idea over the telephone one Wednesday morning while Phyllis cleaned the windows. 'Norman says that if Philippa wants a pony, she'll have to earn the money for it.'

'That's exactly what John said,' lied Joan. 'They can't expect to get anything without working for it.'

Phyllis lugged the bucket of dirty water down the stairs, emptied it and filled it up again. She bristled with resentment as she lugged it back upstairs.

Norman called a meeting with Philippa one Saturday morning in the 3A summer. 'Your mother and I,' he announced, 'have decided that if you are prepared to work hard and save up for a pony and to take full responsibility for the ... er ... husbandry and well-being of the animal, we will support you in the venture.' He must be so good at Board meetings, thought Madge.

'What Daddy means,' she said, 'is that if you really want a pony, you'll have to save up for one.'

'That's all right, then,' said Philippa. 'We already have.'

She unearthed her biscuit tin of savings and biked with it to the Dangerfields'. Ann collected her own tin and they went to find Jenny. They sat in her bedroom and emptied the money all over the floor and counted it. 'Twenty-seven pounds, four shillings and eight pence,' said Ann. They scoured the *Horses and Ponies For Sale* column again: '*Bomb-proof Pony, outgrown; £40. Excellent First Pony: 11.2; £35. Skewbald Gelding: Aged; £32.*'

'We'll have to get an Aged,' Philippa said. 'If we wait till forty pounds, we'll be too old to ride it.'

They knew where they would keep the pony. Arthur's brother, Jenny's Uncle Walter, was cowman at Long Berrow Farm. They mounted their bikes and freewheeled down the lane to Long Berrow. The farmer was entirely understanding. 'How much pocket money do you get?' he asked. 'Half a crown a week each,' said Ann and Philippa. Jennifer did not reply. 'Five bob a week, then,' said the farmer. 'That'll do.'

They found Delilah in the *Horses and Ponies For Sale* column three Fridays later. '*Aged Mare; 13.2; Sound. No vices. £30 with tack.*'

Norman played golf with the Tarminster vet on Sundays. The vet went to look at Delilah and pronounced her aged, but sound in wind and limb.

Delilah was living in a field on the far side of Tarminster. Philippa, Ann and Jenny, armed with their biscuit tins, caught two buses and walked a mile to collect her. 'I tell you what I'll do,' the owner said, 'I'll let you have her for the twenty-seven pounds odd, but bridle only. No saddle.' They settled for it, took the reins and began the six-mile haul back home to Swain's Chard and Long Berrow.

They took it in turns to ride her bareback through the outskirts of Tarminster and up the hills until they reached the farm. No thoroughbred Derby winner had ever looked so beautiful to its owners. They stopped from time to time to let her crop the grass beside the roads; they dismounted when the hills got very steep, they breathed the dusty smell of her and talked to her and patted her and fed her sugar lumps. Delilah sneezed and swished her tail at flies and graciously accepted their devotions.

'She's not very ... pretty, is she?' Joan confided to John across the gap between their beds that night.

'Who?' mumbled John, who had almost been asleep.

All the same, thought Joan, she knew that she was right. Delilah would be something for Ann to get her teeth into, something to keep her away from Boys. And what was more,

20

she thought, and she smiled into the night, Delilah would move them up a notch in Swain's Chard. They would become part of the Horsey Set.

Jennifer, Ann and Philippa rode Delilah into the 4A year.

Jenny was far and away the best rider of the three. She rode like an Indian, fearless and easy, and with Jenny on her back, Delilah shed years. She galloped like the wind; she arched her neck and flared her nostrils and took low walls and fallen tree trunks in her stride. There was no doubt at all that Jenny was a talented rider. That was why Joan Dangerfield sighed when she saw the Cornwood girl galloping the old mare over the hill. Jenny could ride and Philippa had Distinct Talent in Elocution. But Ann? What was Ann going to be best at?

The same thought was going through Ann's own mind as she pushed her bike up the hill in Delilah's wake. Jenny was the best tree-climber and bareback rider; Philippa was the kindest and now had Distinct Talent in Elocution.

So where did that leave her? What could she be best at?

Chapter Six

'Have you talked to Ann yet about ... you know?' Madge lowered her voice as the waitress in the Chalet Suisse brought their coffee and tea.

'I always think these things are best left to Nature,' said Joan airily. The waitress retreated to the cake trolley.

Madge was aghast. 'What on earth do you mean?'

'Well, after all, we do live in the country, for goodness' sake. They can see it happening all around them.'

Madge looked her old friend squarely in the eye. 'Have you ever seen it happen? Honestly? I mean, in all the years you've lived here, have you ever seen a cow or a sheep, or even a chicken ... you know?'

'Don't be revolting, Madge,' said Joan.

'But what do people actually *do*?' asked Philippa on the bus coming home from school after the last-lesson-on-Wednesday Double Biology. They had been doing Reproduction, which involved a lot of pictures on the board of wombs and ovaries and Fallopian tubes, all carefully labelled and under siege from a swarm of tadpoles. Jenny and Ann explained as best they could from their very limited and inaccurate knowledge gleaned from brothers and a sister and from their very unlimited imaginations. 'Yuk,' said Philippa.

'Don't let that dog out,' warned Phyllis sharply. 'She's just come on heat again.' Jenny tried to grab at Finch but she slipped past her and out through the open gate. 'There! What did I tell you? And you've gone and left the gate open.'

22

Phyllis was furious and Jenny dumped her duffel bag on the kitchen floor and ran out in pursuit of Finch, who was heading up through the main street towards the lane that led to the Dangerfields' house. Arthur, who had been reading the early edition of the *Tarminster Echo*, fled from his wife's wrath and followed Jenny.

Ann and Philippa were sitting in the Dangerfield garden trying to work out their Maths homework, John was weeding a flower bed (it was early-closing day in Tarminster) and Joan was making tea in the kitchen. Henry, the Dangerfield Labrador, stood up and wagged his tail. He barked sharply and twitched his nose.

'What on earth's the matter with you?' asked Ann crossly. 'Shut up, you stupid dog, I almost understood this equation.'

Henry was whining and trembling. Finch shot into view, heading for him, straight as Cupid's arrow. With a squeal of lust, Henry, who was hardly more than a puppy, as Joan said later in anguished disapproval, hurtled down the garden and launched himself at the bitch. Joan froze in mid-butter-spread and stared in horror at what, as she said to John later, could only be described as *flagrante delicto*.

At that moment, Jenny appeared at the bottom of the garden, closely followed by a red-faced Arthur. For a full minute, everyone (except Finch and Henry) was paralysed. Then: 'Do something, John,' gasped Joan. John seized his weeding bucket, emptied the weeds out and filled it with cold water. He advanced upon the oblivious dogs and hurled the cold water over them. Yelping and squealing with shock and pain, they separated.

'Well,' said Philippa. 'If that's sex, they can keep it.'

23

Chapter Seven

Madge Foster twisted herself round in the long mirror and bent over backwards to straighten her stocking seams. She crossed the bedroom and perched on the stool in front of her hinged-wing dressing-table mirror. Carefully, she examined her profiles, smoothing base foundation over her jawbone and into her neck, powdering her nose and cheeks lightly. She plucked out a stray eyebrow and smiled her Titania smile.

Titania. She wanted the part very badly indeed. She practised feeling seductive and selfish and petulant and powerful so that when Norman called up the stairs that he was ready to drive her to the Manor for Lady Hennessey's auditions, she rather shocked him by answering in Titania's most alluring voice.

'What did you say, old girl?' Norman's large, solemn face appeared around the bedroom door.

'Out of this wood do not desire to go, Thou shalt remain here, whether thou wilt or no,' breathed Madge-Titania, smiling enigmatically at him in the mirror. Norman blushed. Even after all these years, he still could not quite cope with what he had come to think of as 'the wild streak' in his wife and the response it still called up in him. 'And I do love thee, How I dote on thee,' sighed Titania-Madge, wafting past him onto the landing.

'Jolly good,' said Norman.

''Bye, Mum,' said Philippa, who was doing her History homework and listening to *The Archers* at the same time. 'Good luck.'

Philippa waited for the sound of the Sunbeam Talbot to back

24

out of the drive, change gear and move off down the hill towards the village and the Manor, then she telephoned Ann. 'Has yours left?'

'Yes,' said Ann.

'Mine's gone all Faery Queen,' said Philippa.

'Gor blimey,' said Ann, in a voice she would not have used if Joan had been there, 'so's mine.'

'Could be tricky,' Philippa said and then they forgot about the dangers of *A Midsummer Night's Dream* in the much more immediate excitement of Judith Littlewick's eighth clothes-peg.

Norman dropped Madge off at the Manor front door and turned the car round in the wide carriage-sweep just as John drove up with Joan. 'Good luck,' said both the husbands to their Titanias and then John followed Norman to the Golf Club.

The Swain's Chard Amateur Dramatic Society sat in a large and expectant circle in the Manor House dining room. It was late April and Lady Hennessey had put a notice in the March edition of the Parish Magazine. '*Anybody interested in taking part in a Midsummer Production of* The Dream *by W. Shakespeare is invited to a preliminary reading and audition on April 24th at half-past seven in the Manor House.*'

Lady Hennessey smiled round the circle. Same old problem, she thought. Too many women, not enough men. She explained her plan. 'It will be an open-air production,' she told her guests. 'I shall stage it where the formal garden meets the shrubbery and the Ha-Ha, with the Long Meadow in the background.'

The Swain's Chard Amateur Dramatic Society grew flushed and warm with excitement. Copies of the play were handed round and parts were allotted for the first reading.

'Mrs Dangerfield, perhaps you would take Helena to begin with? And Mrs Foster, will you read Hermia, please?'

And so it went on. Parts were read and swapped and read and swapped again. Lady Hennessey made notes and smiled and corrected pronunciations, and coffee and biscuits were brought in at half-past eight. At nine o'clock, parts were read and swapped again and at ten o'clock, Lady Hennessey thanked them all and bade them good night. Husbands were waiting in the Manor drive. 'How did it go?' they asked. Nobody knew.

The next day, Lady Hennessey telephoned Joan Dangerfield and offered her the part of Helena. Then she telephoned Madge Foster and offered her the part of Titania. Then Madge telephoned Joan and Joan congratulated her through gritted teeth. 'She says she needs a Puck,' said Madge. 'She wondered whether Philippa would do it.'

Joan was speechless. Philippa Foster, nice child though she was, and even possessing Distinct Talent as she might do, could not, by the stretch of anybody's imagination, be thought of as a possible Puck. But Joan was reckoning without Sophia Roncetti.

The first rehearsal took place ten days later in the Manor dining room. Oberon and Bottom had always been foregone conclusions; they were respectively Tom Matthews, a tweedy, pipe-smoking, elegant bachelor who taught at a nearby prep school and Mike Williams, the Drama and Society report on the *Tarminster Echo*, who always took the comic leads. Miss Willow was to play Hippolyta, Lord Hennessey, Theseus and little Mr Whittaker (who gave private violin lessons to Tarminster High School girls on Wednesdays and Thursdays) had been persuaded by Tit Willow to be Flute.

'So I'm short of Fairies, Rude Mechanicals, Lysander and Demetrius and the Changeling Child,' Lady Hennessey said to her Lord over breakfast the next morning. She mounted her bike and set off for the village.

Arthur Cornwood had finished his first round of the day and had nipped home for a quick cup of tea before going back to sort the second post. He had spread out the *Daily Mirror* on the kitchen table and was dunking biscuits peacefully when Lady Hennessey appeared in his front garden. Arthur hid the *Mirror* and swallowed a piece of soggy biscuit hurriedly.

'Good morning, Mr Cornwood,' cried Lady Hennessey breezily. 'I'm so sorry to disturb you, but I wonder if I might have a quick word?' Ten minutes later, Arthur had agreed to be Snout. He was about to usher Lady Hennessey out of the kitchen when her attention was caught by a new school photograph of Jimmy propped up on a shelf. 'Is that your son, Mr Cornwood?' Arthur agreed that it was. 'Is it a recent photograph?' It was. Lady Hennessey had her Changeling Child.

On her way to the Dangerfields, Lady Hennessey remembered that the Cornwoods had a daughter as well. Pretty little thing, she seemed to remember. One Fairy down, three to go.

'Of course you want to be in it,' said Joan crossly to Ann over high tea. 'It was very good of Lady Hennessey to cycle all the way over here to invite you to be Cobweb. You should be flattered that she's asked you.'

'Well I never,' said Phyllis, stooping to pick something up off the front-door mat. 'There's a note here from Lady Hennessey asking if you two'll be in her play.'

'Flippin' 'eck,' said Jimmy. 'I won't All the other kids'll laugh at me.' But he had reckoned without Lady Hennessey.

They rehearsed on Friday evenings. On the third Friday, they reached the scene where the Puck boasts of his exploits to the Fairy.

Joan sat back and waited to be embarrassed by Philippa's large and clumsy elf. But something was happening to Philippa Foster. Her square body was changing shape, becoming taut and angular; the pale face was focusing with wicked concentration and something hypnotic shone out of the navy-blue eyes. She crouched in the middle of the floor and spun her magic.

> 'The wisest aunt, telling the saddest tale
> Sometime for three-foot stool mistaketh me,
> Then slip I from her ...'

Puck stopped and blushed and turned back into Philippa Foster. 'What's the matter, dear?' Lady Hennessey frowned, tapping her script impatiently with her pencil. Snorts of laughter were escaping from Peaseblossom and Cobweb. 'Come along, Philippa. Please continue.' Philippa took a huge breath.

> 'Then slip I from her bum, down topples she.'

All the Fairies were scarlet with laughter and embarrassment, and so was Tit Willow. How could Lady Hennessey have known that the version she always taught her Elocution pupils, the version the girls always read at the High School, had had the offending word cut out of it?

27

'Don't be silly, Philippa,' said Lady Hennessey briskly. 'The word is BUM. Now, everybody, can we all please get over this childish giggling once and for all. Let's face it head on and say it all together, loud and clear. Come along – everybody: BUM, BUM, BUM.'

'BUM BUM BUM BUM BUM,' chanted everybody obediently.

'That's better,' said Lady Hennessey at last. 'I don't think we shall have any more trouble from it now.'

'Whatever was all that nonsense about?' Madge asked Philippa crossly after the rehearsal. 'Fancy being embarrassed over a little word like ... that.'

'It isn't in the version Tit Willow gave me to learn,' explained Philippa.

Madge was outraged. '*What?*' she demanded, blushing hot red. 'What a dreadful thing to call Miss Willow, Philippa.'

Chapter Eight

'I just don't understand her,' said Philippa. 'It's quite all right for Lady Hennessey to say BUM, but she goes up in smoke if I say tit.' A thought struck her. 'I've just realised that *Midsummer Night's Dream*'s nothing but a tit and bum show, Get it?'

'No,' said Ann and Jenny.

Philippa looked at them wearily. 'TITania and Bottom,' she said patiently.

They were riding Delilah and pushing their bikes through the wood on the Saturday after the BUM rehearsal. They had packed sandwiches and Penguins and Schweppes' bottles in their duffel bags to ride off for the day, away from school and Shakespeare and the mothers. But Shakespeare and the mothers seemed to be coming with them.

Jenny and Delilah trotted on ahead along the leaf-mould track and Ann and Philippa pushed the bikes along behind them in silence, until Ann said unexpectedly, 'It's funny watching your mother pretending to be somebody else, isn't it?'

Philippa was puzzled. 'What d'you mean?'

Ann was embarrassed. 'Oh, I dunno. With mine, I sort of get used to her being just my mother and getting cross if I call her Our Mum and fussing about how you eat and how you speak and mind-what-people-think and don't-say-that-it-might-sound-common and don't walk-like-that-it-gives-the-wrong-impression and then she turns into a lovelorn drip like Helena and I don't know which is the real her.'

Philippa roared with laughter. 'I'm used to it with mine. She puts on different people all the time. It doesn't mean anything – it's just like putting on a different dress. But don't you worry. Underneath, there's the real one, the one who wears sensible underwear and who doesn't like boys and deodorants or anything common or sexy. That's our mothers. They only *pretend* to be Helena or Titania. They only said BUM because Lady Hennessey said it first so it's got to be all right because she's an aristocrat. But underneath, they were shocked to their vests.'

A hundred yards ahead of them, Jenny was persuading Delilah into a canter. 'She's a really good rider, isn't she?' Philippa said wistfully. 'I wish I could ride like that.'

'But you're good at acting. Everybody's saying you've got Distinct Talent. It's weird. You just stop being you and you turn into Puck.'

'Only for a bit,' said Philippa, but she blushed and Ann could tell how pleased she was. Philippa (who was always very kind) hunted for something complimentary to say in return. 'You're the sexiest one of us, though.'

Ann let the words seep into her and felt them soak through her. 'What,' she said at last, 'sexier than Judith Littlewick?'

'Well, no,' said Philippa. 'But *as* sexy. In a different way. Not so ... obvious.' She thought again. 'Subtler. And you can do things Judith Littlewick can't.'

'Such as?' asked Ann.

'Well, you're in the Choir.'

It was true, thought Ann. She was a second soprano who could sing the top line and read the alto in an emergency. Judith Littlewick had failed the audition. You're the sexiest, Philippa had said. Perhaps that was it. Perhaps being sexy was her talent. She must work on it.

Jenny circled the old pony and cantered back along the track towards them. 'Your turn,' she said to Ann as she slid off Delilah's back and swapped the reins for bicycle handlebars. Ann led Delilah to a tree stump and clambered aboard, using the stump as a mounting block.

'Finch is having pups again,' said Jenny, trying to balance on the bike without moving. 'You can always tell. She's getting fatter and her eyes have gone dreamy.'

'They must be Henry's,' said Ann proudly.

'I suppose that'll make you sort of Dogs-in-Law,' said Philippa, riding her bike like a scooter over a rough bit of track. They laughed so much that Ann nearly fell off Delilah. She hauled herself upright again and kicked the old mare into a trot.

They came out of the woods onto the low slope of the hill. They climbed, pushing the bikes, for half a mile and then took the track that led below the main peak because it was flatter and easier for Delilah. They wheeled and trotted for another mile through quaker grass and wild scabious until they came to a small coppice where Delilah's hoofs crushed garlic and the smell swam up and filled their heads. Beyond the coppice they reached a narrow lane that plunged down to a brook and up again to open commonland, and then they came to the place they had been heading for – a gently sloping patch of turf and shingle where the brook widened into a clear and shallow pool.

They dismounted. The bikes lay on the ground and Delilah wandered amiably, free of her bridle and bit, cropping the grass and plunging her nose into the pool to drink. The girls unpacked their sandwiches and Penguins and swigged from the bottles. They lay on their backs, swiping at gnats and watching the sun reflected from the kingcups and marsh marigolds. Inside her head, each girl was thinking, but did not say aloud, This is enough. This is all I want. Then something else, some slight restlessness stirred in their minds. Was there more to know? Were there other ways of life to live? Would this be enough to see them through their lifetimes?

They sat up, took off their plimsolls and rolled up their jeans. Then they stepped into the ice-cold water, squealing with the pain of it and surprising the dragonflies that hovered above the marsh marigolds. Yes. It was enough.

Chapter Nine

They were three weeks into rehearsals and Lady Hennessey still lacked Lysander and Demetrius.

'Well, I'll ask him, of course,' said Madge doubtfully, 'but acting's never really been his forte. And he's awfully busy at work.'

'I'll leave it with you, my dear,' said Lady Hennessey and she remounted her bicycle and whizzed through the early evening to the Dangerfields'. John was just putting the car away.

'Ah, Mr Dangerfield, how fortunate.' Somehow, he never quite understood how, John found that he was to play the part of Lysander.

'Lady Hennessey wants you to be in the play, darling.' Madge looked up at Norman pleadingly, her vivid blue eyes gazing into his pale ones.

Norman turned a little pink. 'I'm awfully busy at work, you know.' But Madge could tell that he was flattered.

'She wants you to be Demetrius, darling. He's a dashing young nobleman. A girl called Helena's absolutely potty about him.'

Norman preened a little. 'I'll think about it.'

That evening, when he thought she was downstairs, Madge saw him examining his profile in the dressing-table mirror. He was holding a copy of *A Midsummer Night's Dream* and reading one of Demetrius' speeches. Dear Norman, he'd do anything for her. She tiptoed away.

*

Madge Foster had been right, thought Lady Hennessey. Acting was indeed not Norman's forte. He was wooden and stiff and pompous and he spoke all his lines as if he were addressing a Board meeting. Nevertheless, he was a *man* and Lady Hennessey could not afford to let him go.

'I love thee not, therefore pursue me not,' he said sternly to Helena. It sounded, thought Joan wearily, as if he were reading the minutes of a meeting. And it made it quite impossible for her to get fired up with passion for him.

No, thought Lady Hennessey in bed that night; no, he could not possibly be Demetrius. Then she had a brainwave. Norman would have to swap with Arthur Cornwood, the postman. Norman's impenetrability would be perfect for the Wall, and Arthur Cornwood would make a handsome (if slightly balding) Demetrius.

She telephoned Norman the next day. 'I think, Mr Foster – may I call you Norman? – I think that you have a distinct talent for comedy which would be wasted on Demetrius. Would you mind dreadfully taking on the part of Snout instead? It's a cameo of a comedy part and I know you'd be marvellous.' Mr Foster – yes, she might call him Norman – was entranced.

Lady Hennessey lay in wait for Arthur and the second post.

As so it was, at the fourth rehearsal, that Joan found herself pleading with Arthur Cornwood to love and pity her.

'Do I entice you?' demanded Arthur. 'Do I speak you fair?' Joan sank to her knees and clutched at his. He turned away from her but she clung on. 'I do not, nor I cannot love you,' insisted Arthur, trying to tear himself free of her.

But Joan followed him, shuffling on her knees across the grass. 'And even for that do I love you the more,' she wept. 'I am your spaniel.'

Phyllis chuckled gleefully. Serves you right, you hoity-toity madam. Serves you right. Go on Arthur, make her crawl. She had it coming to her.

It was the Saturday before Midsummer's Day and the first performance of the play. The playgoers of Swain's Chard sat on grassy banks and chewed on blades of grass as they watched the preparations for the wedding of Hippolyta and Theseus and listened to Demetrius rejecting Helena.

'Use me but as your spaniel,' begged Joan, 'spurn me, strike me.' Go on Arthur, spurn her, urged Phyllis under her breath.

'Tempt not too much the hatred of my spirit,' warned Arthur. Whoever would have thought he'd be so masterful, wondered Phyllis.

At last they left the clearing and Puck arrived. Philippa had survived the BUM speech without mishap and had now settled happily into the part. Soon she would squeeze the magic flower juice onto the wrong eyelids and thoroughly confuse most of the characters as well as most of the audience.

In rollicked the Rude Mechanicals, Quince, Snug, Bottom, little Mr Whittaker as Flute and Norman as Snout. He delivered all his lines at a measured pace with a faultless public-school accent. Philippa put the ass' head on Bottom, Titania woke up and the fun began.

'Out of this wood do not desire to go,' whispered Titania Foster to Bottom in tones so dripping with desire that Philippa felt quite embarrassed by her mother.

But everything turned out all right in the end. Demetrius/Arthur fell madly in love with Helena/Joan under the influence of the magic juice. Exhausted by love, he lay down and went to sleep.

He lay exactly on the spot where years and years ago, a seventeen-year-old Phyllis had fallen off the handlebars of his bike on a bee-filled afternoon in early June and had stayed there, waiting for him to join her. Something about the sight of him lying there now in the late afternoon sunlight, made sharp tears prickle at the back of Phyllis' eyes.

Chapter Ten

Finch was lick, lick, licking. Her eyes were wide and pleading as she looked at Jenny and followed her around the house and yard. It was the first day of the summer holidays and Phyllis was out cleaning and Arthur had gone back to the sorting office for his second round. Someone knocked on the back door and Jenny opened it to Ann and Philippa. Philippa was holding Delilah's bridle. 'Are you coming for a ride?'

'Can't,' said Jenny. 'Finch is going into labour and she always has to have one of us here.'

Ann's eyes widened. 'What do you have to do?'

'Oh, I don't do anything. She's very good at it – this is her third litter. But she hates being left on her own while it's happening. She just needs to know I'm there.' Finch lay down in a shady corner of the yard, watching them, her ears pricked even while she licked.

'I've put a pile of newspapers and an old blanket in the shed,' went on Jenny. 'She'll go in when she's ready. We'll just leave the back door open so's she can see us. D'you want some orange?' She put three beakers on the table and snapped open a Schweppes bottle.

'Look,' whispered Philippa. A dark, rubbery ball was appearing out of Finch.

'Is that a pup?' Ann was aghast.

'No,' said Jenny. 'It's the water bag.' Finch licked furiously and the bag burst; water leaked out of it as she got up and made for the blanket and papers in the shed.

'Can we go and watch?' asked Philippa.

'Best not, it'll fuss her. Just keep talking and staying in her

35

view. It won't be long now.' They pulled their chairs near to the back door so that they could see across the yard into the dimness of the shed. 'There's the first one, see?' said Jenny as a small, hideous, flat-headed thing wriggled out onto the newspapers.

'What about the cord? Shouldn't we cut it?' asked Ann, remembering their Biology lessons.

'No need,' said Jenny. 'She bites 'em. Something in her spit seals them off. There she goes.'

Finch nipped expertly and nuzzled the flat-headed thing until it attached itself to her. Three more puppies followed quickly, their cords were severed and Finch lay contentedly on her side, panting a little while the puppies snuffled and nuzzled and sucked.

'Looks like an old sow with piglets, doesn't she?' said Jenny. 'I think that's the lot. I'm glad of that – Our Dad'd have to drown 'em if there'd been any more.'

Philippa and Ann were appalled. 'That's terrible!' they said.

'No, it's not.' Jenny was defensive. 'Finch couldn't have fed more than four and they'd all have died. Our Dad hates doing it; he always sends us away while he does it. But he says it's the only thing to do.' She blushed, sensing they were not convinced. 'I crept back to watch once. I think he was crying.'

They were silent for a moment, thinking of the awfulness of seeing one's father crying. Jenny felt disloyal to Arthur and wished she hadn't told them. But she didn't want them thinking her dad was a cruel man.

'Can we go and look now?' asked Philippa.

'Better not yet,' said Jenny again. 'Let her settle in with them. If she smells us on them, she might turn against them. D'you want a Jaffa cake?' They went back to the kitchen table and topped up the orange squash.

'D'you want to have a baby?' Ann asked suddenly. They ate the Jaffa cakes in silence, pondering it.

'The only thing is,' said Jenny, 'you'd have to do That with somebody first, wouldn't you?'

Later they went out into the yard. Finch lay there, tired and calm and proud while the blind, bald, flat-headed, big-mouthed babies suckled noisily. 'Ugly, aren't they?' said Jenny, laughing.

'I think they're beautiful,' said Ann. 'Wait till I tell Henry.'

'We'd better drink a toast,' said Philippa, 'to you two being Dogs-in-Law.' They drank the rest of the orange. 'It's a pity I'm an atheist,' she went ont, 'otherwise I could have been their Godmother. Or Dogmother,' she added thoughtfully.

Chapter Eleven

Summer Holidays, 1958

Judith Littlewick and Ann Dangerfield were hunting boys. At least, Judith Littlewick was hunting. Ann was not quite sure what she was doing.

She had been alarmed when Judith had asked for her phone number on the last day of the summer term and had promised to ring up and invite herself over to Swain's Chard for the day. Judith was everything that would appal her mother, Ann knew, with her bust and her clothes-pegs and her high-heeled shoes. But she was flattered that the most experienced girl in 4A should want to spend time with her in the summer holidays.

When the phone rang on the third day of the holidays and Ann heard a threepenny-bit clonk down and Judith say, 'I'm coming up tomorrow,' her heart sank.

'I'll have to ask Our Mum.'

'Our Mum?' Joan mimicked, appearing in the hall.

Ann covered the mouthpiece with her hand. 'It's a friend of mine from school. Is it all right if she comes here for the day tomorrow?'

Joan frowned and raised her eyebrows at the same time. 'Is she Nice?' Ann knew exactly what her mother meant and thought fearfully about the clothes-pegs. But then Joan smiled. After all, it was better for Ann to bring her friends to the house than to have her wandering Goodness Knows Where with Goodness Knows Who. 'Yes, that'll be all right.'

'Yes, that'll be all right,' Ann said down the phone.

Another coin clonked. 'I'll be at Swain's Chard by half-past ten tomorrow. Meet me at the main bus-stop.'

At twenty past ten, Ann was sitting on the churchyard wall by the bus shelter, hoping that Judith Littlewick had missed the bus and wishing that today was not happening. It was far simpler to keep her home personality and her school personality quite separate, to speak with the local accent at school and like the Queen and God in Swain's Chard; to be a child who went for walks and picnics at home but who was a rock 'n' rolling juke-box jiver in 4A. Any minute now, the two halves of her life were going to meet under the disapproving eye of her mother, and she was not looking forward to it.

The bus drew up and Judith got out of it. She had dressed herself with psychic insight into what would be acceptable in Swain's Chard. She looked like Doris Day's little sister in turned-up jeans, blue Aertex shirt and a hand-knitted pullover. Her face was free of make-up, her shoes were flat and her bust was almost imperceptible.

They walked up the street and into the lane that led to the private tree-lined road where the Dangerfields lived. 'Blimey, posh,' said Judith. Ann felt ashamed and wished that she lived in a council house.

Judith was absolutely up to Joan. She sounded her aitches and added her ings. She admired the view and the furniture and the books, and was charmingly grateful to Joan for the picnic she'd made up for them. 'Off you go, girls. Have a lovely time.'

At the end of the private road, the lane turned left to the hill or right to the village. 'This way,' said Ann.

'Whatever for?' said Judith. 'There's only countryside up there. Let's go back down to the village.'

They sat in the bus shelter eating their sandwiches and smoking the Woodbines that Judith had brought. Three boys on bikes circled the shelter slowly. Judith pretended not to notice. Then the tallest one rode into the shelter. 'Got a light?'

'Might have,' said Judith. She handed him a box of matches. 'Damn,' she said, 'mine's gone out. Give us a light then.'

The boy lit her cigarette. 'Fancy a walk?' he said, and then Ann found herself trailing awkwardly up the street in the wake of Judith and the Woodbine while the other boys cawed with half-broken voices and wobbled slowly after them.

*

I love this place, thought Jenny Cornwood, coming out of the cool of the woods onto the hillside. I love the way the grass feels short and springy under your feet and the way the shadows of the clouds fly across the fields and I know what Wordsworth and Miss Cameron are on about. But you couldn't say it to the others or they'd laugh, so you just climbed the hills and the special Climbing Tree and listened to the wind in the beech-leaves sounding like the sea, and you knew that that was all that mattered. *All ye know and all ye need to know.*

Her father had carried her up here hundreds of times when she was a baby. She had sat on his shoulders, looking out over the plain and the river to the dinosaur hills, and sometimes they had raced the rainclouds home to the village and sometimes the rain had won and they had arrived home soaking wet and laughing to be scolded by Phyllis.

'Mazed, you are,' she'd say. 'Fancy letting the child get drenched like that.' And then Phyllis would laugh too and cuddle her dry in a towel.

She put two fingers in her mouth and whistled till her little brother Jim and Finch came hurtling down a slope towards her and fell over each other in a heap at her feet. 'The orchid's there again,' said Jim. 'Come on, I'll show you.' They had first found it two years before; a single bee orchid exactly like the insect it pretended to be, growing in a shallow hollow near the old quarry, and they had kept it a secret. There it was, safe and secret still.

They came to the Climbing Tree. Jenny was the best climber in the village, better than the boys. She scrambled up the spiky trunk and Jimmy followed. Finch chased rabbits. 'That's far enough for you,' said Jenny when Jim reached the twenty-foot fork. 'You're only eight. Twenty feet is high enough for eight.'

She climbed on until she reached her viewing point. From here she was even higher than the top of the hill. She looked down onto the great purple range, and at the silver sweep of the river and the flat meadows beyond it. It was always windy up here, no matter how hot the sun was on the ground. Jenny leaned back against the trunk and daydreamed.

A little procession was plodding up the hill towards the

Climbing Tree. A girl was trying to perch on the handlebars of the bike a boy was pushing. She fell off, shrieking and giggling. The boy put his bike down carefully and lay on the grass beside her. There was another girl, followed by two more boys pushing bikes. Jenny watched as the first boy kissed the first girl, and then, as the second girl came closer, she recognised Ann Dangerfield.

Judith Littlewick scrambled to her feet, leaving the boy to pick up his bike and ride away. She brushed grass off her jeans and jumper and ran to catch up with Ann. 'Tell you what,' she said, 'why don't you come back home with me tonight? We can go Down the Dance.'

Chapter Twelve

Down the Dance at Honeyford was a legendary place where Nice Girls didn't go. Joan, who had never heard of it, was surprisingly easily persuaded by Judith's open smile and perfect diction. 'I think I should speak to your mother first, just to make sure it's convenient.'

'I'll ring her, Mrs Dangerfield. May I use your phone?' And Judith had dialled an imaginary number and held an imaginary conversation with her mother who was (a) not there, and (b) not on the telephone. 'That's absolutely fine, Mrs Dangerfield. She'll be delighted.' It would have been ill-mannered of Joan to insist on another phone call.

Ann shoved pyjamas and a toothbrush on top of the secret bra in her duffel bag and she and Judith caught the bus to Tarminster. They spent an hour in Woolworths, wandering up and down the aisles between the long wooden counters. 'I'm starting a Saturday-morning job here in September,' Judith said.

They bought white lipstick and black mascara, pearl nail varnish and bright blue eye shadow. Judith paused at the nylons. 'We'd better get a pair each.'

'I haven't got a suspender belt,' said Ann, feeling silly.

'What are you going to wear Down the Dance then?' Ann looked down at her jeans and pulled a face. 'Tell you what,' said Judith, 'you can borrow my drainpipes and I'll wear my new hooped petticoat.' She bought a pair of fifteen-denier nylons with arrows pointing all the way up the seams, and then they caught the bus to Honeyford.

Honeyford lies on the flat side of Tarminster and its river. In

1958, it was pretty in its own way, which was not the way of Swain's Chard. It was full of chapels and pubs and it had a cider factory and a timberyard and fish factory which overwhelmed the village once a month with the stink of offal. It had the River Tar and a Riverside Road and a single long main street with long rope alleys leading off it. It was the home of Judith Littlewick, Susie Perkins and Jean Scrivener. It had its own gang of Teddy Boys and its own skiffle group and it was where you went if you wanted to go Down the Dance.

The two girls were at work in front of Judith's mother's dressing-table mirror. They lifted up strands of hair from their fringes and punched fine-toothed combs savagely down them so that the hair was bashed into a stiff, matted brush. Then they spread thin layers of unmatted hair back over the brush and gripped the ends back into tall beehives. They borrowed Mrs Littlewick's base foundation colour and spread it thickly over their faces for flawless smooth complexions and outlined their lips with the Woolworths white. Bright wings of blue shadow slanted out from their eyelids and every eyelash was coated in mascara. Ann gazed in delight at her reflection. She'd had no idea that she could look so common.

They teetered along the main street and down to the Nissen hut on the recreation ground where Honeyford went Down the Dance. Ann wore Judith's black drainpipes, a pair of Judith's mother's high stilettos, a tight pink V-necked sweater and white PVC jacket. Beside her, Judith swung her hips in a yellow circular skirt propped up by a hooped and multi-layered petticoat. Her heels were higher than Ann's and her V-neck was lower.

At the far end of the Nissen hut was a stage where the skiffle group of sideboards, bootlace ties, thick-soled suede shoes and drainpipe jeans played Lonnie Donegan songs on flat guitars and washboards. At the end nearest the door was a juke-box. The two ends were connected by drooping lines of low-wattage coloured light bulbs. Teddy Boys stood nonchalantly along one side, eyeing the talent as it tottered in. The talent perched itself on wooden chairs along the other side or leaned sexily against the walls and juke-box.

Ann and Judith sat down near the platform. Judith hitched her petticoats above her knees and crossed her arrowed nylons.

43

Ann crossed her drainpipes. They both assumed the Bardot pout.

The skiffle group scrubbed its way through *The Cumberland Gap* and took a breather. Somebody put *Jailhouse Rock* on the juke-box. 'Dance?' said a large Ted to Ann. All those breaks in 4A had not been wasted; she was one of the best jivers in the class. She shed her shoes and began to dance. The Ted tapped his feet and twirled her beneath his outstretched arm. He spun her back and caught her round her waist then sent her spinning out along his fingertips again. They jived their way through *Jailhouse Rock* and *Livin' Doll* and she rejoined Judith who was smoking a Woodbine and flirting with a little Ted. They drank Coke, and then the juke-box began to play *Fools Rush In* and Big Ted reappeared. 'Dance?'

He got very sentimental and held her close so that she could feel his hot breath on her neck. 'Open up your arms and let this fool rush in,' he crooned, all out of tune.

'Come outside,' he groaned as the music swooned to its end,

'I can't leave my friend,' said Ann, looking round desperately for Judith who was now enfolded in the octopus arms of Little Ted.

'Come on,' said Big Ted, 'Come outside for a while.' He kissed her behind the Nissen hut and stuck his tongue in her mouth. This must be French-kissing, she thought. At least it qualified her for two clothes-pegs. But when she felt his hand fumbling around the V-neck of the borrowed jumper, she pulled away. Not even for three clothes-pegs.

'Dance?' said a voice beside her, and to her enormous relief, Ann recognised Jenny Cornwood's big brother Charlie.

'Just a minute,' said Big Ted dangerously, breathing through his mouth and flexing his drainpipes.

'She's with me,' said Charlie Cornwood, who had never spoken to her before in his life, 'C'mon, Annie.'

The music was smooching again and Charlie Cornwood danced with her. 'I've never seen you Down the Dance before.'

'I've never been before.'

'You're at school with Jenny, aren't you? Our mum cleans for your mum.' He grinned. 'She'd never let our Jenny come down here. Thinks it's a den of iniquity. She could be right. I'd better get you home before Clive Carpenter gets funny.'

'Clive Carpenter?'

'That bloke you were with.' Clive Carpenter.

... Of course – the one Judith Littlewick had scored seven clothes-pegs with last term.

'But I'm supposed to stay at Judith Littlewick's tonight,' said Ann.

Charlie laughed. 'That one – she's too busy to worry about you. Just tell her I'm taking you home.'

Ann wound her way between the dancers to where Judith and Little Ted were still snogging. When they came up for air, Ann said, 'Charlie Cornwood wants to take me home, OK?'

'Don't do anything I wouldn't do,' said Judith and returned to the fray.

Charlie said to Mary Perkins, his steady and Susie Perkins' big sister, 'She's only a kid – same age as Susie and Jenny. Right out of her depth here. I'll run her over to Swain's Chard and be back in half an hour. See ya later, Alligator.'

'Don't do anything I wouldn't do,' said Marlene Wheeler the Honeyford Bicycle who was standing next to the juke-box with her sidekick Yvonne Pratt the Practice Mat.

'That gives me plenty of scope then, dunnit?'

'See you later,' said Mary. She and Charlie had been going steady since they were fourteen at Secondary Modern. She knew him very well.

The motorbike roared through the night along the back roads from Honeyford to Swain's Chard. Ann, high heels wedged onto the chrome foot-rests, clung tightly to Charlie's waist. Under the high August night sky, the single beam of the headlight cut into the blackness of the road. They climbed on out of the river flatland, curved around Tarminster and up towards Swain's Chard. 'We'll go right over the top – over the hill road,' yelled Charlie over his shoulder. They rode up and up until he stopped his bike at the highest point of the road, a hundred yards from the Climbing Tree.

Charlie switched the engine off and they sat in silence, gazing down at the Tarminster lights and the Cathedral spire and the river shining silver in the moonlight. 'There's nowhere in the world more beautiful than this,' said Charlie. Ann sat on the pillion seat, listening to the wind in the beechwoods below them, watching black clouds blow like ragged smoke across the moon then elongate and disperse. She shivered. 'Come on, it's time to get you home.'

Ann came back to reality. She couldn't go home. They thought she was spending the night in Honeyford; they would have locked up by now and she hadn't got a key. She could never explain to them why she had left early and how she had come home.

'I can't go home,' she said in a panic. 'They'll have locked up and gone to bed by now. They'll be furious.' Charlie laughed. 'Oh well, I'll just have to sneak you in to our place then. You can squeeze in with our Jenny.'

They crept past the bedroom where Phyllis dreamed and Arthur snored, and into Jenny's room. 'I've got a friend of yours here,' whispered Charlie, shaking his sister awake. 'Shove over and make room. She'll tell you all about it in the morning.'

He left them, tiptoed downstairs, kick-started the bike and rode back through the night to Honeyford and Mary.

Chapter Thirteen

In the morning, they waited until Phyllis had gone to do her cleaning and then they got up. Ann scrubbed the smeared make-up off and brushed out what was left of the beehive.

'What was it like?' asked Jenny.

Anne winced as the brush caught in a hard tangle of hair. 'It was all right.'

'Only all right? You are lucky. Our Mum'd never let me go there.'

'Neither would mine. You didn't miss much, really,' Ann admitted. 'There was a skiffle group and a juke-box and a lot of Teds.'

'Did anybody ask you to dance?'

Ann giggled. 'You'll never guess – Clive Carpenter.'

'Not Seven Clothes-pegs Clive Carpenter?' Ann nodded. 'Blimey!' breathed Jenny. 'Did he try anything?'

'Yes,' said Ann.

'What did you do?'

'Told him where to get off,' said Ann with more drama than truth.

There was a pause, then Jenny asked, 'Why did our Charlie bring your home?'

Ann rubbed her cheeks with cotton wool and felt them burning. 'I told you. Clive Carpenter was getting fresh and your brother—'

'Rescued you.' Jenny laughed. 'That's typical of Charlie. He's like Robin Hood or some old knight from Camelot. Can't resist a damsel in distress.'

They ate bread and marmalade in the kitchen while Jimmy

47

talked to his frogs in the yard pond.

'He does that every morning,' Jenny said. 'He brought them home in a jam jar when they were just blobs in jelly and when they frogged he put 'em in the pond and now he talks to them every morning before he goes anywhere and every afternoon as soon as he gets home.'

Jimmy squatted on his haunches by the little pond where an elderly gnome perched on a rock and fished for three fat goldfish; there were hutches in the yard full of guinea pigs and rabbits. Finch crouched next to Jimmy, listening with an intelligent mongrel ear to the conversation with the frogs. Grampy Cornwood leaned over the fence from next door and joined in.

'What time will it be safe for you to get home?' asked Jenny.

'Not before eleven. Then it'll look as if I caught the ten o'clock bus.' Ann paused unhappily. 'I've never really lied to them before.'

'Where's Annie then?' asked Phyllis, pushing the Hoover Junior along the hall.

'She stayed the night at Honeyford with a friend from school,' said Joan.

Phyllis tossed her head and tutted. 'They'll have gone Down the Dance then,' she said to the Hoover Junior, just loudly enough for Joan to hear.

'What?' Joan's voice was sharp.

Phyllis dripped disapproval. 'I said, they'll have gone Down the Dance at Honeyford. I wouldn't let our Jennifer go there. Rough sort of place. Riff raff.'

Joan gulped. She had never heard of Down the Dance, but she knew by the Swain's Chard maternal sixth sense that it was not a place where Nice Girls went. 'I'm sure Ann wouldn't go anywhere like that. And her friend seemed a very nice girl.' Phyllis sniffed again and turned the Hoover on.

At eleven o'clock precisely, Ann walked through the back door of her house. At ten past eleven precisely, Judith rang from the Honeyford phone box. 'What happened to you last night?'

Ann, aware of her mother's ears stretching along the hall from the kitchen, kept her voice down. 'He asked if he could take me home.'

There was an impressed silence on the other end of the line and then a clunk as Judith dropped another threepence in the slot. Ann had shot up several rungs on the ladder of her estimation. A girl who could get Charlie Cornwood, heart throb of Swain's Chard and Honeyford and going steady with Mary Perkins, to take her home, was a girl to be reckoned with. 'Did he kiss you?'

Ann paused. 'I'm not telling you,' she said. And she wished very much that he had.

'What was it like?' asked Philippa.

'It was a laugh,' said Ann.

'Did you get off with anybody?'

Ann pulled a face. 'Well ... Clive Carpenter.'

Philippa was aghast. 'Seven Clothes-pegs Clive Carpenter?'

'Yes, well, he took me outside and ...' She paused for effect.

'He didn't ask you to Do It, did he?'

'No,' said Ann, 'don't be silly. But he kept pulling at my V-neck.'

'Gosh,' whispered Philippa, and they were silent for a moment, contemplating the possibilities of Clive Carpenter.

After a while, Philippa said, 'Have you ever seen anybody you could – you know – even imagine doing it with?' When Ann did not immediately reply, she said, 'Blimey, you have! Seen somebody, I mean.'

'Not really,' said Ann.

'But there is somebody you like, isn't there?' Philippa was being very persistent.

'Might be,' said Ann, and blushed. 'But I wouldn't ever do it. Not before I was married, I mean. It's wrong.'

'Oh yes, it is,' agreed Philippa. 'And boys don't respect girls who do, do they? But you have seen someone you wouldn't mind doing it with, haven't you?'

Ann took a deep breath. Her head was full of his name and the back of his neck and the way he danced and the throb of the motorbike on the way home and she was bursting to tell Philippa. 'If I tell you,' she said, 'you've got to promise, cross your heart and hope to die, never to tell anybody else.'

'Not even Jenny?' Philippa was surprised.

''Specially not Jenny.'

Loyalty struggled with curiosity and curiosity won. 'All right,' said Philippa.

Ann took another deep breath and looked away. 'Charlie Cornwood,' she said and blushed.

'Phew,' said Philippa. Then she added, 'Shall we go and get Delilah?'

The wind on the hill and the rain on her bare head washed Down the Dance and Clive Carpenter and Charlie Cornwood out of Ann's thoughts. She cantered along the track and was a child again.

Chapter Fourteen

Phyllis bent over the Dangerfield bath, scouring it with Gumption. She cleaned for women like Joan Dangerfield and gained an intimate and useful knowledge of their lives from the contents of their bathroom cabinets and their airing cupboards and the arrangement of their furniture.

'The Dangerfields sleep in separate twin beds,' she had said to Arthur more than once as she rolled into the comfortable dip in the middle of their own bed. Perhaps it was posher to sleep in twin beds, she thought. Her friend Alice Price, who cleaned up at the Manor, had told her that Lord and Lady Hennessey slept in separate rooms, let alone separate beds. It was not that Phyllis wanted to be posh. Oh no, it certainly wasn't that. It was just that she wanted Joan Dangerfield and her sort to realise that Phyllis Cornwood and her sort were as good as they were any day.

Oh yes, thought Phyllis as she attacked the bath, she was as good as they were any day. So what, then was the difference? Was it the money, or was it more than that? Was it their voices; the way they sounded their 'aitches' and added their 'ings', listened to the Home Service more than to the Light Programme, called dinner lunch and tea supper and the toilet the lav? Was it something to do with reading the *Daily Telegraph* and not the *Daily Mirror* or going on holiday to a cottage in Cornwall instead of doing days out with the motor-bike and side-car?

Phyllis ran the cold tap and slooshed the water round the bath. When she turned off the tap, she could hear the back door being opened and Ann's voice in the kitchen. Phyllis gave the bath a final wipe and the telephone began to ring. The stairwell acted like a funnel. 'He asked if he could take me home,' Ann was saying in a low voice. There was a long pause while another voice crackled on the end of the line. 'I'm not telling you,' Ann said and rang off. Phyllis squeezed out her cloth, hung it over the side of the bath and straightened up. There'd be fireworks soon, she reckoned, what with deodorants and bras and going Down the Dance.

The phone rang again and Phyllis heard Joan say, 'Swain's Chard 2936. Oh hello, Madge. Yes, yes, I'd love to. In ten minutes? At the Chalet Suisse? Lovely.' She called up the stairs, 'I'll leave your money on the kitchen table, Mrs Cornwood. I've just got to pop out for an hour. Could you sweep the stairs and polish in the dining room? Thank you so much. See you next week.'

That was it, thought Phyllis. Yes, that was it. The world was divided into two sorts of women; those who had their hair done at Sharon's Salon every week and met their friends for coffee in the Chalet Suisse, and those who cleaned their houses for them. One day, she thought, Jennifer would have her engagement announced in the *Daily Telegraph*. She would marry a doctor or a solicitor or an architect, and she and her husband would sleep in twin beds. And twice a week a woman from the village would come to clean her house.

She put the lid back on the Gumption tin and moved next door into the Dangerfield lavatory. She lifted the seat and shook Harpic fiercely round the pan. 'Dauntless,' she said out loud and grinned. Daft name for a toilet. She remembered different toilets she had known – Majestic, Eagle, Ambassador ... and what was the name of the one she had scrubbed and bleached all those years ago when she had worked for the Hennesseys up at the Manor? Con something ... Con Brio, that was it! Con Brio. She had always liked the name; it had sounded triumphant and splendid and brave, like the noise of the flush when you pulled the china handle on the end of the heavy metal chain.

Con Brio. The name took her back thirty-five years when she was twelve and just starting work at the Manor. Her mother had been in service there and her father was one of the gardeners, and it had been obvious to them that Phyllis herself would work at the Manor as soon as she was old enough to leave school. But Phyllis herself had had other ideas after one of her poems had been published in the Swain's Chard School Magazine when she was eleven. She would not go into service as her mother had done. She would be a poet and another poet would fall passionately in love with her and would write love poems to her and whisk her away to foreign climes and foreign glamour.

Obviously she did not tell her family about that plan. Hers was not a family for poetry and it was arranged that the day after she left school, she would start up at the Manor. That was all right. Phyllis knew that it was only a short pause in her life, something to do until the poet rode up the Manor drive on his fiery chestnut horse. He would recognise her instantly, see the artist in her, know that she was his destiny and sweep her up into the saddle. He, too, would own a big house near Swain's Chard (she did not want to go away from her family for ever) and they would spend half of each year there and the other half in his château in France.

But he took a long time coming and, in the meantime, young Arthur Cornwood rode up the Manor drive on his postman's bicycle one sunny May morning when she was hanging out the washing. He swept her off her feet and onto his handlebars and for two sunshine-filled years they had ridden perilously and hilariously down the driveway and along the narrow garden paths. She had been fifteen at the start of their courtship and they had hidden from her father (who was very strict) and Arthur had kissed her in the shrubbery behind the formal gardens. He was handsome and dashing and he took her dancing and made her feel like the heroine of a love story, so that she forgot about the poet (who was, in any case, an interminably long time coming).

Phyllis smiled to remember the crazy, wobbling bicycle rides around the hedges and corners of the formal garden and her father's fury when they fell off at his feet one day and squashed a yew hedge he was training to look like a squirrel.

When she was seventeen, Arthur had asked her to marry him and she, finally banishing the poet, had said yes. Her father had said she was too young and they must wait until she was twenty-one. Phyllis' face grew thoughtful as she wielded the lavatory brush and remembered the bee-filled afternoon when they had stopped waiting, and the terrible realisation two months later that something was very wrong. She had never told anyone, not even Arthur, how she had drunk half a bottle of her grandmother's gin and soaked in an unbearably hot bath before she bumped herself downstairs. She could still recall the great gush of relief that had come with the great gush of blood that night. If the blood had not flowed, she would have been sent away to a home for mental defectives and her baby would have been adopted. She sighed and flushed Dauntless. The poet had never turned up. But she and Arthur had been happy enough, in their way.

Chapter Fifteen

The Vicar of Swain's Chard, the Reverend Eric Dobbin, felt himself going hot under the dog collar as he confronted the expressionless faces of the nine young people who had come to his Confirmation Class.

'Welcome,' he said nervously, and his Adam's apple pressed against his dog collar and made his voice squeak. ' Welcome to this new ... er ... session of St Swithin's Confirmation Class.' He paused, hoping in vain for a response. 'Does anybody know the meaning of the word "Confirmation"?' he asked hopefully. Nobody did. 'Ah,' said the Reverend Eric, cheering up a bit. 'Well, at least that gives us a starting point, doesn't it?' Another pause filled by blank faces. 'You are here,' he continued, 'in order that the promises made on your behalf by your parents and godparents at your Baptism may be confirmed by you. Confirmed by you.' He swallowed and cleared his throat. 'That is why it is called "Confirmation".'

Ann and Jenny caught each other's eyes and stared each other out. First one to blink was the loser. Philippa, who was only there under protest, put up her hand. ('I'm not going to Confirmation Class,' she had said to Madge. 'I'm an atheist.' 'Don't be silly, of course, you're not,' Madge had said.) Now the Rev. Eric smiled encouragingly at her.

'How can we confirm promises somebody else made for us when we were far too young to possibly understand what they were saying?' She did not mean to be rude. She would not have dreamed of being rude. She simply wanted to know.

Ann and Jenny stopped staring each other out and transferred their eyes back to the Rev. Eric's face. His looked promising. Poor old Eric was on the run, blushing scarlet now so that his face clashed with his thin ginger hair.

But he stopped running and met Philippa's challenge.

'That is a good question. A very good question indeed. And it is precisely because of that question that we are all here tonight.' He had won himself some time and he took a deep breath as his confidence grew. 'We all need a Way,' he announced. 'Without a Way, we are lost. Without a Way, our lives are chaos – they have no meaning, they make no sense. Jesus Christ is our Good Shepherd who was sent down by His Father, God, to show us that Way. "I am the Way, the Truth and the Life," He said.'

The Confirmation Class glazed over. It knew all this by heart, had been hearing it for as long as it could remember. And the Way that He showed us was the Way of the Ten Commandments that God had given to Moses, with a new idea added onto them. And that new idea is the whole key to the Way that we follow.' Now, he could see that their minds were wandering, 'Who can tell me what those Ten Commandments are?'

Another pause, and then nine hands were unenthusiastically raised. The list of Commandments was recited in bored voices.

'Thou Shalt Not Kill.'

'Thou Shalt Not Steal.'

'Thou Shalt Not Commit Adultery' (sniggers).

'Thou Shalt Not Covet Thy Neighbour's Wife nor His Ox nor His Ass' (more sniggers).

'Thou Shalt Remember the Sabbath Day.'

'Thou Shalt Have No Other Gods Than Me.'

'Thou Shalt Not Bear False Witness Against Thy Neighbour.'

'Honour Thy Father and Thy Mother.'

'Thou Shalt Not Worship Any Graven Image.'

The Commandments ground to a halt. 'Nine out of ten,' said the Rev. Eric, but nobody could think of the tenth.

'What happens if I break them?' asked Philippa. Again, she was genuinely interested and she did not mean to sound insolent. But she suddenly irritated the Rev. Eric and caught him off guard.

'You'll go to Hell,' he snapped.

A shocked silence spread through the Church Room. Then: 'What's Hell like?' asked Jenny casually.

Eric was on unsure ground again. 'Oh, you know – fire and brimstone ... all that sort of thing,' he said, fiddling with his dog collar. He cleared his throat again and tried to smile. 'Let's get back to more cheerful matters, shall we? As I was saying when you were all baptised, your parents and your Godparents promised to bring you up in the Way, the Truth and the Life. They promised to teach you to obey the Commandments (and we've still got one to find), to teach you not to lie or steal or murder, not to covet your neighbour's ox or ass.' ('Or horse,' whispered Ann to Jenny, with a meaningful look at a spiteful girl called Susan who was bitterly jealous of them because of Delilah). 'And now you have reached an age when you can make those promises for yourselves.' This was getting better, he thought.

Then the spiteful girl called Susan put her hand up. 'Do people go to Hell if they've committed adultery?' she enquired.

Eric frowned. 'Well, not if they've repented and promised not to do it again,' he hedged.

'Hmm,' muttered Susan, just loudly enough for him and the Confirmation Class to hear. 'Just as well for Mrs Goodrington, then.'

The class sniggered under its breath. Mrs Goodrington's affair with a neighbouring knight and her subsequent divorce from Mr Goodrington had shaken Swain's Chard to its moral roots two years before. But Mrs Goodrington, now Lady Smythe and the queen of the cocktail-party circuit, had been thoroughly forgiven and took Communion again with the best of them.

The Rev. Eric looked sternly at Susan. 'I must remind you, Susan, that malice is a sin. Perhaps as much of a sin as adultery or stealing.' He was different now, thought the Confirmation Class; stronger, taller, more certain. His colour had settled and he no longer fiddled with his collar.

'Before we close tonight,' he went on, 'I must tell you about the Commandment you forgot. It is probably the most important one of all.' The quality of listening deepened in the room.

'"Thou Shalt Love Thy Neighbour As Thyself,"' said Eric. 'Not more than – *as*. As much as thyself. If you listen to that Commandment and think about what it means and obey it in everything you do, all the others will fall into place. You cannot kill or steal or cheat or bear false witness as long as you love your neighbour as yourself.'

On the way home from the Church Room, Philippa, Jenny and Ann practised walks. Sexy walks with hips and shoulders swaying, tough horsey walks with long strides and straight-ahead toes, motherly walks with toes turned out, religious spinster walks without a wriggle or a curve. Ann wondered which would be her real walk.

Chapter Sixteen

Autumn Term, 5A, 1958

It was the beginning of October. 4A had turned into 5A, 'O' levels were less than nine months away and it was time for Dr Luker's Sex Visit to Tarminster High School for Girls.

Dr Luker, known inevitably as Filthy, was a kind, mild, grey-haired GP who arrived every year to talk to the girls in a gentle, careful way about Love, Loyalty and Sex Within Marriage. The main burden of his lectures was that Virginity was a Good Thing and that Sex Before Marriage was a Bad Thing and so was Heavy Petting which led to something awful called Frigidity. Fidelity and Loyalty were Good Things; Adultery and Disloyalty were not.

He told them an appalling story about a wife's dreadful betrayal of the marriage bed when she overheard her husband boasting at a party that his idea of heaven would be to have six concubines attending to his every need. 'Huh,' the reprehensible wife had sneered, 'listen to old Once-a-Fortnight.' 'If I had been that husband,' Filthy Luker told them, 'I would never have trusted her again. Such things are private between a man and his wife.'

5A listened in awed silence and made private vows never to expose their own husbands in such a humiliating way. 'Any questions?' said Dr Luker.

Someone raised a hand. 'How often are you supposed to do it?'

'It varies,' replied Dr Luker. 'A newly married couple will probably do it every night at first and sometimes more than once a night. Then it will settle down to two or three times a week and after the first year or so, it will probably be just once a week.'

'Or once a fortnight,' came a voice from the back of the room and all the Fifth years laughed. ('Mind you,' said Jean Scrivener at dinner-time after the lecture, 'I should have thought that once a fortnight would be quite enough for anyone.')

'You may be wondering,' said Filthy Luker, 'why virginity is so important.'

5A who, on the whole, hadn't been, looked up in surprise. One bold girl put up her hand. 'Pregnancy,' she said.

'Quite right,' said Filthy Luker. 'Sexual Intercourse Before Marriage Leads to Babies Before Marriage. The family is the basic unit of our society. Babies need the protection and love of both their parents. Any other reasons?'

'VD,' said the bold girl.

'I thought that was something to do with the end of the war,' Ann Dangerfield whispered to Susie Perkins and they both got the giggles and missed the doctor's reply.

It was open question time now. 'Why are people so surprised when they find out they're going to have a baby? I mean, like on *The Archers* and *Mrs Dale's Diary*. You'd think they'd notice and remember if they'd done something like that.'

Dr Luker cleared his throat and turned a little pink. 'It can be quite ... enjoyable,' he admitted, 'and so people do not always think of it simply as a way to have a baby. And quite often they do it and they don't have a baby, you see.' He hurried on. 'Are there any more questions?'

There were. 'How long do people go on doing it for?' 'How old are they when they stop altogether?'

'I know a couple in their seventies who still have intercourse,' said Filthy Luker.

5A was shocked and horrified. How disgusting. Not my parents, thought each girl, Oh no, not mine, not mine.

The lecture moved on to Necking. Where did Necking stop and Heavy Petting begin? Why was Necking all right and Heavy Petting all wrong? Dr Luker explained. Heavy Petting which stopped just short of Going the Whole Way could lead to Frigidity. (What *was* Frigidity, wondered most of 5A. They would have to ask each other afterwards.) The line between Necking and Heavy Petting was somewhere around the base of the neck. Which was why, they supposed when they thought about it afterwards, it was called Necking. Snorts of suppressed laughter were coming from the end of Ann Dangerfield's row. Judith Littlewick was pointing to the clothes-pegs on her blazer lapel. There were eight there now. Was Judith running the risk of Frigidity?

'I am a man,' said Filthy Luker, just in case anyone was not sure, 'and I must tell you that men are made differently from women. Their bodies function differently. A man can be aroused simply by looking at a woman.'

The girls gazed at him curiously. There were a lot of them there for him to look at. Was he aroused? And if he was, how would they know?

'A woman needs to be aroused gently and slowly and tenderly, by words and by touch. And although a man may be urgently and immediately aroused by a woman and may want her very much at that moment, he will soon cease to respect her if she Lets Him Go Too Far.'

And on that final note of warning, Dr Luker left them.

Chapter Seventeen

'For I was an hungered and Ye gave me meat: I was thirsty and Ye gave me drink: I was a stranger and Ye took me in: Naked and Ye clothed me: I was sick and Ye visited me: I was in prison and Ye came unto me.'

The Vicar finished his Gospel Reading. Philippa, despite being an atheist who was only in church because Madge and Norman insisted, was impressed.

After the service, while the parents lingered to chat to the Vicar and Lady Smythe and the members of the Golf Club, Philippa waited for Ann and Jenny to change out of their choir cassocks and join her in a private, yew-tree'd section of the churchyard where a large marble angel perched on a tomb and watched them severely.

'We ought to do that,' said Philippa.

'Do what?' said the others.

'"I was an hungered and Ye gave me meat: I was thirsty and Ye gave me drink" et cetera. If we were anything like real Christians, we'd do that.'

'But you aren't,' objected Jenny. 'You're always going on about being an atheist.'

Philippa looked superior. 'A thinking person can re-think,' she said piously. They thought about it.

'You mean,' said Ann, 'we ought to find somebody who is an hungered and give them meat?'

'Yes,' said Philippa.

'You don't see a lot of it round here though, do you?' remarked Jenny.

Then Philippa was seized by inspiration. 'Mr Johnson – you

know, the poet-tramp. "Gentleman of the Road" my father calls him. He's always hungry and thirsty. He came to our house yesterday and swapped a poem for some bread and cheese.'

'What was the poem like?' asked Jenny.

Philippa giggled. 'It was awful. Come on, he can't be far away.

We'll go and find him.'

They were all three filled with enthusiasm now and a burning desire to do good; to feed the hungry, clothe the naked, visit the sick. Norman, Madge, Joan and John set off for pre-lunch drinks with Sir George and Lady Smythe, while their daughters, plus Jenny, set off in search of Mr Johnson.

They found him sitting on a bench on the Rec, drinking a bottle of beer and writing a poem in a notebook. They approached him a little nervously now, for none of them had ever spoken to him on his own, away from the safety of their own back porches with their mothers in attendance.

'Hello, Mr Johnson,' began Philippa. Mr Johnson grinned and raised his trilby hat courteously.

'Are you writing a poem?' enquiried Ann politely.

Mr Johnson smiled. 'Indeed I am. Would you care to hear it?' They said yes they would, very much, so he finished his bottle of beer, stood up, cleared his throat and proclaimed:

> 'My roof is the sky,
> The ground where I lie
> Is my bed.
> My music is birdsong
> A beautiful heard song.
> My light is the moon
> and (no doubt very soon)
> When I die, I'll be dead.'

The girls did not know quite how to respond to this work of art, but it confirmed their feelings that Mr Johnson was in need of Christian comfort. They clapped very loudly and said nothing.

After a while, Philippa cleared her throat. 'We were wondering ... please don't take offence ... we were wondering if you were hungry or thirsty.'

Mr Johnson looked mournful. 'I certainly am, young lady. Not a crumb nor a drop has passed my lips since the day before yesterday.' He appeared to have forgotten the empty beer bottle lying underneath the bench.

'But Philippa said—' began Ann and stopped when Philippa trod firmly on her foot. ('He probably gets confused,' Philippa explained later. 'Hunger can do that to you.')

'Mr Johnson,' went on Philippa, who was by now completely determined to put the Gospel into practice, 'I should like to invite you to come to my house for Sunday dinner.'

Mr Johnson, Ann and Jenny were amazed into silence. What on earth, thought the girls, would Mr and Mrs Foster say? Much as she wanted to feed the hungry, Ann knew that she could never possibly take Mr Johnson back to her own house, and Jenny knew exactly what Phyllis would have said. 'Don't talk so daft, our Jennifer. Bring a dirty old tramp into the house indeed. You don't know where he's been or what he'll take away with him.'

Mr Johnson himself was dumb with horror and embarrassment. This had never happened to him before and it was the last thing he wanted to do. But Philippa was adamant and he hated to hurt anybody's feelings.

Norman and Madge Foster had returned home after sherry and Madge had laid the table for three for Sunday dinner. The roast beef was absolutely right and the vegetables were almost cooked when Philippa came in through the back door.

'I've brought a guest for Sunday dinner,' she said and her mouth went dry with fear at what she'd done. Normally Madge would have been annoyed at having a surprise guest foisted upon her, but four aristocratic sherries had blurred her reactions.

'I wish you'd give me warning, Philippa. Who is it – Ann?'

Philippa collected Mr Johnson from behind the dustbin and led him firmly into the kitchen. 'It's Mr Johnson. He's hungry. He hasn't eaten since yesterday.' She got in her master stroke before Madge and Norman had had time to recover. 'And the Vicar said in church this morning that we'd got to feed the hungry, didn't he?'

Mr Johnson sat in agonies of discomfort and terror, staring at the Fosters' cutlery, wondering how to handle it. He was beginning to suffer from claustophobia and panic, but he did not want to be rude and hurt the young lady's feelings. He could sense her parents' embarrassment and shock, and he knew that he should not be there. At the same time, it would be impossibly rude to go now.

'Drink?' asked Norman. Mr Johnson grinned gratefully. 'Beer? Whisky?'

'Both,' Mr Johnson wanted to say, but he settled for whisky which would be stronger and numb him more quickly. He hoped that Norman would make it a large one. Norman did. Mr Johnson downed it in one go and braved the knives and forks.

They ate in silence, trying to ignore the slurping and chewing noises that came from Mr Johnson's side of the table. Once, Madge tried to think of something to say. 'How long have you been a ...' oh no, she mustn't say 'tramp' '... poet?' she remembered just time.

'All my life,' said Mr Johnson grandly, and that was the end of the conversation.

When the meal was over, he wondered desperately how he could leave without being rude. 'Ah well,' said Norman. 'I expect you've got a lot of poems to write. We mustn't hold you up.'

'Oh I have, I have,' cried Mr Johnson gratefully, leaping to his feet so that he knocked his chair over behind him. 'Goodbye,' he said, 'and thank you for the dinner.' He rushed out of the house, gasping with relief as he breathed in the air and felt the ground under his feet again. He hurried through the garden and headed for the hill.

The next morning, when she opened the back door to bring in the milk, Madge found a piece of paper torn out of a notebook and propped between the bottles.

Thank you for dinner
I would have been thinner
Without it.

Thank you for luncheon,

'Twas something to munch on,
Don't doubt it.

Thanks for the plateful,
I am deeply grateful
About it.

So thank you kind Mister, dear Miss and good Missus.
I thank you again for the loaves and the fishes.

Yrs truly,
A. Johnson.

'That last bit doesn't rhyme properly,' Ann pointed out.

Philippa thought for a minute. 'It probably would, the way he'd be saying it after all that beer and whisky.'

'He could've said, "Thank you again with love and with kisses",' suggested Jenny and they exploded into laughter.

Mr Johnson never came back to Swain's Chard again.

Chapter Eighteen

5A sat in the Music Room, staring out of the windows at the snowflakes, playing under the tables with folded paper fortune-tellers ... choose a number ... choose a colour ... choose a boy's name. Miss Freeman put a record on the gramophone and the great slow strides of Elgar's *Nimrod Variation* filled the room. Miss Freeman closed her eyes, tipped back her chair and leaned against the wall behind the piano. 5A watched her. She always did that, went into a trance whenever she played Elgar or Dvořák or Beethoven to them. 5A held competitions after the lessons to see who could come up with the most outrageous idea of what she was thinking about.

The music swelled and climbed and plunged and climbed again, and Jenny climbed with it, up to the top of Swain's Chard Hill, riding high on her father's shoulders, watching the black clouds looming and threatening until they broke and poured and drenched her. They began to run back down the hill and the music diminished into quick, light rain which gave way to diluted sunlight on leaf-dappled ground underneath the trees. 'It's like sex, isn't it?' whispered Judith Littlewick to Ann Dangerfield who had no idea whether it was or not, but who nodded and giggled and passed the message on.

They watched Miss Freeman. What *was* she thinking about? Had she once been wonderfully wooed while an orchestra played this music in the background? Or had she played it in an orchestra herself and yearned for the love of the First Violin? (She was always going on about First Violins, they noticed.) Or, even better, had she perhaps known and loved Elgar (or Beethoven or Dvořák) himself? (They were hazy about dates.)

Had she walked with Elgar over the tops of his hills while he composed his music? Perhaps she was one of his Enigmas.

Behind her closed eyelids, Miss Freeman rode the music as it carried her again towards her truths. Life is like music, she thought as Elgar swooped and soared and wept and triumphed and Nimrod reached his magnificent conclusion. Miss Freeman opened her eyes, looked straight at 5A and dared to say it. 'Life is like music, girls. We are not alive without our tune, our spirit, our feeling, our colour. But we must have the rhythm and the structure too. If we do not, all that feeling and colour spills and overflows and runs out of control and we end up in meaningless chaos.'

Batty, thought 5A. Utterly loopy. Sex-starved, poor old thing. 'But if you only have the rhythm and the structure without the tune and the colour and the feeling, then you are dead; a form without a content.'

5A yawned and rustled but Miss Freeman persisted. 'A piece of music is like a life,' she said. 'There are loud parts and quiet parts, calm stretches and stormy passages, heights and depths and plateaux and peaks and troughs. But containing them all must be the framework, the pattern, the structure.'

The bell rang. 'Good afternoon, 5A.'

'Good afternoon, Miss Freeman,' said 5A and hurried to the cloakrooms. It was Wednesday, the night for going Down the Dance at Honeyford.

After school on Wednesdays, Philippa Foster went to her elocution lesson with Miss Willow. The elocution studio was a large, bare, light rented room above the Tarminster Bakery and 300 yards up the road from the Tarminster Brewery. For the rest of their lives, Miss Willow's pupils were to associate poems like 'Cargoes' and 'Home-Thoughts from Abroad' with the too-sweet smell of warm yeast and the breathless fumes of hops.

'Take a deep breath, Philippa. Fill your lungs from the diaphragm; the intercostal diaphragmatic method of breathing, you remember. Don't lift your shoulders. Keep your mouth shut and hum the air out. Keep your throat open and your lips closed. Fill your lungs with the air and your mouth with the sound until you feel your lips vibrating. MMMMMMMMM-MMMM.'

'MMMMMMMMMMMMMM,' hummed Philippa.

Miss Willow had just come back from four days at an Elocution Teachers' Refresher Course in London. The course had been led by a tall and brilliant woman called Melissa Creely, who wore bright, swirling clothes and who spoke in a thrilling voice.

'MMMMMMMMMMMMMM,' she had called to the spiky, fluffy and elasticated women who had come from rented elocution studios and private schools all over the country. 'Hum from your bowels; hum from your genitals.' The spinsters had blushed and hummed obediently, not exactly sure where their bowels and their genitals were.

Now Miss Willow wished that she had the confidence to ask these same things of her Tarminster pupils. But it was quite out of the question, of course.

Philippa's hum ran out of air. 'Very good, dear. Now take another breath – deep as you can but don't move your shoulders – good . . . and let the sound out to MAAAAAAAAAAAA.'

Philippa Maaaaaaaaed and Mooooooooooooed and Mawwwwwwwwwwwwwed and Mayyyyyyed and Meeeeeeeeed her way through her mouth and her nose and her sinuses until her voice was round and flexible and full. Now she was ready to be Viola.

> 'If I did love you in my master's flame,
> With such a suffering, such a deadly life,
> In your denial I would find no sense,
> I would not understand it.'

Pale square Philippa Foster was turning before Miss Willow's eyes into the slender tough little girl in boys' clothes.

'Why, what would you?' Now Philippa was the tall and dark and arrogant Olivia, and then again she turned back into the boy-girl and spoke the lines of passionate love:

> 'Make me a willow cabin at your gate,
> and call upon my soul within the house,
> Write loyal cantons of condemned love
> And sing them loud, even in the dead of night.'

Tit Willow felt the words sink into her and shiver up her spine. How she longed to speak words of love like that to someone who would understand and respond to them. To Mr Whittaker perhaps, who came to give private violin lessons to Tarminster High School girls on Wednesdays and Thursdays when she (Laetitia) was there for Country Dancing. Laetitia had so much passion walled up inside her highly-strung bosom, but nobody had, as yet, released it. It was as if she were a dam, she thought, with a great river of love waiting to burst through her in a terrifying and glorious flood. She would be thirty-six next birthday, she reflected. Thirty-six, with all that passion still walled up inside her, waiting for someone like Mr Whittaker to release it ...

Philippa stopped being Viola and resumed her normal shape. 'Excellent,' said Miss Willow, and she meant it. 'And now I'd like to hear your poem.'

Philippa stood at a three-quarters angle to the front of the studio, breathed deeply without lifting her shoulders and began to recite a poem by Louis MacNeice. It was called 'Les Sylphides' and it was about a short-sighted young man who had fallen madly in love with his girlfriend during a performance of *Les Sylphides* and proposed to her, thus dooming them both to a lifetime of toast and marmalade, morning papers, respectability and bills.

Is that how it would be, thought Laetitia, being married to Mr Whittaker? Would she face him across the cornflakes and only see the back page of *The Times*? Oh, no, no, surely it did not have to be like that! Surely Mr Whittaker would play his violin to her at breakfast and bring her flowers, no matter how long they had been married.

Not for her, thought Philippa, as she finished the poem. Not likely. No marriage and ordinariness for her. She, Philippa Foster – *Sophia Roncetti* – would do something extraordinary, remarkable, memorable with her life. She thanked Miss Willow for the lesson and caught the bus home to Swain's Chard.

Chapter Nineteen

The Reverend Eric Dobbin looked out over the hats and moustaches and the powdered, confident faces of his congregation and wondered again, as he preached his message of poverty and humility, what these people would have done if Jesus and His gang had turned up in church one Sunday morning, muddy from Galilee, rowdy from the pub and with Mary Magdalene in tow.

All the same, thought the Rev. Eric, they were good people, the churchgoers of Swain's Chard. They did not steal or murder or commit adultery, and if they ever coveted their neighbours' Humber Hawks or wives or golf clubs, they kept quiet about it. They would not have dreamed of letting anybody (including God) know if they were less than satisfied with their lot. And most of them were. Absolutely satisfied. No (in the Name of the Father and of the Son and of the Holy Ghost, Amen, turn and walk down the pulpit steps), they were good, kind people who spoke the Queen's English, read the *Daily Telegraph* and believed wholeheartedly in God, Who also read the *Daily Telegraph.* All the same, thought the Vicar again, he would love to see their faces if Jesus and Co walked in.

'I believe in God the Father Almighty, Maker of Heaven and Earth,' Ann Dangerfield yawned as the choir swivelled and faced the altar. 'And in Jesus Christ His only Son Our Lord.' Of course she did and so did Jenny Cornwood who stood behind her in the Choir and so did all the rest of them, chanting the words through the church. Miss Bugle could rabbit on about cabbages, but it was a relief to know that God was up

71

there, looking down at Swain's Chard and smiling on St Swithin's and its congregation ...

'Conceived by the Holy Ghost, Born of the Virgin Mary ...' She and Jenny had had conversations about the practicalities of the Immaculate Conception and the Virgin Birth and had wanted to ask Miss Bugle about them in R.I. But there were some things one did not mention to Miss Bugle. Conception and birth were two of them.

They had broken up on the Wednesday for the Christmas holidays. On the Thursday morning, Philippa, Ann and Jenny had been down at Swain's Chard Post Office, sorting the Christmas post into pigeon-holes and string-tied bundles. Now it was Sunday. Tomorrow night the dancing lessons would begin.

The mothers of Swain's Chard, namely Joan Dangerfield and Madge Foster, had worked out their marvellous plan one Wednesday morning in November. They sat, drinking coffee at the window table of the Chalet Suisse, after an invigorating shampoo and set at Sharon's Salon.

'We'll hire the Institute every night for a week,' Joan had said in a flash of inspiration.

'What on earth for?' Madge asked.

'Dancing lessons. We'll pay Letty Willow to bring her gramophone along and give the children ballroom dancing-lessons every evening for a week. Then, when Christmas is over, we'll hold a Small Dance.'

Madge tried unsuccessfully to envisage her daughter as the Belle of the Ball while Joan's brain went into top gear.

'We'll invite some Suitable Boys – the boarding-school children will be home by then ...' She paused to crumble a piece of scone excitedly. 'And Lady Hennessey's grandsons will be home from Eton. I'm sure she could be persuaded to give a Small Dance at the Manor ...'

She was quiet then, absorbed in a daydream of the Manor drawing room and Ann in the arms of one of Lady Hennessey's grandsons, dancing the Last Waltz to a soft tune played on piano, sax and drums. Madge, too, sipped her coffee in silence. She was trying to work out what on earth Philippa could wear.

Chapter Twenty

And so it was that, on the Monday evening of the last week before Christmas, a row of Suitable Girls sat along one side of the Institute, facing a row of Suitable Boys on the other. 'I feel like something out of *Pride and Prejudice*,' said Philippa. They were doing it for 'O' level. The door opened and Lady Hennessey's grandsons entered.

Miss Willow set up her gramophone on the little stage. 'Good evening, Ladies and Gentlemen.' The mothers of Swain's Chard were paying her five shillings an evening to teach their children the Waltz, the Quickstep, the Cha-Cha-Cha and the etiquette of the dance floor. 'The first dance I am going to teach you is the Waltz. Gentlemen, will you please take your partners.'

Nobody moved.

'I can see that I shall have to begin at the beginning. Gentlemen, stand up.'

They stood up.

'Now go up to a lady and say to her, "May I have the pleasure of this dance?"'

Ann had a sudden memory of Big Ted Down the Dance. 'Dance?' he had said, jerking his head towards the juke-box.

'May I have the pleasure of this dance?' enquired a gangly youth from the Boys' Grammar School, meandering across the floor and stopping in front of her.

'And Ladies, you must say, "Thank you very much",' ordered Miss Willow.

'Thank you very much,' Ann said, and got to her feet. At least she was not a wallflower. Philippa, who was, grinned bravely and pretended not to mind. (Jenny, who was not considered suitable by the mothers of Swain's Chard, was not there.)

'There are still some people without partners,' called Miss Willow reproachfully.

A very small boy who had been press-ganged into the classes by his mother, walking jerkily across the floor to Philippa. 'May I have the pleasure of this dance?'

'Thank you very much.' She stood up and the top of his head was level with her chin.

'Gentlemen, place your right arm around your partner's waist, with the palm of your hand flat against her back. Ladies, place your left hand on your partner's shoulder.' Philippa bent her knees and her partner peered out desperately from beneath her armpit. She wished she knew his name. 'Now Gentlemen, hold out your left hand with the palm facing upwards, and Ladies, put your right hand, palm downwards, in his hand and stand with your feet together.' The Suitable Boys and Girls of Swain's Chard gripped each other.

'Smile,' urged Miss Willow. 'Imagine that you are making triangles with your feet – but don't look at them. Look at each other – and *smile*. Gentlemen, move your right foot forwards; Ladies, move your left foot back.'

Right feet trod on left feet, faces smiled bravely, eyes stared past ears. Philippa's partner stared in terror at Philippa's bust.

'That is the first side of your triangle. Now move your other foot until it is about ten inches away from the first one and parallel to it. That is your hypotenuse.' How rude, thought Philippa, and began to giggle silently. 'The next part is easy,' said Miss Willow. 'You simply move the first foot to meet the second foot and that makes the base of the triangle.'

Philippa was shaking and tears of pent-up laughter were running down her cheeks. Her very small partner stared manfully ahead of him and then he too began to shake.

Slowly and carefully, the dancers plodded around the edge of the floor. One two three; forward to the side join up. *Da* da de *da*; forward to the side join up. After three rounds, Miss Willow put a record on the gramophone and the flowing melody of the *Skater's Waltz* slid around the Institute.

'Don't look at your feet. Keep your arms up. Smile at your partner. Relax!' cried Miss Willow.

74

Eventually the *Skater's Waltz* skidded to its final chord and they dropped their partners thankfully and fled back to their chairs. 'Good gracious me, no!' Miss Willow cried. 'No, that won't do at all. You can't just drop your partner like some old parcel, Gentlemen. You must thank her and lead her back to her place.'

'Thank you,' said the gangly boy from the Grammar School. 'Thank you,' said Philippa's very small partner.

On the Saturday after the final Friday lesson, a simple white card arrived through the Dangerfield letter-box. Lady Hennessey, it said, requested the pleasure of the company of Miss Ann Dangerfield at a Small Dance to be held at the Manor House on Thursday, January 4th at 8 p.m. RSVP. Miss Ann Dangerfield, under the strict supevision of her mother, thanked Lady Hennessey for her kind invitation and had much pleasure in accepting it. With a sense of achievement, Joan propped the card up on the Welsh dresser and telephoned Madge to see if Philippa had had one. She had.

'Our Jennifer's got one of them,' said Phyllis with satisfaction, moving the invitation to dust the Willow Pattern plates on the dresser. Jenny had not been invited to the Institute dancing classes and Phyllis had fumed with resentment. 'Snobby lot,' she had raged to Arthur. 'Our kids are as good as theirs any day.' And then she had gone out and climbed the hill to watch the rain clouds crossing Tarminster until they had broken furiously over her head. 'Blow winds and crack your cheeks,' she had said out loud. Funny thing to say, she thought. Wherever had she got that from?

Jenny's post-round included the Manor. On the Tuesday after the Monday of the *Skater's Waltz* lesson, she trudged up the long driveway, crunching Wellington sole-marks into the new fall of snow, past the lopsided cedars and berried holly bushes, round the sweep of the drive and off up the pathway to the Tradesmen's Entrance. NO HAWKERS NO CIRCULARS.

'Hiya,' said a cheerful voice. The front door was open and Guy Hennessey was standing at the top of the steps, barefooted and wrapped in a tartan dressing grown. 'I can't come out,

I've lost my slippers. Could you bring the post up here?'

She carried the bundle of cards up the steps and handed them to him. They had known each other by sight all their lives and they knew each other's names, but this was the first time they had spoken.

'Why aren't you coming to the ghastly dancing classes at the Institute?' he asked. And that was why the simple white invitation had been posted through the Cornwoods' letter-box two days later.

Chapter Twenty-One

'You can wear the white dress if you like,' said Ann's big sister
Mollie, home for Christmas from Domestic Science College.
'I've grown out of it anyway.' The white dress had arrived by
surface mail three years before, wrapped in massed layers of
tissue paper and strung and sealed in heavy-duty brown parcel
paper. A wealthy second cousin in America had worn it once
and then had posted it across the Atlantic to her Dangerfield
relations.

They could still remember opening the parcel. The dress
was different from anything else they had ever seen or worn. It
was ballerina length, tight-waisted, full-skirted and scoop-
necked. Pleated net swung out in a hip-high circle when
Mollie twirled, and she had twirled many a time in front of her
bedroom mirror wishing for a chance to wear the dress in
public. But the mothers of Swain's Chard had not got into their
stride in time for Mollie, and the white dress had never left the
house. Ann had tried it on secretly when Mollie, now too tall
and too wide to fit into it, was safely away at Domestic Science
College. It was not a dress to wear Down the Dance, but it was
exactly the dress for a Small Dance at the Manor. Ann was
shamed by her sister's generosity. She knew that Mollie would
have gouged out her eyes if she had caught her wearing it
without permission.

Ann took off all her clothes and stood in front of the mirror.
What a waste, she thought. What a waist. She looked very
good with no clothes on. What a waste that nobody else would
see how good she looked. Apart from the rest of 5A in the
showers, of course. But that was not what she meant. Mollie

had put an Everly Brothers' record on the gramophone down-stairs. *When I feel blue, In the night, And I want you, To hold me tight*. The plaintive notes came up through the bedroom floor. Ann began to dance, naked and smiling at her reflection. She ought to become a stripper or a night-club dancer but, of course, that would never happen. Nice Girls from Swain's Chard could not be strippers. She heard her mother coming up the stairs and stepped into the white dress, pulling it up over her shoulders. Demurely, she looked at her new reflection.

'It's beautiful, darling,' Joan exclaimed. 'It's perfect. You'll never be a wallflower. Now remember, always let the man do the chasing. Never show him that you are interested.' There was a pause and she put on her meaningful face. 'And don't get Emotionally Involved.'

She smoothed out a ruck in the frock and lowered her voice to a confidential whisper. 'You've got IT, you know.'

Ann was puzzled. 'It?'

'*IT* – you know – S.A. A girl's either got it or she hasn't. And if she's got it, she'll never lose it. And you have.'

'What is it?' Ann was whispering too.

Joan lowered her voice still further. 'S.A. *Sex appeal*.'

Ann went hot with horror. Her mother had used the forbidden word. Her mother, who still denied the need for bras and deodorants and boys. How on earth could her mother know about Sex Appeal?

'You see, I had it too,' said Joan. She blushed and left the room.

Phyllis Cornwood, her mouth full of pins, knelt on the dining-room floor while Jenny turned in slow circles on top of the table. 'It's up a bit on the left. Stand still, Jennifer,' mumbled Phyllis through the pins, tweaking the untacked hem level. 'Now go on turning.'

Jenny turned, very slowly, keeping her feet level and her knees straight, wincing when a pin-point scraped the back of her legs. The material was a heavy, satin-like midnight blue. Phyllis had spent her cleaning money recklessly to make sure that her daughter would shine at the Manor House dance and prove that the Cornwoods were just as good as the Dangerfields, the Fosters, the Hennesseys and all the rest of them.

'Go upstairs to the bedroom mirror and see if it's right.'

Jenny looked at herself critically. She always wore jeans. Now she saw a girl in a gleaming dark-blue dress – the same colour as Philippa Foster's eyes, she thought – with a scooped neck and narrow shoulders, a tight bodice and bell-shaped skirt that swung to just below her knees.

Phyllis came into the room and pulled a face at her. 'You'll be climbing trees again by Sunday.'

'It's a bit too short, Our Mum. Sorry. Can you do the hem again, two inches longer?' Phyllis sniffed and took another mouthful of pins.

'I'm not wearing *that*,' said Philippa Foster.

'Don't be so silly, Philippa,' said Madge irritably.

'Look at me,' Philippa insisted. 'I'm not exactly the dazzling beauty of the dance floor, am I? I'm not some demure heroine who will blossom in the light of a romantic hero's love. *Am I?*'

For days, Madge had been hunting through copies of *Vogue* and *Tatler*, trying to find good ideas for a dress. From every page, slender, petite, expensive girls looked coolly or flirtatiously over their shoulders, bent sideways from their hips, laughed brightly into their admirers' eyes. None of them looked remotely like Philippa.

In desperation, the day before Christmas Eve, Madge telephone Miss Gibson who ran the haberdashery shop in Swain's Chard and took in dressmaking. Miss Gibson sketched out a box-like dress with huge puffed sleeves and a panelled skirt. 'I'm not wearing that,' hissed Philippa, while Miss Gibson was out of the room. 'It'll make me look like Henry the Eighth. Or Dan Dare.'

Chapter Twenty-Two

The dining room at the Manor was forty feet long and twenty feet wide, with bow-windowed recesses along one side of it, glass-shaded gas brackets down the other side of it and French windows opening onto the formal gardens at the far end.

The Henry Morrison Dance Trio (piano, sax and drums) smiled and nodded above its bow ties and played sprightly music in the dining room as the Suitable Girls and Boys of Swain's Chard arrived in the hall and were shown to the bedrooms which had been set aside as cloakrooms for the evening. Lord Hennessey stood at the dining-room door, ladling steaming and potent fruit punch into goblets and handing them to his young guests.

The girls, nervous and smiling in scoop-necked dresses and silver sandals, in borrowed necklaces and bracelets and sequinned evening bags, sidled into the dining room, sipping at the punch. They sat in chilly little clusters on window seats and chairs. *Dance with me*, they prayed inside their heads, *Please, somebody – anybody – dance with me, Don't let me be a wallflower*.

Boys in white shirts and dinner jackets fiddled with their bow ties until the band began to play a Waltz and, 'May I have the pleasure of this dance?' said Suitable Boys to Suitable Girls who smiled with relief and granted them the pleasure. *One two three, one two three,* called the voice of Tit Willow in their heads; *back to the side join feet*. The Waltz ended and the boys thanked the girls and returned them to their window ledges. Lord Hennessey ladled out more punch and the gas brackets glowed with a warmer light.

Ann Dangerfield shone in the white lace dress, with a dusting of her mother's powder on her nose and a smear of deodorant under her arms. 'If your hands get hot, run your wrists under a cold tap,' Joan had said, as she touched the inside corners of her daughter's eyes with a bright red Leichner stick. She stepped back to inspect Ann. 'You look wonderful, darling ... so just remember that. Believe that you look wonderful and you will. Off you go and enjoy yourself. You've got IT. Never forget that. IT.'

Ann still found it difficult to reconcile these two halves of her mother. The old one blushed at the very thought of bras and boys. And then, quite without warning, the new one poked her head out and said, 'You've got IT.' And, just as suddenly, she disappeared and the old one took over again.

Jennifer Cornwood's midnight-blue dress swung like an upside-down flower halfway between her ankles and her knees as she crossed the dining-room floor. Phyllis and Arthur had given her dark-blue shoes with little heels for Christmas and there had been a suspender belt and a strapless bra in her stocking. Now she felt the unaccustomed tightness of the belt around her middle and she wriggled a little in time to the music. Guy Hennessey came across the room towards her.

Philippa Foster sat, large and square, a cross between Henry VIII and Dan Dare. The stiff navy velvet corduroy of Miss Gibson's dress stuck out on either side of her and bunched up in her lap. She had been there for half an hour. Desperately, she tried to summon up the soul of Sophia Roncetti, but even Sophia could not battle her way out of the awful dress.

Ann Dangerfield danced past her, radiant with Sex Appeal. 'Who on earth wants Sex Appeal?' Madge had scoffed. 'It's very common. You've got more than that. You've got Distinct Talent.' But that night all that Philippa wanted was S.A. Partner after partner queued to dance with Ann and the white dress. Jenny Cornwood floated by, a dreamy blue flower in Guy Hennessey's arms. They had danced with each other all evening.

Dan Dare sat on, alone.

A late arrival skulked through the door of the dining room. It was Jeremy Carruthers, the very small boy from the dancing class. He stood uncertainly on the edge of the dance floor, eyeing passing belles with dismay until he sighted Philippa. With obvious relief, he made his way towards her and sat down beside her. Lord Hennessey bore down on them with two steaming goblets of punch. Philippa and Jeremy Carruthers inhaled the steam and sipped. At once the room was cosier, the music grew more urgent, the glow of the gaslights warmed them. Sophia Roncetti uncurled a little.

'Would you like another drink?' asked Jeremy Carruthers. Sophia Roncetti smiled. What extraordinary eyes she has, thought Jeremy Carruthers. He had never seen them properly before because his face had never been on a level with hers before. At the dancing classes, the top of his head had barely reached her chin. But now, sitting beside her in the glow of the gaslight, the punch and the music, he could look into her extraordinary navy-blue eyes.

Feeling slightly dizzy, he picked up the goblets and meandered towards Lord Hennessey. 'Refill?' asked the Lord. 'Thank you, sir,' said Jeremy Carruthers. He returned to Philippa. He could not stop looking at her eyes. Sophia Roncetti smiled out of them, dark and wild and dangerous.

The Henry Morrison Trio played on. The Suitable Boys and Girls danced Quicksteps (one two three four), Veletas and Eightsomes and Waltzes. There were Ladies' Excuse Mes and Paul Joneses and Tea for Two cha cha and Two for Tea cha cha. St Bernard waltzed, White Sergeants Dashed and 'May I have the pleasure of this dance?' said the Swain's Chard boys to the Swain's Chard girls.

The band began to play a Tango. But Tit Willow's classes had not got as far as the Tango; a Waltz and a Quickstep, a Veleta and a Cha-Cha-Cha ought to have been enough to see them through these holidays. The rhythm of the Tango throbbed in the dining room and the gas flames trembled in response. 'Come on,' said the punch in Jeremy Carruthers to the eyes of Sophia Roncetti, and he led her out onto the floor. Nobody else was dancing. How could they? Nobody knew the steps.

But now, out there in the middle of the floor, wild and exotic, released by the music and five glasses of punch, Sophia Roncetti, alias Philippa Foster (who, as well as being very kind, had suddenly discovered co-ordination and natural musicality) danced a Tango with Jeremy Carruthers.

And then it was half-past eleven and midnight was in sight. 'May I have the pleasure of the Last Waltz?' Guy Hennessey asked Jenny. 'May I have the pleasure of the Last Waltz?' Jeremy Carruthers asked Philippa. 'May I have the pleasure of the Last Waltz?' so many people asked Ann that she pretended not to hear and shook her head and laughed. The Last Waltz was special. She would wait and see.

At ten minutes to midnight, Charlie Cornwood walked across the Park and climbed the wide steps to the front door. 'Go and pick your sister up, our Charlie,' Phyllis had said. 'I don't want her walking back on her own.' Now Charlie knocked on the Manor front door and was welcomed inside by Lord Hennessey. 'Punch?' said the Lord, pouring it out and ushering him into the dining room.

At five minutes to midnight, the first parents knocked on the Manor front door. Soon a group of them clustered in the hall, drinking fruit punch and smiling nostalgically as they tapped their feet to the music of Henry Morrison.

The mood changed as Lord Hennessey turned the gaslights down. 'And now, take your partners for the Last Waltz,' murmured Henry Morrison seductively. Guy took Jenny's hand, Jeremy took Philippa's hand and the gangly youth from the Boys' Grammar School headed across the room towards Ann. 'May I have the pleasure of—' he began.

'Dance?' interrupted Charlie Cornwood and Ann was in his arms. She felt electric, magnetic, light and beautiful and all the other things that she had ever dreamed of feeling when the band played the music for the Last Waltz. The lights were very dim and Charlie Cornwood held her very close. He bent his head until their cheeks were touching as the Waltz tune carried them round and round the room. Parents came into the dimness and smiled benignly and anxiously at the indistinguishable shapes moving gently to the music. The Waltz reached its final bars and Charlie Cornwood kissed Ann Dangerfield. She remembered the touch of his lips on hers for the rest of her life.

The gaslights were turned up again and the mothers smiled and peered. Madge saw Philippa holding hands with a rather small boy and breathed a sigh of relief; then she saw Jennifer

83

Cornwood in the arms of Guy Hennessey. And then, Good Lord, who on earth was that, over in the far corner of the dining room, near the French windows, locked in a passionate embrace, oblivious to everything? Joan saw Jennifer Cornwood in the arms of Guy Hennessey, Philippa Foster holding hands with a very short boy, and then ... Good Lord!

Chapter Twenty-Three

Charlie Cornwood walked his sister home. 'I saw you kissing Ann Dangerfield in the Last Waltz,' said Jenny accusingly. Charlie puffed out his best and swaggered like a pigeon. 'Don't fool about, our Charlie. I mean it. She's my best friend and I don't want anybody getting hurt.'

Charlie grinned and punched her affectionately. 'I don't think it hurt her,' he said. 'Anyway, you can talk. Who was that bloke you was all wrapped up in?'

'Shut up, Charlie. You know what I mean. What about Mary? I know it doesn't mean nothing to you. I know it's only a bit of fun. But people do get hurt.'

'Nobody's going to get hurt. Your friend's a nice kid. And she's pretty, too. There's nothing wrong with a kiss for Christmas, is there?' And Charlie delivered his sister through the back door, climbed aboard his motorbike and roared back down the hills to Honeyford and Mary.

It snowed again that night. At first it came in tiny fast flakes that spun and clung to the cold ground and covered it with a thin white skin. Then the big flakes came, whirling and dancing over the sleeping villages, settling on bare branches and roofs and hills and hedges. A rough wind leapt across the hill and through the wood and blew the snow into waves and drifts, so that Swain's Chard awoke to a sea of snow that called a glorious halt to work and school and responsibility, and sent the whole village into its sheds and outhouses to dig out toboggans and old tin trays. The school bus could not run, the fathers could not get to work. The snow was a white blessing that gave them an extra week of holiday.

'Come on, Philippa,' called Jeremy Carruthers, shifting back on his racing toboggan to make room for her in front of him. Philippa squeezed onto what was left of the seat, bending her knees and braking the sledge with her feet. Jeremy's view was completely blocked. 'OK?' he asked.

'OK,' said Philippa, lifting her feet and wedging them against the uprights of the runners.

Jeremy had greased the metal strips and the sledge flew down the first slope of the run, skimming the snow and leaping ruts and pitches as it gathered speed. 'Lean over!' yelled Philippa, leaning to the right as Jeremy leaned to the left; the toboggan veered, swerved and tipped them off into a deep drift on the edge of the run. For a minute they lay there, laughing and breathless, glowing with speed and the bite of the wind in their faces. And then, for the second time in a week, Jeremy found himself on the same level as the navy-blue eyes of Sophia Roncetti and electricity trembled in the air between them. Then, hurriedly, Sophia clambered clumsily onto her feet and turned back into Philippa Foster, brushing snow off her coat and gloves and Jeremy remembered that he was five feet four and she was five feet seven. They turned and trudged back up the slope, towing the sledge behind them.

Both the Cornwoods carried tin trays under their arms. Guy watched them climbing the slope; Jenny in front with Jimmy and Finch in tow. He waved and waited for them to catch him up at the top of the run. 'Hiya,' he said. 'Race you.' And he lay belly down, flat on his sledge.

Jenny laughed and lined up alongside him on her tray. 'Go on, Jim. We'll give you a start.'

Jimmy launched himself, they counted to five and followed, surfing the snow and steering with their feet. Jimmy came to a sudden stop in a deep drift, but Jenny and Guy raced on, neck and neck, gasping and laughing into the wind until the ground flattened out and slowed down. 'Dead heat,' said Guy and they turned and began to climb the slope again. Philippa yelled and waved from the Carruthers' racer.

Ann pulled her sledge up the lane from the house, smiling to herself and dreaming of Charlie Cornwood and the way that he had kissed her in the Last Waltz. She re-lived the way it had made her feel. Perhaps he would have scorned the snow and ridden through it up the roads from Honeyford, like some impossible knight in shining armour. Perhaps he would be waiting to claim her at the top of the toboggan run.

'Hello, Ann.' It was the gangly boy from the Grammar School. She could never remember whether he was called Andrew or Adrian. 'Going sledging?'

What, she thought irritably, did he imagine she was doing, walking through the snow in Wellington boots and gloves, pulling a toboggan behind her! He had a sledge in tow as well and he plodded along beside her.

'There's a good film on at the Hippodrome next Saturday,' he said, looking away from her. 'I wondered whether you might like to come and see it?'

A boy was asking her to the pictures, thought Ann. It must be her S.A.

Jennifer Cornwood and Jimmy Cornwood and Finch Cornwood and Guy Hennessey just seemed to somehow happen to meet every day of that snow week. By chance, they always chose the same times to walk up the lane from the village and out onto the snow-covered slopes. 'Look,' said Jimmy, 'There's that bloke again. I reckon he likes you.' Jimmy took it upon himself to shadow his sister relentlessly. One day, Guy said, 'Shall we go out for a walk this evening?'

'Where you going, our Jennifer?' asked Phyllis that evening after supper.

'Taking Finch for a walk.' said Jenny, praying that Jimmy wouldn't hear.

'I'm coming too,' said Jimmy.

'No, you're not.'

'Yes I am.'

Phyllis grabbed her son. 'No, you're not. It's dark, far too late for you to be out. Mind you wrap up warm, Jennifer.'

Jimmy was furious. 'She's gone to meet that Lady Hennessey's grandson.' Phyllis smiled.

He was waiting for her near the churchyard wall. She saw the light of his cigarette and smelled the foreign smell of it before she reached him. It was a clear, still, frosty night; the sky and the stars were millions of miles away and Swain's Chard shone white and clean in the streetlamps. They set off towards the hill. Jenny could think of nothing to say now that there was no tin tray to ride, no little brother to shout at, no music to dance to. Then Guy reached out and held her hand and there was no need for her to say anything at all. They walked on through the snow and starlight, listening to a small wind soughing in the branches and watching Finch as she chased night smells and scrabbled in snowdrifts.

The next evening, Guy took her to the Flying Pig in the village. It was the first time a boy had invited her out for a drink and she didn't know what to ask for. Then she remembered that Judith Littlewick always said she drank Babycham when a boy took her out to a pub, so she asked for one.

She watched Guy as he stood against the bar and her heart lurched with love for him. He was tall and very good-looking, with thick brown hair and grey eyes that laughed to her when he glanced back and caught her watching him. She blushed and looked away. His mouth was wide and generous and he was handsome and he was with her.

'What are you smiling at?' He put the drinks down on their table. She shook her head and smiled again. On the way home, he kissed her and she thought that she would melt like warmed snow.

'I'm not going out on my own with him,' said Ann to Philippa. 'I wouldn't know what to say.'

'You probably wouldn't get a chance to say anything,' said Philippa sagely. 'He'll probably lure you into the double seats in the back row, leap upon you and have his wicked way.'

When they had stopped laughing, Ann said, 'In any case, my mother'd never let me go to the pictures with a boy.'

'All right,' said Philippa, 'I'll come with you – if the buses are running by then. Pity it wasn't Charlie Cornwood who asked you to go, eh?'

'Don't be daft,' said Ann, looking at something a long way off so that Philippa wouldn't see her blushing. 'Why on earth should I go to the pictures with Charlie Cornwood? Anyway, he's got a Steady.' And she remembered the electric shock of Charlie's lips on hers at the end of the Last Waltz.

'Who are you going to the pictures with, Ann?' asked Joan.

'Philippa,' Ann replied. It wasn't a lie.

The ground began to thaw on the Friday and the main roads were passable by the evening. 'One of my schoolfriends is having a party tomorrow night,' said Guy to Jennifer. 'Will you come with me?'

Adrian or Andrew found himself sitting in a middle row of the Hippodrome at Tarminster, between Ann and Philippa, sharing a bag of popcorn with them both.

Jenny wore the midnight-blue dress and the low-heeled shoes again. 'You look beautiful,' said Guy Hennessey when he collected her in his tinny old Austin Ten. But at the party in a big house three miles out of Swain's Chard, she did not feel beautiful at all; she felt like a dull little country bumpkin. The other girls were sleek and slim and groomed like show thoroughbreds and they eyed her with suspicion and turned their backs on her and talked of hunting and Oxford and ski-ing and balls and boarding schools in Switzerland. Guy held her close to him. 'You're prettier than any of them,' he whispered.

One of his friends tapped him on the shoulder. 'Excuse me – don't hog this girl all night.' He smiled at Jenny and slid himself between them. 'I'm Philip Smythe. I don't believe we've met. Who're you?'

'Jenny Cornwood,' said Jenny.

'Well, Jenny Cornwood, I must say old Guy's been very secretive about you.' He was a good dancer and they moved easily round the room to a fast Quickstep. 'Are you up yet?'

'Up?'

'At University.'

Jenny laughed. 'Oh no, I'm still at school.'

'Where's that?' asked the young man called Philip Smythe.

'Tarminster Girls' High,' said Jennifer Cornwood and something rose in her so that she said, 'And my dad's a postman and my mum goes out cleaning houses, before you ask.' The young man called Philip Smythe smiled politely, but he blushed and finished the Quickstep in silence.

Afterwards, when Guy drove her home that night and stopped in the road outside her gate, he said, 'I think I'm beginning to fall in love with you.' He kissed her in the tinny darkness of the Austin Ten and she knew that he meant it, that it was true.

But all the time, beneath the kissing and the touching and the gazing and the murmurs, they both knew that there could be no future in a love affair between a High School girl from the council houses and the boy from Eton whose grandmother was the Lady of the Manor.

The snow melted away and so did the magic time of snowballs and sledging and falling in love. Guy Hennessey kissed Jenny Cornwood goodbye and went back to Eton; Jeremy Carruthers threw a last snowball at Philippa Foster and went back to wherever he had come from. Adrian or Andrew gave up on Ann and turned his attentions to a girl in 4A who was very impressed by him.

The school bus ran again and the girls returned to gabardine macs and berets and slip-on shoes. Sometimes Charlie Cornwood rode past on his motorbike while Ann was waiting for the school bus. He always waved and wolf-whistled.

Chapter Twenty-Four

Ann was on Dinner Duty, serving stew and gravy from a huge metal pot on a trestle table to the queue of Junior girls who received it with groans of disgust. Philppa and Jenny had collected their cutlery bags and were already eating their dinner at the far end of the Hall. 'We'll see you in the cloakrooms after dinner,' they had said to Ann. The Senior Cloakrooms were a favourite and forbidden gossip place for fifth-year girls in winter.

'This is revolting,' said Philippa. 'How we can be expected to be truly thankful for it defeats me.'

Jenny chased a carrot through her gravy.' 'Phil ...' she said uneasily and stopped.

'Yes?' said Philippa.

Jenny speared the carrot. 'You know at the Manor dance?'

'Yes,' said Philippa patiently.

'Did you see – well, did you see my brother Charlie with Ann?'

'Yes,' said Philippa.

'The thing is,' said Jenny, staring at her stew, 'I can't really say anything to her about him – he is my brother and that – and there's no meanness in him or anything ... but Ann isn't taking him seriously, is she?' At last she had said it. 'I mean, Charlie'd never hurt anybody on purpose – but he's kind and funny and quite good-looking, I suppose, and girls fall for him all the time. He's a flirt, but he doesn't mean anything by it. And he's been going steady with Mary for years and years and everybody knows they'll get married one day and I want to tell Ann not to go and fall for him but I'm too embarrassed.'

Philippa blotted up gravy in some mashed potato thoughtfully. She was bursting to part with Ann's 4A confidence after the night Down the Dance. 'Promise me you won't tell her if I tell you something?' she began, 'She'd kill me if she knew. But she told me once that your brother was the only person she – well, who she really liked.'

Jenny sighed. 'Lots of girls like Charlie.'

Now Philippa could not stop. 'Ann said he was the only person she had ever seen that she could imagine – you know – doing it with.'

They both went red with shame. It was different when you talked about Gregory Peck or Cliff Richard or Dirk Bogarde. Then it was distant and impossible and safe. But when you talked about your best friend and your brother, you had moved onto the dangerous territory of the possible.

'I shouldn't have told you.' Philippa was deeply ashamed of herself. 'Promise you won't say anything.' Jenny promised.

Later, in the privacy of the Senior Cloakrooms, the three of them sat on the wooden lids of the shoe-lockers, shrouded by gabardine macs. 'I never knew you could dance like that,' Ann said to Philippa.

'Like what?'

'When you and that little bloke got up and did the Tango.'

'Oh,' said Philippa, 'was that what it was? I didn't know; I just did it. I think there must have been something in that fruit punch. I had a terrible headache in the night.'

'What's he called, your little bloke?' asked Jenny.

'You keep on asking me that. He's called Jeremy Carruthers. And he's not mine.'

'Oh, yes. It's just that he's so little I keep on forgetting. D'you like him?'

'Don't be daft,' retorted Philippa. 'He only comes up to my knees. If I stepped backwards, I'd tread on him.'

They re-lived the dance, remembering who had looked good and who had looked awful, who had worn what and who had got off with whom and who had been left out. But when they approached the time of the Last Waltz, the conversation faltered then veered away to the safer ground of the snow and the toboggan rides and the extra white week of the Christmas holidays.

'So what about you and Guy Hennessey?' Philippa said to Jenny. (They were safely out of the Manor dining room and the slow one-two-three of Henry Morrison and out on the helter-skelter of the toboggan run.) Charlie was firmly back in Honeyford with Mary and no one had mentioned him. Jenny felt herself go warm at the sound of Guy's name and the others laughed.

'He's gorgeous, isn't he?' said Ann and she began to hum *I'm as Corny as Kansas in August*.

'He seemed pretty keen on you,' said Philippa, whose shape and generous spirit allowed her to say things that other girls might hesitate to say.

'I think he was a bit,' said Jenny, remembering the night walks in the snow, the bar at the Flying Pig, the kissing in the car after the party at his friend's house.

'You didn't ...'

'No, of course I didn't,' said Jenny immediately. The others sighed with relief. They did not want to see her in the light of one who had. All the same, they would have liked to know how far she had gone with Guy Hennessey. It was, of course, quite out of the question to ask.

Later on, when Ann and Philippa were on their own at the Fosters' house, Ann said, 'I think she's really keen on Guy Hennessey.'

'Yes,' said Philippa, and because she was generous-spirited, she added, 'And I think Guy Hennessey's really keen on her.' They were quiet for a moment, mulling it over.

'That would be something, wouldn't it? thought Ann out loud. 'Say they really fell properly in love and got married and Jenny turned into Lady Hennessey?'

'I expect her mum'd stop cleaning for your mum then,' said Philippa. It was an interesting idea.

At home, in her bedroom, reading *Jane Eyre* and dreaming of the way Guy Hennessey had kissed her, Jenny knew all over again that nothing would come of a love affair between a postman's daughter and a Lady of the Manor's grandson. It was all right for Jane Eyre, she came from a posh background, even if Mr Rochester didn't realise it. She yawned and got up and took Finch out for a walk.

Philippa was away from school with a cold. At dinner-time,

Jenny and Ann sat in the forest of gabardine macs and talked about her. 'She's changing, isn't she? I don't mean nastily. But she's getting more ... confident,' said Ann.

Jenny agreed. 'I think it's since she's found she's good at acting. It doesn't matter any more that she's no good at Games or Maths or Music. She knows what she can do and she's doing it.'

She's lucky, thought Ann. And then she thought, But I'd sooner be sexy.

In the next silence, Jenny almost said to Ann: 'I want to talk to you about Charlie and tell you not to fall for him because he's good-looking and a flirt and he kissed you in the Last Waltz.' But she couldn't say it. It would have been too embarrassing. So she thought about Guy Hennessey instead.

And all the time, Ann was aching to say, 'I want to talk to you about Charlie. I want to say his name and tell you I think about him all the time and go all fuzzy when I remember how he kissed me. But I can't because you're his sister and because he's twenty and I'm fifteen and he failed the eleven-plus and I'm at the High School and you live in the council houses and we live up a private road. And your mum cleans for my mum.'

How could she possibly say all those things to Jenny?

Chapter Twenty-Five

It must have been spring, something in the air, something that rose like the sap in the trees, that made Norman Foster leave his office before lunch one Wednesday and drive home to Swain's Chard. He felt skittish and restless, full of energy, in need of a change. Perhaps Madge would come out for a sandwich at the Golf Club.

But Madge was not at home; he had forgotten that Wednesday was her day for Sharon's Salon and coffee at the Chalet Suisse. Now she and Joan were walking the dogs over the hill.

What could he do? A round of golf perhaps? But something stirred in Norman. He wanted a change from golf, a mini-adventure. Without even bothering to change out of his office suit, he wandered into the shed and saw Delilah's bridle and halter hanging from their hook.

Norman frowned. He did not understand bridles. He had never even sat on a horse. Horses were not his forte. But perhaps one should change one's fortes in one's forties. He smiled ponderously at the pun; it was really rather good. He must remember to tell it to Madge when she came home.

Well, he thought, unhooking the bridle and halter, without really noticing what he was doing, there was nothing to stop him from strolling over to Long Berrow to get some fresh air.

Lambs skedaddled and skipped in the fields, birds shouted at him and catkins brushed his face as he wandered along the Long Berrow lane. 'Younger than Springtime,' he hummed under this breath and out of tune. The sun shone onto the primroses and the birds sang along with him. He turned left along the bumpy track that led to Delilah's field and followed it away from the farm buildings and down a slope to a five-barred gate. There was Delilah, aged and drowsy, snoozing against a chestnut tree and swishing her tail to brush away flies.

Norman put one foot on the bottom bar of the gate, thought better of it, removed the foot and opened the gate. He closed it again carefully (always close a gate behind you) and walked cautiously up to Delilah. 'Good afternoon,' said Norman. Delilah flared her nostrils and sneezed at him. He looked at the bridle in his hands. Never turn your back on a challenge. He reached out an awkward hand and patted the old mare's nose. The brand-new leaves of the chestnut tree sparkled and waved at him and lambs cried in their babyish voices from the next field. Delilah smiled.

Norman looked at the bridle again and tried to remember how the girls had put it on. (Always face a problem head on.) But as soon as he got the top strap over the top of the old mare's head, the bit rested halfway up her nose. He didn't know how to open her mouth. Delilah yawned a gap-toothed yellow yawn and Norman decided against the bridle and picked up the halter. This was much easier. He slipped the noseband up Delilah's long face and the other bit behind her ears. He smiled with satisfaction. If at first you don't succeed...

'Come along, old girl. We're going for a walk.' Surprised but amiable enough, Delilah plodded along beside him. 'A four-legged friend, a four-legged friend, he'll never let you down,' droned Norman tunelessly. The lambs laughed from the next field.

They came to the water trough. 'Drink?' asked Norman. He might have been at a Swain's Chard cocktail party. Delilah plunged her nose into the water and drank. Norman looked at her. The side of the trough was two feet high and she was standing at an angle close to it. If he stood on the edge of it he could ...

Delilah raised her head in surprise at the unaccustomed weight on her back. She sneezed and shrugged her shoulders phlegmatically and wandered away from the trough. 'Whoa,' said Norman nervously. Delilah flicked her ears and wandered on. Norman's stout legs in their office trousers stuck plumply out on either side of her.

96

Hoofs clip-clopped along the lane on the far side of the field. Delilah pricked her ears and ambled into a lopsided trot towards the sound. 'Whoa. Oh whoa, whoa,' panted Norman. Meet your problems head on, he reminded himself. But it wasn't his head that was the problem. Delilah was broad in the beam and he bumped about painfully as she ambled towards the lane and the clip-clopping sound, whinnying gently at the glossy horses and their glossy riders who trotted briskly past.

'Good afternoon,' they cried in horsey voices, raising their crops and touching the peaks of their hard black hats.

Stiff upper lip, thought Norman. 'Good afternoon,' he answered breathlessly, praying he wouldn't fall off until they had gone by.

They vanished up the lane and Delilah slowed down to a walk again. Thank goodness for that. Now he could get off and go home. He had had his springtime adventure. In future, he'd stick to golf and to standing on his own feet.

But he couldn't work out how to get back onto his own feet. His legs simply refused to bend in the right directions. He pointed one foot towards Delilah's tail, but it would not come up in line with her back. She stopped and bent her head to crop at the grass and her neck stretched in front of him like a slide in a children's playground. But Norman had never liked playgrounds much, even as a child. Delilah lifted her head again and set off on her vague wanderings.

Norman tried to steer her back towards the water trough, but she ignored his tugs on her halter rope and simply wandered, slowly and solemnly round and round in vague circles. The lambs bleated from the other field and their mothers stared through the hedge at the curious sight.

Madge was pleasantly surprised to see the Sunbeam Talbot in the drive when she came back from her walk with Joan. 'Hello darling,' she called through the back door, but nobody was there. Madge frowned. Funny. It was unlike Norman to come home early. She hoped he was all right.

Philippa banged into the kitchen. 'Mum, have you seen Delilah's bridle and halter? They aren't in the shed.'

'No, of course I haven't. Don't be silly. Have you seen your father? The car's here but I can't find him.' They stared at each other.

'Surely not,' said Madge. 'He doesn't know the first thing about horses.'

Nevertheless, they collected their bicycles and set off urgently down the Long Berrow lane, turning left past the farm towards Delilah's field.

They saw him long before they reached the gate. Watched by a line of fascinated sheep, he was circling the field slowly and importantly on top of a patient Delilah.

'What on earth is he doing?' asked Philippa. She was about to open her mouth to shout to her father when Madge made a silencing gesture and got off her bike.

'Don't let him see us. He'll think we're laughing at him.' They looked at each other and collapsed into helpless giggles.

'I don't think he can steer,' gasped Philippa. At that moment, Delilah felt thirsty. She turned around and broke into her trot, lumbering at last towards the water trough.

'Oh dear,' whispered Madge anxiously. 'I do hope he doesn't fall off.'

Delilah reached the trough and sank her nose into it. Norman stretched out one plump, stiff leg and managed to touch the edge of the trough with this toes. Delilah moved a sideways step closer to the trough and Norman was able to lower his weight onto the foot. Very, very carefully, he slid the remaining leg up until it was flat across her back and then down, until it too touched the edge of the trough. At the same moment, Delilah lifted her nose and nudged him affectionately into the trough. He clambered out, soaked and stiff, but safe.

Madge and Philippa turned their bikes and fled up the track, aching and speechless with silent laughter. But when they got back to the house, Madge said very sternly, 'You must never, ever tell him that we saw him. It would hurt his feelings very badly indeed. Your father doesn't like to be laughed at.' Again she shook with helpless laughter.

Norman slunk into the shed and returned the bridle and halter to their hook. Thank goodness no one had noticed they had gone.

Madge was in the kitchen boiling something and Philippa was doing her homework, so he was able to creep unseen up the stairs and shed his soaked office suit before anybody saw it. He put it in a bag and hid it in the car. He would take it to the cleaners tomorrow.

That night, in the darkness of their room, Madge reached out a hand. 'Darling Norman,' she whispered, 'I do love you.'

Norman flinched. His encounter with Delilah had temporarily unmanned him. 'Jolly good,' he said.

Chapter Twenty-Six

1960

'O' levels were over and done with and passed and failed, and 5A had turned into the Lower Sixth. 'Jane Austen never went beyond the bedroom door,' announced Miss Cameron suddenly one day, 'because she simply had no idea of what lay on the other side of it.' She paused just long enough for the Lower Sixth to have time to wonder whether or not Miss Cameron herself had any idea of what lay there. 'D.H. Lawrence, on the other hand, dispensed with the bedroom altogether and did everything that had to be done *en plein air*.'

The Lower Sixth smiled and blushed. It was 1960 and *Lady Chatterley's Lover* had just leapt out of the courtroom and onto the shelf of the Sixth Form Library at Tarminster High. The single paperback copy had been so opened and re-opened at pages 141 and 185, so gasped and blushed and giggled over in quiet corners during study time, that within a week it fell open at those pages of its own accord as soon as anybody lifted it off the shelf.

The Lower Sixth gazed in awe at Miss Cameron. Could she, this slender, splendid, exotic yet utterly pure schoolmistress of theirs, could she possibly have read those words before she put them on the shelf? The Lower Sixth devoutly hoped not.

King Lear was another set text. One day they read the great storm scene. 'Blow winds and crack your cheeks,' cried Philippa in her best contralto.

'This, girls,' their teacher told them, 'is an example of the Pathetic Fallacy.'

Laughter snorted along the back row. 'I thought that was something Lady Chatterley saw,' whispered Jenny. 'No, it's what Judith Littlewick would have said Clive Carpenter was an example of,' replied Philippa. They passed the joke along until the whole back row was rocking with suppressed mirth.

'*Hysterico passio*, down,' said Miss Cameron briskly. 'Have you anything enlightening to add, Philippa? Another example of the Pathetic Fallacy, perhaps?'

The room returned to near silence and the mad scene on the heath. Only occasional snorts and shaking shoulders showed whereabouts the joke had got to.

*

'*And the spirit of God moved across the face of the waters*
And God said
"Let there be light"
And there was
LIGHT.'

It was Choir Practice. Miss Freeman tapped her baton tip on the top of the piano and brought Haydn's *Creation* to a ragged halt. 'Those first bars must be very quiet and mysterious. We'll take it as slowly as we dare, smoothly without a break. No breath between "God" and "moved", please. Then, when we come to "Let there be light", let the light shine high and clean and pure in your voices, but still keep it quiet. And I do not want to hear about any "loight". The word is "*light*". Keep it quiet, quiet, quiet for "And there was" and then hit it double forte, give it everything you've got on that second LIGHT. Make the light explode. Ready? "*And the spirit. . ."*'

Ann and Jenny stood side by side and sang the soprano line. Ann saw a picture of the view from Swain's Chard Hill with the river flowing silently in the dark and then bursting into silver as the moon shone out over Tarminster. She and Charlie Cornwood sat astride the motorbike as they had done two years ago on the night when he had rescued her from Clive Carpenter Down the Dance.

Miss Freeman tapped the piano with her baton again. 'Much better, much better,' she said, 'but you must come off the note together. Once more and then we'll move on.'

The *Creation* moved into its second phase as despairing, cursing rage attended the rapid fall of chaos and its demons and then, lightly and flirtatiously, a new created world, tiddly pom, a new created world, sprang up, sprang up at God's command.

They were rehearsing for an Easter concert in Tarminster Cathedral, which was to be performed by the massed school choirs of the county and the County Youth Orchestra under the baton of the County Music Adviser. Hired soloists would sing the chief roles, and those who, like Philippa, still lacked natural musicality but who like to be helpful, would sell programmes and usher parents to their seats.

It was the evening of the concert in Tarminster Cathedral. The massed and school-uniformed choirs of the county stood on specially erected rostra at the East end of the Nave while the County Youth Orchestra tuned up in the wide space beneath the organ. Joan and John Dangerfield bought a programme from Philippa and sat down near the front. Ten rows behind them, Arthur waved to Jennifer until Phyllis told him not to be so ignorant.

A silence fell. The First Violin appeared and took his seat and then the conductor mounted his stand, bowed in greeting to his orchestra and chorus and then turned and bowed to the congregation. The soloists arrived, large and confident and smiling in dinner jackets and low-cut evening dresses, the Dean said a prayer, the conductor raised his baton and the creation of the world began.

It was another of those evenings that the girls would remember for the rest of their lives. The orchestra played the representation of chaos, and black demons and appalling storms screamed and flew and rumbled round the huge old building. The bass soloist sang the formlessness and emptiness and darkness of the earth, the Chorus drew its breath ('Keep your shoulders still and breathe from your diaphragms,' Miss Freeman reminded them for the thousandth time) and quietly, very quietly and mysteriously, the Spirit of God moved upon the face of the waters. And then there was light and the sound of the light rose up and filled the whole Cathedral, and the conductor, like God, saw that it was good.

Phyllis was only just in time to stop Arthur from clapping after the Heavens were telling the Glory of God at the end of Part One. It made her sweat for weeks afterwards to think how close he'd come to embarrassing her in front of all those people. The choir was going at it hammer and tongs, displaying the firmament over and over again and Arthur had been quite carried away. And then, quite suddenly, they had stopped singing and the orchestra had played four chords and the conductor had relaxed and lowered his arms and there was silence. That was when Phyllis saw Arthur lifting up his hands to clap and she had grabbed the left one and hung onto it.

'Downright mean, I call it,' Arthur said later. 'They put their hearts and souls into it and don't get so much as a clap.' But Phyllis had been right. The first part of the *Creation* had been greeted by absolute silence and she would have died of shame if Arthur had made a fool of himself in front of all those people.

Chapter Twenty-Seven

The day after the *Creation*, Jenny, Philippa and Ann were playing Three Card Brag round the table in the Cornwoods' kitchen. Phyllis and Arthur were out and Jimmy was playing football on the Rec. The girls gambled with the Cornwood poker pot money – a collection of pennies and halfpennies and farthings that were kept in an old china teapot on the mantelpiece. They always put the money back afterwards. Philippa dealt and they all inspected their cards carefully, wearing their poker faces.

'Where are you going?' Joan and Madge had asked their daughters as they had left their houses. 'Out for a walk,' the daughers had replied. It was not a lie. They had to walk to Jenny's house, but it was quite impossible to say to Joan or Madge, 'I'm going to play poker in the Cornwoods' kitchen.'

'It's stupid, isn't it?' Ann said. 'We can go for a walk, we can go for a ride, we can go and play tennis on the Manor House courts. We can even go to the pictures as long as we go with each other or Somebody Suitable. So why can't we go and play cards at Jen's house? Why could we never go Down the Dance?'

'It's Posh or Common,' said Philippa simply, and they began to do posh and common walks.

After the first hand of Three Card Brag, which Philippa won with a six-seven-eight run, Jenny suddenly said, 'It was beautiful last night, wasn't it?'

Ann paused in mid-deal and heard again the huge music as it climbed and soared and echoed around the vaults of the Cathedral.

'It was,' agreed Philippa. 'It sent shivers down me. And I've got no natural musicality. Give me another card, Ann.'

Jenny put her cards face-down on the table. 'They really believed it, didn't they?'

'Who?'

'Whoever wrote those words in the Bible: "And the spirit of God moved across the face of the waters. Let there be light."'

'And there was LIGHT,' sang Ann, very forte.

'They really believed it, word for word, though, didn't they?' Jenny persisted. 'Six days to create it all and then a rest.'

'Don't you?' asked Ann.

'I don't know.'

'I don't,' said Philippa.

'Oh you, you're just an atheist,' said Jenny.

'Yes,' said Philippa proudly, 'I am.'

'And *I* want to get on with this game of cards. Lead on, Macduff. Get on with the deal.'

'It's "Lay on, Macduff", actually,' said Ann. 'Anyway, how can you be so sure? How can you be certain about your atheism?'

Philippa, who had not ever really thought about it very deeply, but who always enjoyed the effect it had on other people when she said it, was momentarily silenced.

'I'd like to be sure,' said Jenny. And then she added fiercely, 'I want to know. I really want to know the answers. I keep thinking I'll meet somebody who'll give me the definite answers, like Miss Bugle or the Vicar. But Miss Bugle sees God in cabbages and the Vicar never gives us proof. I think I'll go to university and read Philosophy.'

Ann looked up. 'That's a good idea,' she said, and she dealt the rest of the cards thoughtfully.

'Now look at that,' said Philippa, throwing down her hand in disgust. 'Nothing. Nothing at all. A six of Clubs, an Ace of Diamonds, a four and a ten. What a useless hand. I'm stacking.'

The other two played on; a penny, two pennies, sixpence, a shilling. 'Two shillings to see you,' Jenny said to Ann. Ann put down a pair of sixes. 'Hell's bells and buckets of bloody blood,' she said as Jenny put a ten, Jack, Queen down on the table. 'That's what I mean,' Jenny said. 'Is there any sense in that? Is that Fate or Chance or God or what?

'What?' said the others, who were counting out their money.

Jenny tried to explain. 'Well, is being alive at all like playing cards? I mean, is it just a matter of luck what hand you're dealt? Or is there something watching? Something that works it all out beforehand? Saying, "I'll give *her* a lousy hand and *her* a wonderful one and *her* a middling one?" And what are we supposed to do about it?'

'You'd definitely better go and study Philosophy,' said Philippa. 'Come on, it's your deal.'

Chapter Twenty-Eight

1961

It was the last day of the summer term. 'A' levels had been taken and fates were being decided by the godlike men and women who marked examination papers; university and nursing and teacher-training places had been promised, secretarial courses had been booked.

Miss Bugle and her staff stood in a long, curved line along the stage in the Hall. The Honours board, with its carved names of those who had gone on to glory – BA (Hons) – shone in the sunlight. The bare space at the bottom of the board was waiting for more names.

The High School mistresses were splendid in black gowns and mortar boards, and some were even exotic in white furs or scarlet, silk-lined hoods.

Miss Freeman played the opening bars and the Choir and Orchestra led the way into, '*O Jesus I have promised To serve Thee to the end, Be Thou for ever near me, My Master and my Friend; I shall not fear the battle If Thou art by my side, Nor wander from the pathway, If Thou wilt be my guide dum dum dum-de-dum.*'

Miss Bugle stood and faced her girls.

'This is an exciting, an important and in some ways a sad day for some of you and for the School. It is sad, of course, because we shall be saying goodbye to you and we shall miss you; but much more than that it is exciting and important. It is exciting because you now stand on the brink of your new lives; it is important because what you have learned during your seven years here is what you will be taking with you out into that new life.' She hoiked at her strap and her glasses flickered. 'You have learned many things at this school, but I believe that the most important of them all is the firm moral standpoint we have tried to give you – the solid rock on which your characters are built. It is a moral standpoint that cannot be better illustrated than by this story.' She moved to the lectern and opened the school Bible.

'A certain man went down from Jerusalem to Jericho, and fell among thieves, which stripped him of his raiment and wounded him, leaving him half dead ...'

The story that they knew so well and had heard so many times before took on an extra ring and shine as the girls realised that this was the last time they would stand in the Hall in their summer dresses and ankle-socks with the batty old spinsters in their batwinged gowns listening to The Bugle trumpeting.

'But a certain Samaritan, as he journeyed, came where he was; and when he saw him, he had compassion on him, and went to him, and bound up his wounds, pouring in oil and wine, and set him on his own beast and brought him to an inn and took care of him...' When Miss Bugle reached the end of the parable, she looked down at her girls and commanded, 'Go thou and do likewise.' Then she closed the Bible.

'It always occurs to me,' she continued more quietly, 'whenever I read that parable, that it is far easier to be kind to a perfect stranger than to the people you know and live with and see every day. I always think, But what if that Good Samaritan had gone home and beaten up his wife, or refused to give his brother the money for his rent? Would that have invalidated the good he had done to the man who came down from Jerusalem to Jericho?'

She paused for another hitch of her shoulder strap. 'Yes,' she went on. 'Yes, I believe that it would. Public, dramatic acts of goodness are no more important than small, private acts of compassion and generosity. It is the everyday goodness, the little, nameless, unremembered acts of kindness and love (Wordsworth) that will lead us into the Kingdom of Heaven. So go thou, my dear girls, and do likewise.'

With a final, firm hoik and a grin at Miss Freeman, she sat

down. Miss Freeman played a bar, the orchestra joined in and the choir rose and sang 'God be in my head, And in my understanding.'

Miss Freeman smiled radiantly at her choir as the sung prayer came to its quiet ending. Jenny remembered the music lessons and the great slow movement of the *Enigma* when it had seemed as if Elgar was striding across her own hills and gazing down at Tarminster and the river and the valleys. '"*Beauty is truth, truth beauty,*" – *that is all Ye know on earth, and all ye need to know*,' whispered Miss Cameron and Keats.

'Go forth into the world in peace,' ordered Miss Bugle briskly. The orchestra began to play part of the *New World Symphony* and the Upper Sixth girls of Tarminster High filed out of the Hall for the last time and went forth into their own new worlds.

Part Two

Chapter One

October, 1961

Ann

The Philosophy lecturer introduced himself and took something out of his jacket pocket. Twelve Philosophy-with-English students put on intelligent expressions and watched him alertly. This was the first seminar of the first week of their new lives at university; they had come from Grammar schools throughout the length and breadth of Britain to find the key that would unlock the meaning of the universe.

It looked as if the Philosophy lecturer had just taken it out of his pocket.

He held it face-on to his audience. 'What do you see?' he asked them. Ann avoided his eye.

'Half-a-crown,' said one foolhardy student.

The Philosopher smiled thinly. 'What you see is a circle – a silver circle. That is all you perceive. You only *assume* it to be half-a-crown.' The foolhardy student blushed and shrank.

The Philosophy lecturer turned his hand around so that only the edge of the coin showed between his thumb and forefinger. 'Now what do you see?' They were beginning to understand his game. 'A straight line? Exactly.' His voice was as thin as his smile. 'Looked at in one way, this object is a circle. Looked at in another, it is a straight line. What does that tell you about the nature of reality?'

He looked at them with dislike. Nobody dared to answer him. 'I'll put it another way.' Every syllable was cold and clear and clipped. 'What does it tell you about the nature of Truth?'

'"*Beauty is truth, truth beauty,*" – *that is all Ye know on earth, and all ye need to know*', called Miss Cameron from a great distance, but she and her poetry lessons had nothing to do with where Ann was now.

The philosopher grew bored. 'It tells you that there is no such thing as objective reality, and that therefore there is no such thing as "Truth". Objective truth cannot exist since everything is only a matter of perception. Truth is only the subjective angle from which we look.'

In the silence that followed this declaration, a boy sitting next to Ann muttered, 'There's a party in one of the second-year houses tonight. Are you going?'

They danced differently here. In the dim red light of stolen road-lamps, drinking beer and harsh red wine to the beat of *Hit the Road, Jack*, they danced at each other in a wild, free, look-at-me-aren't-I-exciting? kind of way. You can do whatever you like, realised Ann, as long as you stay with the beat.

She swung her hips and stretched her arms high above her head, while the boy from the Philosophy lecture stamped and sweated and shook his head, caught up in his own rhythm and thoughts. There was something a bit ... separated about it, thought Ann, and then she shook her hair across her face and stamped and danced with herself in the way that she had danced at home, in front of the mirror when nobody was looking and she had wished that she could be a stripper.

Delilah died that night. Uncle Walter found her stretched out peacefully under the autumn chestnut tree and he bicycled straight over from the farm to tell his sister-in-law. The mothers telephoned the daughters and told them what had happened.

They came home at the weekend and walked the woods and climbed the hill in silence. They took the lower track through the garlic coppice and followed the steep lane down to the brook. They climbed up to the open commonland and down again to the kingcup pool where they had picnicked and watched dragonflies, while the old pony had cropped the grass and plunged her nose into the water. They hardly spoke. Nothing would ever be the same again.

They walked home and caught separate trains back to their separate lives.

In 1962, Ann went on the Pill. All the girls did. 'Are you on it?' they asked each other. Ann was still only at six clothes-pegs, but not to be on the Pill was like not passing your eleven-plus, so she went on it too, and kept her eyes open for someone to justify it.

Pete was a third-year engineering student and Ann met him in the second term of her first year on a protest march. Two policemen picked them up from the middle of the road where they were sitting side by side, carried them to the pavement and dumped them on it. They got up and went back to Pete's flat where he cooked them spaghetti Bolognaise and played Miles Davis records while they ate it. 'Well,' said Pete, after they had done the washing up, 'I suppose we'd better go to bed.'

It wasn't a bit like *Lady Chatterley's Lover*, thought Ann, on her way back to her digs. Still, she'd shed her virginity at last; that was another hurdle overcome.

Ann and Pete went out together and stayed in together for the rest of the year, until Pete decided that he ought to concentrate on revision for his Finals. He was succeeded by a second-year Sociologist called Mike who was followed by a second-year Economist called Dave. It was never like *Lady Chatterley's Lover*.

Then Damien Cruikshank came to the University.

Damien Cruikshank was a Postgraduate student from Cambridge who was writing a thesis on The Philosophy and Social Relevance of Twentieth-Century Art. He was tall and dark and handsome. He wore tweed jackets and Old Spice. He smoked a pipe and drove a Ford Popular.

Chapter Two

1962

'The purpose of Art is to challenge and destroy,' said Damien Cruikshank. He had brought Ann and the Ford Popular to the Festival of Contemporary Arts in Shimmerton-on-Sea.

'WAAAAAABLAAAAAAAAWAAZAALAAAAA ADEDAAAAAAAAAAAAAAAAAAAAA!' A contemporary poet stood, hairy-chested and waist-deep in the sea and howled his existential message at the holidaymakers and Art-lovers on the beach.

'Amazing, isn't it?' said Damien. 'You see? He challenges all the accepted bourgeois clichés about Art; he breaks down all the structures, all the barriers. "Balls," he screams at the middle classes. "Balls!"'

'Balls,' grunted a middle-aged holidaymaker from Butlin's to his wife. They had come away for a few days without the kids and had not expected to land in the middle of the Shimmerton Festival of Contemporary Arts. The poet reared up higher in the water.

'I don't think he's wearing any swimming trunks,' said the man's wife and they caught the bus back to the camp and settled in with relief to a cheerful afternoon with a Max Bygraves lookalike singalong.

'AAAAAAAAAAAAAAAAAAAAAAAAAAAAAAAAAAA AAGH!' continued the poet in the sea. He was a bit like John the Baptist, thought Ann. Or something out of the *Beano*.

'There's a yearning in it, isn't there?' Damien was entranced. The poet (who was wearing swimming trunks after

116

all) was coming closer, wading out of the sea towards them.

'Don't just look at me,' he yelled angrily to his watchers, waving his arms and pulling faces at them. 'Join me, join me. Shake off your bourgeois inhibitions, shake off your chains of good behaviour. This is theatre, this is Living Art. Join me.'

'Art is for everyone,' said Damien and, for an awful moment, Ann thought he was going to tear off all his clothes and rush into the sea. 'It is blasphemy to shut it up in theatres and concert halls and galleries, where only the rich and privileged can see it. Art is for all of the people all of the time. Art is the great "Why?" and "How?" – the agonised cry of humanity which is being stifled and ignored.'

Tulips from Amsterdam sang the lookalike in the holiday camp and all the campers sang along with him. 'BLAAAA BLAAAAAABLAAAABLAAAAAAA!' wailed the poet, and then he came up out of the sea and got dressed.

That night, Damien took Ann to a theatre to see a contemporary play where two people sat in silence for a very long time and then talked very fast about Nothingness and then took all their clothes off for a very brief moment before the lights went out for the interval.

'It's brilliant, isn't it? said Damien.

'Brilliant,' Ann agreed. 'I particularly liked the tension of the silences.'

He smiled at her approvingly but when at the end of the play, they played the National Anthem and Ann stood up, Damien rolled his eyes in horror and embarrassment and pulled her back into her seat. 'It's a joke,' he hissed. 'God, you are so middle-class.' She blushed with shame.

Next day, they went to a Contemporary Art exhibition in a disused warehouse on the Quay at Shimmerton. Giant empty canvases were spread across the floors and viewers were invited to don Wellington boots and paddle in puddles of bright oil paint and then to hop, skip and skid across the canvas.

'Living Art,' insisted Damien. 'It's alive, it's vibrant, it's exciting, it's democratic. Do you see? You can do it; I can do it. Anybody can do it. It challenges all our deep-rooted, élitist prejudices about talent. We are all artists. Come on. Create.'

Obediently, Ann jumped about in her paint-covered

Wellingtons and discovered that she too was an artist, that there was nothing to it at all.

'There is no such thing as talent,' cried Damien, 'We are all artists!' He lay down in the paint puddles and then he rolled great blurry streaks of yellow and red across the canvas.

Chapter Three

1961

Philippa

'Hum from your genitals, hum from your bowels,' implored Miss Creely, the tall, dark, brilliant Principal of the Melissa Creely School of Speech and Drama. Philippa blushed and giggled inwardly at the thought of poor fluffy Tit Willow and her elocution lessons in the room above the bakery. 'Now hum from the roots of your being, hum from the base of your soul.' A few half-hearted hums rumbled out of the roots of the beings of the first-year voice class.

'No, No, No, *No!*' cried Melissa Creely. 'Try to remember. Try to remember grief. Remember your own greatest moment of loss.' The class tried. The best Philippa could come up with was the sudden and unexplained death of her guinea-pig.

'That's the trouble with these children,' sighed Melissa Creely to her husband, Señor Vittorio in bed that night. 'They have not suffered. They have not been Wounded by Life. How can they be actors and actresses when they have never plumbed the depths of grief and passion?'

Melissa Creely knew all about passion. She had found Señor Vittorio ten years before when she was doing a summer season in cabaret in Sitges and he was a Flamenco dancer in a night-club. She had fallen madly in love with his clicking heels and his arched back and his tiny, compact body, and she had brought him home to England when her aunt died and left her enough money to found her Drama School. Vittorio was her Movement and Dance coach. Girls from Grammar and small

119

private schools from all over England came to them to learn how to be actors and actresses.

'Ladies and Gentlemen,' Vittorio smiled his Flamenco smile, arched his eyebrows and his back and quivered his heels. His accent was even more Spanish than it had been when he left Sitges. 'The very first lesson I must teach you is the Posture. Everything is held within the Posture. Everything depends upon the Posture. And the Posture ...' his eyebrows rose even higher '... is rooted in the buttocks.'

There was an astonished silence and Philippa knew that she was going red. Vittorio noticed, as he noticed every year. 'Hello, English Rose,' and he spun towards her in his tight trousers. His buttocks were the main thing you noticed about him, thought Philippa, going even redder. Even when he was facing you.

'You can speak your soul,' he was very close to her now, 'through your buttocks. Yes. I want you to imagine, each and every one of you, that you hold a lemon between your cheeks. Go on. Take a lemon and place it between your cheeks.'

Philippa put out her hand and reached for the imaginary lemon. Then she opened her mouth and stuck the lemon in it.

'Señorita, what is it that you are doing?'

Philippa removed the lemon before she answered. 'I've put a lemon between my cheeks,' she said humbly.

Vittorio threw up his hands and clutched his head. 'Nononononono, Señorita. Not between the cheeks of your face. Between the cheeks of your *bottom*.'

The class was motionless. This was not at all like Miss Willow, Philippa thought again.

Vittorio was becoming impatient. He stamped his little Flamenco feet. 'Do as I say. You take a lemon. Where from? From where?'

'From the vegetable rack?' suggested someone timidly.

'Very good,' said Vittorio and he clapped. 'You take the lemon from the vegetable rack ... so ... *excellente*. I too, I take it – we all take it. So ... we take the lemon from the bottom shelf of the vegetable rack, and we hold it between our fingers and our thumbs and then, we place it ... very, very carefully ... between our buttocks.'

With enormous care and concentration, the class followed his instructions. When everyone had got their lemons safely in position, Vittorio said briskly: 'And now; squeeze your lemons. Squeeze them as hard as you can and hold them there. And that is your position, that is the basis of good posture.'

The next exercise involved turning into a tree. The class had to imagine that it was a particular sort of tree – an oak, a Christmas tree, a sycamore, a beech. 'Feel your roots. Feel them spreading, spreading, spreading through the earth. Let them clutch and twine, let them stretch and grow. Is the soil sandy? Is it rocky? Is it damp? Feel the soil. And let your roots reach out through it, let them touch its texture, drink its moisture, curl around its rocks.'

Philippa tried very hard to let her roots stretch and grow. She tried very hard ('*Philippa always tried hard*') to feel like the Climbing Tree near the top of the hill at Swain's Chard, but the tightly held lemon between her buttocks got in the way.

Señor Vittorio came close to her to see how she was getting on and she lost her balance, fell towards him, knocked him over and trod on him. He gave an exotic yelp, scrambled to his feet and limped around in exaggerated agony. 'Señorita, Señorita, I implore you to be careful. Señorita, you have trodden on my bloody roots!'

'It's the lemon, Señor,' gasped Philippa, near to tears with shame. 'The lemon gets in the way of being a tree.'

Vittorio flung up his hands and eyebrows again and drummed his heels. 'Nononono, Señorita, nononono. Throw away your lemon, throw it away. That was a different exercise!'

With relief, Philippa extracted the lemon and threw it across the room. Then she turned into the Climbing Tree.

'There is one,' said Vittorio to Melissa in bed that night. 'There is one – the large pale one with the navy-blue eyes. She has no co-ordination yet. But she has comedy. She has fire. She has talent.' He drummed his heels and fell asleep.

That was the night Delilah died.

Chapter Four

October, 1961

Jenny

All over England, in the first weeks of the first term in October 1961, Philosophy lecturers were taking half-crowns out of their trouser pockets and performing the now-it's-a-circle-now-it's-a-straight-line routine before the very eyes of answer-hungry undergraduates. The Truth. Now you see it, now you don't. The Truth is an illusion, a trick, a sleight of mind. The truth was that the Truth did not exist. 'There is no such thing as objective Truth,' they recited, delighted. 'Truth is merely a matter of perception. Nothing exists. Nothing matters.' All over England, Philosophy lecturers slipped their magic half-crowns into their cosmic fruit machines and came up with a bunch of bananas.

Jenny's first lecture was over and the new Philosophy students moved in an uneasy and self-conscious body out of the lecture theatre and into the coffee bar. Jenny walked beside an auburn-haired, beautiful and self-possessed young woman who shared digs with her. She was called Ginger McKinley, she came from London, she was twenty and both her parents had been to university. She was coldly and silently unimpressed by everything and everyone. She sat deliberately and aloofly alone in the coffee bar and Jenny joined a short, serious bespectacled girl who looked safer. Her name was Sarah Hartmann.

'Did you understand a word of that?' asked Jenny, as they drank frothy coffee from the Espresso machine. It was the kind of thing she would have said to Ann or Philippa.

'Of course,' Sarah Hartmann replied. 'It was only the standard introduction to the concepts of perception and of subjective versus objective realities.' She got up and walked purposefully towards the library. I should not be here, thought Jenny. I am not one of these people. I don't even understand the words they use.

A thin, dark-haired, vivacious girl sat down beside her. 'Did you understand a word of that?' she asked Jenny tentatively.

'I think it was just the standard introduction to the ideas of perception and objective versus subjective reality,' said Jenny. The dark girl looked worried and Jenny relented. 'I've only just heard that from somebody else,' she confessed. 'I don't understand any of it. Think I'll leave.'

They decided to go and look up 'objective' in the dictionary, and in the library they found the serious bespectacled girl called Sarah Hartmann bending over 'O' in the *Shorter Oxford*. She blushed and closed the book.

That was how it worked. They listened carefully and they learned new words and phrases and they repeated them and passed them on and, after a while, they almost understood them. And after another while they really did understand them because they had moved into a tiny, exclusive, private world of words and phrases and they used them like a secret code. 'Existentialism', they said, 'empirical', 'eclectic' and 'yoghourt'.

'There is no such thing as true altruism,' said Jenny's Philosopher teacher who was also her personal tutor and moral guardian and whose name was Gabriel Woolf. 'No such thing as a genuinely altruistic action. We only perform acts of apparent unselfishness because we have been brainwashed into believing that it is "good" to do them. But what is "Good"? How do we know the meaning of the word? Is there some great concrete block of "goodness" somewhere out there beyond the sky that we can recognise? So that all we have to do is tune into it and hear it on our own personal moral radios? Or is it that we have been told, over and over again by generations of those in power over us, by our parents, our teachers, our political and military masters, that what they want us to do is "good"? For centuries, they have rewarded us for doing what pleases them and punished us for doing what offends them. Is not that all that "goodness" means? If I am right, if that is true, then we have been brainwashed into believing that kind, unselfish actions are good because they make us feel good. And so it must follow that all such actions are necessarily and essentially *selfish*.

'And that is your essay for this week: "All apparently altruistic actions are really selfish ones. Discuss." That is the end of the tutorial. Good afternoon.'

'Good afternoon,' said Jenny and the dark-haired girl whose name was Theresa Smith.

So Miss Bugle was wrong, thought Jenny after she had looked up 'altruistic' in the dictionary. The Good Samaritan was only kind to the beaten-up man from Jerusalem because it had made him feel good to be kind. If he had been taught from babyhood that it was good to stamp on people's faces then he would have stamped and that would have made him feel terrific. There was no such thing as 'good'. A safety net of certainty fell away from the universe and life yawned for a moment – a meaningless black hole. And all that Brownie stuff about Doing a Good Deed a Day and all that Sunday School stuff about Loving Thy Neighbour was nothing more than an adult conspiracy to keep children in order by making them feel virtuous.

That was the night Delilah died.

So Truth and the Brownies and the Good Samaritan were quietly killed off as the fledgling philosophers digested their diets of logic and proof and spat out anything that could not be empirically verified.

'What is the meaning of "empirical verification", Miss Cornwood?' asked Gabriel Woolf towards the end of another Wednesday morning. Two hundred miles away, Jenny's mother was wiping Gumption around the Dangerfield bath and Miss Bugle was reading the Parable of the Sower to 4A.

Jenny was ready for him. 'It is the proof of an objective reality and such proof can only be obtained by way of the senses.'

Gabriel Woolf nodded approvingly. She was learning fast, this little country bumpkin. 'That is correct. In other words, if

I can see it, smell it, taste it, touch it or hear it, I have proof that it exists. If I cannot recognise it through my senses, I have no such proof.'

He turned to Theresa who was afraid of him and who therefore irritated him. 'Now, Miss Smith, define "meaning". What is the meaning of "meaning"?'

Theresa was flustered and she blushed and floundered. 'It means ... I know what it means, but I can't explain it.'

Gabriel's sigh was scornful. 'Meaning, Miss Smith, can only be attached to those things which have been recognised by the senses. The only purpose of language is to communicate meaning. Therefore, it must follow that only those things which have meaning can be talked about and those things which have no meaning *cannot* be talked about. It therefore follows that we cannot talk with meaning about God or religion because neither of them can be recognised by the senses. Therefore they have no meaning.'

He gazed at Theresa through his dark glasses. 'Take down this statement, please.' The girls poised biros above their A4 pads. 'All statements,' announced Gabriel Woolf, 'about God and religion are meaningless. Discuss.'

Theresa went very red. She was a Catholic and she believed deeply in God. Gabriel Woolf's logic sometimes cut too deep. 'You can't say that,' she said bravely; she knew that he despised her.

Gabriel smiled coldly and raised one eyebrow. 'Don't bluster at me, Miss Smith,' he said. 'I want reasoned logic, analytical thought – not hysteria.' But Theresa believed in God with all her heart and soul and she told him so. 'Prove him to me, Miss Smith. Show him to me. Can you see him? Touch him? Taste him? *Smell* him?'

'No,' said Theresa Smith and her voice was shaking. 'But I believe in Him. That's why it's called Faith.'

Gabriel raised his other eyebrow. 'Has it not occurred to you, Miss Smith, that this touching devotion to an unseen fairy tale is no more than a child's devotion to Father Christmas? What proof have you that either of them exists?'

'None,' said Theresa, and her voice was stronger now, although there were tears of humiliation in her eyes. 'That is why we call it "Faith".'

Gabriel Woolf raised both his eyebrows at the same time and turned to Jenny. 'And you, Miss Cornwood?'

Jenny was learning not to be afraid of him. She could separate herself into two people. One was her mind, that understood the concepts and argued intellectually and logically. The other was herself and her life and her friends and her family. She kept them apart and enjoyed the intellectual crossword puzzles.

'What about you?' asked Gabriel Woolf. 'Do you agree that all statements about God and religion are, by their very nature, meaningless?'

Jenny hooked her brain around the sentence. 'If meaning *can* only be attached to those things which can be recognised by the senses, and if language *is* only about meaning – then it must follow that any statement about God or religion is meaningless.' She knew that Theresa felt betrayed and she felt a pang of disloyalty to God and Miss Bugle.

'Excellent,' said Gabriel Woolf. He liked her more and more. She had a brain. She had a body too, he noticed.

Chapter Five

Theresa and Jenny grew fond of each other during their first year. They could admit their weaknesses to one another, confess when they did not understand a new word, confide when they were falling in love with a new man, grumble when they had period pains or spots.

'Were both your parents brought up as Catholics?' Jenny asked one day after an early Philosophy tutorial. They were lying flat on their backs on Theresa's bedroom floor, trying out a yoghourt and cucumber face mask they had found in a magazine. Her mask cracked as she spoke.

'No,' replied Theresa without moving her lips. They waited half an hour, then peeled off the yoghourt and returned to Theresa's parents. 'My mother is a convert. She converted so's she could marry my father. Catholics always joke that converts are more fierce about it than born-ins. It's certainly true of my mum.' There was affection in her voice.

'It means a lot to you, doesn't you?'

Theresa shrugged. 'I suppose it's everything. I mean, it's always been the basis of my whole life.'

'So does it hurt when the Big Bad Woolf says all these things to you?'

'Nope,' said Theresa, 'I just know he's wrong.'

Jenny spread marge thoughtfully on a slice of bread (they kept secret supplies under the bed) and munched it slowly. 'He's dishy though, isn't he? In a distant sort of way.'

Theresa pulled a face. 'Not my sort of way. He likes you, though.'

Jenny blushed. 'Don't be daft. He must be nearly thirty.

Anyway, he's a lecturer.' She bit into her bread and marge again. 'I wish I could be as sure of it as you are. The God thing, I mean. I believe in God, of course – or I always used to. But when all these things get argued at us, I have to ask questions and now I can't be sure of the answers any more.'

Theresa shrugged again. 'That's when you have to hang on to faith. You'll put on weight if you eat any more of that bread. You see, I always knew that people would challenge my Catholicism and laugh at me about it, so I was sort of prepared. I just shut my mind to Woolf. I just know that without my faith, the whole thing'd seem pointless and empty and I don't want it to.'

Jenny nodded. 'I know what you mean. I often feel like that when I write these essays. If I believed what I wrote, it'd make everything empty. So I just switch off and think, It's only to do with my brain; it isn't real. Then I can write it. But I don't know what I do believe in any more. Do you? Do you honestly believe in things like the Virgin Birth and the Resurrection and Hell and the Devil and everything?'

Theresa spread jam thickly on a slice of bread. 'Oh yes. And in Purgatory and Limbo.'

'What on earth are Purgatory and Limbo?'

Theresa bit into her bread and jam. 'Not on earth at all, actually. Purgatory's the sort of halfway house between earth and Heaven. You see, if you're a saint with an absolutely umbesmirched soul, you'll whizz straight to Heaven when you die. It's very rare, of course. And if you've committed a mortal sin like murder, then your soul will plunge straight down to Hell and nothing you can say or do will stop it. But for most people, ordinary halfway people, who do some good and some bad but who mostly try to be good, there's Purgatory. It's like Hell but not permanent and not so hot or awful and you'll stay there until you've atoned for your sins and you're clean enough to go to Heaven.'

Jenny had never heard anything like it. It had certainly not been part of Miss Bugle's scheme of things. 'How d'you get out of it? Purgatory, I mean.'

Theresa wrinkled her nose. 'I expect they sling down a rope-ladder or something and then they heave you up. Don't be silly, Jenny. How would I know?'

'Then how do you know any of it?'

'I don't know it,' said Theresa. 'Not factually. Not empirically. But I believe it. That's why we call it "Faith".'

God, how I loathe these smug little Christian Virgins who come up here all protected by their crucifixes and their chastity, said Gabriel Woolf to his reflection as he shaved that evening. He had had a particularly tedious tutorial with the Smith girl that morning. Still, the other one was coming along nicely, he thought, and he smiled at the reflection and put his dark glasses on again.

'And what's Limbo? I never heard of that before,' said Jenny, examining her yoghourt-cleansed skin in Theresa's mirror.

'It's where the souls of unbaptised babies go. They can't go to Heaven, of course.'

'Why not, for crying out loud?'

'You can't get into Heaven if you haven't been baptised. You're still in a state of original sin. That's the whole point of baptism; it wipes the baby's soul clean. A baby with original sin still on it couldn't go to Heaven, so it has to go to Limbo.'

'And what's Limbo like?' Jenny was appalled.

'Sort of nothing, I suppose. Like an everlasting waiting room.'

Jenny shuddered. 'I think that's horrible. Poor little sods. Just because they haven't got the right passport ... it's disgusting. You'd think He'd let them in without a ticket. Come on, Theresa, you can't really believe it's true.' But Theresa said she could.

It just depends who tells you what, thought Jenny, smearing cream on her face before she got into bed that night. If you've grown up with Theresa's parents telling you without doubt that you've got a Guardian Angel and an immortal soul, and that Heaven and Hell and Purgatory and Limbo are waiting for you somewhere beyond the sky, then you believe them. And if you've grown up with the Vicar telling you God lives in the church, or with the Bugle telling you He's in a row of cabbages, then you believe them. And if you've grown up with Gabriel Woolf telling you that there's absolutely nothing and it's all a ridiculous fairy tale because the universe is empty and meaningless, then you'll believe him.

So where does that leave me? thought Jenny, turning over in bed. And she found herself repeating the *Our Father* rather urgently, and wondering at the same time why she was doing it.

Chapter Six

1962

Jenny

In the second year, the students were allowed to move into flats as long as there was a responsible adult living on the premises. Jenny, Theresa and Sarah Hartmann moved into a cold and cavernous bedsitter with bathroom and kitchen attached. Their responsible adult was a motherly prostitute who operated from the first floor and who kindly agreed to sign the official form from the University to say that she was over twenty-one, resident on the premises and prepared to be their moral guardian.

They loved the bedsitter. It meant freedom and adulthood and independence, and they were very serious about shopping lists and weekly budgeting and saving shillings for the electricity meter.

Their social lives changed. It was no longer necessary for them to be back in their digs by eleven-thirty before outraged landladies locked them out. Now they could sit up until two or three in the mornings discussing the nature of the universe, the impossibility of God, who had gone home with whom after the last party and who was going to wear what at the next.

'Let's give a dinner party,' said Jenny. They invited an earnest third-year poet who gave readings of his own work before selected audiences (which had once included Sarah), the Roman Catholic Chaplain who was a friend of Theresa and who seemed nice but a bit lonely as she was his only customer, and Gabriel Woolf.

'You can't invite Gabriel Woolf,' said Sarah, shocked. 'He's a lecturer. He must be at least thirty.'

'He's only twenty-nine,' said Jenny.

'And he's got a thing about Jenny,' said Theresa.

They cooked moussaka because it was the only exotic thing they knew how to make, and they did a fruit salad for pudding. They bought four bottles of cheap red wine from the off-licence and hoped that their guests would bring more. The Chaplain did, but the poet, who was broke, and the Philosopher, who was mean, did not. They stocked up with shillings for the meter and they put Ella Fitzgerald on the record player. Halfway through the evening, Jenny, realising that they were going to run out of wine, ran down the road and bought two more bottles of cheap red wine with the rest of the week's supply of meter money.

There was no table in the bedsit and so they sat on the beds to eat the moussaka. They lit candles to save the electricity for Ella Fitzgerald, and after a while, the poet, who was drunk, asked Sarah, who was drunk, if she would like to dance. Theresa and the Chaplain talked about horse racing and then Gabriel Woolf, who was drunk, asked Jenny, who was drunk, if she would like to dance. They all drank more wine and then Jenny and Gabriel sat on the bed with Theresa and the Chaplain and talked about gambling and Fate and predestination and the Meaning of Life.

'All statements about God and religion are meaningless,' said Gabriel Woolf, and hiccoughed.

'Define "meaningless",' said the Chaplain and giggled.

'Any statement that is not empirically verifiable is, *per se*, meaningless,' chorused everybody else and they all laughed uproariously and fell onto the floor.

'I have composed a poem in honour of our revered Philosopher,' said the third-year poet, clambering to his feet and waving his glass grandly, 'and I should like to recite it to you, here and now.'

With sensitive timing, the electricity ran out and Ella Fitzgerald slowed down and stopped.

'A poem, a poem ... let's be hearing it,' cried the Chaplain from the floor and the poet recited his poem.

'The Professor of Philosophy smiled at me;
"You"ve got to understand that God is dead," said he.
"Have a little wine
And we'll talk of Wittgenstein,
Or I'll teach ya
Some Nietzsche
Instead,
So you really get it stuck into your head."

The Professor of Philosophy laughed, "Tee hee"
As he snuggled in his cosy university,
Talking of Jean-Paul
Till the iron bit my soul.
A.J. Ayer
Was there
As well.
And they really opened up the road to Hell.'

There was loud applause from the floor where the Chaplain lay waving his legs in the air to the rhythm of the poem. Then the philosopher rose, swayed majestically, took a swipe at the poet and missed. 'Blessed are the peacemakers,' belched the Chaplain, and the dinner party was over.

Chapter Seven

Dear Philippa,

How's life and showbiz? Your mum told my mum that you've got a job on a pier theatre for the summer. I think that's fantastic. Damien wouldn't approve, but I do. He's terribly serious about The Nature and Purpose of Art ... he's doing it for his Ph.D. Did I tell you about the Festival of Contemporary Art we went to in Shimmerton last year? Everyone kept taking their clothes off and rolling in paint and wailing. I wanted to giggle but Damien said it was terribly significant – all about breaking down barriers and destroying the middle classes. Did I tell you about Damien ha ha only about five million times yes I know. He's twenty-three now, and I've been with him for over a year. His thesis is coming along well, he says – it's about The Social Relevance of Twentieth-Century Art ..., ha ha again yes I know I told you that before as well. I dunno what he'd make of your Pier Show – it's a bit outside his area, to put it mildly. I don't think I'd ever be able to persuade him to come and see it and I can't think of any way to get there without him.

What I really wanted to ask you is have you heard anything from Jenny lately? She hasn't written to me for months. We used to write and compare notes about our

Philosophy lectures. I wondered if you knew whether she's OK or if I've offended her or something? She wrote ages ago about a hilarious dinner party she and her flatmates had given for some pretentious gits at the university. One of them was her Philosophy tutor ... he's got a very odd name. She talked about him quite a lot. She sounds as if she's doing really well on the course. She was always the brightest of the three of us, wasn't she?

I'm plucking up courage to take Damien home to Swain's Chard to meet the parents. HELP.

Lots of love,
Ann

17 Station Road
Duckworth
30th June

Dear Ann,
No, I haven't heard anything from Jenny for months either. I expect she's just got tangled up in Philosophy and giving dinner parties. You said you found it pretty intense didn't you? (Philosophy, not dinner parties.) That man's name was Gabriel Woolf. I noticed it because she mentioned it at least three times on one page. Damien sounds serious if you're thinking about taking him home to meet your parents. IS THIS WISE???? No. I definitely think you should NOT bring him to the Larry Laronde Summer Extravaganza on Duckworth Pier. We've just started rehearsals and I'm sure it would *not* fit into any of his theories about Twentieth-Century Art. He sounds a bit daunting. Are you thinking of marrying him?

Lots of love,
Philippa

Dear Philippa,
Damien says marriage is an unnecessary bourgeois formality created solely for the economic advantages of the already economically advantaged. He says that a piece of paper is not necessary to sanctify the union of two reasoning people. Are you thinking about marrying anybody?

Lots of love,
Ann
P.S. I still haven't heard from Jenny. I wrote to her again last week.

Chapter Eight

Summer, 1963

Philippa

'Cut me a couple of thirty-sixes, darling,' called Larry Laronde across the stage to Philippa. Panic flooded her. What the hell was a thirty-six and where would she find one – and what should she cut it with?

Steve the Stage Manager, who looked like a Greek god and who planned on being a film star, came to her rescue. 'Gels,' he said, handing her a sheet of pale lilac film and a Stanley knife. 'Cut two squares of this to fit into the follow spot.'

Philippa kissed him in gratitude and he backed away in alarm. Had she left a dent in the after-tan on his cheek? 'It's all right, Steve,' she said. 'I haven't smudged you, honestly.' '*Philippa Foster is always very kind*,' her school reports had said.

Larry Laronde was cursing one of his dancers on the other side of the stage. 'Did I advertise for somebody with three left feet?' he spat and the dancer missed the step again. 'Play the bar again!' yelled Larry to the pianist. 'Now, you flat-footed imbecile, ONE two three four, CROSS two three four...'

The dancer crossed on the second beat and Larry leapt at him and grabbed him. 'With me ... keep going!' he screamed at the pianist who had stopped to light another cigarette. 'ONE two three four, CROSS two three four, TURN two three four, BACK two three four and DOWN two three four. Hoo bloody ray. Has that screwed it into your tiny brain? Now go away and do it and do it and do it until it's filtered down to your fucking flat feet.'

The wardrobe mistress flew onto the stage in tears. 'There's a whole trunkful of glitter gone missing, Larry,' she wailed.

Larry smiled and his teeth were like a sharks.' 'Well, go and find it, darling. Don't stand there whimpering at *me*.'

A bored voice spoke from the auditorium. 'Larry, darling, I hate to be tedious, but we haven't run through my silent-movie number yet and I really need the practice with the lights.' It was Freddy Farraday, the show comic, the show star, the show queen, who topped the bill for the whole summer season of the Larry Laronde Summer Extravaganza on the pier at Duckworth. Freddy Farraday was the only person in the company who Larry feared, for if Freddy left his show, audiences would cease to come.

'I know, love,' said Larry appeasingly. 'Why don't you take a break while I sort out some technical things? Come back in two hours and we'll run it then.'

The company had arrived in Duckworth very early that morning. They had the day to get the show installed and to run through the acts before eight o'clock, when the holidaymakers of Duckworth would be sitting in their seats waiting to be transported.

Freddy looked at his watch. 'It's high noon now, my sweet. I'll be back at two.' He skipped out of his seat with a merry wave. 'See you all later, my darlings. And Heaven preserve you if you're not ready for me.'

The pianist played on and the three-legged dancer struggled to get his steps right. The wardrobe mistress found her trunk of glitter dumped near the dustbins behind the theatre and began ironing and sewing on new bits of sparkle and Velcro. The electrician carried heavy lights up steep ladders and clamped and screwed them into place.

'Where're those thirty-sixes?' demanded Larry. 'I need to see the limes working.' Philippa had cut her squares of film and given them to the electrician. Suddenly two pools of lilac light appeared on the floor of the stage.

Larry pointed at Philippa. 'You, go up to the projection floor and follow me with one of those limes.' Philippa did as she was told. 'Focus it on me,' yelled Larry and she took hold of the big lamp and pointed it at him. '*Focus* it!' bawled Larry. 'It's too bloody big!'

The electrician came to her rescue and showed her how to move a lever so that the beam of light grew narrower and narrower until it surrounded Larry with a lilac halo.

'That'll do,' said Larry. 'Now follow me across the stage.' She followed him with the lilac spot. 'OK,' Larry said. 'You're on the limes for the show. Get your running order from Steve.'

At two o'clock precisely, Freddy reappeared. He stood in the wings, waiting for a total blackout. 'Right,' yelled Larry to Philippa who was back in position behind her limelight. 'I want everything in total black for the start of this number. Then, when you hear George play the opening bars of Freddy's music, bring your spot up onto him. Open white for this one. Got it?'

Philippa was aware of her heart beating in the dark silence. George began to play some quick, light, tripping music and she switched on her light. A pool of white shone on the right-hand side of the stage.

'OTHER SIDE!' screamed Larry. Something was scuttling about in the darkness of the other side of the stage. She swept her white light until it picked up Freddy in the beam.

'Do it again,' said Freddy in a dangerously patient voice. 'You know where I am now, dear, so pick me up straight away. As the actress said to the bishop.'

Sweating, Philippa pointed the light in what she hoped was Freddy's direction, and when she heard the mincing notes on the piano, she switched on. Spot on. There was Freddy creeping like a villain in the white light. Philippa relaxed. There was another scream.

'Where's the fucking flicker?' Freddy demanded.

'Where's the fucking flicker?' Larry echoed.

Philippa stuck her head over the edge of the projection balcony. 'How can I do a fucking flicker if I haven't *got* a fucking flickerer?' There was a shocked silence. No one spoke like that to Larry Laronde or Freddy Farraday.

'It's a reasonable question,' said Larry at last. 'Give the girl a flicker-wheel.' But no one had a flicker-wheel to give her and the rehearsal ground to a bad-tempered halt.

Then Steve had a brilliant idea. 'She'll have to wave bits of cardboard very fast in front of the light. Very fast. It'll have the same effect.'

So they gave her the top of a cardboard box and showed her how to waggle it very fast in front of the white light, so that it looked as if Freddy was an actor on a very old silent screen. Larry Laronde was never rude to Philippa again.

The full dress run-through was scheduled for three o'clock. Philippa stood behind her limelights, her list of the running order of the acts Sellotaped to the ledge in front of her, her cardboard flickerer beside her.

1: Overture. Open white on George.
2: Tabs out; no spot; full chorus for opening number.

The curtains of the Duckworth Pier Theatre flew up and the chorus line of the Larry Laronde Summer Extravaganza smiled and shook its shoulders at the empty auditorium. 'Something terrific, Something specific, Something for everyone,' it sang. Smiling, the chorus backed and kicked its way offstage and Philippa slid a rose-pink gel into her follow spot and shone it onto Janice, the lead singer, who languished by a plastic palm tree against the backdrop of a tropical beach.

'Born on opposite sides of the sea, We are as different as people could be,' she sang wistfully, and the baritone slid up behind her. 'It's true,' he murmured. She turned and smiled into his eyes and Philippa kept the pink spot steady. 'And yet you want to marry me.' 'I do.'

Romance trembled through the auditorium and reached Philippa up on her projection platform. It was hard to believe that they loathed each other and that the baritone (whose name was Barry) would far rather have been gazing into the eyes of Steve the Stage Manager. They finished the song and wandered off, his arm around her waist and her head upon his shoulder while Steve rushed on in the blackout and took the palm tree away.

Lights up again and a centre-spot for the company magician who did a lot of things with top hats and handkerchiefs and coloured scarves.

'Leave that, it's fine,' called Larry Laronde. 'Straight into the Morris Dancing, George.'

George picked up an accordion and squeezed it. Freddy

140

Farraday skipped onto the stage, all socks and bells and hand-kerchiefs, followed by the six male chorus dancers. They cantered and hopped and cavorted and frolicked, bending their knees up to their chins and flirting with their handkerchiefs. Larry applauded, they skipped off and the magician came back and did a juggling act.

Red spot for this!' yelled Larry to Philippa. 'Please,' he added.

The juggling ended and Barry the Baritone returned to the rose-pink spot and sang a selection from *Fiddler on the Roof*. Philippa glanced down at her running order. Freddy's silent-film number was next. She was ready with her cardboard flapper.

'Sunrise, sunset,' sang Barry and Philippa closed down the pink spot sensitively, slid out the gel and pointed the lamp towards where Freddy ought to be. There he was, creeping and threatening, intent upon some evil deed.

Philippa flapped her cardboard until her wrists were aching with tiredness. She followed Freddy across the stage and watched him turn and straighten up and become a damsel in distress who wept and pleaded, clasping her hands and implor-ing. And then he was the cruel villain again, crouching and pouncing, stabbing and laughing, with no sound at all except for George on the piano. And then he was the girl, distraught, shrinking and crumbling with terror.

All the time, George improvised on the piano, tuning into Freddy's different characters, manipulating the mood. Just when it seemed that all was lost, the music changed again and became mighty and heroic, and as it did so, Freddy, too, gained height and stature. He was the hero, the rescuer, the destroyer of evil, the saviour of virgins.

At the moment when Philippa knew that her wrist could not take one more single flicker, George played three mighty chords on the piano, Freddy bowed and the silent movie was over. It took Philippa several seconds to remember that there had been only one actor on the stage.

The Summer Extravaganza (nightly except Sundays, twice on Saturdays with change of programme on Wednesdays) ran all through the Duckworth season and closed down in the first week of September. Guest-houses and hotels closed their doors on their last visitors, children went back to school, undergraduates who had worked as ice-cream sellers or deck-chair attendants, waitresses and chambermaids, opened their last wage-packets and went back to their books. Philippa went home to Swain's Chard.

The woods were turning orange. Philippa kicked the fallen leaves and breathed in the childhood smells of leaf-mould and damp earth. 'Cut me a couple of number 5As, darling,' Larry's voice whispered. It was one of the legacies of his Summer Extravaganza that she now saw every colour in terms of a numbered square of coloured film. A brown leaf fell and spun through the air and she caught it and wished for an acting job. Somebody was scuffing through the leaves behind her, walking fast, trying to catch her up. She turned around.

'Hello,' said Jeremy Carruthers, who had grown so tall that she did not recognise him at first. 'Hello, Philippa, it's me. Don't say I've grown.'

He walked along beside her and she thought with interest that somebody looked very different when you could look up into his face rather than staring down at the top of his head. The thought made her laugh and she told him about it and he laughed too, and they scuffed their way together through the woods and out onto the lower slopes of the hill.

'It'll all be covered in snow in a couple of months,' said Jeremy, and they remembered the helter-skeltering toboggan rides of the winter of the Small Dance. He really had grown very tall for a boy who had been so small, thought Philippa, and he was very good-looking too.

'What are you doing now?' she asked.

'Theology degree. Don't laugh – I'm going to be a parson.'

'I wasn't going to laugh,' said Philippa, who wasn't. Another flurry of leaves fell towards them and Jeremy caught one. 'Now wish,' said Philippa.

'I am wishing.'

'What?'

'It won't work if I tell you.'

Philippa said, 'I'm not sure if embryo parsons are meant to be superstitious, you know.'

They climbed on into the grey wind. She told him that she

was an out-of-work actress and about the summer season with Larry and Freddy and Steve and Barry the Baritone. On top of the hill, Jeremy Carruthers said, 'If I write to you from Theological College, will you write back?'

'All right,' said Philippa.

Chapter Nine

Beech House
Swain's Chard
September 17th

Dear Jeremy,
Thank you for your letter, it was great to hear from you. I shouldn't worry too much about the doubt. I've been an atheist since I was fourteen, but I suppose it doesn't matter so much as I don't want to be a parson. Still, I should think most people, even parsons, must have doubts about God sometimes – 'specially if they think at all. I dunno. Sorry. I'm not being much help.

I'm still at home in Swain's Chard as you can see, buying *The Stage* every Friday and hunting for acting jobs. One season on Duckworth Pier doesn't look very impressive, but at least I stand a better chance for a job in Rep now I've got my Equity card. Oh dear, this must all look very trivial when you're lying awake at night wondering whether God exists after all.

Love,
Philippa

Dear Philippa,
Thanks for the letter. I don't really lie awake at night worrying about God. Only when I've drunk too much in the evening. What's an Equity card? I thought it was something to do with horses.

Yours,
Jeremy

Beech House
Swain's Chard
September 30th

Dear Jeremy,
You are an idiot. Equity's the actors' union. You've got to be a card-carrying member of it before you can get a job, but you can't get a job till you've got an Equity card. I didn't think parsons were supposed to get drunk.

Love,
Philippa

North Carrington Theological College
October 1st

Dear Philippa,
I don't get badly drunk. Only beer. Two or three pints and I start to ask questions. Do I really believe in the Resurrection of the body? Do I really believe the stories about the moving stone and the women in the garden and Doubting Thomas in the upstairs room shoving his hands into the wounds? And then I think, if I can't honestly,

145

utterly believe in those things, how can I ever stand up in a pulpit and ask other people to believe them?

There's an old bloke here – he lectures part-time at the College and he's interesting. He said the other day that it was time we grew up out of the GOD-IS-A-BIG-MAN-IN-THE-SKY childishness and into more mature ideas. He said he wasn't interested in a God who did cheap conjuring tricks with water and wine and bread and fish. I liked what he said, but some of the other students were outraged and said you couldn't be a Christian if you thought like that. Thanks for explaining the Equity card. How did you get yours?

Yours,
Jeremy

Beech House
Swain's Chard
October 23rd

Dear Jeremy,
Thanks for the last letter. Sorry I haven't written back sooner but things have hotted up on the job front and I've got an interview next week for a new experimental play. It sounds very peculiar and it's for DSM (Deputy Stage Manager in case you didn't know), not an acting job. But it's a job and it's paid and it's experience. Larry Laronde got me my Equity card when I took the job with him – they weren't so hard to get, even last summer. Now they're like gold dust. But at least I've got one and I've got it for life unless I forget to pay my dues. Is there a Parson's Union? How's the Big-Man-in-the-Sky debate?

Love from
Philippa

Dear Philippa,

By the time you get this, I'll probably have been struck down by a thunderbolt. I said in a seminar yesterday that the theme of Virgin Birth was found in most religions and that I was still having difficulties with the miracles and the Resurrection unless I thought of them as allegories rather than as literal truths. All the others started foaming at the mouth and having the vapours and waving crucifixes and garlic at me. But the old boy I told you about, the Big-Man-in-the-Sky one, said he absolutely understood my point of view and shared most of it.

Then there was uproar and some of the students practically burst into tears and said I had no right even to call myself a Christian, let alone be training as a priest. They're probably right. Then they stormed off and reported the old man to the Principal. The rumour is that they've demanded his resignation and he'll probably get the sack and it'll all be my fault. Trouble is, he's the only one here who makes any sense for me. Maybe I ought to give up this lark and go in for soliciting or pimping or accountancy or something sensible like that.

Write and let me know how you get on with the DSM interview. Sorry to go on so much about my life and times. Would I be any good as a DSM if I stop trying to be a parson?

Love,
Jeremy

Dear Jeremy,
You mustn't stop now. This is your tame atheist speaking.
If people like you stop thinking and challenging and ques-
tioning and moving the ideas forward, it'll all collapse
into a heap of candy-floss fairy tales that are no use to
anyone. I think what you say is amazing; it's really made
me stop and think again so it must be something else.

I got that DSM job and no, you wouldn't be any good
at it. There are too many people chasing too few jobs in
the theatre already without taking on runaway parsons. I
was right – it's a *very* peculiar play about a balloon as far
as I can work out. Ha ha. Why don't you come and see
it? I'll let you know the dates as soon as I do.

Love,
Philippa

Chapter Ten

Summer, 1963

Jenny

'I think,' said Dr Gabriel Woolf to Miss Jennifer Cornwood, 'that I should like to go to bed with you.' This statement, made at the end of a Philosophy tutorial when Theresa was away with flu, coincided with one of the times when Jenny was thinking that she really ought to do something about getting rid of her virginity. To lose it to a lecturer would give it some status – like a posthumous award. 'I can promise you that it will be a memorable experience,' said Dr Woolf.

It was. Jenny remembered it for the rest of her life. Dr Woolf breathed a lot and bounced about a lot and Jenny was visited by a brief but unnerving vision of Phyllis and Filthy Luker perching along the top of the brass bedstead and looking reproachful. They were joined by Miss Bugle and the Virgin Mary. Then Jenny got terrible cramp in her right foot and had to pull on her big toe to ease it. Dr Woolf must have thought that this was some sort of rural exotic position and he breathed and bounced even more, but Jenny was so preoccupied with her cramp that all other sensations withdrew and faded into the background.

Dr Woolf rolled off her and lit a cigarette. Jenny's cramp stopped. 'That was wonderful,' Gabriel said, and she got the impression that he said it a lot. 'Was it good for you?' he added, putting on his dark glasses, and she got the impression that he had forgotten her name.

'Oh yes,' she said politely, not wanting to hurt his feelings. I

149

don't want to have breakfast with him, she thought desperately. Gabriel turned over and went to sleep, snoring gently, and with great relief, she slipped out of his bed, dressed quickly and tiptoed out into the night and back to Theresa and Sarah, who were sitting up in their beds writing essays.

'Where on earth have you been?' asked Theresa.

It was only then that Jenny realised that she must have lost her virginity at last. She remembered Judith Littlewick. Ten clothes-pegs to you, she thought and grinned. 'Extra Philosophy tutorial,' she said. 'Something I had to sort out.'

Theresa was over her flu in time for the next tutorial. It was her turn to read an essay out loud, which meant that Jenny could simply sit and listen and wait for the hour to pass without having to talk directly to her teacher, seducer, moral guardian, lover, whatever he was.

Dr Woolf went into the familiar attack again. 'Does it never occur to you, Miss Smith, that your determined attachment to the concept of a benign god is no more than a small child's attachment to its father? If the child falls over and cuts its knee, it runs to its father for comfort and sticking plaster. The religious believer runs to her god for spiritual sticking plaster because she cannot bear the idea of life without him. What have you got to say to that, Miss Smith?'

'I think you're a bastard,' said Miss Smith surprisingly and she got up, left the room and changed her course from Philosophy to Literature.

'Oh dear, oh dear,' said Gabriel Woolf. 'These poor little Christians. They come up here with their Bibles and their Scripture Union badges and they take it all so personally. One should not take anything personally, Miss Cornwood.'

The dark glasses stared at her and then he set her an essay for the following week and made no further reference to their memorable experience.

She felt the first swell of sickness when she was emptying the rubbish into the dustbin one Wednesday morning. It hit her again two mornings later when Theresa was frying kippers in honour of it being Friday. Two weeks after that, the non-appearance of her period ('*You had a period last week*,' said Tit Willow. '*And the week before. Get into the showers*.') began to suggest that the surges of sickness were not what her mother called a 'tummy bug'. Surely she could not be ... not after one, unmagical bedding. It would pass. She would say nothing. It would pass. Six weeks passed without a period and in the end she spoke to Ginger McKinley. Ginger would know what to do.

She did. 'You go to the chemist and buy these special pills.' She wrote the name on the back of an old essay. 'If you don't have a period within three days, you'll know you're pregnant.'

With a sense of unreality, Jenny bought the pills and swallowed them. Four days later, a great lurch of nausea convinced her that she was going to have a baby. *Going to have a baby*. It was there inside her, tiny and real and growing every second. A baby.

'Of course it's not a baby,' said Gabriel Woolf angrily. 'It's am embryo, a foetus, a collection of cells.'

'When does a baby get a soul?' Jenny said carelessly to Theresa.

'From the moment it's conceived,' replied Theresa.

'How do you know?'

Theresa shrugged. 'It's what we're taught. Why are you so het up about it, anyway?'

'It's a Philosophy question I've got to work out.'

Alone in the night, she talked to the baby. 'I wish I knew what you are. Gabriel says you're just a bundle of cells. A growth. I wish you didn't feel like a baby. I wish you'd just fall out of me.'

In the morning she knocked on Gabriel Woolf's door. He was in the middle of a tutorial on the Absurdity of Being and he was annoyed at the interruption. 'Come back in half an hour, Miss Cornwood. I can see you for five minutes then.'

'I don't know what to do,' said Jenny, facing him across his desk.

He sighed. 'I'm not a complete bastard, Miss Cornwood. I will pay for you to have an abortion.'

From a long way off she heard herself say, 'I don't want to have an abortion.'

Gabriel became impatient. 'This is a ridiculous conversation. I certainly have no interest in having a child, and you, I imagine, are in no position to bring one up on your own.' She would not cry. She would *not* cry in front of him. 'Well?' he asked. 'Are you?' She shook her head.

A new thought struck him and he leaned back in amazement, tilting his chair. 'You are not, surely, expecting me to marry you?' She shook her head again. He looked at his watch. 'I've got another tutorial in a minute. I'll meet you in the bar at lunch-time.' His voice was kinder. 'I really will pay for the abortion.'

Chapter Eleven

Jenny

She found Theresa eating yoghourt and reading D.H. Lawrence in the flat. 'Do you really believe in the existence of the human soul?'

Theresa nodded. 'Are you still worrying about that essay?'

The confession beat against Jenny's lips, but she could not tell Theresa. Theresa would hate her for even thinking about an abortion. 'What was it you said about the souls of unbaptised babies? Where do they go?'

Theresa wiped yoghourt off her mouth with the back of her hand. 'Limbo – the non-place. The waiting room.'

'But what's it like?'

Theresa stared at her, frowning. 'There was one old nun when I was about seven. She said it was a desert, a nowhere place where nothing ever changes. No corners or hills or future or past. Oh, I dunno. Shut up and let me get on with this book. I've got an essay to write, too, you know.'

Jenny took her baby to see a doctor. 'I can't help you to get rid of the child,' he said. 'You understand that, don't you? It's against the law.'

'What can I do?' she asked, putting herself into the doctor's hands.

His voice was kind. 'The best advice I can give you, Miss Cornwood, is to go home, tell your parents what has happened and ask them to let you have your baby at home. Have it and give it a loving childhood. It will be best for you both.'

She asked for a week's sick-leave from the university and caught a train to Tarminster and a bus to Swain's Chard. There

153

was nobody at home when she arrived at the house and she sat in the yard beside the gnome and stared into the pond. One of Jimmy's frogs stared back at her from underneath the water lily.

Finch laid her head on Jenny's knee and Jenny rehearsed the words she was going to say to Phyllis. 'I'm going to have a baby, Mum. I'm really sorry to have let you down.'

And Phyllis would put her arms around her and say, 'That's all right, my love. Of course you must come home. We'll take care of you and the baby. Of course you must come home.'

'Good gracious me,' said Phyllis, coming out of the back door into the yard. 'Whatever are you doing here? You didn't half give me a fright. I wondered who it was.'

The prepared speech froze. 'We've got a bit of time off. Reading Week, they call it.'

Phyllis sniffed. 'Reading Week? I thought that was what you students did all the time.' But she smiled proudly at Jenny. This was the one who would get her BA and sleep in twin beds and have a cleaning woman. 'You all right, Jennifer?'

'Yes, Mum, I'm fine. I've had a bit of a tummy bug or something, but I'm fine now.'

'Good,' said Phyllis. 'I'll buy another chop for tea.'

Jenny walked out of the village and up towards the hill. *I'm going to have a baby, Mum. That's all right, my love. That's lovely. You come on home and have your baby. Me and your Dad'll take care of you.*

The wind flurried the trees. It was late spring and there were small frogs in the ponds and lambs in the fields across the valley. The climb grew steeper and she left the woods behind and came out onto the open stretch above the quarry. She began to climb her tree. Twenty feet up to the fork where she used to make Jimmy stop, and on up to the branch where she could look out to Tarminster and the river and the plain and the dinosaur-shaped hills.

'This is where I grew up,' she told the baby. 'This is my view. I want you to be here. I want to carry you up the hill on my shoulders and show you the dinosaur and the sun on the river. I want you to catch tadpoles in a jam-jar and bring them home and put them in our pond.'

The ground was thirty feet below her. Violently she wished

that the branch would break and thump her to the ground so that the tadpole life would be jerked out of her and become a small, accidental puddle of blood on the earth which would sink into the hill and become a part of the place. So that she would not have to make the decision. Then she hurt with grief in case the baby really *was* a baby and it could read her thoughts.

She spoke to it again. 'One year it was so cold here that every single twig on the beech trees froze and when the wind blew, they tinkled together like frozen bells. I was only four, but I remember it. Come on, let's go home and tell your Nan about you.'

They sat quietly round the kitchen table, eating the lamb chops. 'So what d'you do at university?' asked Jimmy, who was going to leave school as soon as he possibly could and be apprenticed to a plumber.

'You read books and think,' said his sister.

Jimmy pulled a face. 'Can't see how that's going to earn you a living,' he retorted. 'What's the point of it?'

'Don't talk with your mouth full,' said Phyllis. 'The point of it is that she'll be educated and qualified and able to earn a good living.'

'What, by thinking a lot? Who's going to pay anybody for thinking a lot?'

'She can be a schoolteacher or something,' said Phyllis crossly. 'Now shut up and eat your tea.'

While they did the washing up, Phyllis filled her in on the Swain's Chard gossip. Ann Dangerfield was doing well at her university, or so her mother said. She'd got a boyfriend who was a Ph.D, whatever that meant. Philippa Foster had finished at her acting school and was working on some pier somewhere. A couple of girls from the estate were in the family way. 'Oh well,' said Phyllis, 'I suppose they've got to be good at something.'

Time and again through the week, Jenny drew a breath and opened her mouth to say the words, but they would not come out. One evening she walked up the hill with her father. The three of them.

'You seem a bit quiet, our Jen. Is everything all right?'

'What d'you think it's all about, Dad?'

He laughed. 'You should be telling me that. You're the philosopher.'

They stood against the wind and watched the rainclouds building up over Tarminster. Beauty is truth, truth beauty, – that is all ye know on earth, and all ye need to know. *There is no such thing as Truth. Everything is a matter of perception.*

She caught the next train back to the University.

Chapter Twelve

It was Arthur's Saturday off. 'I tell you what,' said Phyllis, sitting up in bed and seeing the sunshine through the net curtains, 'let's go off somewhere today. I'll pack us up some sandwiches and a flask and you get out the motorbike and side-car and we'll go.'

Arthur looked at his wife admiringly. What a woman she was ... always ready with an idea, always ready to have a go. She made corned beef and pickle sandwiches and wrapped a chunk of fruit-cake in greaseproof paper while Arthur went out into the yard to wipe a layer of dust and damp off the inside of the side-car. Phyllis was laughing as she carried the picnic out. 'Makes me feel like a kid. We haven't done this for years.'

'Where you going, Our Mum?' asked Jimmy.

'Out for the day. You'll have to fend for yourself. There's cold meat in the larder. Don't go bringing mud into the house, mind.'

They turned out of the yard and into the road that ran along the back of the council houses. Arthur had taken the top off the side-car and Phyllis felt the wind lifting her hair as they drove through the village. Past the 30 mph sign and out the other side, past the de-restriction sign and Arthur pressed the accelerator until the speedometer touched 33. He turned to grin at Phyllis through his plastic visor and she laughed back at him. She looked like a young girl, he thought.

'Where're we going?' he shouted above the rattle of the old bike.

'Anywhere – I don't care.' So they drove on and on, out of Swain's Chard, beyond Tarminster and on into alien country of

157

flat meadowlands where cows drank from streams lined by poplar and willow. Then the landscape became hilly again and Phyllis looked down banks and gaps in hedges and saw glimpses of the river.

Arthur turned the bike along a rough, neglected track that came to a dead end at the top of a steep bank. They scrambled down it, spread the old tartan rug they kept in the side-car underneath a willow and sat down to eat their sandwiches. The river dawdled past them and sunlight dappled through the willow branches.

'Look,' said Phyllis, 'there's a dragonfly.' They watched the electric-blue creature as it darted and hovered around them, settling briefly on twigs and bulrushes, skimming the water, disappearing around the bend in the river. Phyllis lay back and let the sun soak into her. She closed her eyes. This is all it needs to be, she said to herself. She began to doze.

She became aware of Arthur leaning over her, of his hands touching her gently. She opened her eyes and stared straight into his. 'Don't be so soft, Arthur. We can't – not here. Someone'll see us.'

But nobody did see them, and later, as she cradled Arthur's (slightly balding) head in her arms, smiling dreamily and feeling the warmth of the sun on her bare legs, watching the dragonfly that suddenly hovered above them again, she remembered that other afternoon when she had lain with Arthur in the open air and there had been bees, not dragonflies.

Madge Foster stood in front of the cheval mirror and admired herself. It was the evening of that same Saturday and the night of the Swain's Chard Golf Club Summer Dinner and Dance. Madge was getting dressed.

Some people may have wondered why Madge Foster, petite and pretty and vivacious as she was, had ever married Norman, who was large and solemn and important. But Madge never wondered; she knew exactly why. Norman was solid and dependable and he adored her and wanted to take care of her and Madge liked being adored and taken care of. And so they suited one another very well indeed.

Madge had been seventeen when she arrived in the typing pool at Crawford's. One day, Norman's permanent secretary, a fearsome woman encased in kirby grips and corsets, had had a day off to go to a long-distance funeral and Madge had been sent up to Norman as a substitute. (At twenty-seven, Norman was already an important figure in the firm.) He had fallen in love at first sight with Madge and had wooed her ponderously and relentlessly. She had returned his love and they had got married and lived pretty happily ever after, producing Philippa in the process. Madge's kittenish flirtatiousness and acting talents could still stir Norman to passion, even now, nearly twenty years later.

Now, Madge looked at herself critically in the long mirror. Her body, in its new white Marks & Spencer petticoat, was still slim and taut and her legs and ankles, in dark stockings and high sling-backs, were, if not as outrageously long as Joan's, still shapely and unmarred by varicose veins. She stretched her arms above her head and shivered slightly as she slipped the long dark cotton summer evening dress over her head and felt it slither over her back and thighs.

Norman walked into the bedroom, resplendent in his dinner jacket, purple waistcoat and shining white shirt. 'All set, old girl? We don't want to keep the Crawfords waiting.'

John Dangerfield was a mild man who had never wanted much excitement out of life. Security, well-upholstered certainties and long-term respectability were what he asked for. Perhaps it was because his name provided him with enough excitement, or perhaps it was simply that he liked the quiet comfort of the family business (Ladies' Outfitters inherited through three generations). The business was his life and it gave him his life-style; a nice home in Swain's Chard, a wife and two daughters, a comfortable income and a pleasing standing in the business community of Tarminster and District.

Now he sighed and folded away his *Daily Telegraph*. He would have to go upstairs and get ready for the Golf Club Summer Dinner and Dance. Joan had bought a new dress and had her hair done a new way, and it would be one of her chances to Shine. John sighed again. It was sometimes a little wearing, having a wife who Shone. But then again, he thought, if he had married a dim wife, they would probably have faded completely into the background of Tarminster and District,

159

which would not have been so good for business.

He climbed the stairs and went into the bedroom. Joan looked ... splendid, he thought. Not pretty, nothing so chocolate-boxy as pretty, and not exactly beautiful either. Striking

'Do I look all right?' she asked, turning towards him. He remembered her Helena in *Midsummer Night's Dream*.

'Very nice, dear.'

Joan pouted. 'Is that all you can say?'

'You look ... splendid,' he said, and she accepted the word and turned back to the mirror.

'You'll have to hurry up, John. You know it always takes you ages to get your tie right.'

He changed obediently into his white shirt and black socks, fiddling awkwardly with his collar stud and cuff-links, twanging himself on the chin with one of his braces, taking the bow tie by the throat and forcing it into an untidy and lopsided bow.

'Come here,' said Joan impatiently, 'I'll do it for you.' She undid it and fixed it and kissed him lightly and unexpectedly on his cheek, leaving a patch of red lipstick behind. And all of a sudden, she was not only splendid and striking, she was beautiful as well, and John remembered how he had seen her in the Tarminster Operatic and Dramatic Society, the best dancer in the Chorus with the best legs in Tarminster. How surprised and alarmed he had been when she had accepted his offer of marriage three years later.

'You look beautiful,' he said gruffly, and something in Joan melted in surprise.

'Come along, darling,' she said. 'We don't want to be late for the Dinner.'

After the Dinner was eaten, the tables were cleared and the Henry Morrison Band (now a Quintet, with Piano, Sax, Drums, Bass Guitar and Clarinet) took up its position on a small raised dais and began to play a slight cha-cha.

'Would you care for another drink?' said Norman to Joan (The Fosters and the Dangerfields were sharing a table with the Vicar and his wife and Mr and Mrs Crawford.)

'Thank you. I'd love a Martini,' replied Joan, who had already had two as well as three glasses of wine with the meal.

'May I have the pleasure of this dance?' the Vicar asked

Madge. The Reverend Eric was no dancer, but he was willing, and Madge, who had also drunk several glasses of wine, took him in hand. Mrs Dobbin, a timid, tired woman, smiled hopefully at John.

'Ah,' said John. 'May I have the pleasure of this dance?' They bobbed dutifully around the dance floor. Norman came back with the drinks and asked his boss' wife for the pleasure and Mr Crawford stood up with, and sometimes on, Joan.

Madge was enjoying herself. She was a talented flirt and dancing the cha-cha with her, the Reverend Eric began to remember a part of himself that had become a trifle strangled when he had first put on his dog collar. The dance ended and all the couples returned to their tables. They sat down, smiling and fanning themselves and sipping at their drinks, and Henry Morrison changed gear. 'Gentlemen, please take your partners for a Quickstep.'

Mr Crawford stood up and offered himself to Madge. She smiled and took his outstretched hand. There was something about this little woman, he thought, as he found himself doing surprising things in reverse, that made you realise that you were quite a good mover after all. But when he returned her to their table and she was claimed by Norman for a lumbering Waltz, Mrs Crawford smiled sweetly at her husband.

'Funny to think how she was nothing but a little typist in your pool twenty years ago,' she whispered quietly in his ear as he led her onto the dance floor.

There was a bit of a wild streak in Madge Foster, thought John Dangerfield as she wheedled him into an improvised Samba. Was she altogether a good influence on Joan, he wondered.

Is that it, wondered Joan in the car on the way home. Is that what it's all about? You grow up and go to school, then leave and have a few years of glitter and glamour. And then you settle down and get married and have children and then they grow up and go away and you are left with the Golf Club Dinner and Dance and a cha-cha with Mr Crawford and a Quickstep with the Vicar.

'I'm going for a walk,' she said suddenly to John as he turned the car into their drive.

'At this time of night? It's half-past one in the morning.'

'I don't care. I need some air.' She saw his anxious, hurt expression and squeezed his hand so that he wouldn't take it personally. 'It's all right, John dear. I think I'm a little bit tipsy.'

'I'll come with you,' he said nobly, because he was dying to get into bed and go to sleep.

'No, don't. I'll be all right. I won't be long.' She slipped off her shoes and left them on the floor of the car, then she opened the door and slid out into the summer darkness.

It was a clear, warm, soft night and Joan had never been afraid of solitude or of the countryside at night. Light-headed from Martini and wine, stocking-footed on the springy grass of the hill paths, she wandered up the familiar slopes, past the toboggan run, alongside the drystone wall that edged the wood, up and up and on until she found herself standing at the top of the hill, looking down at a few lights that still shone from Tarminster and at the glint of the river in the moonlight. Full moon for lunatics, she thought. Am I a lunatic, she wondered, sobering up in the night air and seeing herself from the outside – a middle-aged woman with no shoes, wearing a summer ball-dress, alone on the hill in the small hours of the morning.

No, not a lunatic. Up here she was saner than anywhere else. Up here, she could answer the question that had troubled her at the dance and come to a head in the car. Dancing with the Vicar and Mr Crawford was not the end of it all, not what it was all about. She leaned against the night and felt the spring of the grass beneath her feet and lifted her face to the moon. It was all right. She turned and went back home.

John sighed again, with relief this time, when he heard his wife opening the front door and climbing the stairs in her stockinged feet. Perhaps she had caught something of Madge Foster's wild streak, he thought. Or perhaps she had reached the Difficult Age. He must remember to be patient with her.

Chapter Thirteen

Jenny

In the bedsitter, she opened her mouth to tell Theresa, but the words jammed again. How could she say it to Catholic Theresa, of all people? So she went to find Ginger McKinley who was very practical. 'Make two lists,' said Ginger. '"Reasons for having it" and "Reasons for not having it".'

Under 'Reasons for not having it', Jenny wrote: *No Job, no money, no home.* Under 'Reasons for having it', she wrote nothing because she could only think *I love it* – and that was neither logical nor practical.

Ginger looked very hard at her. 'You're not thinking it's a baby, are you? Because it's not. It's nothing. Only a bundle of cells.'

She trained herself to think of the thing inside her as an inconvenience, a growth, something to be removed, like tonsils, so that she could get on with the rest of her life. As always, Ginger knew what to do. There was an expensive, hygienic, private clinic where they did it in one day, cash over the counter, superb conditions but keep your mouth shut. 'Do you want me to make an appointment for you?'

Jenny, whose life had slowed down to an unreal dream, nodded. Ginger, who, despite the cool façade, had become very kind, made the appointment. 'Do you want me to come with you?'

Jenny nodded again. Everything seemed to be happening on the outside of her, to be carrying her along with it, while she, like a small child, drifted along in the wake of the grown-ups who knew what was best for her.

They arrived at the clinic which was disguised as an exclusive private dental surgery. Rows of impressions and moulds for false teeth gaped along windowsills and three or four rich, elderly and toothless patients went in and out of different doors. A receptionist led Jenny into a back room where two thin, dark-suited, bespectacled men sat behind a desk. Ginger was left behind with the false teeth in the reception area.

'Good morning, Miss ... ah ... Cornwood,' said one of the men. His voice was thin and cold. 'Do you understand the purpose of this interview?' Ginger had explained it to her. Two psychiatrists would sign a certificate to say that she was mentally unfit to have a child, so that if any questions were asked later, the clinic was covered.

They took it in turns to ask in bored tones about her age, occupation, family background, financial position, physical well-being and state of mind. Then it came. 'Have you ever considered taking your life because of this pregnancy?'

Jenny was amazed. 'No,' she said.

The men were obviously irritated. 'Miss Cornwood,' said the one on the right, 'we are trying to help you. Please answer the question again.' He paused and then repeated it, slowly and emphatically: 'Have you ever considered taking your life because of this pregnancy?'

There was not a glimmer of warmth or kindness in their faces and they were losing patience with her. 'Come along, Miss Cornwood, we cannot help you unless you give us a satisfactory answer.'

Again the sense of slow-motion unreality floated over her. These were the grown-ups. They were doctors; they knew what was best. She suddenly understood what she had to say.

'Yes,' she whispered.

The men relaxed and signed a form, then rang for the receptionist. She bustled in, smiling and competent, and led Jenny back to the false teeth and Ginger. 'That's lovely then, Miss Cornwood. We'll see you again in three days' time. Ten o'clock. No need to bring anything, you'll be out in a couple of hours.'

She lowered her voice confidentially. 'Have you got ...' Ginger paid a deposit of twenty pounds and they left the dental clinic.

Gabriel gave her the money in ten-pound notes and three days later, Ginger took her back to the place. The cosy receptionist greeted her and took the money. There was no receipt, no record of anything. A plump, jolly nurse in a white cap came in to take Jenny to her room. She was comforting and reassuring.

'I don't want to do it,' Jenny said suddenly.

'Listen,' said the kind nurse, 'there's really nothing to it. It's perfectly safe.' She squeezed Jenny's hand. 'I know it's hard, dear, but once it's over, you'll forget it ever happened and get on with your real life.'

Jenny undressed and put on a white theatre gown. She sat on the edge of the bed and waited, swinging her bare legs. Funny, she thought. The same legs she had swung from the Climbing Tree. Now they seemed to belong to somebody else entirely.

The nurse led her into a small operating theatre where a genial man greeted her. 'All set, my dear?' He was very well-spoken. Her mother would have approved of the way he spoke. 'Don't look so worried. There's nothing to it.' His voice changed. 'Have you told your parents?'

'No,' she replied.

'You must promise me that you will never tell them. It might upset them. Don't ever say anything about it to anybody.'

He put a needle into Jenny's arm and she felt herself fly away, out of her body, up towards the ceiling of the room. It was very pleasant and all of a sudden she began to laugh and the nurse and doctor laughed too as they worked on her body, lying there below her. She floated, light-headed, careless and carefree, and from a great distance, she watched the painless process. There was nothing to it, nothing at all. Scrape, scrape, scrape, scoop, scoop, scoop and out it came, a small lump of liver in a silver dish.

'It looks like a sliver of liver,' she said, and giggled at the rhyme. 'Just a sliver of liver. Not a baby at all.' And they all laughed together at her rhyme. 'Only it isn't a liver, it's a dier.' She almost wept with laughter at her wit and the doctor and the nurse laughed with her as she flew around the ceiling of the operating theatre.

Later, back in the bedsitter, lying awake in the night and listening to the peaceful breathing of Theresa and Sarah, she

165

felt as if her whole life had been scraped out of her. Everything that she had ever been had been cut out of the very centre of her, and she was dead inside. She could hear the baby crying for her, abandoned in the desert Theresa had called Limbo. She wanted to reach out and pull it back to her, to comfort it and tell it that she loved it. Theresa moved in her sleep and muttered something and Jenny wished that she could be Theresa, whole and strong and certain of her beliefs.

In the morning, after the other two had gone to their lectures, she shoved some clothes into a duffel bag and caught the train to Tarminster again.

Chapter Fourteen

Ann

'Ann's bringing a Man home for Reading Week,' Joan shouted at Madge from underneath her dryer.

Half an hour later, shampooed and set in the corner of the Chalet Suisse, Madge asked, 'What on earth is Reading Week?'

'It's a week when they come home to read,' explained Joan airily.

Madge pulled a face. 'I should have thought,' she said, 'that that was what they did all the time. You mean half term.'

'He's doing a Ph.D in The Social Relevance of Contemporary Art,' said Joan, then wished she hadn't when Madge asked what on earth that was supposed to mean, and was it coming out of Norman's taxes.

Ann and Damien wandered through the nave of Tarminster Cathedral. 'It's beautiful, isn't it?' she whispered, suddenly remembering the evening they had sung the *Creation* and the way that Haydn's music had exploded and flown up into the arches and fan-vaulting of the roof.

Damien scuffed his feet angrily along the great stone slabs which covered the bones of English lords and knights and bishops. The scuffing noise echoed rebelliously. 'It disgusts me,' he said loudly. 'It's the perfect example of the Capitalist use of superstitious fear to keep the working classes in their place.' A passing parson stared at him in surprise. 'It says, "Be good, hand over all your money to us; don't complain, don't ask questions or rise up. Do as you're told, fear God, the

167

Church and the ruling classes and you'll get your reward in Heaven. Challenge us and you'll go to Hell. The worse it is for you now, the better it will be after you've died. Enjoy your proverty and misery and sickness in the knowledge that Heaven is waiting for you. And in the meantime, we'll enjoy our wealth and privilege and power. We'll have a fucking ball." Come here.'

He grabbed Ann's hand and almost ran with her towards the Choir Screen. 'Look at these bloody great tombs – see? They told the poor that it was good to be poor, that poverty would lead them to Heaven. But all the time they were giving vast amounts of money to the Church to buy their own way there. Look at them.' He stamped on one of the gravestones. 'The nearer to the altar you were, the nearer to God you were – on the Central Line to Heaven. It makes me want to spit.'

For a moment she thought that he really was going to spit, then and there. A verger in a red dress approached them. 'Would you like to take your seats in the Choir for Evensong?'

'Fuck off,' snarled Damien, and swung back down the nave as a procession came into view. A white-robed man carrying a great gold and ebony cross led men and boys in parallel lines towards them and then he turned and glided through the gates of the Choir Screen. In pairs, they bowed to the altar and then looped off to take their places in the Choir stalls. It reminded Ann of something. Of course – Strip the Willow.

'It's a farce, isn't it?' said Damien. 'A primitive ritual based on fear to appease some terrible Creator.'

'He's terribly nice,' said Joan to Madge down the telephone. 'Very good-looking and frightfully bright, of course. Ph.D. And he seems genuinely fond of Ann. I wouldn't be surprised to hear wedding bells on the horizon.' (Can you hear things on the horizon, Madge wondered.) 'I've booked tickets for them for this evening.'

The Swain's Chard Amateur Dramatic Society's production of *Blithe Spirit* starred Joan Dangerfield as Ruth and Madge Foster as Elvira. Damien stretched his long legs out into the aisle of the Institute and yawned osentatiously. He covered his eyes with his hand and uttered just-audible groans when anybody needed a prompt or the maid's accent slipped.

'I don't think I can stand any more,' he said to Ann in the interval.

'But they're taking us out for a meal after the show,' whispered Ann.

'It's jolly good, isn't it?' said her father, handing Damien a cup of tea and a Rich Tea biscuit.

After the kisses and congratulations, Joan and John took their guests out for a meal in Tarminster's new and only Indian restaurant. The next day, Joan, who noticed these things, said, 'He doesn't say please or thank you much, does he?' She and Ann were washing up after Sunday dinner. 'And why wouldn't he stand up for the National Anthem? Everybody noticed.'

Ann, who had adopted a bent-kneed, crouching compromise between her father and her lover, was irritated. 'He thinks conventions like that are an affectation – a sign of middle-class hypocrisy and manipulation,' she explained, drying the Willow Pattern plates furiously. And I agree with him, she said to herself.

'Ah,' said Joan.

That afternoon, Ann took Damien for a walk to the top of Swain's Chard Hill. She led the way, climbing ahead of him up the narrow white track, until they stood with the wind in their faces, looking out over Tarminster and the river and across to the jagged line of the hills.

'Why have you brought me here?' Damien asked.

Without looking at him she replied, 'I don't think there's anywhere in the world more beautiful than this.'

He laughed and put his arms around her. 'You're so bloody romantic. You'll be quoting Wordsworth any minute now.' And he kissed her.

When he stopped, she said, 'You will remember to tell my mother she was good in the play and to thank her for the meal and everything, won't you?'

Damien looked at her in disbelief. 'Your mother? She epitomises everything I loathe about middle-class England. Church-going, Tory-voting, amateur-dramatic, cocktail-drinking, smug, prejudiced ignoramuses. You are all so full of middle-class charm ... you suffocate me.'

She hit him hard across his superior face and he was very

169

surprised. 'I despise violence,' he announced, rather blurrily, when he could speak.

He collected his things from the house and drove away in his Ford Popular without seeing Joan or John. 'Has he gone already?' Joan asked indignantly. 'I really do think he might have said goodbye, Ph.D or no Ph.D.'

'God, Mother,' shouted Ann, 'why can't you just shut up? You're so ... fucking *middle-class*!' She turned and strode back towards the hill.

Chapter Fifteen

Jenny

It would be all right once she was home again. She would climb the hill and look out over the wide miles to the dinosaur range. The wind would blow through her exhausted brain and clear it of all this misery and confusion and guilt. The sound of the woods in late-summer leaf and birdsong would fill up the empty space where the baby had been. It was over. She would go home and Swain's Chard would mend her.

She got off the bus before it reached the village and set off up a steep, narrow lane that would bring her to the top of the hill from the Tarminster side. She could look down the homeward slopes to the Climbing Tree and the first roofs of the village.

It was very hot and her duffel bag was heavy. She toiled on against a terrible sadness, driving herself to the top, waiting for the relief to come, waiting to get to the top and know that everything was all right, that she was forgiven, that she was the same as she had always been. At last she reached the top and looked down towards her home.

The Climbing Tree had gone. It lay like a a great dead animal, sawn-off and hideous, with snapped branches and dying leaves spread around its stump.

'Council felled it yesterday,' said Jimmy. 'Some kid was climbing it last week and one of the branches snapped and he broke his arm. He's all right, but everyone said the tree was dangerous so the council cut it down yesterday. We all went up to watch. What you doing here again, anyway? You only just went back.'

'I've chucked it, Jim. I'm not going back.'

Even Jimmy was shocked. 'Blimey,' he said, 'Our Mum's not half going to be mad at you.' Then he punched her gently. 'I'm glad though. It's been boring here without you now Charlie's with Mary over at Honeyford all the time. You can live at home again and get a proper job.' He grinned at her. 'I told you all that reading and thinking wasn't no good to anybody.'

Phyllis was furious. 'What d'you mean, not going back? What's the matter with you? You ill or something?'

Perhaps she could just be ill, thought Jenny. She felt ill enough. Being ill would be the easiest way out. But then they'd send her to the doctor and the doctor would see there was nothing wrong with her.

'I'm no good at it, Mum. I haven't got the brains for it, after all.'

No good, no good, no good. The words echoed in her head like a shout in a cave. Or a tomb. Funny that womb should rhyme with tomb. No good. *No good, no good, no good.*

But there was no such thing as good or bad or right or wrong. It was only a matter of how you looked at things; only a matter of whether the half-crown was a straight line or a circle. Good and bad and right and wrong were nothing but man-made ideas. How then could it be that she felt so utterly bad and wrong? Day after day she climbed the hill, past the amputated tree, waiting for the place to heal her; but the skies were grey and the sound of the wind in the woods only reached her outer ears. Nothing could touch the inside emptiness of her.

One afternoon she stood and waited while the rainclouds raced towards her and broke into a fierce downpour on her head. All the pain and guilt and loss rose up inside her and she began to cry. *I'm sorry. I'm sorry.* But nothing changed. It was as if the landscape she had loved and grown in had turned its back on her because she had sinned against it. 'Blow, winds, and crack your cheeks! ... You cataracts and hurricanoes, spout ...' A huge black cloud hunched above her and emptied itself furiously over the hill. 'You think 'tis much that this contentious storm invades us to the skin' ... it was true. The mad old king was right. The pain in her mind was so great that she hardly noticed what was happening to her body.

172

She stood on in the raging rain. Perhaps it would wash her clean, wash away the terrible thing she had done, let her be forgiven, even though there was Nothing there to forgive her. Suddenly she knew she must confess; that was what Theresa had said. 'Confess your sins and repent, and you will be forgiven.'

Jenny turned and ran back down the hill with an energy and an urgency she had not felt since the baby. She came to the village and walked in through the side door of St Swithin's and knelt down in the back pew and tried to pray. But the words were stuck in her head and refused to fly away, and when she dared to look up at the crucifix, it seemed as if the nailed and twisted body had turned Its face away from her.

A door opened at the back of the church and she heard footsteps. They hesitated at the end of her pew and then continued on up the nave and Jenny saw the back view of the Reverend Eric Dobbin moving up his church. He stopped and turned, and she covered her face with her hands again, pretending she was praying. The Rev. Eric walked on towards the altar, frowning; the lonely figure in the back pew made him sense that something was very wrong, but he would not interrupt its solitude. He wandered about near the organ, pretending to look for music and orders of services and prayers for the sick until the figure in the pew lifted her head from her hands and stared in front of her.

The Vicar realised that she was Jenny Cornwood, the postman's daughter, who had been to his Sunday School and Confirmation classes and who had sung in his choir. He had probably even baptised her, he thought. He began to walk slowly and casually down a side aisle, to give her the chance to speak. As he drew alongside the end of her pew, Jenny turned her face towards him and he was shocked. In the dimness of the church, she looked like that terrible picture by – Munch, was it? He never knew quite how you ought to pronounce it. Yes, that picture called *The Scream*; the white, terror-filled face on the end of some pier where people strolled at sunset and the white face screamed out all the fear of all time until you answered it with all your own innermost terrors.

'Hello, Jenny,' said the Reverend Eric quietly. She tried to smile at him. There was something quite desperate about her eyes, he thought, and she was soaking wet and white-faced. 'Are you all right?'

'Yes, thank you,' said Jenny Cornwood, and she got up and slid out of the far side of the pew, heading towards the church door. Just as she was about to leave, she said, 'Can I talk to you a minute?'

He walked beside her across the graveyard and steered her into the Vicarage, praying that the Flower Committee Ladies would not have arrived yet. They had not. 'Thank You, God,' said the Reverend Eric. He meant what he said and he had no doubt in his mind that God had heard him.

They sat either side of the fireplace, in comfortable armchairs. 'What did you want to talk about, Jennifer?' asked Eric.

She came straight out with it. 'Do you believe in Limbo?'

Eric was startled. Twenty years in Swain's Chard had accustomed him to angry altercations about the Flower Rota, Parish Council elections and the Organ Restoration Fund, but no one had ever asked him about Limbo before. He thought for a minute and tried to remember the lectures at Theological College all those years ago. The trouble was, they kept changing the ideas, and if you hadn't got time to read the *Church Times* thoroughly, you could easily miss something vital about the Afterlife.

'It's a Roman Catholic concept,' he said eventually and doubtfully.

'So you don't believe in it?'

The Reverend Eric sensed that he must tread carefully. 'No.'

'But the Roman Catholics do,' said Jenny Cornwood.

'Um,' said the Rev. Eric.

'And Purgatory?'

'Certainly not,' replied the Vicar with more confidence. 'Absolutely not. The Church of England abolished Purgatory at the Reformation.'

The white face and desperate eyes stared at him. 'But do you believe in Heaven and Hell?'

'Oh yes, most certainly we do.'

Jenny sighed impatiently. 'I don't understand. You say that the Church of England has definitely cancelled Purgatory and Limbo?' The Vicar nodded. 'But that it still believes in Heaven and Hell?' Again the Reverend Eric nodded. He was beginning to wish that the Flower Girls would arrive. 'But Catholics believe in all of it, and philosophers believe in none of it. So how can you be sure, any of you, that any of it is true?' With enormous relief, he heard a cheerful knocking on the Vicarage front door. 'That's why we call it "Faith",' he said, slipping with gratitude into the platitude. 'Blessed are those who have not seen yet who have believed.' The bright voices of the Flower Committee were twittering in the hall. 'Look Jenny, I've got a meeting now. But please do come back, any time, if you would like to discuss this again.'

She seemed calmer now, he thought, as he let her out into the hall and through the front door and returned to usher the Flower Committee into the study. But he felt guilty as well, aware that he had failed her, that he had not done all that he should have done. He would give the matter more thought when the Flower meeting was over.

'They none of them know; none of them really knows,' said Jenny to herself as she walked away from the Vicarage. But that in itself was some comfort. If there was no such place as Limbo, her baby could not have gone there. And he (she always thought of him as 'he') could not possibly have gone to Hell; the poor little sod had done nothing to deserve that.

She remembered the Baptism services she had sung through when she was in the church choir, and shuddered. All that stuff about casting out Satan. She should have asked the Vicar that. If unbaptised C of E babies didn't go to Limbo, where the hell did they go? If there was a Hell (and the Vicar had been very certain on that point), presumably she was heading there, and serve her right, she thought. But there again, who knew? Who could possibly know?

The Church of England had abolished Purgatory and Limbo; the Catholics still believed in them. Who was right? And suddenly she saw very clearly why the philosophers were right. It was nonsense to discuss and argue and agonise about things that nobody could give the answers to. The answers people gave were only bandages to fill up the terrible gaps in the universe. There were no answers, she understood now, only questions.

She shrugged and shook her wet hair. In a funny way, the

visit to the Vicar had done her good. All that was left in her now was a deep, deep grief for the baby. The grief stayed locked inside her because she had promised the men at the clinic that she would never tell anyone else what had happened.

Chapter Sixteen

She was dead inside, but she got a live-in job as a chamber-maid, kitchen assistant and cleaner at the Three Bells in Tarminster, where Charlie's girlfriend, Mary Perkins, was the cook. Mary came up on the early bus from Honeyford every morning, but living in saved Jenny from the eyes and tongues of Swain's Chard.

She moved slowly in a grey nothingness where she did not hope or dream or see colours any more. Nothing shone. Being a live-in worker gave her a roof over her head and food in her mouth although, most of the time, she could see little reason for either. But she gritted her teeth and kept her eyes down and cleaned shelves and floors and toilets and changed sheets and served meals. If only she might one day reach her baby and tell him that she was sorry and that she loved him, then he might forgive her. In the meantime she would clean and clean until she was too exhausted to do anything but sleep.

She banked the money they paid her at the Three Bells. Now she understand why people said 'for love or money'. When there was no love inside you because you did not deserve love any more and you had no love to give, you turned to dead, cold money.

Phyllis was beside herself. 'Why did she leave?' she kept asking Arthur, night after night in bed.

Arthur, who was grieving for the grief he sensed inside his daughter, sighed. 'Perhaps it was just wrong for her,' he said hopelessly. 'She's a village girl; perhaps she was just out of her depth with those kind of people.'

Phyllis bristled beside him and he could feel her hackles rising through her brushed nylon nightie. 'Of course she wasn't out of her depth. That's exactly what Madam Snooty Dangerfield's saying to her hoity-toity friends. Our Jennifer's got more brains than any of them.'

But underneath her anger and disappointment and hurt pride, Phyllis too was grieving for some injury she instinctively felt but did not understand, some wrong that had been inflicted on her child. She took it out in rage against Joan and Madge. She knew what they'd be saying under their dryers and over their morning tea and coffee.

'Poor little Jenny Cornwood. Out of her depth, I suppose,' said Joan in the Chalet Suisse. It was the Monday morning after Damien's departure from Swain's Chard.

'How was Ann's man?' asked Madge.

Joan gazed intently into her tea leaves. Was that a motorbike? 'Not what I had expected for a Ph.D,' she said curtly, and changed the subject.

'I'm pregnant,' whispered Mary to Jenny as they peeled potatoes together in the Three Bells kitchen. 'Hold onto your hats for a wedding. Don't say anything to your mum yet, though; Charlie still needs a bit of time to get used to the idea.'

'You're so ... fucking *middle-class*!' Ann had said to her mother after Damien had driven off angrily in the Ford Popular. Then she had turned and walked back up the hill. She stood at the top, leaning against the wind to steady herself against her rage and frustration. She was equally furious with Damien and with Joan, both of whom seemed to think it was their duty and their right to turn her into something they wanted her to be. And she was furious with herself for being the rope in their tug-of-war.

From this height, she could look down on Damien and her mother and see them clearly at last, moulded by their own prejudices, blinkered by their theories and ideologies, insisting that she must feel and think and be what they were. They were strong, both of them, and they were pulling her in opposite directions, refusing to allow her to be herself. *Herself*. And who on earth was that? Who was she, Ann Dangerfield, aged twenty, anyway? She was nothing but a confusion of upbringing and education; a mixture of other people's utterly incompatible ideas. A mess.

A motorbike was climbing the long road up from Tarminster. She could see it rounding the bends and coming nearer, glinting in the afternoon sun. Something about it held her attention, made her watch until it reached the high part of the road and began to cross the slope of the hill itself.

Charlie Cornwood slowed down. He had kicked the bike into action and roared along the lanes out of Honeyford towards Tarminster. 'I'm going to have a baby,' she had said. Just like that. This morning. She was having a baby. *His* baby. It would be born early next year, she said. They would get married. It would be all right, she said; they could live on his wages in a room in her parents' house until they could get a council house of their own and it would be all right, she promised. He loved her, didn't he? Of course he loved her; he had loved her since she was fifteen and everyone had always understood that they would get married one day. *'But not yet, not yet!'* he yelled above the shout of the engine. Not fatherhood yet, not husbanding yet; there was life to be lived, fun to be had, dances to be danced, roads to be ridden. He was not ready yet for the council estate and the rent and all the steadiness they would expect from him.

He roared round the Tarminster by-pass and took the road to Swain's Chard. He must get to some air, get to some space where he could breathe; he must turn some corner before the cage doors closed, find some adventure before he was claimed forever by family life.

The road out of Tarminster was steep and the bike slowed down. He changed into a lower gear and drove the machine as hard as he could until the top of Swain's Chard Hill came into view. He glanced up and saw a figure silhouetted against the afternoon sky. For some reason he slowed down again. The figure moved. It was running down the hill towards the road, jumping over dips in the ground, moving easily and quickly, knowing the place, coming towards him all the time. Something about the way it moved ... He could see now that it was a girl – someone he knew. He stopped the bike and waited until Ann Dangerfield, breathless and laughing, with her hair

179

all blown across her face, ran out into the road. 'Coming for a ride?' said Charlie.

They rode and rode, out through the other side of Swain's Chard and onto high stretches of commonland where trees and hedges were bent permanently sideways by the force of the wind. Ann clung to Charlie as he raced the bike faster and faster and she felt the power of the engine and the rush of the wind in her face.

They rode for an hour or more until they were quite lost and dusk was beginning to blur the outlines of the hedges. Charlie turned the bike off the road onto a high, flat, lonely place and then he stopped. Ann leaned her face against the back of his jacket and waited for him. Very gently, he helped her from the bike and held both her hands. He kissed her as if he hardly dared to at first, as if she were something very precious, as if he were not sure he was allowed to touch her. When he knew that it was all right and they lay on the high, springy ground in the open air and he touched her, she knew that she was special and magical and rare to him. He touched her and it felt as if her body was flying away, singing some high, impossible note that went on and on and on until it flew into the sky, trembled and exploded into shooting stars and golden rain that fell and sank silently into the earth.

Afterwards, he drove her back to Swain's Chard and he returned to Honeyford and Mary and the baby.

'Where on earth have you been?' asked Joan crossly.

For a second Ann thought she might blurt out: 'I've been making love to Charlie Cornwood.' Instead, she said: 'I went for a walk.'

'All this time?'

'I met an old friend and we went for a drive.'

'Who?' asked Joan.

Ann laughed. 'Come on, Mother. I'm a big girl now. Almost grown-up.' For the first time in either of their lives, they both realised that it was almost true.

Phyllis sniffed when Charlie told her the news. 'Oh well, we knew they'd get married sometime,' she said and went out and bought patterns for matinée jackets and bootees and great quantities of yellow and lilac two-ply wool.

Jenny watched her mother with amazement. Was this how Phyllis would have reacted if she had told her about the baby? Would she have started knitting and catching the bus to Tarminster to hunt for a pram and a cot and a carrycot?

Jenny watched the preparations for the wedding – Mary in white at St Eustace's in Honeyford and a reception at the Three Bells (special rates for staff). She listened to Phyllis thinking up and trying out names – Sarah, Matthew, Paul, Louise ... 'Mine would have been your first,' she kept wanting to say. 'He would have been your first grandchild. He could have had a name and worn your matinée jackets and ridden in your pram.' But she had promised to say nothing and so she went on peeling vegetables and cleaning basins and vacuuming floors and preparing the food for other people's weddings and crying for her unnamed child in the nights.

It was a November wedding. Mary wore a full, white dress with a white fur cape and the bridesmaids had muffs and white fur bonnets. Jenny sat with her parents and Jimmy on the Groom's side of the church and watched Mary ('You would never have guessed if you hadn't known,' said Honeyford) walk radiantly up the aisle to join Charlie. They promised lifelong fidelity and love, they promised to honour and cherish and, in Mary's case, obey, and then they knelt down, side by side, at the altar rails to be blessed. How funny the soles of their shoes look, Jenny thought. Somebody ought to tell people to clean the soles as well as the tops of their shoes before they get married and kneel down.

And that is the difference, she thought, as Mr and Mrs Charles Cornwood signed their names in the vestry and left the church to be greeted by confetti and cameras. There was no one to wait for me at the end of the aisle, no one with dusty soles to his shoes to make me and my baby respectable. That was one blessing, she realised, as she threw a handful of confetti over her brother and sister-in-law. At least she had not married Gabriel Woolf.

Everyone got into cars and climbed onto motorbikes and drove out of Honeyford to Tarminster and the three-course sit-down meal at the Three Bells. Jenny had peeled the potatoes and criss-crossed the sprouts that very morning.

Chapter Seventeen

1964

Ann

Ann took her Finals and emerged with a lower-middle-class degree in Philosophy-with-English. Joan and John went proudly to her Graduation Day and watched her walk through a hallful of other proud parents in her hired gown and mortar board, shake the hand of the Vice Chancellor and return to her seat, clutching the piece of paper that said she was a BA (Hons).

'The world is your oyster now,' said Joan happily. 'What an extraordinary phrase,' she added. 'We must remember to let Miss Bugle know.' They were eating strawberries and cream in a quadrangle. 'She'll put you up on the Honours Board.'

Ann got a job teaching Religious Education (with some English) at a Secondary Modern school in the Forest of Dean. The staffroom was full of ageing, exhausted and irritable men and women, and Ann was a shock to her pupils because she was young and had long hair and long legs and short skirts, and she sat on the edge of her desk strumming four chords on a guitar while they sang *Sloop John B*, *Kingston Town* and *Yellow Bird* in their R.E. lessons.

'Do you believe in God?' she asked one day.

'Yes, Miss,' they chorused.

'What does He look like?'

'He's got a long white beard,' said one girl.

'And long white hair,' said another.

'And a long white nightie,' said a boy, 'and a long white...'

The class cackled raucously and Ann felt herself blushing. She decided to ignore the boy.

'But why do you believe in God?'

'Everybody does, Miss. It's what you're taught when you're a kid.'

'But say you'd never been taught it? What if nobody had ever told you?'

That made them think for a minute. 'Then you wouldn't know, would you?'

'So that would make God not true?'

They were shocked now. 'What you on about, Miss?'

'Would not knowing about God mean that God doesn't exist?'

4A was most emphatic. 'Oh no, Miss. It'd still be true. You just wouldn't know about it.'

Another day she showed them the now-it's-a-circle-now-it's-a-straight-line trick with the half-crown to illustrate the theory of perception. 4A was very unimpressed. 'That's daft, Miss. Anybody can see it's really a half-crown. It's only the way you hold it makes it look like a straight line.'

They demolished the philosophical theories of perception before break and taught her card tricks instead, which were much more tricky and much more interesting. They took her into their confidences and told her about their home-lives and their love-lives, because she was young with long brown hair and legs, and because she wore mini-skirts and played the guitar and they all sang Beatles' songs in her English lessons.

Roger Bennett taught Art and Crafts at the school. He was a strong and silent Mills-&-Boon-and-Mr-Darcy-enigmatic, handsome man of thirty with a shadowy wife and two or three children in the background of his life. He gazed moodily across the smoke-filled staffroom when the grey, exhausted teachers collapsed into coffee cups and ash-trays at morning break. He was thirty with a mortgage and a lifetime of staffrooms and Art and Craft rooms ahead of him. He thought he yearned for something to happen and fly him away from the timetable of his life.

Sometimes he caught Ann's eye and then they would both look away. She is so wild and strong and free, he thought. He had been like that once, he thought, before the children and the mortgage and the pension. She is what I really wanted, what I dreamed of, what I deserved. He dreamed on safely. Nothing would come of it, nothing would happen. He did not even want it to. But looking at her across the smoky staffroom brightened his days and coloured his dreams.

In the afternoons, when the last bell had rung, he went home to his wife and his two or three children and they all ate tea together and then he marked sketchbooks and helped to put the children to bed. Then he and his wife watched television and went to bed, and in the mornings he got up and drove to Morning Assembly and the Art Room. And now there was the girl with the long legs and the mini-skirts who strummed Beatles' songs on her guitar in lessons and was deeply disapproved of by the exhausted ones.

He really was very handsome and enigmatic, thought Ann. And he looked so moody and disappointed sometimes. Like Mr Rochester. His wife probably did not understand him. *She* would have understood him, Ann thought, if she had got there first, and she began to fall privately and enjoyably in love with Roger Bennett. It was perfectly safe, perfectly all right. Nobody, least of all Roger himself, would ever know. It coloured her days.

4A watched with interest.

At the Staff Christmas Party, when the shadowy wife stayed at home to look after the children who were cutting teeth or developing rashes or both, Roger and Ann found themselves next to each other at the table of bits prepared by the Domestic Science teacher and the Headmaster's wife. He poured her a glass of white wine and lit a cigarette for her, and when the party was over, they somehow found themselves in a bar in the town, drinking beer and smoking and talking about Life and Art.

'You are so wild and strong and free,' said Roger.

Ann felt misty and wild and free and she lit another cigarette. 'And you?' she asked.

His moody eyes gazed into hers. 'I'm in a cage,' said Roger Bennett, and he breathed smoke out of his nose. He looks like a dragon, thought Ann, like a sad, handsome, enigmatic dragon. 'I was strong and free once, too. Like you.'

He drank his fifth pint of beer. They both blew smoke rings

and thought about the sadness and waste of it all. He told her of his need to create, to express himself through his Art, of his creative spirit which was caged and withered by the restraints of teaching and marriage and the mortgage. She reached out and held his hand sympathetically. Much later, he kissed her in a haze of wine and beer and cigarette smoke, and then he went home to his wife and children.

'Nice party?' asked his wife, who was covered in Bonjela and Calamine. 'Bloody awful,' said Roger and he helped her to dab Calamine on the rashes.

Their affair was a wild free thing of exciting and guilty secret meetings, of long, tender gazes across the staffroom at break and of coded messages left on blackboards and notice-boards. It was quite harmless, Nobody knew – there was nothing *to* know. Nobody was going to leave anybody or hurt anybody.

4A watched in fascination and disbelief and delight. Whispers grew into murmurs and murmurs spread into the staffroom and out of the school and into the town. They hurried up Roger's garden path and through the back door and into the ears of Roger's wife, who burst out of the shadows into glorious Technicolour and was waiting for Roger with a carving knife when he came back from school one Thursday afternoon.

'Get out of this house!' she screamed at him, pointing the knife like a fencing foil. (She had been good at fencing when he first met her; it had been one of the things that had attracted him to her.) All at once he remembered how wild and young and free she had been in the Drama and Fencing classes at Teacher Training College, and now here she was again with her hair flying and her eyes ablaze with rage.

'Darling,' he said

'Don't you dare to "Darling" me,' she spat and he backed away, alarmed. 'Get into your car – oh, and hand over all the money in your pockets first ...' Again the knife came close. She was like a highwayman, Roger thought admiringly as he obeyed her. 'Now get into your car and go back to your whore. You can have as many women as you like, you ... *fornicator* – but I will not be one of them!'

Ann had just climbed out of the bath. She had washed her

hair and wound the ends into spiky plastic curlers and dabbed Calamine onto an outcrop of spots on her chin. She lay on the floor, preparing a poem for the next day's first lesson and thinking how pleasant it was to have a flat and time and space to herself. Somebody was knocking timidly on the door of the flat. Ann pulled out the curlers, wiped off the Calamine and went to the door. 'Who is it?'

'It's me, Roger, Please let me in.'

'I'm working, Roger.' She glanced at her un-made-up face in the hall mirror.

'Please Ann, I'm desperate. I've got to talk to you.'

Reluctantly she opened the door and let him in. He looked rather peevish and short all of a sudden, she thought.

'She's thrown me out,' he said, and burst into tears. 'I've got nowhere to go.'

Ann brushed her hair hurriedly while he washed his face in the bathroom. He noticed the bottle of Calamine on the shelf and it filled him with grief and longing for his children, so Ann took him into her bed and comforted him.

In the morning, they drove in separate cars to school, and afterwards he went home to see if his Technicolour wife had returned to the shadows. She was ready and blazing still. 'OUT!' she yelled, standing guard at the kitchen door while his children clung to her knees and whimpered.

'Please can we talk?' he begged.

'There's nothing to talk about. You want her, you have her. We'll manage. You bastard.'

He had never seen her like this before. She was magnificent. 'I haven't got any clothes or the cheque-book or anything ...' he said feebly. She handed him a bag packed with a few under-pants and socks and his toothbrush. The cheque-book for their joint account was in it. He had never imagined that she could be so strong and wild and wonderful and he dithered in the drive.

'Get out,' she hissed. 'We don't need you. You bastard.' Shaking and astonished, he drove back to Ann's flat.

On Monday, in the dinner break, he went to the bank. His wife had emptied the joint account.

The school shivered with the shock. Ann and Roger were

asked to leave after an emergency meeting of the Governors and another of the PTA and two supply teachers were rushed in to fill the gaps in Art and R.E. 4A was shocked and delighted. If the R.E. Mistress could run away with the Art and Craft Master, who could be certain of anything any more? They giggled and gossiped and gloried in the scandal. Anything could happen now.

Chapter Eighteen

1965

Ann and Roger moved to Shimmerton with its echoes of Damien Cruikshank and the Festival of Contemporary Arts, where people were more liberal and progressive than they had been in the Forest of Dean. Ann took a temporary two-term maternity-leave cover and Roger took odd days of supply work when Shimmerton teachers got 'flu or stress or dismissed.

When Roger was not teaching, he stayed in their flat over a newsagent's and painted. They slipped into a pattern whereby Ann worked regularly and Roger stayed at home regularly and painted. It began to suit him very well indeed.

'You are wonderful for me,' he said one day. 'You have released me. Because of you I can paint again.' He was wearing a fisherman's smock and his hands were patchy with oils. Ann was tired from a hard day's struggle with 3P, 4D and 2Y, who were not the slightest bit interested in theories of perception, the existence of God or whether a half-crown was a straight line or a circle, and there was no food in the fridge.

'Look,' said Roger, and he showed her a large, splattered canvas full of lines and smudges and exploding fireworks. 'It's us,' he cried. 'It's our life, our freedom, our adventure.'

Oh *blaaablaaaaablaaaaaablaaa*, thought Ann and wished she was on the back of a motorbike riding over the hills and far away. 'Terrific,' she said tonelessly, and went out to buy two chops and a packet of frozen peas.

The maternity-leave teacher decided that she liked her baby and wanted to stay at home and look after her, so Ann's job became permanent and Roger's canvases grew larger and more colourful. 'I have found my freedom again,' he kept telling her, 'and it's all because of you. I was in a cage and you have set me free.'

Every day she got up at seven o'clock, made the tea and left him in bed, drawing up his creative energy. She took registers, fought for control and drank instant coffee in the smoke-filled, exhausted staffroom. She watched a new, young English teacher who had long red hair and even longer legs, playing *Hey Jude* on the guitar and havoc with the emotions of the Geography, Maths and P.E. masters. In the late afternoons, she came home with a bagful of exercise books to Roger and his creativity. 'You are wonderful,' he said.

'How's Ann getting on?' shouted Madge from under a dryer one morning.

'Fine,' replied Joan from beneath her own dryer. 'She's got a new teaching job on the South Coast.'

'Any Man on the horizon?' Madge was on the scent of something and Joan had to duck and swerve to throw her off.

'Not as far as I know. I think she's carving out a career for herself,' Joan said firmly.

'Like Philippa,' said Madge happily.

Chapter Nineteen

1963–4

Philippa

Philippa sat on the edge of her chair and chewed the end of her pencil. (*'Philippa Foster, don't chew your pencil,'* Miss Bugle said.) She was taking notes for the positioning of props for the play, which was a very exciting, experimental one with a lot of symbolism. It had never been performed before and it posed a great many unanswered and unanswerable questions, as the playwright had explained when the company had gathered for the first reading.

It was called *Hot Air*, and it was about three characters, a Clown, a Professor and a Housewife, who had somehow met each other for the first time in the basket of a hot-air balloon. The whole of the first act was performed in the basket in mid-air above some tree-tops and consisted of deeply existential discussion between the characters (who were only visible from the waist up, leaning over the edge of the basket) about the nature of Man and God and of their identity once they were removed from all the normal surroundings that usually defined them.

'Take the Chair from the Professor, the Circus Ring from the Clown and the Kitchen from the Housewife, and what are they?' the playwright had written in his introduction. *'Take God from His Heaven and what is He?'*

In the second act, the balloon flew higher and bumped into God, Who turned out to be a huge inflatable dummy with a white beard and a white dress, sitting on a fluffy white cloud. The discussion turned into a blazing row which reached its climax when the Professor seized a safety pin from the Housewife and stabbed the inflatable God, who collapsed slowly with a reproachful farting noise and floated limply to the ground.

The Housewife tried to seize back the safety pin because her skirt was falling down without it and, in the ensuing struggle, the balloon got punctured so that it, too, collapsed, the basket fell to the ground and everybody was killed. Dead Blackout. Its whole point, as the playwright had explained after the first reading, was to illustrate the Absurdity of Our Existence.

It was a difficult play to stage, which may have accounted for this being its first performance. Philippa's job, as Deputy Stage Manager (DSM) was to sit in on all the rehearsals and make notes in the script about cueing in lights and sounds and Special Effects (such as where to pull the plug on God so that His air came out and He folded up at precisely the right moment). At the same time she had to signal to the sound operators to stand by and then to GO on the farting noise.

She had to supervise the buying of the props and make sure that the ASMs had put them in the right places for the actors to find them, and she had to remind the Director about what he had told the actors to do in the previous rehearsal and where they had to stand. (This was not too difficult as they were in the balloon basket when the lights went up and they stayed in it until they all fell out and died at the end.)

She had to signal the light changes to the board operators in the lighting box – stand by and GO – then cue the stage-hands on the fly floor to lower the balloon and basket for the final climax and the Dead Blackout.

The actors stood inside the chalked square on the floor of the rehearsal room; the Clown on the left, the Professor on the right and the Housewife in the middle.

'You are floating,' the Director told them. 'You are sixty feet above the ground, looking down upon the tree-tops. The balloon swells above you, the fire roars in your ears. Be there.'

191

The actors switched on their acting feelings, braced their legs to the sway of the basket and gazed into space.

'Good,' said the Director. 'That's good.' The actress who was playing the part of the Housewife put out a hand to steady herself against the side of the basket. 'But,' went on the Director, and his voice was sensitive and artistic, 'where have you come from? How did you get here?' They floated on blankly. 'Gina?' The Director focused his question at the actress. 'How did you arrive in this balloon?'

Gina came back to earth and looked bored. 'I walked, on my feet, from that chair and I stepped into this square.'

'No, Gina. In the other reality. In the reality of the play. Where have you come from?'

'I haven't got the foggiest, darling. You tell me.'

There was an embarrassed pause as the Director hesitated, saddened. 'No, love, it has to come from you, from her, from this woman you are becoming. I can't tell you. You must feel it, inside you.'

Gina looked even more bored; she was older than the Director and had been around a lot longer than he had. 'Pass me the Stanislavski,' she muttered sulkily.

The Director blushed and turned to the Clown. 'Willy, what about you?'

Willy was ready. 'I was trampolining in the middle of my circus ring and I bounced too high, flew through the roof of the Big Top and here I am!'

'What you could call *over* the top,' said Gina to the Professor. She said in a loud voice, 'Well, darling, if that's the way you want it, I was screwing the milkman on the new double bed with the supersprung mattress and we bounced so high that I landed in the basket.'

'Aha,' said the Professor, who was played by an actor called Patrick, 'but what happened to the milkman?'

'Floated away in his float, of course,' said Gina, 'What d'you think?'

The Director waited patiently. 'And you, Professor, how did you arrive in this situation?'

'Easy,' said the actor called Patrick who had had time to think of something. 'I was giving a lecture and I talked so much hot air that it carried me up, up and away to my beautiful balloon.'

The Director looked much happier. 'Well done. Good,' he said again. 'Now let's get on with it.'

They stumbled through the first act, forgetting their lines, cursing when practice props were in the wrong place and prompts were too late or too early. They broke for coffee after an hour and a half, and the Designer came in carrying God. They blew Him up with a bicycle pump and He floated awesomely in the air, eight feet tall with a lilo stopper in the middle of His back to keep the air him.

Ten days to go until the first night and they still had to make the balloon and the basket.

Chapter Twenty

It was the first night of *Hot Air*. The balloon went up and the house-lights went down. The Professor and the Housewife and the Clown swayed in their basket above the tree-tops and debated the Meaning of Life until the stage-lights went out, the house-lights came up and it was the interval. So far, so good. Invited members of the audience (West End Managers, Agents and Critics, plus the company's friends and relations, including Madge and Norman) sipped wine in the Private Bar and discussed the play.

'Can't see the Swain's Chard lot doing this one, darling,' said Norman loudly to Madge. 'Bit slow, isn't it?'

Madge tried to pretend that he was not with her and to think of something sophisticated and knowledgeable to say to the theatrical-looking man on the other side of her. How could she have known that he was the playwright?

A bell rang through the bars, recalling the audience to its seats. Philippa cued the house-lights down and the stage-lights up and there was the balloon again, rising higher still into the clouds. But what in Heaven's name was this? My goodness, it was God, floating along all smug and smiling on His cloud. Norman nudged Madge. 'Looks like Winnie the Pooh.' Madge ignored him. God collided with the balloonists.

The debate changed gear. God must be true, the Housewife said, because how could they bump into Him if He wasn't? Nonsense, replied the Professor, seizing her safety pin and pointing it challengingly at God.

Philippa pressed the Standby button to signal to the special-effects boy to get ready to pull the plug on God. Then she pressed GO. Somewhere out of sight, a frantic stage-hand was tugging on the piece of string that was attached to the wooden bung that kept the air inside God. It had worked perfectly at the Technical Rehearsal the day before; the plug had popped out, God had farted and deflated and floated to the ground. But now the stage-hand tugged and tugged and nothing happened. God ignored him and stayed firmly aloft, all blown up and plump and smiling.

The stage-hand tugged again, desperately. The string broke and God floated on, free from all restraints, benign and bland, beyond the proscenium arch and out above the heads of the audience. The actors had by this time run out of script and were improvising furiously.

I'll show You what You are,' stormed the Professor, waving the safety pin and leaning dangerously far out of the basket. But God was a long way out of his reach by now.

'Gimme back my safety pin, my skirt's falling down,' shrieked the Housewife.

Something had to be done, thought Philippa and she gave the GO signal to the stage-hand to lower the balloon. There was a lurch and a scuffle in the basket as the actors felt themselves going down. The balloon was stabbed by the pin and the stage-hand managed to pull the plug on this one. The basket landed with a slight bump on the ground and the last thing that the audience saw on the stage was the basket lying on its side with the Clown, the Professor and the Housewife lying in twisted corpse-shapes around it.

Philippa signalled the Dead Blackout and there was a long and awkward pause while everybody wondered what happened. At last the house-lights came up and the Director led the audience into puzzled applause while God still floated, completely out of control, above their heads.

The playwright wept into a glass of whisky at the bar, which was where Madge found him while Norman was in the Gents.

'Wasn't it wonderful?' said Madge, recognising him as the theatrical man from the interval but still not knowing that he was the playwright. He looked at her with adoration. Madge would never know that she was the person who had stopped him drinking himself almost unconscious and jumping into the sea. He kissed her passionately as Norman emerged from the Gents.

'Who on earth was that?' asked Norman crossly as he drove her home through the night to Swain's Chard.

'I haven't the faintest idea,' replied Madge truthfully. But the man and his worshipping kiss stayed with her for the rest of her life.

The theatre critics came up with all sorts of different theories about the symbolic and cosmic intentions of the play the next day. One called it 'deeply religious,' another said that it was 'deeply blasphemous', another described it as 'absurdist' and a fourth called it 'medievalist'. Nobody outside the company knew that the real truth behind it was that a bit of string had broken, a plug had refused to come out and that by refusing to deflate, God had completely overturned the playwright's intentions.

Chapter Twenty-One

Jeremy Carruthers came to see *Hot Air* on the Saturday night of the end of its first week. This time, God did as He was told and deflated obediently and on cue.

'What did you think?' asked Philippa when she met Jeremy at the stage-door after the performance.

'It feels a bit like me,' said Jeremy.

They went out to dinner with the rest of the company at a late-night restaurant called Curtain Call. It was popular with actors as it was the only eating place in the town that stayed open after eleven-thirty, and its Encore Bar was oblivious to the licensing laws.

Jeremy and Philippa sat along the side of a candle-lit table with Willie, Gina and Patrick and the stage crew, who were all telling stories of theatrical successes and failures in glorious Technicolour and lit with gossip and scandal. As the word spread along the table that Philippa's guest was a trainee parson, the stories grew more risqué and outrageous and the carafes of red wine multiplied, were emptied and refilled. 'Just like the Marriage Feast at Canaa,' said Patrick with a knowing wink at Jeremy.

As the meal went on, Philippa felt as if she were standing with her feet on two separate islands that were floating further and further apart. She tried to talk to Jeremy about Swain's Chard and Theological College, and all the time the jokes and stories stabbed their conversation, punctuated by shrieks of laughter from Gina and Willie. What a wanker. What a corpser. Died on stage just before the interval. Had to bring the tabs in smartish. Talk about a DBO. What a piss-artist. You had to prop him up against a flat to keep him upright while he said his lines. And they had to have an extra ASM to catch him in the wings when he came off. All actors required this morning, even those with small parts. Something wrong with his balls. They used to swell up whenever he got nervous. Couldn't play Shakespeare at all in the end – couldn't wear the tights. Terrific for school matinées. She used to fart in the wings every night when she got older. Just before she went on. We used to wait for it ... pop-pop-pop-pop. Harry, Joan, Paddy, Dottie, Molly, Jimmy, Bobby, Alan, Molly, Harry, Jimmy, Joan ... When they were not gossiping and scandal-swapping, Gina and Patrick took it in turns to flirt with Jeremy. Philippa hoped he didn't notice.

'I'm sorry,' she said when the meal was over and she and Jeremy were walking back to her digs. 'They aren't really like that.' But they are, she thought, only I don't usually notice. 'I think they were sort of putting on a performance for your benefit.'

Jeremy laughed, but she knew that he had been out of his depth and not comfortable with her friends and her life.

'I expect it'd be the same for me if I went out with a crowd of your Theological friends,' she added hopelessly. She felt very sad when he said good night and walked off into the night to his hotel.

All through that night, Philippa kept waking up and wondering which life was really hers, which one she really belonged to. Was it Swain's Chard and Ann and Jenny and Miss Bugle and the High School? All the things their growing up had been? Or was it this brightly coloured, transient world of flats and tabs and lamps and velcro and gels and cues and grease-paint?

In the morning, she saw Jeremy off at the station and then she went on to the theatre to run through some new ideas the director had just come up with. She noticed church bells ringing.

Chapter Twenty-Two

1965

Ann leaned over the basin and was sick. Roger was being very sweet. 'It must be something you ate yesterday. I'll ring the school and say you're ill. You go back to bed and I'll bring you a hot-water bottle.' He was full of love and warmth. A gallery had just offered him his first solo exhibition. But when Ann bent over the basin again the next morning, he experienced a shiver of déjà vu.

On the third morning, after she had finished being sick, Ann took a deep breath and telephoned Swain's Chard. 'I'm pregnant, Mother.'

'Sorry?' said Joan. 'This line's not very good.'

'I'm going to have a baby, Mother.'

There was a swallowing noise on the end of the line, followed by a sniff. 'Don't be silly, Ann,' said Joan briskly. 'You can't be going to have a baby. You aren't even married.'

And that had been it. They continued to communicate by telephone and stilted letters, but the baby was never mentioned.

'I think she believes that if she doesn't think about it, it'll go away,' Ann said Roger. But if that was what Joan thought, she was wrong.

Joan put down the phone and thought she must have dreamed what Ann had said. Like that terrible sense you get after somebody tells you that somebody else has died, but you don't like to write a letter of condolence in case you'd imagined it – and so you wait until more people tell you and then you can be absolutely sure. But there was nobody else who could tell her this particular piece of village scandal.

Perhaps she should ring Ann, now, straight away, and have a normal, cheerful, matter-of-fact conversation with her so that she would know that she had dreamed the other one.

But for some reason, she could not pick up the telephone again. She called to Henry and unhooked his lead from the back door. She must get out of the house and into some fresh air. She slammed outside and across the garden, heading for the woods.

How could her daughter be going to have a baby, be going to be an unmarried mother? There was a Home for Unmarried Mothers in Swain's Chard where, twenty and thirty and forty years ago, families who could not bear the disgrace of an illegitimate pregnancy had sent their sullied daughters to be shut away for life, out of gossip's reach with the other unacceptables – cripples and mental defectives. They walked through the village in twos and some of the more able ones went out to clean. They came to church every Sunday, walking in a sad crocodile under grey pudding-basin haircuts and round felt hats; fallen women, imperfect women whose families did not want them any more. Was that what Ann was now, Joan wondered.

Don't be ridiculous, she answered herself. Times have changed. We don't do that any more. But what do we do then? Do we have our fallen daughters and their bastard children back at home to live with us? She flinched from the thought of the low-voiced comments of the Flower Committee and the Golf Club wives and the cocktail parties.

She strode on, trying to outpace her thoughts. If Ann was pregnant, there must be a Man involved. But Ann had not talked about any men since the day that Damien Cruikshank had run away in his little Ford Popular. She calmed down a little. There must be a Man after all and perhaps he, whoever he was, would marry Ann and make it all right, so that the baby would not be illegitimate after all and they would be able to welcome it home to Swain's Chard at Christmas and have it christened at St Swithin's.

But still she did not dare to ring and ask her daughter in

case the Man had run away, in case he was married, in case Ann was going to be an unmarried mother after all. Again the slow, sad, two-by-two procession of felt-hatted, lisle-stockinged women walked hopelessly across Joan's mind.

She must talk to somebody about it, find out what people would think, how she ought to react, what she ought to do. But who could she talk to? Not Madge. Madge would be so smug. That sort of thing would not have happened to Philippa – oh no, thought Joan bitterly, never to Philippa. The Vicar, she thought. I'll go and talk to the Reverend Eric.

But when she was sitting in the Vicarage study on one side of the fireplace with Eric sitting patiently on the other, she found it quite impossible to come to the point. 'We – some of the my friends – we were having a ... theological discussion,' she began improbably, 'about the nature of – things...' she trailed off vaguely.

'Things?' prompted the Reverend Eric, wondering what on earth she was leading up to.

'About the definition of sin – adultery, for instance,' continued poor Joan.

The Vicar looked at her with interest. Had Joan Dangerfield been tempted, he wondered for one hilarious moment. 'The definition of adultery,' he repeated thoughtfully, and he got up and pulled a dictionary out of the bookshelf.

'"Adultery: the act of fornication by a married person with another person who is not their lawful spouse,"' he read.

Joan frowned thoughtfully. 'Does that mean that the ... adulteree ... if she is not married, is not guilty of adultery?' she asked.

The Rev. Eric knew that he was on thin ice. 'I suppose not,' he said doubtfully. 'Nevertheless, she is *participating* in a sinful act – fornication.' Joan blushed painfully. What on earth was all this about, he wondered. He had never seen her so distressed before. This was in a different league from Flower Committee wrangles or spite over the chairmanship of the Women's Institute.

'And ... fornication?' Joan could hardly bear to speak the word and her voice was faint.

Eric grinned to try and cheer her up. 'Ah, I know about fornication. It comes from the Latin. It means, literally, "goings-on underneath the arches".' He smiled rakishly at her. 'Doesn't sound nearly so bad put like that, does it?

Joan tried to be comforted. 'Thank you,' she said, 'You've been most helpful,' and she left the Vicarage.

It was raining outside in Swain's Chard and she had not bothered to put on a headscarf, but she could not bear to go back into the house where Ann's telephoned words would press in on her, no matter where she went. 'I'm going to have a baby, Mother.' An unmarried mother, a fornicator or, at the very least, one who had indulged in goings-on underneath the arches. An adulteress? No, not an adulteress, only an adulteree. But no matter how you look at it, or what you called it, there was something multiplying and growing inside her daughter that would make the Dangerfields the talk of Swain's Chard for years to come.

Joan climbed the hill desperately and stood at the top in the mist and the rain, hoping that her thoughts would fly away into the spaces. But they simply hung there like the mist itself, so that in the end she had to give up and go home to make John's supper.

'John,' she said, 'I've got to talk to you.' John put down his *Tarminster Echo* and smiled patiently. Joan was being unusually tentative, he thought.

She hunted for the right words. 'Do you remember when we allowed Ann and Philippa to buy Delilah, we thought it would be good for Ann ... that it would keep her away from ... Boys?' John nodded vaguely.

Joan swallowed. 'Well, I'm afraid it didn't work.'

John was puzzled. 'But Delilah died four years ago.' He was trying to be helpful.

Joan nodded miserably, the news swelling up like a huge balloon in her throat. Then the balloon and Joan both burst and dissolved into huge sobs and tears. 'She's going to have a baby, John.'

For the first time in years, John had to get up and put his arms around his wife and comfort her. As he patted her back in a vague, numb, helpless way, he kept thinking to himself, This is going to have a bad effect on business if it gets about round here.

Chapter Twenty-Three

On the fourth morning of the sickness, Roger had had a vision of a cage door opening and drawing him magnetically towards it. He wrenched himself free. 'You could have an abortion,' he said.

'No,' said Ann.

The cage door opened again. 'All right,' said Roger. 'I'll stay at home and work and be a house-husband. It's happening all the time. They call them New Men. I can take care of the baby and paint at the same time, and you can go on with your career.'

Her career? Was that what it was? Was this weekly battle for discipline a career?

'You are so lucky,' said the exhausted men in the staffroom. 'At least you've got a valid excuse to stop.' 'I wish *I* was pregnant,' grumbled the Maths master.

And then it all became gloriously clear. She would stop teaching and stay at home and bring up her baby. She would read Dr Spock and watch *Playschool* and have other mothers round to coffee and gossip and listen to *Woman's Hour* and *Morning Story* and the repeat edition of *The Archers*.

'It'll be all right,' promised Roger. 'Men are just as good as women at taking care of babies. I've just read an article about it in the *Guardian*.' He was getting more ideas for his exhibition and he was excited. He bought a book on Modern Childbirth and another one on Modern Child-Rearing and his paintings took on a sperm and womb dimension. Ann marked essays on World Religions and got fatter.

*

203

There were fourteen pregnant women in the ante-natal class in the hospital. They sat in a semi-circle around an elderly midwife who was stretching a thin piece of transparent rubber between her clenched fists. 'I want you to imagine,' she said 'that this piece of stretched rubber is your pelvic floor.' Without letting go of the pelvic floor, she stuck a pin into it and held it up to the light so that they could see the tiny hole she had made. 'This tiny little pinprick of a hole is your cervix.' Some of the women winced.

'I need a volunteer,' said the midwife. 'You,' she said, pointing at a husband. He stood up sheepishly and the midwife handed him one side of the pelvic floor. 'Keep it taut,' she instructed, picking up a tennis ball.

'Now this tennis ball,' she continued merrily, 'is the head of your baby.' She held the baby's head playfully between her thumb and forefinger. 'Now,' she went on dramatically, 'the baby's head has got to *squeeeeeze* through the hole in the cervix,' and she pressed the tennis ball against the pinprick in the very thin sheet of stretched rubber.

One of the husbands put his head between his knees. 'Are you all right?' whispered his wife. 'I think I'm going to faint,' he whispered back.

'But of course,' went on the midwife, 'we can all see that this is quite impossible. So what has to happen is that the hole in our cervix has got to stretch and stretch and *stretch* ...' With every stretch, she pulled the thin piece of rubber and, as she pulled, the hole in the middle of it grew larger. The faint-hearted husband dared to raise his head for a moment and then he was out cold on the floor.

'Dear me,' said the midwife, and she roared with laughter, 'There's always one, isn't there?'

They brought him round and revived him with sweet tea while the midwife showed them how the tennis ball would eventually push its way through the hole in the rubber.

'It's called "dilation",' she announced. 'There we go.' She pushed the ball through and the rubber split. 'Bob's your uncle!' and she dropped it. 'Whoops, silly me! See you all next week. We'll work on the breathing exercises then.'

Mothers and fathers and unborn babies filed out into the evening, thinking nervously about cervixes.

Ann went every Tuesday evening to her Contemporary Childbirth classes at Shimmerton Hospital, while Roger, who had seen it all before, went to the Shimmerton pubs. He met a crowd of contemporary artists and musicians, cheerful, care-free people who played guitars on the beach and disappeared suddenly and without premeditation for six months at a time to Greece or Spain or Crete. They were free, exciting people who never seemed to be worried by the tedious minutiae of ordinary life like mortgages, rent or gas bills, and Roger drank with them and sang with them on Tuesday evenings and felt free and creative and untrammelled with them. Sometimes they were joined by the young English teacher with the red hair and the long legs. She sang Greek songs when they played their guitars and she reminded Roger of his wife and of Ann and of all the other women he had once known and never known and now would never get to know.

One Tuesday night, when Ann was almost eight months pregnant and still working and still going to the heavy breath-ing classes, Roger met the guitar-playing artists at the pub. 'Don't worry, I'll be with you when the time comes,' he told Ann. The English mistress had brought the Maths master with her (he had a shadowy wife and a child or two back home) and something about the way they looked at each other and held hands secretly under tables when they thought no one was looking made Roger feel uneasy. He almost thought he heard the Maths master say to the girl, 'You are so wild and strong and free.'

Roger drank two pints of beer very quickly and was seized by any extraordinary longing to speak to his wife and children again. He drank another pint and wove his way unsteadily to the end of the bar where a coin-box telephone was tucked into an alcove. He dug loose change out of his pocket and dialled his old home number. A man answered and, frozen by shock and embarrassment and a confused mixture of other emotions he did not want to think about, Roger could not speak. The man said, 'Who is there?' and Roger heard his wife's voice in the background. 'Who is it, darling?'

Red and sweating with outrage, Roger rang off. How dare she? How *dare* she, in his house, at this time of night (it was half-past nine) with his children there? It was disgusting, appalling. What was she doing to his children, behaving like that? He returned to the bar and slouched moodily against it, gazing morosely into his fifth or sixth pint of beer.

'Cheer up, Rog. Come on, we're off to the beach. We'll have a party.'

They piled into VW Campers and Beetles and old Ford Transits and headed for the beach, loaded up with bottles of wine and cans of beer and guitars. They collected driftwood and a wrecked rowing boat and they built a fire on the sand. They lay on the beach, drinking in the summer moonlight and somebody began to play 'Yesterday, All my troubles seemed so far away ...' Couples were up and dancing barefoot in the sand, silhouetted against the firelight.

'Will you still feed me, When I'm sixty-four?' called one voice. 'Think I'm going back to San Francisco,' sang somebody else and then The Girl from Ipenema danced by, young and lovely and tall and slender. Roger looked again. No, it wasn't The Girl from Ipenema, it was the girl who taught English, the one with the hair and the legs. All the same, he thought wistfully, she was young and lovely and tall and slender and everyone she passed went '*Oohhhhhhhhhhhh.*'

People took off their clothes and ran into the sea and the guitars played on. Roger flung off his clothes and galloped recklessly into the sea. He was a good swimmer and soon he was a hundred yards beyond the others, swimming along a path of moonlight. Something splashed beside him. Was it a porpoise – a mermaid? No; tall and slender and young and lovely and wet and naked with her sea-soaked hair plastered to her face and shoulders like seaweed, was The Girl from Ipenema, who had left her mathematical admirer on the beach to swim along the moonlight to Roger. She was laughing as she twisted herself around him and crossed her long legs behind him and pressed her mermaid's body against his. Roger lost all sense of time as he swam her out of the moonlight.

Then they heard splashing and a jolly shout nearby and there was the Maths master swimming along the moonlight path to find them. The girl laughed again and peeled herself off Roger. She dived beneath the surface of the water and came up again into the moonlight and the Maths master.

Roger waded out of the sea and back to the singers on the

beach. They threw more driftwood onto the fire and then a circle of dancers surrounded it, hands on shoulders, knees bent, heads turned sideways, stepping in time to the slow, slow chords of *Zorba's Dance*. Da da ... da da ... diddle da da ... da ... da da da ... they went and the circle speeded up ... dadadidididididadadadididdidi diddleeedadadidi ... Roger was in the circle, knees bending and straightening, bending and straightening as the music got faster and faster and faster and then died away in the slow, slow diminuendo. Some of them were off to Corfu the next day, they said.

Roger got a lift home to Ann and the flat in one of the camper vans with The Girl from Ipenema and the Maths master. They delivered him safely back to Ann who was fast alseep on her back with her belly rising like the full moon above her. Then they drove back to the girl's flat where the Maths master made frantic love to her for thirty-give minutes before driving back home to *his* wife and family. She, too, was fast asleep and he climbed quietly in beside her and lay for a while, listening to the gentle breathing and snuffling of the baby alarm.

How sad and curious it was, thought Roger, just before he went to sleep against the warmth of Ann's bulging body. These girls ran wild and strong and free, like moorland ponies or high-flying birds. And you fell in love with them for their freedom and strength but, by falling in love with them, you wanted to cage them and keep them. And once you'd done that, they turned into wives and mothers and all the flying wild horse in them died down and shrivelled up. That was rather a good thought, he thought, and turned over onto his side. He must remember to tell Ann about it in the morning.

But there was no time for thinking or talking in the morning. Ann and her womb had to be up and off to school and she was far too rushed to want to know about his thoughts. He would paint them instead, he decided, and he began to rough out sketches of open moorland landscapes and cages and bars. He would call it *Allegory*.

Chapter Twenty-Four

Ann was completely unprepared for the extraordinary and overwhelming rush of love that washed over her as soon as they put her daughter into her arms. Her name was Jane. She held her, gazing in disbelief at the cap of black hair, the squashed nose and the skinny fingers with their perfect nails and she knew that this was living in the present (and perfect) tense. Everything else up to now had been a looking forward or a looking back; Jane was here and now. Roger gazed at them both and thought how much he wanted to paint them.

When Jane was four hours old and Roger had gone home to catch up on the sleep he had lost through the hours of helping Ann breathe through the labour, Ann slid gingerly off the edge of the hospital bed, picked up her purse and, leaving her daughter fast asleep in her see-through crib and honeycomb blanket, went in search of a telephone.

'Swain's Chard 2936?' said Joan.

'Hello, Mum. It's me, Ann. I'm just ringing to tell you you've got a grand-daughter. She's called Jane.'

John Dangerfield arrived home from the shop to find no evening meal awaiting him for the first time in twenty-eight years, and a note on the kitchen table, scribbled on the back of an old shopping list. *Gone to see Ann. You're a grandfather. I'll ring tonight.*

As John poured himself a drink and wondered what it meant to be a grandfather, his wife smiled sideways at her reflection in the train window. She wanted to tell everyone she saw about this baby, to announce to the whole world that she was a grandmother. 'I'm going to meet my first grand-daughter,' she confided to the woman in the opposite seat.

The woman smiled. 'I've got six,' she said. 'They're all beautiful. But there's nothing quite like the first. What's she called?'

'Jane,' said Joan, and it was the most beautiful name she had ever heard. She smiled at the sound. It was the only thing she knew about this baby, she realised. She didn't even know the father's name. Would she be Jane Dangerfield or Jane Something else? Had Ann married this man secretly in some register office without telling her and John?

'Jane,' she said again, and the name blotted out all the other thoughts. She had a grand-daughter whose name was Jane.

'That's nice,' said the woman in the opposite seat.

Ann was dozing when her mother walked through the swing doors of the maternity ward. A nurse showed Joan where to go and for a long minute she stood and stared down at the tiny grandchild who lay on her side, swaddled up in the hospital baby sheets and honeycomb blanket, rosy and squashed with a cap of long black hair.

When Ann opened her eyes, she saw Joan bending over the see-through cot and touching the baby's head. 'Hello, Mum.' It was the closest they had been since Ann was a child.

The baby woke, complaining, and Joan held her expertly. 'You never forget what to do,' she said.

Ann, who was not at all sure what to do, was impressed by the deft way her mother handled and soothed the baby. 'I'm still scared I'll drop her or break her.'

'Don't be silly,' said Joan, in the way she always did, and Roger walked into the ward.

'This is my mother. This is Roger,' said Ann and they shook hands around the baby.

Joan's rushed departure without toothbrush or cheque-book meant that she would have to spend the night in the flat. The world had changed gear; the life and manners of Swain's Chard had nothing to do with the life of Shimmerton or the new life in the see-through cot. It had nothing to do with the approval of the Flower Committee or the Amateur Dramatic Society or Phyllis Cornwood.

Roger drove Joan (what relation was he to her, she wondered.

209

In-law? Outlaw? What the hell, she thought) through the wet and shining evening streets of Shimmerton, up steep hills behind the sea-front. They reached a little crop of shops – a pub, a general store, a chemist, a bookie, a newsagent. Roger stopped the Mini outside the newsagent and leaned across Joan (what relation was she to him, he wondered) to open her door. 'I'll drop you off here and go and park.'

He let her in through a narrow red door at the side of the newsagents; she read one of the advertisements while he fiddled with his key. *Gina will give Home Massage*, it said, and offered a phone number.

Joan followed Roger up two flights of uncarpeted stairs, past a smell of cooking on the first landing, and let her in through another door at the top. 'Make yourself at home,' he said. 'I'll have to move the car – it blocks the street here. I'll only be five minutes. Please make yourself at home.'

Joan stood in the living room, looking at the books in orange boxes against the walls, at the big orange and navy oil paintings above them, at the piles of records, the guitar, the sagbags, the rag rugs, the stripped pine table and chairs. There was a smell of something like incense, she noticed, and she touched a burnt-out stick that still smoked gently in a lump of clay. This was unlike any room that she had ever been in before and it excited her. It was as if she were travelling out of Swain's Chard and all its comfortable certainties and cocktail cabinets and chrysanthemum-ed gardens into another place where the ice was thin and the air was clear and bracing and there was a smell of adventure and danger that made her feel curiously at home.

What would John make of this, she wondered. The gas-stove needed a good clean and so did the bath – but so what? thought Joan. They were not her gas-stove or bath and Roger might be offended if she got going with a J-cloth. And anyway, there were more things in life than clean stoves and baths. She wondered what they were.

She wandered out of the living room onto the landing and opened a door; a double mattress lay on the floor and there was a battered carrycot beside it. Joan blushed and closed the door; there were some things she preferred not to think about.

Further along the landing was another, half-open door. Joan

peered round it cautiously, ready to back away if it looked threatening. This room was small and had obviously been intended as a spare bedroom, but now it was full of easels and canvases and the smell of oil paint and white spirit. She looked at a large, unfinished painting of girls and young women flying and running and dancing like butterflies and birds and wild horses over open moorland, pursued by men with lassos and butterfly nets. In one corner, in the foreground of the picture, one of the butterfly girls crouched sadly in a cage. Her face was not clear yet, but something about the body and the pose reminded Joan oddly of Ann. And then, even more oddly, of herself.

There were other paintings in the room that were most certainly of Ann; Ann sitting at the pine table, marking books, Ann playing the guitar (I didn't know she was musical, thought Joan), Ann with no clothes on in an advanced state of pregnancy. Joan blushed again and left the room. Only just in time; as she crossed the landing, she heard Roger coming up the stairs.

'I've bought some wine to celebrate,' he announced. 'Do you like red or white?' Joan, who usually drank sherry, said she thought she'd like some red and Roger poured her a large glassful. The telephone rang and he went to answer it. 'Some friends of mine ... they've heard the news. They want to come round to celebrate. I hope you don't mind?'

He poured her another glass of wine, which she did not refuse, although she had only eaten a sandwich on the train. Roger looked at her. 'Hell's teeth, I should have offered you some food.' He went to the fridge, but it was empty apart from a pint of milk and two cans of beer. 'There's a chippy just down the road. I'll get us both some cod and chips – OK?'

'OK,' said Joan, who was beginning to feel very cheerful, and Roger disappeared again.

'Ciao,' he called back from the stairs. Chow? Pondered Joan. Had they got a dog? She poured herself another glass of wine and wandered back to the spare room and the paintings.

More footsteps climbed the stairs from the street and a young couple appeared on the landing. The girl wore a long, flowering garment with fringes hanging from its edges and the youth wore a tasselled leather jacket and long hair. 'Hiya,' they said and walked past Joan into the living room.

'Shit, it's cold in here,' said the young man.

'Light the fucking fire then,' said the girl and he knelt down and turned a gas-tap in the wall and held a lighter to the fire. Blue flames danced.

'Wine – great,' said the girl, and the man poured some into two beakers and topped up Joan's glass.

More people were laughing on the staircase and coming through the door into the living room. 'Hiya,' they said to Joan. They plonked bottles of wine onto the table and one of them picked up the guitar and began to play it. Joan sat on a sagbag and watched and listened through an agreeable haze of wine, hunger and tiredness and then fell into a daydream about Jane's Christening. The guitarist played on. He had very long hair and was thin and enigmatic. A large girl in a purple smock sang in a deep voice to the tune he played. Roger returned with the cod and chips and poured Joan another glass of wine.

More and more people arrived for Jane's birthday party. Some brought guitars and one brought a set of bongo drums and another brought a mouth organ. 'There's a joint in the other room if you want one,' somebody whispered to Joan.

'Oh, thank you very much, but I've just had fish and chips,' she replied. It was very late for a meal, she thought. But she supposed these people ... they were all artists and musicians, of course ... lived a freer, more Bohemian life than the one she was used to in Swain's Chard. But at least they had the sense to cook a hot meal, even if it was very late at night.

Joan smiled and felt interesting. If only Madge could see her now. And after all, if she had had her way, if she had been allowed to lead the life she should have led, if she had followed her talents and danced her way onto the stages of Europe, she would have lived like this, surrounded by artists and actors and musicians. She would have been wild and free and Bohemian instead of being a businessman's wife who found her excitements with the Swain's Chard Amateur Dramatic Society and the church Flower Committee.

Then she remembered that she had completely forgotten to ring John. She swayed to her feet. 'May I ring my husband?'

She dialled the number and John answered almost immediately. 'Is Ann all right? Are you all right?' He sounded agitated.

'Yes, yes, yes. Everything's ... amazing.'

'You sound a bit odd,' said John.

'Nonono, I'm absolutely fine,' said Joan and she slurred slightly on the 'absolutely'. 'Ann's got a beautiful, absolutely (*there it was again*) beautiful little girl called Jane. She's your grand-daughter, John. Isn't that amazing?'

'Are you in a pub?' asked John. 'I can hear music.'

'Nononono. They're having a bit of a party to celebrate. Don't worry about a thing. Come and get me tomorrow.'

'But I don't even know where you are,' said John.

How peevish and middle-aged he sounded, Joan thought. 'Oh dear no.' She giggled. 'Neither do I. I tell you what. I'll ring you again in the morning and tell you how to get here when I know where I am. Chow.'

'Chow?' repeated John.

'Yes. Chow,' said Joan and rang off.

She returned to the party and sank into the sagbag, dozing to the chatter and the music and the sweet smell of the joss-sticks they were burning and the cigarettes they were smoking. 'Where Have all the Flowers Gone?' played the boy on the guitar. 'The Answer, my Friend, is Blowing in the Wind,' they replied and Joan fell asleep.

The next day, she telephoned John again to give him the address. She gazed at the chaos of filled ash-trays, empty beer cans and half-empty wine bottles, but she did not tidy them up. In the afternoon, John arrived and she took him to meet his grand-daughter. In the evening, they drove home to Swain's Chard.

Sometimes, walking alone on the hill, Joan thought about Roger's painting of the dancing, flying women and the unfinished girl in the cage. She wondered why she remembered it so clearly.

Chapter Twenty-Five

Jane woke up for the third time. It was four o'clock in the morning as Ann, her eyes still closed, sat up, leaned over and lifted her daughter out of the carrycot to feed her. She half-opened one eye and squinted at the alarm clock. Three minutes past four. It was not possible. The last feed had been at half-past one and in three hours she would have to be awake and dressing for school, changing Jane's nappy, and expelling milk into feeding bottles to put in the fridge for Roger to do the daytime feeds. She would pack unmarked exercise books into a plastic bag and climb, exhausted, into the Mini to face 3Y, 4J, 2L and 1M. A door opened in the side of her brain and let in a crack of light which illuminated two words on the floor of her mind. STUFF IT, they said. She looked at Roger's sleeping back with rage. It's all right for you, you bastard. All you have to do is paint life. I've got to live it.

Jane fell asleep against her and Ann lowered her gently back into the carrycot, switched off the alarm clock and went back to sleep, with the wonderful words STUFF IT still glowing in her brain. At 8.21, Jane began to whimper and make snuffling sucking noises and Roger sat up in bed. 'Hell's teeth,' he said, 'it's twenty past eight. You should have gone to work half an hour ago.' Ann ignored him and he poked her.

She opened her eyes very slowly. 'I'm not going,' she told him, clearly and deliberately. 'I'm not going ever again. I've had no sleep for three months, I've been back at work for one month, I'm so tired I can hardly stand up straight and I'm not going back. You'll have to go back to work instead.'

Roger was appalled. 'But I'm working towards my exhibition! This could be the big one. It'd ruin my career to go back to teaching now.' Ann rolled away from him and closed her eyes. Roger became very sweet and understanding.

'I tell you what. Take the rest of this week off and catch up on your sleep. You'll feel quite different once you've had some rest. I'll ring the school and tell them you've got a touch of something. It's probably post-natal depression. Yes, that's it – I'll tell them you've got a touch of post-natal depression.'

She was furious. 'Don't you bloody dare. Tell them I've got impacted nipples and a hole in the head and I'm so tired I can't speak or walk, but don't you dare say I've got post-natal depression.' She lifted Jane again and began to feed her. Roger made a pot of tea and went back to his painting. It could be a turning point for him, this exhibition.

When she got up, very slowly, two hours later, Ann went to look at the picture he was working on. The thought slid sideways into her head and would not go away. 'He's not as good as he thinks he is,' it whispered. 'He's not a great artist at all. He's not a real thinker, not a real creator. He's a cliché.' The telephone rang and she listened while he talked Art with one of his cronies. 'What a squeaky voice he's got,' whispered the thought. 'And what a load of pretentious tripe they talk. Art Art Art. What about getting up in the morning and going out to work and getting up in the night to feed the baby and going out to work the next day and getting up all through the next night?'

When Roger rang off, she said it again, very slowly and clearly. 'I don't want to go out to work any more. I want to stay at home and take care of Jane and think.'

The next day, while Roger was meeting the gallery owner about the exhibition, she packed the carrycot, the babygros, the bath, the Napisan and a change of her own underwear into the Mini and set off for Swain's Chard.

Joan woke up that morning in a strange mood. She looked across at John's feet sticking out of the end of the eiderdown and thought how pink and silly they were. Instantly she banished the thought. It was very unfair and disloyal of her to think it, and it was certainly not John's fault if he had small pink feet. The feet stirred and flapped about a bit and John woke up. He got out of bed and did his morning exercises and then he brought the tea tray in to her, balancing it carefully on the little table that separated their beds. He kissed her goodbye and drove away to Tarminster and the shop.

Joan heaved a luxurious sigh and poured herself a cup of tea. She sipped it lazily as she listened to the eight o'clock news; Rolling Stones hysteria in America, rows about the nature of God in the General Synod, strikes in car factories. Joan swilled the tea leaves round the bottom of the cup and turned it upside-down into her saucer. All the tea leaves came out with the slops, leaving an empty white space where her future should have been. She poured a second cup and thought again about John's feet.

The night in Shimmerton had unsettled her, had reminded her of a part of herself she thought she had forgotten – the part that had danced on the landing in the impossibly high heels, the part that had dreamed of glamour and audiences and music and applause. A neglected door had opened in her mind and she had looked through it. There she was again, in the front line of the chorus, bang in the middle, high-kicking her way downstage, away from Swain's Chard and the Flower Committee and the Amateur Dramatic Society and the housework.

The lights were bright and an orchestra was playing in the pit. From each side of the stage came the girls, tall and leggy, proud as racehorses, glittering in six-inch heels and nodding plumes and skin-tight, body-hugging costumes. And the tallest, leggiest, most glittering of them all was Joan. She kicked her racehorse legs above her head and flirted with her audience, and she knew, beyond a doubt, that this was what she had been born for.

'Don't be silly, dear, of course you don't want to be a chorus girl. Good gracious me, whatever next,' her family had said as they booked her in to Miss Fawcett's Secretarial College. And John had come along on his small feet and she had married him and they were happy. All this restlessness, these silly memories must be the Change of Life. She would get something from the doctor for it.

She drank the second cup of tea and swirled her fortune for the second time that morning. There she was again, the dancer. Or was she a tree? The third cup gave her something that could have been a half-moon. Or a rocking cradle. Or a question mark, if she looked at it from another angle. She climbed out of bed and looked out of the window. Four magpies. *Four for something better*. Silly superstitious nonsense. She went to run her bath.

She was hanging out a few pieces of washing when Ann's Mini appeared in the drive. 'Good heavens,' said Joan through a screen of shirts and pyjamas, 'are you on holiday?'

'I've come home for a few days,' said Ann, manoeuvring Jane and the carrycot out of the back seat.

'Is everything all right?' asked Joan.

Ann burst into tears and Jane joined in.

Chapter Twenty-Six

1965

Ann

Ann moved back into her old room, where she had once danced naked in front of the long mirror and put on the white dress for the Small Dance at the Manor. Roger telephoned every evening for a week from Shimmerton and Joan and John wondered every night for a week across the gap between their beds, exactly what was going on. 'She just needs a break,' they decided.

Two days after the retreat to Swain's Chard, Joan girded up her loins, tied her headscarf under her chin, fixed the carrycot onto its transporter wheels and strode out of the house and into the village. Rounding the corner into the main street, she nearly collided with a pushchair driven by Phyllis.

'Oh my,' said Phyllis, 'I didn't see you coming.'

'Sorry,' said Joan.

Phyllis peered into the carrycot. 'Who's this?'

'This is Jane,' said Joan and the whole of her prickled with pride in her grandchild. 'She's Ann's baby.'

'Well, I never,' said Phyllis. 'I never even knew Ann was married.'

Blast Swain's Chard and the gossip and the Flower Committee and all of it, said the secret side of Joan. 'She's not,' she said.

Phyllis smiled sympathetically. 'They none of them are, these days. This is Charlie's first and they got married three months before he was born. Never mind. We love 'em just the same, don't we?'

For the first time in their long and complicated relationship, the two women looked at each other as equals, as women, as grandmothers. Charlie's toddler smiled at Joan who smiled back. 'He's beautiful,' said Joan.

'Yes,' said Phyllis. Still smiling, the women and the babies went their separate ways.

Phyllis pushed on along the main road out of the village towards the Manor and the woods. A hearse moved slowly down the road towards her and she stood still as a mark of respect. Charlie's baby waved enthusiastically and pointed at the flowers. Who was it, Phyllis wondered. Nobody local or she would have known. More likely to be some retired newcomer who had lately come to Swain's Chard and died before anybody had got to know them.

How sad, thought Phyllis, to die in a strange place where nobody knew your name or your family or even knew what you had looked like or cared that you were dead. I should like to do one big thing before I go, she thought, so that they would say, 'There goes old Phyllis Cornwood – you know, the one who ...' But she couldn't think what it would be. Perhaps she would start writing poems again and they would be her big thing. In the meantime, she must give this child his dinner and get him off to sleep.

Joan came out of the chemist's with a packet of Napicleanse. She was loading it onto the transporter as the hearse drew level with her and paused, signalling left before it turned towards the church. Two old men standing on the corner stopped talking and removed their caps until it had passed them. Jane smiled up at her grandmother and something in Joan high-kicked.

I don't want to die without achieving one extraordinary thing, she thought suddenly as the hearse turned off the main street and stopped at the churchyard gate. I don't want to die without anyone noticing that I was even here.

She let off the brake, turned round and headed for home.

Chapter Twenty-Seven

October, 1965

Ann swung the carrycot onto the top step of the bus and folded the transporter wheels into the container space beside the driver. 'Return to Tarminster, please,' she said to the driver and carried Jane to the back seat of the bus. The Mini was seriously unwell in the Swain's Chard garage. Three days ago, a postcard had arrived from Roger. He had given up the flat in Shimmerton and was living in a camper van on a beach in Greece.

'Hello,' said the woman in the back seat of the bus.

'Hello, Mrs Cornwood,' said Ann. She thought of Charlie and blushed.

Phyllis held out her hand over the carrycot and Jane clutched her finger. 'She's got a good grip,' said Phyllis approvingly. 'I've met her before, when she was out with your mum. Hello, my love, hello, my beautiful.' She bent her head over Jane whose face split into a huge grin. Phyllis fished about in her purse and found half-a-crown. 'Here you are, my darling. A lucky silver coin.' She held it within Jane's reach and the baby reached out and curled her fat fist around it. 'That's a girl. That's a good, strong grip. Now you hang on to that and you'll have luck all your life.'

A hundred miles away, Gabriel Woolf held out half-a-crown between his thumb and forefinger and showed it to a new class of embryo Philosophers. 'What am I holding in my hand?' he asked.

220

*

'Thank you very much, Mrs Cornwood,' Ann said, taking the coin from her daughter's hand. I'll keep it safe for her. Her lucky half-crown.' There was a pause in the conversation as the bus skirted the lower slopes of the hill and rounded the bend where she had seen Charlie's motorbike shining in the sun on the day she had fled from her mother and Damien Cruikshank into Charlie's arms. What on earth would Mrs Cornwood think if she knew, she wondered and a bubble of laughter grew inside her.

'Going shopping?' asked Mrs Cornwood.

'Only window-shopping,' said Ann. She realised how desperately short of money she would soon be. There were no more monthly pay-cheques; Roger had no money to send her and now the repairs to the Mini would use up what was left of her savings. She was almost entirely dependent on her parents again and it was not a state she liked.

Mrs Cornwood explained that she was going to buy knitting wool for Charlie and Mary's second baby who was expected in two months.

'That'll mean another Christening,' she said, and smiled. 'Will you have her done here?'

Christening was not something Ann had ever thought about in connection with Jane. She wondered whether Charlie had known about his first child that day he had made love to her, and she changed the subject by asking about Jenny.

Phyllis frowned. 'Oh, she's all right,' she said.

Ann knew that Jenny had dropped out of university mysteriously and had come back to the area to live, but the complications of her own life had occupied her too fully for her to remember the details. 'She's not living at home, is she?' she asked.

'No,' replied Phyllis shortly. 'She's living-in at the Three Bells in Tarminster. She works there.' Mrs Cornwood turned and looked out of the window. The bus was descending the hill into the first suburban scattering of the city. Jane made a crying noise and Phyllis turned back to smile at her again. 'I expect she'd like to see you,' she said suddenly. 'You could just ask for her in Reception.'

The receptionist at the Three Bells was a little surprised by

221

the young woman with the carrycot asking to see a member of the kitchen staff, but she rang through obligingly and said that yes, Jenny was working that morning and if Ann cared to go round to the tradesmen's entrance, she would find her there.

There was an awkwardness at first when Ann Dangerfield, BA (Hons) and mother of Jane met Jennifer Cornwood, Kitchen Assistant, for the first time for over two years.

'Mum said you'd had a baby.' Jenny tucked a wisp of escaping hair into her cap and wiped her hands down the sides of her overall.

'She's called Jane,' said Ann. They did not know what to say next.

'Look,' said Jenny, 'I finish for an hour in twenty minutes. Let's go and have a coffee somewhere then.'

They sat in a Espresso bar near the Cathedral, eating bacon sandwiches and drinking Coke. 'How long are you home for?' asked Jenny.

Ann pulled a face and rubbed Jane's back with one hand. 'I think I've left him. Or perhaps he's left me.' She was frightened when she heard herself say it. She had never said it before, she thought – not even to herself. Saying it out loud changed everything, stopped this being a kind of holiday, made it real.

Jenny was shocked. 'Left your husband?'

'He's not my husband. He's someone else's – only nobody knows that here, specially not my parents. He left his wife for me – sort of – and now I think I must have left him. Except that now he's gone abroad, so perhaps he thinks he's left me.'

Jenny swigged at her Coke and wrinkled her nose. 'It all sounds a bit uncertain.'

Jane belched expertly and a dribble of milk ran out of her mouth. Ann wiped it away with a corner of her skirt. 'Oh come along, Miss Cornwood. You did Philosophy too, didn't you? What is the meaning of "certainty"? How can anything be "certain"?'

She opened her purse to pay the bill and fished out the half-crown Phyllis had given her on the bus. She held it up between her thumb and forefinger. 'Did they teach you this one? Now-it's-a-straight-line-now-it's-a-circle-now-you-see-it-now-you-don't. Now there's the Truth; now there's nothing.'

Everything is how you see it; nothing is true, nothing is false, nothing is right, nothing is wrong, nothing matters, thought Jenny, and the memory of Gabriel Woolf stabbed her where the baby had once been. 'Nothing is right, nothing is wrong. There are no truths; reality is only what you make it,' she repeated aloud and looked at Ann and her baby. 'Is that what you'll teach her?'

An angry-looking woman came to wipe their table and take their money and Ann realised that she had handed over Jane's lucky half-crown. She got to the till just as the angry woman was ringing the money in. 'Excuse me,' she said, feeling silly, 'but that's a special half-crown. Can you swap it for this two and six?'

The woman looked at her with scorn and dislike, chewing on a lump of gum. Silently, despisingly, she handed back the half-crown and put the florin and the sixpence into the till instead. As she returned to the table where Jenny was holding Jane, Ann realised that the angry woman was Yvonne Pratt the Practice Mat from Down the Dance at Honeyford.

Ann put her name on the list of available supply teachers for schools within a ten-mile radius of Tarminster and waited for the telephone to ring. It never did. She caught the bus to Tarminster again and met Jenny in the Espresso bar. 'I've got to get a job,' she said.

'There's a vacancy for a part-time kitchen worker at our place,' Jenny told her. Which was how Ann Dangerfield began her new career.

Chapter Twenty-Eight

Joan was extraordinary and unexpected and magnificent. For two and a half days a week she took sole charge of her grand-daughter and pushed her proudly through Swain's Chard. For two and a half days a week, Ann caught the early bus to Tarminster (having expressed the day's supply of milk into sterilised bottles) and joined Jenny Cornwood in the kitchen of the Three Bells.

It was a Wednesday morning. Jenny had already cleared the early-morning tea trays from the hotel bedrooms and served breakfast to commercial travellers and autumn honey-mooners. Now Ann was piling plates and cereal bowls onto trays and posting them through the hatch for Jenny to begin the washing up. She folded tablecloths cornerwise and shook breadcrumbs out of the French windows onto the lawn. One or two of the cloths were greasy with butter or stained by spilt tea, but she could put most of them back for the next meal. She finished in the Dining Room and joined Jenny at the sink.

'Thrilling, isn't it?' she said.

'It's work,' said Jenny, 'It's money in the bank.'

'What are you saving for?'

Jenny laughed humourlessly. 'I haven't a clue. But it's there. I know it's there. Like an escape route.'

'What would you escape to?' The mood of the conversation had changed; something was going on underneath the surface of the words and neither of them knew where it was leading.

'Don't ask me,' said Jenny. 'Don't you remember? There are no answers, only questions; so what's the point of asking the questions?' They washed and rinsed and dried in silence for a while.

'How long have you been working here, Jen?'

'Over two years, I suppose.' Ann squeezed out a dish-cloth and spread it to dry across the tap tops. 'You'll poke holes in it like that,' said Jenny. 'Drape it over the side of the bowl.' She moved the cloth to the washing-up bowl.

'Why?' asked Ann.

'I told you – you'll make holes in it otherwise.'

'No, I mean why did you come to work here?'

Jenny did not reply at once, and then she said, 'I could ask you the same question. You're here too.'

'You know what I mean, Jen. Why did you leave university? You're better than this. You deserve more than this.'

She was taken aback by the rage in her old friend's voice. 'No, I'm not. No, I don't. What d'you mean, "better than this"? This sort of work's always been good enough for us; for my mother and my grandmother and my sister-in-law. I'm sorry if it's not good enough for *you*. It's quite good enough for me.'

'I didn't mean that ...' But, in a way, she did. Here it was again, the awful, unspoken difference between their mothers and, however hard they tried, between them – the thing that had always got in the way when they were children.

Ann began to bluster. 'Come on, Jen, you know I didn't mean it like that. But I've got to earn money to feed and clothe Jane. I've got a baby to take care of – she's my reason, she's my responsibility. But you haven't got that, have you?'

Something tore in Jenny and she hated Ann Dangerfield. 'No, I haven't, have I? Aren't I lucky? I'm free to get on with my life, no ties or responsibilities or commitments. The world is my oyster, my horizons are limitless. Well, this is my oyster and don't you bloody well sneer at it. It's good enough for me, good enough for my sort. And that's the difference between you and me, Ann Dangerfield. You can do this for a fill-in, for a temporary laugh till something better turns up or till your man comes back or Mummy and Daddy give you a hand-out. But it's not like that for me. I haven't got a degree or a man or a mum and dad who can afford hand-outs. So for me it's real and it's for ever and don't you dare to tell me that I'm better

225

than it, because I'm not and I don't want to be. It's where I belong.'

She ran out of the kitchen and up the stairs to change the sheets and make the beds. Ann was shaking and tears pricked in her eyes as she swept the kitchen floor.

It was the first lesson of the afternoon for 4A – Religious Instruction and Personal Hygiene with Miss Bugle. 'Behold, a sower went forth to sow; and, when he sowed, some seeds fell by the wayside and the fowls came and devoured them up ...'

A girl called Patricia leaned over and whispered to her neighbour: 'Are you going down the discothèque tonight?'

Miss Bugle fixed her with a bright stare. 'Some fell upon stony places where they had not much earth, and sometimes, Patricia, I know exactly how that sower felt, and forthwith they sprung up because they had no deepness of earth; and some fell among thorns; and the thorns sprang up and choked them.'

'Yes,' Patricia's neighbour whispered back.

'But others,' continued Miss Bugle with relief, 'fell into good ground and brought forth fruit, some an hundredfold, some sixty fold, some thirty fold.' 4A planned what to wear to the discothèque in Honeyford that night.

Gabriel Woolf leaned back in his chair and watched the first-year girl as she read her essay out loud. It was *All Statements about God and Religion are Meaningless. Discuss*. She had very good legs. He yawned and fished half-a-crown out of his pocket. Heads he would ask her for a drink that evening; tails he wouldn't. He tossed the coin surreptitiously. *Heads*. She read on, intent upon the task he had set her.

Jenny shoved the last set of dirty sheets and pillow slips into the laundry bag and hauled it down the stairs. Ann went into the Lounge to empty the ash-trays and dust and vacuum. Then she caught the bus home to Swain's Chard and Jane.

Chapter Twenty-Nine

Dear Jeremy,

Yes, I'm home again. Resting!! I'm sorry I haven't written for three million years (neither have you), but we were touring to so many different schools that there was never any time to think about anything else. Are you all right?

I'm writing to you because I can't think of anybody else I can say this to, and I'm not even quite sure what I want to say. So forgive the rambling.

Last week I went to have coffee in Tarminster with Ann and Jenny – you know, Ann Dangerfield and Jenny Cornwood. We were all best friends at school. I know people always say two's company three's a crowd but it was never like that with us for some reason. I haven't seen them properly together since the first year after we all left school. They went to different universities and I went to the Melissa Creely and we all just drifted apart a bit. We kept in touch by letters for a while and saw each other if the holidays coincided, but my course was only a two-year one and theirs were three and I had much shorter holidays than they did. But they were still always my best friends from home if you see what I mean.

Something went wrong for Jenny at university. I never knew what it was and Ann didn't either. She didn't want

227

anyone to know. All I know is she left mysteriously after two years and came home and really cut herself off from everybody. I heard she'd got a local job somewhere but nobody seemed to know where. And she didn't want to have anything to do with me or Ann so in the end I gave up writing to her, except for Christmas cards (me to her).

Anyway, it turns out she's been working at the Three Bells ever since she gave up university and now Ann's working there too, so Ann said why didn't we all meet for coffee. Did you know Ann's got a baby? She's a beautiful little girl called Jane. And there's another mystery there. I'm not gossiping, honestly, Jeremy. My mother keeps probing me about Ann's baby and who the father is and why isn't she with him and I don't know but she obviously thinks I do and I'm just not telling her. The amazing thing is that Ann's mother Joan (I don't know if you met her) was the most strait-laced, chastity-belted anti-sex-and-illegitimate-baby one of all the mothers and she's being amazingly cool about this baby.

The point is, the three of us and the baby met in an Espresso bar yesterday for a coffee. It was very strange and I'm still feeling odd about it. There we all were, the three of us and the baby, and I just felt that we none of us knew each other any more. Something happened to Jenny and it's changed her so much that it sort of looks as if a light's gone out in her. She was always straightforward and lively and pretty and happy-go-lucky. And now she's quiet ... grey and she doesn't seem to be there a lot of the time. If you see what I mean. And Ann's a mother of a baby with a father nobody wants to talk about and then there's me.

I don't know why I've written you all this. Sorry. It made me feel a bit sad and lonely, I suppose. But I may as well post it now I've written it. No work on the horizon. I'm staying at home getting bored and broke. How's God????

Love,
Philippa

Chapter Thirty

The day after her outburst, Jenny said, 'I didn't mean all that. I'm sorry – I shouldn't have said all those things. They aren't even true.' They had been true, but now they both wanted them not to be. *There is no such thing as the Truth; it is all a matter of perception.* Later she said, 'It wasn't about that – about class, I mean. It was something else.'

Ann took her cue. 'What?'

'I don't know if I can tell you,' Jenny said. 'I've never told anyone about it.'

On the Sunday, Jenny telephoned Ann and said, 'Let's go for a walk. Up the hill at home, like we used to when we were kids. We can take turns to carry Jane.' She caught the bus to Swain's Chard and met Ann and Jane at the church-wall bus-stop.

'I remember meeting Judith Littlewick here one day. She took me out boy-hunting. I didn't know what to do.'

'I saw you,' said Jenny, suddenly remembering. 'I was up the Climbing Tree and I saw you coming up the hill. Judith was on the handlebars of some boy's bike.'

'I wonder what happened to Judith Littlewick?' said Ann.

'She did exactly what she always said she'd do,' Jenny told her. 'Shorthand and typing at the Tech, job in a solicitor's office, married the solicitor and now she lives in one of those big posh houses with trees in the garden on the Honeyford side of Tarminster.'

They climbed on and thought about 4A and the different ways life worked out. 'That was the one and only time I went Down the Dance at Honeyford,' Ann said wistfully. 'Your brother rescued me from some awful Ted and brought me back to your place.' They laughed and climbed on slowly; it was warm and Ann had Jane slung across her in a blue canvas sling thing from Mothercare.

'There was a bee orchid here once,' said Jenny. 'It grew every year when we were kids, but I haven't seen it for years now.' They passed the stump of the Climbing Tree and that was when she began to tell Ann the story of Gabriel Woolf and the Philosophy tutorials and the baby and Theresa and her Catholic beliefs and the coming home and the not being able to tell Phyllis what was happening to her. They stood at the top of the hill and looked down at Tarminster Cathedral and the river and the dinosaur hills in the distance.

'So I had an abortion,' said Jenny Cornwood simply, and the tears began to stream down her face and Ann felt tears in her own throat and eyes and Jane woke up and cried and there they were, the three of them, standing in the Sunday sunshine at the top of Swain's Chard Hill, weeping for the baby Jenny had never had.

'D'you think he's all right?' sobbed Jenny. 'I worry about him in the nights. I know you'll think I'm mad, but I wish I knew where he was. I don't want him to think that no one ever loved him, because I did, I loved him terribly. But I didn't know what else to do.'

Then she blew her nose and sniffed loudly, smiling at Ann and Jane. 'What a load of rubbish, eh? I know he wasn't a baby. I know he wasn't anything more than a bundle of cells. But he felt real, you see. And I used to talk to him. Was it like that with her?'

And Ann had to say, truthfully, that no, it hadn't been at all like that with Jane. Her pregnancy had come as a shock and a very unwelcome surprise. She had felt very sick and cross and the growing thing inside her had never seemed like a real person until the moment they had put her into Ann's arms.

'So if you'd lost her, had a miscarriage, I mean, you wouldn't have minded so much?'

'No,' said Ann. 'I'd have been relieved.'

'But you never thought of getting rid of her?'

'No,' said Ann again. 'It just never crossed my mind. Probably too scared of breaking the law.'

Jenny sat down on the grass on the top of the hill and picked a blade and chewed it thoughtfully. 'It just goes to show that those philosophers are right, I suppose. Nothing is real and solid. Everything's only a matter of how you look at it. But I still wish I'd never done it. Nothing has felt right since. Nothing looks entirely beautiful any more. It's as if I'd killed off the most important part of me.' Ann wondered what to say and could find nothing. 'I even went to see the Vicar,' went on Jenny. 'I asked him if he believed in Hell and Purgatory and Heaven and Limbo and he said he believed in Hell and Heaven but not in Purgatory or Limbo.'

She pulled at another blade of grass and chewed it slowly. 'Do you remember all those things we used to chant in church? "He descended into Hell; He ascended into Heaven. I believe in the Resurrection of the body and the Life everlasting, Amen." I don't believe in all that any more. I daren't believe in it now, after what I've done.'

'The forgiveness of sins,' said Ann suddenly, and from years before, she heard Miss Bugle telling them: *The Kingdom of Heaven is within us. And consequently, I suppose, girls, the Kingdom of Hell is also within us.*

'D'you remember The Bugle, Jen, hitching up her shoulder strap and telling us to wash under our armpits?' '*The God I follow*,' Miss Bugle said across the years, '*is nothing if not forgiving. If He were not, I'd have nothing more to do with Him.*'

Jenny was remembering too. 'What was it she used to say about Pie in the Sky when you Die?'

Suddenly Miss Bugle was there on the hill with them. '*The Kingdom of Heaven is within us. Here and now. I won't believe in Pie in the Sky when you Die. It's here and now in the way we live our lives, with reverence and awe and wonder. The God I follow*,' she continued, standing four square on her laced-up feet, '*is nothing if not forgiving. Don't forget to wash underneath your arms, girls.*' And then she was gone.

'Batty old spinsters, all of them,' said Ann and she began to feed Jane, on top of the hill in the weak sunshine. Jenny lay on her back and gazed at the sky. Theresa used to talk about forgiveness, too, she thought. To be forgiven, she had said, you must truly repent. You must confess and repent and do a

231

penance. She had confessed to Ann and God only knew how much she repented. Her penance must be to tell her mother.

Jane finished her feed and they walked slowly back to Swain's Chard.

At six o'clock the next morning, while Arthur was sorting the post for his first round, before Jimmy was up, while Phyllis was doing her chores before she went out to do other people's, Jenny came downstairs from her old room, where she'd spent the night, and said, 'There's something I've got to tell you, Mum. I got pregnant at university and I had an abortion, that's why I left.' She said it very fast, straight out and quiet and awful but straight out and true.

Phyllis stopped preparing vegetables for the evening stew, turned round and put both arms around her daughter. She still smells of Gumption, Jenny thought as she leaned against her mother and wept the tears of grief and loneliness and guilt into the flowered overall.

'It's all right, my love, it's all right, my love, it's all over now, it's all right, it's all over ...' She rocked her daughter as she used to do when some childhood grief had grown too much to be borne alone. Great shuddering sobs broke out of Jenny as Phyllis rocked her on and on and on. Later she said, 'Why didn't you tell me?

'I couldn't. You'd have been so ashamed of me. You were so proud that I'd gone to university. I thought it'd be all right. I thought I'd just have the operation and forget about it and everything would go back to being how it was before. I never knew that it would be so ...' she sought for the word '... sad.'

They heard Jimmy whistling upstairs. 'Go and wash your face. Don't want him seeing you in this state.'

'I'll be late for work.'

'You can miss work for one day. I'll ring in. You go back to bed and sleep.'

Later still, after Jim had gone to work, Phyllis went to Jenny's room and sat on the edge of the bed. 'I've never told anybody this before, our Jen. Not even your father. And I don't never want him to know.' She frowned and picked at a loose thread on the bedspread. 'I had to bump myself down the stairs once – three years before your dad and I got married. I was only seventeen and I'd missed twice before I realised what was going on.'

Jenny lay with her eyes closed, letting her mother's words sink into her. Phyllis was silent, remembering the afternoon when both her parents were away at the agricultural show and she and Arthur had lain in the grass of the hidden garden in the bee-filled afternoon. She remembered the other afternoon, grey and rain-battered, two months later.

'When I realised, I drank half a bottle of my nan's gin and lay in a boiling-hot bath in her outhouse. Then I went upstairs and bumped myself all the way down to the bottom. That shifted it. That shifted it,' she said again. 'It was the only thing I could have done, Jennifer. My dad would most probably have taken a gun to your father if he'd found out, and they'd have sent me away to a home and made me give up the baby. It was the only thing to do.'

Jenny kept her eyes shut and let waves of relief wash over her again and again and again. At last she said very quietly, 'And you didn't think you'd done anything wrong? You didn't wonder what would happen to it ... to the baby?'

'I never thought of it as a baby,' Phyllis said. 'And it was for the best. I'd have had to have given it away, you see, and I couldn't abear that. I married your dad and we had Charlie, then you and then Jimmy. I've thought about it sometimes, since. Everything grows in the end, you see. Families are like trees, I always think. They put out branches and some get chopped off or frost-bitten ... but the tree goes on growing and putting out new shoots. There'll be other shoots for you, my love.'

That afternoon, Jenny climbed the hill and sat on the stump of the Climbing Tree. 'Everything grows again,' she said. 'Even you and me perhaps. Go on, Tree, do us a favour. Put out a shoot again.' In the late-afternoon light, the shadows and dips of the hill and the outlines of the woods against the streaked sky looked as beautiful as they had ever done. She got up and climbed the rest of the pitch until she could see Tarminster Cathedral and the plain and the river and the dinosaur range beyond them. They blazed with light and colour.

Something had changed inside her. She had been forgiven

and now she was allowed to come alive again. She would not have to close the doors on the rest of her life so that she could never lift her eyes above kitchen-floor level. She could lift up her eyes unto the hills again. For the first time since the baby, she felt reconnected to the earth and to her childhood. She felt the spring of the moss and grass against the soles of her feet and she heard the whispering in the trees. The white undersides of the hornbeam leaves flickered and danced and the sky was huge and high and laughing with skylarks.

She heard the sound of horses galloping towards her and felt the tremble of the earth as she turned to watch them. The animals were big and strong and powerful and their riders handled them well. But not as well as I could, said something proud in Jenny Cornwood. They veered off onto a track twenty yards before they reached her and she realised that the rider in the lead was Guy Hennessey. He was followed by an expensive, confident girl. Guy had not noticed Jenny or, if he had, he had not recognised her. She smiled when she remembered the Small Dance at the Manor and the week of snow when they had sledged and kissed and walked through the starlight that had been her childhood. Now here it was again, restored to her with all its promises.

She watched the horses and their riders until they galloped out of sight. It would be fine to ride again, to thunder across the hills, further and further into new landscapes. Over the hills and far away.

The next morning, as she shook the breakfast crumbs out of the tablecloths and swept the Dining-Room carpet, she thought about the money she had saved. There must be enough almost to buy a horse.

Jenny smiled.

Chapter Thirty-One

Philippa

When *Hot Air* had closed for ever, two weeks after it had opened, Philippa came home to Swain's Chard for a short break while she hunted through *The Stage* each week for jobs for actresses and DSMs. 'She's resting,' Madge explained to Joan.

One afternoon, when Philippa had been resting for five weeks and was beginning to wonder about the meaning and purpose of Life, the telephone rang. 'This is Jeremy Carruthers,' said the voice of Jeremy Carruthers. 'Please may I speak to Philippa?' Madge said yes he might and handed him over to her daughter.

Jeremy Carruthers said that he had now finished his theological training and was about to start work as a curate. He stopped talking and took a deep breath. Philippa heard it gasping all the way down the line. 'I was wondering whether you might possibly think about marrying me some time,' he said casually.

Philippa roared with laughter.

'It's not that funny,' said Jeremy Carruthers, and then he began to laugh too so that Philippa realised that he was serious. And then she realised something even more surprising. She rather like the idea of being married to Jeremy Carruthers.

'You've taken my by surprise, Mr Carruthers. I'll need a week or two to think about it.'

'You're going to say "Don't ring us, we'll ring you," aren't you?' said Jeremy.

'Yes,' said Philippa and put the phone down.

She went for a walk through the woods, scuffing the leaf-mould, remembering how he had caught her up here after the Summer Extravaganza and asked if he might write to her. Mrs Jeremy Carruthers. The Reverend and Mrs Jeremy Carruthers. The Very Reverend and Mrs Carruthers. They would live in creeper-covered Vicarages and she would give fund-raising garden parties. They might even end up in Tarminster Cathedral Close and she would be a Cathedral wife at bigger, grander garden parties. She liked Jeremy. He was funny and wise and kind and strong, and he had grown very tall. She had known him for years and she trusted him utterly and he made her feel happy. She imagined, vaguely, being in bed with him (what exactly did you do?) and getting up in the morning and having breakfast with him, of helping him with his parish work, of bringing up his children in the Vicarage garden, of being a slightly scatty, but much-loved Vicar's wife. Dean's wife. Bishop's wife.

Wife rhymes with life, thought Philippa. Or is it instead of it? she wondered. Is it living it at second-hand, in the passenger seat? So far, in her life, there had always been the sense of an open door, of an ongoing road, of the possibilities of new corners to turn, new hills to climb, new waters to cross, new skies to fly. If she said 'Yes' to Jeremy Carruthers, she would have to walk along *his* roads and turn *his* corners, she would have to forgo her own hills and waters and skies. If she married Jeremy, she would never again flap bits of cardboard in front of a white follow spot, or press the Standby button to let the air out of God.

Philippa went home and wrote two letters. One was an application for a job in *The Stage*. It was Acting ASM in a touring play for children about a White Knight and a clown who went on quests to save the world. The other letter was to Jeremy Carruthers. In it she said that she could not marry him or anybody else for a very long time as she had things to do (like waving bits of cardboard in front of lights, she thought). She hoped that they would always be friends and that they would go on writing to each other.

Jeremy wrote back sounding far more hurt and unhappy than she had expected him to be, and said he was not sure about writing any more. In the same post, Philippa received a letter inviting her to an audition for the tour. She got the job of ASM and the parts of Second Pirate, Inventor's Wife and the Head of the Loch Ness Monster.

They rehearsed the play and toured it to primary schools in the North of England, and when it was over, Philippa came back to Swain's Chard again.

Philippa was tired of resting, so she asked her father for a job at Crawford's, the small light-engineering factory in Tarminster where he was Deputy Managing Director. The firm employed about sixty workers who made and assembled parts for small electric clocks. Philippa got a job as a tapper. This involved standing in front of a sort of drill-thing from eight o'clock in the morning until half-past five in the afternoon with an hour off for lunch in the works canteen and two ten-minute tea breaks.

The noise of machinery on the factory floor was deafening. On Philippa's right side was a cardboard box filled with 2000 small metal plates called castings. Each casting had a hole drilled in it. On her left side was an empty cardboard box. Her job was to pick up the castings, one at a time, and to fit them, one at a time, onto a thing called a jig. She had to line the drill up with the hole and pull a handle down until the drill went through the hole. She was hugely relieved and proud to discover that she could do it. She had to pull the handle up again so that the drill came out of the hole and then drop the re-drilled casting into the empty cardboard box, pick up another one and start all over again. Two thousand times. She never understood, in all the months she worked at Crawford's, why anyone should have to drill a hole into a hole that was already drilled.

When she had put all her tapped castings into her empty box, Philippa lugged them to Marge the Chargehand to be emptied onto the scales and weighed. Marge took Philippa under her wing. She mended the drills that Philippa kept breaking and showed her how to use a gauge to measure the holes she was tapping. 'Riveting, isn't it?' she said.

Whenever Marge the Chargehand heaved a box of tapped castings off the floor and emptied them onto the scales, Philippa noticed the thin gold wedding ring on her left hand. 'Where does your husband work, Marge?'

'He's dead,' Marge said.

Philippa was embarrassed. 'Sorry, I shouldn't have asked.'

'Why ever not, dear? You weren't to know, were you?' She signed the work-card to say that Philippa had tapped her quota and heaved another boxful over to the drill. 'Poor old Bill,' she said. 'He went eight years ago – just like that. I was only part-time up till then, but after he died, I had to go full-time.'

'Do you like it here?'

Marge grimaced. 'What's liking got to do with anything? It's a job. It pays the rent and heats the flat and buys me food. I survive.' She said it matter-of-factly, without a glimmer of self-pity.

Philippa switched on her machine and began on her next box-load. One, two, three, four, ninety-seven, ninety-eight, ninety-nine, two hundred and thirty-seven and the drill broke again. 'Sorry, Marge.'

'Stop saying sorry. You've picked it up brilliant.' She fixed the drill skilfully in place. 'Sometimes I do wonder what it's all in aid of, though. Day in, day out at this place for eleven pounds a week. Like I said, it keeps a roof over my head, but sometimes I do wonder if there wasn't meant to be a bit more to life than that.'

She tested the drill agains her finger and laughed. 'Hark at me going all philosophical. Survival, that's the name of the game.'

Chapter Thirty-Two

Ann was emptying ash-trays and plumping up cushions in the Lounge of the Three Bells. She wanted to Hoover the carpet, but the resident pianist, a genial, middle-aged man called Peter Preston, was trying out some new numbers and it seemed rude to interrupt him. Ann wandered vaguely around the Lounge, wiping surfaces unenthusiastically and humming the tunes that Peter Preston was playing.

'Don't mind me,' said Peter Preston, nodding his head towards the Hoover. 'Carry on. You won't disturb me.'

'Thanks,' said Ann and pressed the ON switch. She followed the machine around the floor and heard the notes of *Summertime* soaring above its roar. Ann joined in, riding the high notes easily and dropping down on the low ones until they mingled with the sound of the vacuum cleaner. 'So hush, little baby, Don't you cry ...'

Peter Preston played the song through twice and Ann, safely drowned by the noise of the cleaner, sang it with him. Peter Preston changed his tune. 'You're my world,' he played, 'You're every breath I take,' sang Ann, 'You're my world, you're every move I make ...' and she pushed the Hoover into the corners of the floor. *Anyone Who Had a Heart*, played Peter Preston, and then he went into a selection of Rodgers and Hammerstein hits. Ann sang her way along with them until the floor of the Lounge was cleaner than it had been for years. Then she stopped and switched off. *Trains and Boats and Planes*, played Peter Preston, but Ann was as silent as the Hoover now.

'Why have you stopped?' he asked.

'I've finished in here; it's clean.'

'No,' said Peter Preston. 'I meant, why have you stopped singing? You've got some voice.'

'Have I?' Ann was pleased. 'I didn't think you could hear me.'

'Come on,' said Peter Preston, 'Come over here and let's hear what you can do.'

It was not the church choir, nor was it Miss Freeman and the *Creation* but, to her delight, Ann discovered that she could belt out Cilla Black and Dionne Warwick and Gershwin and BeeGee songs in a way that would have amazed Miss Freeman and the Vicar.

'Hang on a minute,' said Peter Preston and went out of the Lounge. He returned with the Manager who cast a critical eye over the carpet and then ran a forefinger along a shelf. For once, there was nothing he could complain about.

'Sing,' ordered Peter Preston and he played the opening bars of *Summertime*. Unprotected by the Hoover, Ann's voice shook on the first three notes, but Peter smiled encouragingly and within three bars she was soaring and flying and swooping as easily as the song itself.

'Yes,' said the Manager, 'I see what you mean.' And Ann found herself with two jobs. For two days a week, she was chambermaid, cleaner and waitress and for two evenings a week, she became the Fabulous Ann Dangerfield, Resident Singer at the Three Bells.

'I'm not sure that I ought to leave her any more than I do already,' Ann said doubtfully to Joan as she wrapped her daughter in a bath towel and cuddled her dry.

'Of course you can,' said Joan. 'It's only for two evenings, after all, and she's perfectly happy here with me and her grandfather. If you've got a talent, darling, you mustn't waste it.' Once again, Ann found herself being amazed and confused by her mother, but she smiled at her gratefully. 'What are you going to wear?' asked Joan.

'I can't imagine. I'd better go in early tomorrow and look for something then.' She prayed that Joan would not suggest coming in with her and helping to choose a dress for the first night.

Her prayer was answered. 'You might find something suitable in your father's shop,' suggested Joan.

But Ann went nowhere near her father's shop. The Fabulous Ann Dangerfield was not the sort of girl to be kitted out by John Dangerfield, Ladies' Outfitter.

She found a sleek, tight-fitting black number that hugged her bust and hips and came to a stop four inches above her knees. Her mother must not see her in it.

'Did you find anything, darling?'

'Yes,' said Ann.

'Let's see,' said Joan, coming into Ann's bedroom hand-in-hand with Jane.

'I left it at work, hanging up in Jenny's room. I didn't want it to get crushed on the bus.'

That afternoon, she took Jane for a walk in the woods. 'I do love you more than anything else in the world,' she said. Jane smiled. She had never doubted it.

There were only about twelve people staying at the Three Bells and only a handful of them were in the Lounge after dinner. But a notice outside the hotel, announcing the début of the Fabulous Ann Dangerfield had attracted some mild attention, and a few more people had come into the non-residents' bar that led into the Lounge.

Jenny had persuaded Mary and Charlie to come. Charlie had been oddly unwilling, his sister had noticed, and now he was looking awkward and uncomfortable on a sofa beside his wife. It was probably because she had told him that they wouldn't let him in without a tie. Little clusters of winers and diners and drinkers sat around on stools and armchairs and sofas, sipping coffee and Tia Marias. Peter Preston played a few numbers and then he slowed to a pause.

'Ladies and Gentlemen,' he said into the lull in conversation, 'tonight I want to introduce to you an exciting, new, and what is more, a local talent. Please give a very warm welcome to Tarminster's Own, Sensational Ann Dangerfield!'

A few people smiled and clapped politely, Peter Preston played the opening bars of *Summertime* and Tarminster's Own, Sensational Ann Dangerfield began to sing.

241

As soon as she heard her voice, she knew that she was good enough. Not sensational perhaps, or even fabulous, but good enough. This was her thing. Jenny had always been the best tree-climber and bareback rider, Philippa was best at Elocution, but Ann Dangerfield could sing. She smiled across at Charlie, who was staring at her with an expression in his eyes that she remembered.

Then *Summertime* was over and Peter Preston began to play the opening of *Always Something There to Remind Me*.

Chapter Thirty-Three

Charlie Cornwood, husband of Mary and father of two, drove a lorry for Crawford's. Everybody at the factory loved Charlie, just as everybody everywhere always had done. He was still ridiculously, heart-stoppingly beautiful and he was still crazy and kind. He wolf-whistled and danced and sang and flirted his way through life, pinching whatever bottoms and rescuing whatever distressed damsels came his way. He loved his wife and children deeply and was surprisingly faithful to them. He was a knight in shining armour and a donkey jacket for the Crawford's girls, riding his articulated lorry through the county in search of chivalrous adventures.

Marge leaned over to pick up a box of milled and tapped plates. Charlie, who happened to be whistling by, reached out and pinched her bottom as she bent. 'Bugger off, you cheeky sod,' squawked Marge, straightening up and laughing at him.

'Get out of the way,' said Charlie, 'I'll carry 'em for you.' She grinned and ruffled his hair, grateful for his help. Her back was giving her gyp these days. 'Give us a kiss and I'll shift the lot for you,' he teased.

'What about demarcation?'

'Bugger that – you go and get a cup of tea.'

Another day he sauntered down the line of millers and tappers and stopped to watch Philippa at work. 'Screwing well?' he enquired.

'Fuck off, Charlie,' she said cheerfully.

Charlie was deeply shocked and offended. 'You should speak to her about her language,' he said in a low tone to Marge. 'People'll get the wrong idea about her.'

Marge was intrigued. 'Why? What she say?'

Charlie blushed. 'The F word. Girls shouldn't swear like that.'

'Don't be so sensitive,' Marge teased him. 'She doesn't mean nothing. She's a bit theatrical, that's all.' Nevertheless, the next time she met Philippa in the Female Toilets, she had a quiet word. 'I shouldn't say that to Charlie,' she said. 'It upsets him to hear girls swearing. Really hurt his feelings.'

Abashed, Philippa apologised to Charlie.

'That's all right, my darling. I just wouldn't want people thinking you was common.'

'Charlie,' said Philippa, 'do us a favour. Don't tell any of them here that my dad's one of the bosses. I don't want them treating me any differently and they would if they knew.' Charlie promised to keep his mouth shut and he did.

A new driver joined the Crawford's team. His name was Derrick. 'They must've named him after his cock,' said Marlene Wheeler scornfully. 'Got a cock like a crane – or so he says. Picks up anything it sees in front of it.'

Derrick was big and brawny and covered in tattoos. 'You wouldn't believe where I've got 'em,' he boasted to the girls.

'There are some things I'd rather not think about,' said Philippa's co-tapper Shirley to her mate Dawn.

'Come on, Granny,' Derrick said to Marge one day. 'Get a fucking move on with those fucking boxes. I haven't got all night to load up. I've got—' but before the factory floor could learn what he had got, Derrick's feet had left the ground and he found himself being swung round to stare straight into Charlie's furious blue eyes.

Charlie carried him out by the donkey-jacket lapels and plonked him down in the yard. The girls left their drills and followed them outside. Charlie swiped at Derrick. Derrick ducked and answered with a wild swing which Charlie deflected with his left hand. Then he lowered his head and charged at Derrick like an enraged young bull. As they fell into a thrashing heap on the ground, a great roar went up from the circle of watching women. Charlie emerged, victorious, hauling Derrick to his feet and holding his arm in a fearsome half-Nelson.

'Apologise to her,' he demanded.

Derrick snarled an apology at Marge and slunk off to his cab as Management came out onto its balcony to see what the disturbance was about. Derrick and Charlie were both sacked, but the girls went on strike in support of Charlie and stayed out for two days until he was reinstated. Derrick was never seen again.

Chapter Thirty-Four

'Spinsters and widows are our best bet,' said Mr Crawford. It was Friday night and Norman and Madge were giving a small dinner party for Mr and Mrs Crawford and a pink young man with pale ginger hair and pale blue eyes and a pale pink wife. His name was Colin Palfrey and the dinner party was part of his interview for a middle-management job at Crawford's. His wife, who was called Mrs Palfrey and who was tense and worried about the cutlery, sat beside Philippa and watched her carefully at the beginning of every course.

'Why?' asked Philippa.

'Don't talk with your mouth full, Philippa,' said Madge.

'Why what?' asked Norman.

'Why are spinsters and widows your best best?'

'They've got to keep their horizons low,' explained Mr Crawford, pleased to be able to expand on the subject he knew best. 'They can't afford to think of anything except their bonuses, so they keep their minds on the job and work fast.'

'Is that good?' asked Philippa.

'It's good for us,' said Mr Crawford, and everybody except Philippa laughed.

When they had stopped laughing, Philippa said, 'But isn't it a terrible way of life for them? Boring and repetitive and pointless?

'Not at all,' said Mr Crawford firmly. 'It keeps a roof over their heads, and the ones who don't need the money quite so badly – the young marrieds who do it for pin money – they've got their daydreams. They live in their daydreams, you see.' Smiling, he accepted a second helping from Madge.

'What sort of daydreams?' asked Mrs Crawford, who had never heard anything like it and who had almost forgotten what daydreams were.

'Oh, they dream that the Beatles or Dirk Bogarde will come driving down Tarminster High Street one day and whisk 'em away to passion and glamour. Or the older ones dream of the new three-piece suites they'll buy on the never-never with the bonus money. They're quite happy.'

'How extraordinary,' said Mrs Crawford, who was having a passing vision of Dirk Bogarde rescuing her from Tarminster High Street and whisking her away to Gerrard's Cross.

'I think that's horrible,' said Philippa, who had drunk two sherries before the meal. 'It shows a complete disregard for the quality of life of the women who work for you!'

Mr Crawford smiled benignly. He had had daughters himself. But later on, after their guests had gone home and Madge and Norman had done the washing up and gone to bed, Madge said, 'I'm beginning to wonder if all this theatre life is good for Philippa. She's beginning to get quite Bolshie.'

The daydreams on the factory floor were considerably more complex than anything that Mr Crawford had imagined. 'I do arithmetic in my head to keep me going,' said Philippa's left-hand tapping neighbour, Dawn, a young married woman. 'I always liked mental arithmetic when I was at school. I work out the rates of return on my savings so's I can put down a deposit on a house.'

Shirley was the tapper on Philippa's right. 'I work out dances for *Top of the Pops*. You know, like Pan's People. Daft, isn't it?' she said. 'I see them really clearly in my head, but I dunno how to write them down.'

Philippa kept quiet about her father's position in the factory and none of the women guessed she was his daughter. Norman was Management and Philippa had realised very quickly that Management was the Enemy. Management watched you from its balcony floor twenty feet above you and then disappeared through doors into offices where the others had never been. Management parked in a superior car park which was quite separate from the one where the works' buses unloaded their workers every morning and picked them up every evening.

Management ate in a separate canteen which it called The Mess, talked with a different voice, saw life through different eyes.

In Philippa's life there had always been an open door, an open road and new corners to turn, but now, at Crawford's, she worked alongside women whose lives were in cages enclosed by the factory gates, by the clocking on at eight and the clocking off at half-past five, whose only freedom lay in daydreams or in wildcat strikes.

One day they had a wildcat strike. Philippa was never sure how it came about, only that it was something to do with a query about one of the girls' bonus figures. Suddenly, above the noise of the machines and *The Sun Ain't Gonna Shine Any More*, a whistle blew. Everyone except Philippa switched off their machines and the whole floor whirred to a slow halt. Philippa, oblivious to everything except her drill and castings, went on tapping, intent on earning her very first bonus.

Shirley poked her on the shoulder. 'Switch off. We're coming out.'

Solemn-faced and silent, the girls filed out between the rows of still machines, watched by irritated eyes from the bosses' balcony. They left the shop floor and stood in grey drizzle in the dreary yard where delivery vans were waiting for the next consignment of small parts.

'What's going on?' Philippa whispered to Shirley.

'Strike,' said Shirley.

They stood in the drizzle and listened to Marlene Wheeler, who was the shop steward, making a speech about exploitation. Management watched from behind upstairs closed windows. The shop steward finished her speech and everybody cheered a lot and the drizzle stopped and the sun came out, so the girls brought sandwiches and drinks from the dispenser out into the yard and they all had a picnic. When the after-dinner hooter sounded, they all stayed put.

Mr Crawford himself came out into the yard. Marlene Wheeler explained the grievance, which was that one of the tappers had been accused of faking her bonus figures. Mr Crawford apologised on behalf of Management, honour was satisfied, the sun went in and the drizzle began again so everybody went inside and switched on their machines again.

'Breaks up the day a bit,' shouted Shirley cheerfully above the noise of the drills.

'Wildcat strikes,' snorted Norman angrily that night at supper. 'Typical of that mentality. They'll jump on any little thing just to give themselves an excuse to stop working. And if we dock their pay for the time lost, they'll strike again. I hope you're beginning to understand the sort of thing we're up against, Philippa.'

Philippa thought about Marge and her eleven pounds a week and Shirley and her choreography and Dawn with her mental arithmetic and said nothing.

'What were you doing before you came to work here?' asked Shirley one tea break.

Philippa blushed. 'I was in a play.'

It sounded flippant and silly compared with the lives of the women here, but Shirley was enthralled. 'Are you an actress, then?'

'Not yet,' said Philippa. 'I want to be. I was Acting ASM for the last thing I did.'

'What's that?'

'It means Assistant Stage Manager with a bit of acting thrown in. It's not as important as it sounds.'

Dawn joined them. 'She's going to be a film star,' said Shirley. 'Don't forget us when you're famous.' They laughed, delighted with the glamour of it.

'Do you know any famous people?' Shirley asked. 'You know, anyone from television?'

Philippa thought and then remembered that Patrick, who had played the Professor in *Hot Air* had once had a small part in an episode of *Dixon of Dock Green* and that an actress who had been in the children's tour had been a temp in *Compact*. Then the morning break was over and the girls returned to their machines to dream of another way of life.

Lift the casting, drill the hole, drop the casting, take another. Why, wondered Philippa for the thousand-thousandth time, do I have to drill holes into holes that are already there? A Boss wandered down the staircase from his office on the balcony and stood behind her, watching her drill the holes. She turned round and smiled at him; then she recognised him as Colin Palfrey, the man with the pale ginger hair and the pale blue eyes who must have got the middle-management job, despite his wife's uncertainties about the cutlery.

'Why am I drilling holes into holes that are there already?' she shouted at him above the noise of the machines. He drew back, appalled. Tappers did not speak to Management.

'Silly sod,' said Marge when Philippa took the next batch of tapped castings up to be weighed. 'Was he rude to you? Because if he was, we'll come out.'

The firebell rang. 'Fire practice,' said Philippa and all the girls switched off their machines and filed out into the delivery yard.

'Breaks up the day,' said Shirley.

Chapter Thirty-Five

Jenny was on her hands and knees on the floor of the kitchen in the Three Bells, swabbing the tiles with a cloth. Something was different in her now; she could daydream again. She smiled as she thought about the dream horse she would buy and ride out of the wood and over the hills and far away. And then what? she thought. What when she had ridden as far as the dinosaur range? What would she do then? Would she turn round and come back to the kitchen floor and the ash-trays and the dirty-linen basket?

She straightened up and wrung the floor-cloth into a bucket of dark grey water. Time to chuck this lot and fill the bucket with some fresh. She carried the bucket into the yard and emptied it down the drain. I want to know about things, she said inside her head as she ran hot water into the bucket and poured some bleach in with it. I want to understand. I want to ask the questions and to know that somewhere there are real, solid answers. I've had too much of theories and myths and other people's word games. I want to ask the questions and find out the answers.

In front of her, on the kitchen windowsill, a shabby geranium sat rather hopelessly in a pot. It looked thirsty, Jenny thought, and she gave it some water. She picked up one of its leaves and examined it closely; its shape, its ridgy veins, the way the stem divided into a flower head. The geranium drank the water gratefully and she gave it some more. Osmosis, she remembered from 'O' level Biology. How does it know how to do that? The leaves of the plant were a tired and dusty green. Photosynthesis, she remembered, and washed them off with a dishcloth.

Jenny picked up her bucket of bleach and water and got down onto her knees again. 'Those are the things I want to know,' she said to the bucket. 'Why do some things grow geranium-shaped and some grow into trees? What made the bee orchid disguise itself as a bee? Why do plants put out roots and shoots and breathe in carbon dioxide and breathe out oxygen?'

Ann walked into the kitchen. 'It is a serious worry,' she said, 'when one's friends begin to talk to buckets. Are you coming out for lunch?'

'No,' said Jenny. 'I've got to do something.'

She finished the floor, washed her hands, took off her overall and walked out of the Three Bells into Tarminster. It took her a quarter of an hour to reach the entrance to the High School. For a moment she hesitated, watching the uniformed schoolgirls who bounced tennis balls, whizzed on roller skates, galloped over hurdles or sat on the grass and gossiped. Was she still the child who had done all these things, or was she someone else entirely now? It didn't matter through. She had been forgiven, and now she was free to look for real answers.

She walked through the gates and in through the back entrance of the High School, past the Senior Cloakroom and along the corridor that led to the Hall and the Towel Room and the Library. A figure marched purposefully towards her, hitching her left shoulder strap as she approached. 'May I help you?' asked Miss Bugle.

In an instant, Jenny was Jennifer Cornwood of 4A. 'Please Miss Bugle,' she began.

The Headmistress' glasses glittered. 'Good gracious me,' she cried, 'it's Jennifer Cornwood! How very glad I am to see you.'

Jennifer gulped. 'Please may I look at the university prospectuses in the Library?' she asked. Her voice sounded high and childish, she thought.

'Most certainly you may,' replied Miss Bugle and the bell rang for the end of the dinner-hour. Miss Bugle hitched her strap again. 'Can't stop now. Got a date with the Prodigal Son and 4A.' She grinned delightedly. 'Splendid to see you again, Jennifer. So sorry I can't talk properly now. Come back another day – Tuesdays are usually good. You know where the prospectuses are – still on the table in the far corner of the

Library, just where they always were. Tuesdays are good.' She hoiked again and galloped off to 4A and the Prodigal Son.

Jenny walked into the Library where Sixth-Form girls were whispering. She sat down at the table in the far corner and opened a prospectus.

Chapter Thirty-Six

£BILLION BOOST FOR TARMINSTER shouted the front-page head-line of the *Tarminster Echo*. HUGE NEW ROAD SCHEME PUTS CITY ON NATIONAL MAP. 'Guaranteed Growth,' says Minister.

'*Plans for a massive ten-mile stretch of dual carriageway to link Tarminster to the London trunk road were released today,*' continued the lead story. An outline map showed the route of the link road. It cut straight through the woods and across the lower and middle slopes of Swain's Chard Hill and joined the main road to Tarminster again, two miles beyond the village.

'It'll be an excellent thing for us,' said Norman Foster over dinner that evening. A copy of the *Tarminster Echo* lay on the table beside his plate. 'It'll mean much more access for lorries, more trade with the rest of the country, more jobs, bigger profits – a higher standard of living altogether.'

John Dangerfield was delighted. 'It'll be a tremendous boost for business,' he said to Joan that evening. 'Let's face it, Tarminster's a bit of a backwater. Now we'll be able to move upmarket – attract a more sophisticated clientèle.'

Ann reached across the table for the copy of the *Tarminster Echo* that he had brought home with him that evening. She looked at the map. 'Have you seen this, Dad?'

'Yes,' John replied.

'But look,' Ann pointed to the line of the road. 'This road goes right through our woods and over the hill.'

'It's the only possible route,' explained John. 'It'd cost millions in compensation to take it anywhere else. There'll be a Public Inquiry, of course, just to go through the motions. But the road's got to come if this area's going to move forwards commercially.'

Ann pushed back her chair. 'Thanks for dinner,' she said to Joan. 'I'm going for a walk.'

'But you haven't had your pudding yet,' complained her mother.

'I've had enough. I'll do the washing up when I get back.'

'But what about Jane?'

'I'll take her with me.' She lifted Jane out of her bouncing baby seat and strapped her into the pushchair.

'It's a funny time to take her for a walk,' objected Joan. 'It's nearly her bathtime.'

'It's a beautiful evening. A walk before bedtime'll do her good.'

Ann pushed her daughter up the bumpy track beside the woods and out onto the open slopes. Now the rise was too steep for the pushchair so she dumped it at the edge of the wood and carried Jane on up. She found Jenny standing by the stump of the Climbing Tree and together, in silence, they climbed their hill until they stood in the evening wind, staring back down at the way they had come, at the green rise and fall of the hill as it dropped to the woods, at the darkening shapes of the trees against the sky and the run of the drystone wall that edged the wood, and the dips and the outcrops of stone and wild flowers. 'They can't do it,' said Jenny at last. 'We can't let them do it.' Philippa was climbing the last slope of the hill towards them.

There would be, said the *Tarminster Echo*, a Public Inquiry at 7.30 p.m. on October 4th in Swain's Chard Institute. Interested parties were invited to attend to hear representatives of the Ministry of Transport and the County Council explain their plans. Objections should be lodged with the Department Inspector.

It was dinner break next day in Crawford's canteen. Philippa sat with Shirley and Marge, eating sandwiches and talking about the road scheme.

'I don't know,' said Marge. 'I suppose it's a good thing for the area – bring more money in, I mean, but it seems wrong. Like killing something.' She swallowed thoughtfully. 'We used to catch the bus up there nearly every Saturday in summer when we was kids. And in the winters, we'd pull our sledges all the way from Tarminster. Mother'd pack us a picnic and we'd be gone all day. It's like destroying your childhood somehow.'

That was it, thought Philippa. That was exactly what she'd been feeling ever since her father had brought home the news. The road would destroy her childhood and all the things she had ever believed were permanent and beautiful and necessary. 'We've got to stop it,' she said.

Marge laughed. 'How can we stop it? The authorities have made their decision already. They won't listen to us.'

'There's going to be a Public Inquiry,' Philippa said, 'on October 4th in our Institute. We've got to go and tell them they can't do it.'

'I'd never dare,' said Shirley.

'No,' said Marge, 'but Philippa would, wouldn't you, Phil? You're not scared of standing up in front of people, are you? You'd do it, wouldn't you?'

'Yes,' said Philippa. 'Yes, I would.'

Chapter Thirty-Seven

Every evening, since she had read the news, Jenny had climbed the hill and stared down at the shape of the land that had been imprinted on her since she was a baby. It had been this place she had returned to after the abortion and, in the end, it had been this place that had forgiven her. She saw in her mind's eye how it would look after they had built the road. Seventy feet of dual carriageway would slice through her trees and cut its way through the earth that was part of her. The wind in the leaves would be drowned by the whine and roar of traffic, the air would smell of petrol and the bee orchid would never grow again. 'You bastards,' she said out loud. 'You stupid, greedy bastards.'

'Are you going to this meeting tomorrow night?' Joan asked John on October 3rd across the gap between their beds.

'Oh yes. We must show solidarity. They're saying there's a group of romantic sentimentalists and beatnik types who are trying to oppose the scheme. You've seen all those hysterical letters from batty old spinsters and neurotics in the local press.'

'Will it go to the vote then?' asked Joan who had, in her secret heart, applauded the letters but did not want John to think she was neurotic and hysterical.

'Oh, good heavens, no. There'll be spokesmen from both sides and the Inspector from the Department will listen to the arguments and read all the correspondence. Then he'll go away and make an informed decision.'

'So there's a chance that the road might not go ahead?'

'Good heavens, no,' said John again. 'It's a foregone conclusion, but the democratic process must be seen to be gone through. No, no, this road's got to happen if we're to have real growth.'

Joan smiled oddly. 'Growth,' she said. 'Funny word to choose, when it means cutting down the real growing things. . .'

John lay in the darkness and wondered about his wife. She had changed in some intangible way, ever since their granddaughter had been born and she had spent that night in Shimmerton and come home saying 'Chow'. He supposed she was at a funny age.

'Be realistic, Joan,' he said patiently. 'In the real world, you've got to have money and growth and commercial expansion. That's what it's all about.'

Joan thought to herself, 'What very small feet you have, John.' Out loud she said, 'I don't know that I like the real world much.' Then she turned over and stared at the dark rectangle of the bedroom window. An owl began to hoot.

It was October 4th and the last lesson of the afternoon. 'Wisdom and Spirit of the Universe,' said Miss Cameron as the last bell rang. Miss Freeman played the final glorious bars of the *New World Symphony* and took the record off the turntable. Miss Bugle read, '"I will lift up mine eyes unto the hills from whence cometh my Salvation." Close your Bibles, girls, and put away your things. And don't forget to wash underneath your arms.' High School girls in gabardine macs and berets streamed out of the school gates while Miss Bugle cranked the starter on her Austin Seven and Miss Freeman climbed into Miss Cameron's green MG.

The Institute doors were open from half-past six to allow plenty of time for interested parties to arrive and seat themselves. A long trestle table had been set out on the stage with metal and canvas chairs along it, ready for the local MP, the Department Inspector, the Chairman of the Chamber of Commerce and the Chairman of the County Council Planning Committee. A reporter and photographer from the *Tarminster Echo* were there and a hundred metal and canvas chairs had been arranged in rows in the hall.

Norman and Madge were already sitting in the front row when John and Joan arrived and sat down behind them. 'Good Lord,' said Madge to Norman ten minutes later, 'Philippa's just come in. Who on earth are all those women with her? They look as if they've just come straight from your factory.'

Philippa waved to her mother and sat down with Marge and Shirley in one of the back rows. They were joined by Ann and Jane (Why on earth has she brought the baby with her? John through irritably. I hope to goodness she doesn't start feeding her in front of all these people), and finally by Jenny. At twenty past seven, Miss Bugle, Miss Freeman and Miss Cameron, who had had supper in the Flying Pig, made their entrance. Nearly all the seats were occupied by now.

The Public Inquiry opened with a speech made by the MP in which he introduced the Inspector and thanked the Chairman of the Chamber of Commerce and the man from the County Council for giving up their valuable time to explain matters to the good people of Swain's Chard. He himself, he assured them with an oleaginous smile, was there to ensure fair play. A murmuring chuckle ran around the Institute and he sat down.

The County Council man then stood up and outlined the road scheme and spoke of its enormous and indubitable advantages to the wealth and development of the whole community. 'Hear, Hear!' said Mr Crawford and Norman and John and the owner of the Three Bells and all the other people who knew and understood about Growth and Progress.

The County Council man sat down and the Chairman of the Chamber of Commerce stood up and said the same things all over again. 'Hear Hear!' said all the people who knew about how to make money.

'Are there any questions from the Floor at this stage?' enquired the MP, smiling benignly down at the Floor. Lady Hennessey stood up.

'Is any attention being paid,' she asked, 'to the aesthetic questions that this scheme raises?' There was an embarrassed pause while the men on the platform tried to remember what aesthetic meant. 'What I mean to say,' continued Lady Hennessey, not wishing to embarrass anyone, 'is, has anybody thought about what this road will do to the appearance and the atmosphere and the spirit of Swain's Chard and the countryside around it?'

The MP rose, smiling and bland. 'A great deal of consideration has indeed been given to this aspect of the matter, Lady Hennessey,' he assured her with glutinous courtesy. 'While it is accepted that there must inevitably be some … alteration to the landscape, it will be kept to a minimum, and it is overwhelmingly felt that any such alteration will be completely justified by the huge economic advantages that our whole community will reap.'

'Hear, Hear!' said Norman and John and Mr Crawford and the owner of the Three Bells again.

Philippa stood up at the back of the hall. 'I disagree,' she said and her voice was high and nervous until she remembered how Tit Willow had told her to breathe from her diaphragm and relax her throat. 'If you cut down the trees and build the road across the hill, you will destroy something you can never replace.'

Norman turned round and glared at his daughter; Marge and Shirley smiled admiringly at her. The men on the stage, apart from the Inspector, who had remained expressionless all evening, smiled tolerantly. They had met these young women before; hopeless, over-educated romantics, not yet married, not enough to do with themselves, looking for excitement and a purpose until they found husbands and children for themselves.

'I understand your concern,' said the MP, putting on his wise and understanding face, 'but there will be plenty of countryside left; and in the Real World,' he paused to allow the reverberations of the Real World to sink in, 'we have to be concerned with the practicalities of economic survival.'

Jenny was on her feet. 'But our piece of countryside won't be left for us or for our children. And what is the point of economic survival if it means that we only survive into ugliness?' she said. Her face was scarlet and she was shaking with nervousness and anger. 'If you build this new road, you will destroy something deep inside all of us who grew up here. You will kill something that is alive and growing and beautiful and that none of you can create, no matter how much money you make. You can destroy living beauty, but you can't make it grow again. If you put buying and selling and greed and ugliness above living beauty, then we are all lost. You only care about making profits and getting rich – and you lessen yourselves and you lessen all of us. If you ignore our need for beauty, you will ... diminish ... the human spirit.'

She stopped and stared around her. She had made a complete fool of herself; she had been hysterical and naïve and the men on the platform were looking amused and bored. But Ann and Philippa and the women from the factory were on their feet and clapping, and so were Lady Hennessey and Miss Bugle and Miss Freeman and Miss Cameron. 'Hear, Hear!' they cried. 'Hear, Hear!' echoed Joan and she too stood up and clapped.

The Public Inquiry was over.

The Inspector went away and weighed up all the evidence before him.

Six weeks later, the front-page headline in the *Tarminster Echo* announced: INSPECTOR GIVES GO-AHEAD FOR NEW LINK ROAD.

Chapter Thirty-Eight

It was dinner-time again in Crawford's canteen, the day after the Inspector's decision to allow the new road had appeared in the *Tarminster Echo*. The first dinner-shift had already eaten but had remained in the long room, squashing into extra chairs or sitting on the floor between the tables. Marge rapped her table with a spoon-handle and waited until silence fell upon the eaters and those still waiting in the queue.

'Everybody who reads the paper knows,' she said, 'about the plans for the new link road to Tarminster and that the authorities have just given the go-ahead for it to happen. We have called this meeting because we want to discuss with all of you what the road will mean for us and for our families and for our children and grandchildren. You all know Philippa here and you've probably heard about what she said at the public meeting at Swain's Chard six weeks ago – about the way the road will destroy the countryside we most of us grew up in. On the other hand, I know that some of us – including me – are worried about money and job security, and that this road will probably make our jobs safer and bring more jobs and money into the area. That's why we've called this meeting, so's we can thrash it all out now, between us, and decide whether or not we want the road and if we don't, what we're going to do about it.' Marge sat down.

Philippa stood up. This was much worse than the Public Inquiry. This time she was talking to people whose livelihoods would be affected by the coming of the road. This was no longer about a poetic, romantic view of the countryside and suddenly she felt very large and plain and pale. Sophia

Roncetti, wild gypsy dancer, came to her rescue.

'You're probably sick to death of hearing me say things like this,' she began, 'but I believe that there are more important things than making money to buy bigger television sets and faster cars and newer furniture. It's hard to put it into words because it's such an abstract thing, but Marge sort of summed it up weeks ago when she talked about being a child in the summertime and catching the bus to Swain's Chard Hill with a picnic her mother'd packed up for the whole family so's they could run wild for the day. It doesn't sound much, but without it her childhood would not have been so ... bright. That hill and the woods and the view from the top are something mighty and beautiful and grand and fine that we *all* need. If we allow them to be killed in the name of growth and progress and profit, we shall be allowing them to murder something ...' she hestitated and blushed to hear herself say the world '... holy,' she said at last, looking very embarrassed. This was not Sophia Roncetti speaking; this was plain Philippa Foster. 'That's all, really. I want to stop the road because I believe that if we let it happen, we'll all be smaller and meaner and poorer.' She sat down amid some awkward clapping from some of the tappers.

The shop steward, Marlene Wheeler, stood up. 'It's all very well for you to talk like that. You come here with your posh voice and your posh ideas, rabbiting on about the beauties of nature and holiness, but we aren't talking here about extra money to buy new cars or televisions. We are talking about paying the rent and buying the food.' There was a loud murmur of agreement from the Assembly Line girls. Philippa looked at Marge who nodded to her to speak.

'Hang on a minute,' said Marlene Wheeler angrily.

'Philippa to speak,' said Marge firmly and Marlene sat down, scowling.

'I understand that,' said Philippa nervously, 'and I don't know how to answer it, except to say, when we've all got enough to survive on, enough to pay the rent and buy the food, what then? Is it tellies and cars and then bigger tellies and faster cars? Is that it? Is that the only thing we're aiming for? Or is there something else? If we destroy this beauty, what are we going to survive *for*?'

There was more applause from the tapping line and then Shirley stood up. 'I'm not much good at this,' she said apologetically, 'but I think I know what Philippa's trying to say. It's sort of, what's the point of anything if you haven't got—'

The door of the canteen swung open and Mr Crawford barged in. 'What the hell is going on here? Is this an unofficial union meeting? You should all have been back at work nineteen minutes ago. I'm docking half an hour's pay from everybody's wage-packet.'

There was an astounded silence. Nobody moved. Then Marge said quietly, 'We'll go back to our machines when we are ready, Mr Crawford. We have some important business to conclude.'

She turned back to the packed canteen 'I suggest that we give ourselves three days to think this over,' she continued. 'At dinner-time on Friday, we'll all meet here again and take a vote on whether to do nothing or whether to fight.'

With silent dignity, not looking once at Mr Crawford, his workers moved towards the canteen door. As the first ones reached it, Mr Crawford said, very loudly and clearly, 'I don't know how many of you are aware of the fact that Philippa is Mr Foster's daughter.'

Mr Crawford's untimely entrance had the surprising effect of swinging his workers' votes against the road and in favour of the trees and Swain's Chard Hill. It was his revelation about Philippa which finally rallied the Assembly Line and the Tappers behind the Spirit and Wisdom of the Universe when they held the vote on the following Friday. Far from seeing Philippa as a bosses' spy, a traitor and a paid informer, the Crawford's women admired her for being a girl who wasn't afraid to defy her class and her family, to ger her hands dirty and to speak her mind.

'And after all,' as Marlene Wheeler said at the Friday meeting, 'we'll never see any of these great profits that they're on about. We'll just go on grinding away here, day after boring bloody day, year after boring bloody year so's they can line their pockets and put up our rents. So we may as well fight for the trees and have a bit of a laugh.'

*

264

It was breakfast-time in the Three Bells and Ann was on the early shift, serving grapefruit to shiny-suited businessmen who were converging on Tarminster like hungry starlings to see what pickings were to be had when the new road came to the city and brought new money with it. They talked loudly and importantly about Five-Year Plans and Investments and Growth. 'It's an exciting prospect,' they chattered, greedy-eyed and sparkly-faced in their shiny dark blue suits. 'It'll boost trade no end. It'll bring Growth to the area.' Growth Growth Growth they said.

'Like cancer,' said Ann, putting down a plate of sausage, egg, bacon and fried bread in front of the loudest, fattest starling.

'What did you say?' demanded the starling, and his bright little eyes popped at her.

'I said,' repeated Ann, 'like *cancer*.'

There was an appalled silence in the Dining Room as Ann picked up a tray and slung a tea-towel over her shoulder defiantly. 'You talk of growth and trade and profits all the time, but you never stop to look at what you are killing to get it. You and your lot are carving up my childhood and the firm ground of my life, and all the money you make for yourselves will never make the hills and trees come back. Yes you're just like cancer. You grow out of control and you kill anything that gets in your way.'

The chief starling's eyes grew brighter and brighter and almost popped out of his head with fury. 'Fetch me the Manager. I insist upon seeing the Manager immediately,' he squawked.

He and all his shiny, glittering flock demanded their money back and went to find another hotel, the Manager of the Three Bells sacked Ann on the spot and Jenny gave in her notice.

Chapter Thirty-Nine

One the evening of the day when Ann got the sack from the Three Bells, Philippa arrived home from Crawford's to find a telegram from her agent waiting for her. URGENT STOP RING IMMEDIATELY STOP. She rang. 'You've got an audition at Hamilton Rep tomorrow. They need a young comedy actress for their next season. Vivian Day's picked you out of *Spotlight* and he phoned me this morning. Can you get a train tonight? I'll sort out a hotel and ring you back.'

She caught an evening train to Hamilton Spa, an elegant watering place a hundred miles away to the North, whose repertory theatre was one of the best in the country. '*Hamilton Rep, Hamilton Rep, Hamilton Rep*,' said the train all the way there. A season with Hamilton Rep would change her life. It would mean that she was a real actress, a serious actress with a passport to London and Stratford. '*Hamilton Rep, Hamilton Rep, Hamilton Rep*.' Philippa took her audition pieces out of her bag and went through them in her head.

She found the hotel the agent had booked and went to bed early. In the morning, at half-past nine, she walked to the theatre. 'I'm Philippa Foster,' she told the stage-doorman. 'I've got an appointment with Vivian Day.'

Don't get too hopeful, she had said to herself in the night when she could hardly sleep for excitement. They'll have asked lots of girls to come. You're an outsider still; the odds are all against you, '*Don't count your chickens*,' said Norman's voice in her head and she smiled at him.

The stage-doorman led her up ancient winding staircases and along corridors lined with dressing-room doors. Framed

266

pictures of actors and actresses gestured and glowered from the walls, famous and hallowed names from the nineteenth century; engravings of Macready as Shylock, Kemble as Hamlet and Kean as King Lear. Old posters and play bills from a hundred years of comedy and tragedy and music hall and pantomine smiled a welcome to Philippa Foster.

The stage-doorman stopped outside a door and knocked on it. 'Come in,' said the voice of Vivian Day.

They talked for twenty minutes and she felt at ease with him, despite his fame and his reputation for a terrifying temper and a cruel wit. She could tell that he liked her. He stood up. 'Well then, Miss Foster, I think it's time we went downstairs to see what you are made of.'

She followed him back along the corridors, noticing how they sloped and creaked. This was one of the oldest theatres in the country, where ghosts of the greatest actors of all time were said to float through the corridors and into the dressing rooms and above the stage into the fly tower.

Vivian Day led Philippa down the winding stairs again and then she found herself in the wings of a set. He spoke to an electrician who was adjusting a pageant lamp. 'Go up into the box and give me a general stage cover,' he ordered, then turned to Philippa. 'I'll go down into the auditorium. Wait until you get some light and go when you are ready. Take your time.'

He left her and disappeared into the darkness. Then white light flooded the stage. 'Thank you,' came the disembodied voice of Vivian Day as the electrician descended the ladder. 'Whenever you're ready, Miss Foster.'

Forget about him, forget about where you are. You are Viola. *I* am Viola, washed up on the shores of Illyria, soaked and lost and terrified, desperate to know where my brother is.

Now I am Audrey from *As You Like It*. Poor old ugly Audrey. A poor thing. An indifferent virgin.

And now I am Honey, the vacuous little wife in *Who's Afraid of Virginia Woolf*: I am blonde and stupid and I keep on throwing up.

'Thank you, Miss Foster,' said Vivian Day, and his voice gave nothing away. Nevertheless, she knew that she had done her best and that if that was not good enough for him, then she was not good enough for Hamilton Rep.

She could hear him moving in the darkness of the auditorium and then he broke through the barrier of light that separated them and handed her two scripts. He showed her where they were marked and where he wanted her to read. 'Thank you,' he said again when she had finished. 'House-lights,' he called, and she heard the electrician hurry through the darkness and climb the cat ladder to the lighting box.

The house-lights came up in the auditorium and the white lights dimmed from the stage. Philippa gazed around her. Hamilton Rep was a red velvet, steeply raked theatre with ornate boxes and pillars and hangings, like the Pollock Toy Theatre her parents had given her for Christman when she was ten.

'You can come down now, Miss Foster,' said Vivian Day, and she walked down the steps that led from the stage and went towards him. He smiled and indicated the seat beside him. She pressed it down and sat on it, looking at the stage with its elaborately decorated proscenium arch where gilded cupids held up the looped curtains and black footlights crouched along the floor.

Vivian Day smiled at her again. 'As your agent probably told you, we are looking for a young actress who can play the comic roles in our next season. But there will be scope for some straight work as well. I have four more young women to see today. I will let your agent know by tonight.'

He shook hands with her and she left the theatre. All the way home on the train she could see it in her mind's eye, red and gold and velvet and black, wooden and winding, alive with the ghosts of actresses who had played Lady Macbeth and Juliet and Ophelia. '*Don't count your chickens*,' she heard Norman say again in her head. '*He's got to see four others*.' But when the telephone rang two hours after she had arrived home and her mother's voice was calling her to it, she knew that she had got the job.

'Are you all right, Philippa?' asked Shirley before they switched on their machines the next day. 'They said your mum rang in to say you couldn't get in for work. Are you ill or something?'

Philippa shook her head. 'No. I went for an audition. I've got a job in Rep.'

'What's Rep?' asked Shirley. 'I thought that was something you made curtains out of.' Then her face changed. 'When d'you start?'

'In about six weeks, I think,' said Philippa. 'It'll be for the whole year.'

And then she realised what Shirley meant. The phone call and the audition and the getting of the job had all happened so fast that she had been flown into a world where Crawford's and the link road and Swain's Chard did not exist. '*Hamilton Rep*,' the train had said, and she had turned into Viola and Audrey and Honey and there had been no room in her head for anything else until now.

'Oh God,' said Philippa and she switched on her drill.

'But you *can't* turn it down!' said Madge. She was very angry. 'It's the chance of a lifetime. It'll make all the difference to your career.'

'I cannot believe what you are saying,' said her agent. 'Hamilton Rep? Any young actress would kill for an offer like that.' He was very angry indeed. 'I've got not time for schoolgirls who just want to play at being in the theatre. You won't get another chance like this, you know.'

'Are you sure?' said Ann and Jenny as they walked with her through the woods that evening. Philippa wanted to cry, but she wouldn't. She swallowed hard and Sophia Roncetti came to the rescue.

'What's happening here is more important,' she said firmly. 'You know it is. What's the point of me showing off on a stage while they chop down all this? And anyway,' she said, 'at least I know now I've got the talent. At least I can be sure of that. If someone like Vivian Day wants me now, then someone else'll want me when this is all over.'

She wished she could be sure.

Chapter Forty

The road cut and thrashed its way across the farmland towards Swain's Chard. On May 12th, the *Tarminster Echo* announced: '*Work will begin to fell the first trees in Swain's Chard Wood on May 18th.*' It was written in a very small paragraph on a left-hand inside page and hidden between reports of Women's Instititute meetings and a weekly nature column.

Trees would bleed their sap into the earth; nestling birds, too young to fly, would smash to the ground and their nests would be crushed. Wild orchids and bluebells would be wiped out. Earwigs and woodlice, slugs and earthworms, slow worms and centipedes, beetles and weasels and shrews and voles and moles and hedgehogs, rabbits and fieldmice, squirrels and spiders and toads would be flattened and sliced and squashed and mashed as the massive boost for Tarminster rolled and scythed its way into the Swain's Chard Woods.

On May 13th, Marge the Chargehand called another meeting in Crawford's canteen. It was quick and quiet. 'They're planning to start cutting the trees early next Wednesday morning,' she told them. 'Don't say nothing to nobody about what we're going to do. That's very important. We've got to take them by surprise. We clock off as normal on Tuesday, but we don't come in on Wednesday. Be up at the main road gates to the woods as early as you can. Then we'll see what they'll dare to do.'

All through the week, men in donkey jackets worked in the woods, marking chosen trees with chalked crosses. On the night of 17th May, Jenny and Philippa and Ann took a tent and sleeping bags and Jane and pitched camp just inside the entrance to the wood. Opposite them, on the torn farmland, the diggers waited like sleeping monsters, savage and gormless with their necks bent and their mouths hanging open. A notice stood beside the gates:

DANGER. NO ENTRY. TREE FELLING.

Jane grizzled to be fed and Ann leant against a tree and unbuttoned her shirt. 'Where on earth are you taking her?' Joan had asked. 'I want to take her to sleep in the woods before it's too late,' Ann had replied.

They lay in a sleeping-bagged row inside the tent. The flaps were still open, facing away from the gaping monsters and into the wood. The night air smelled of earth and moss and fern, and a full moon glimmered through the beech leaves.

'Full moon for lunatics,' said Philippa. 'Is that what we are?' They lay on their backs without speaking, watching the clouds blow across the moon's face and listening to the light swaying of the branches. Jane snored and snuffled, snug against her mother's side. Something rustled at the back of the tent.

'My God, what's that?' whispered Philippa, and then the thing tripped and sneezed and giggled and Marge's voice said, 'It's all right, girls, it's only us.'

Philippa crawled out like a large green caterpillar, still zipped inside her sleeping bag and found Marge and Shirley struggling to put up another tent.

'We didn't want to be late for the action,' Marge explained. 'The first bus up from Tarminster doesn't leave until six-fifteen and I suddenly thought they might make an early start and we didn't want you here on your own without reinforcements. The others'll come on the bus.'

They lay awake through most of the night, listening to the screech owls and a nightingale who sang out in the open where the woods met the slope of the hill, hearing strange rustles and snuffles around the tents, watching the moon until it faded and the sky grew slowly grey and the dawn birds shouted, hundreds and hundreds of them, greeting the sun.

'It's half-past five,' said Jenny. 'We'd better get ready.'

271

Chapter Forty-One

The men arrived at seven, in a van, with chainsaws and hard hats. There were six of them.

'Bloody hell,' said the driver when he saw the tent. 'What we got here?' A movement above his head made him look upwards. Twenty feet above him, on the first chalk-marked tree, he saw a young woman sitting astride a branch, leaning back against the trunk and swinging her legs. She smiled down at him and waved. The driver nudged his mate and pointed, but his mate was staring to where Marge, two trees away but only four feet off the ground, was clinging nervously to a forked branch.

'Bloody hell,' the first man said again. 'It's women. Roosting.'

'There's another one,' said his mate, pointing to a third tree where Ann and Jane perched on a broad, natural platform where the tree had divided itself into two.

'Blimey,' said the first man. 'That one's nesting.'

The double-decker bus from Tarminster rattled along the road and stopped opposite the entrance to the wood. Women were streaming off it, all the tappers and millers and drillers and assemblers from Crawford's, armed with Thermos flasks and sandwich boxes, some in jeans and Wellingtons, others in high heels and summer dresses.

'Your dad isn't half going to get a shock when he goes into work today,' said Dawn to Philippa. They tucked their skirts into their pants and their boots or high-heeled shoes into notches and stumps of branches and soon the astonished tree-fellers were gazing at forty roosting women, bright in the sunlight, laughing and chattering like a late dawn chorus.

'Bloody hell,' said the first man again. 'What are we going to do with them?'

The foreman arrived. 'Get the police, of course,' he said crossly. 'Dial 999, you mean?' The foreman did not find him funny. 'No. I mean get into that van, drive down to the village and bring the local Plod back. *Now!*'

Fifteen minutes later, the van returned with Swain's Chard's PC Coles in its wake, puffing and sweating up the hill on his bicycle. PC Coles had known Jennifer Cornwood since before she was born. In fact, he sometimes thought ruefully, if Arthur Cornwood hadn't got there first, he himself might have claimed the hand of Phyllis all those years ago. He smiled to think of the way he had mooned with hopeless love on top of Swain's Chard Hill when he was a lad of sixteen. He had secretly carved his initials above hers on one of the beech trees. . .

'Now come along, girls,' he called, holding his helmet on his head as he craned his neck backwards to peer up into the branches. 'Be sensible. They're only trying to do their job, so come on down and let them get on with it.'

'I'm ever so sorry, Mr Coles,' said Jenny from her high perch, 'but we've got to stay here. We're fighting for our lives, you see.'

PC Coles very much wished that he could forget his position as upholder of Law and Order in Swain's Chard, especially when he realised that Jenny's tree was the one that had *H.C. 4 P.S.* carved halfway up its trunk. But the stern voice of duty recalled him.

'I shall be forced to call in reinforcements if you refuse to come down,' he said solemnly, and waited. Nobody moved and so, with dignity, PC Coles remounted his bicycle and departed slowly back towards the village. He would go and find Phyllis, he decided. She would know what to do.

He knocked at the Cornwoods' door. 'Oh my,' said Phyllis when she saw his uniform. 'Whatever's happened?'

'Nothing serious,' said PC Coles, for he was a kindly man who hated causing distress. 'It's just that your Jennifer and a whole flock of other women have climbed the trees in the woods and there's going to be a Situation if we don't get them down.'

'What d'you mean, climbed the trees?' Phyllis was impatient. He'd always been slow, Harold Coles.

'She says they're fighting for their lives,' said PC Coles, blushing a little. Phyllis flared her nostrils. How magnificent she was, he thought.

'Quite right, too,' she said, and she got her bike out of the yard and rode straight past him.

'I'm sorry, Mrs Dangerfield,' she said to Joan at the back door, 'but I can't come to work this morning. 'I've got to go up to the woods to help the girls.' She explained the situation quickly and Joan donned Wellingtons and headscarf and was just closing the back door when the telephone rang.

'Coffee?' said Madge's voice.

'Sorry,' said Joan, 'there's something urgent I've got to do up in the woods.' She caught up with Phyllis outside the Manor gates, just as Alice Price was turning into the drive for her morning's cleaning session at the Manor.

'Come on, Alice,' Phyllis cried, 'We've got to go and save the woods.'

'I'd better tell Her Ladyship first,' said Alice, and hurried on up the drive to the Tradesmen's Entrance. 'There's a bit of a revolution going on, Lady Hennessey,' she explained apologetically, 'so I'm afraid I can't come and clean for you this morning. I've got to go and save the trees.' Immediately, Lady Hennessey mounted her own bicycle and followed Alice down the drive.

Police reinforcements in Panda cars had arrived from Tarminster and were addressing the roosting women through a loudhailer. 'You are breaking the law,' announced a Sergeant. 'Come down now, all of you, or we shall take steps to remove you.' His threat was greeted with birdsong and laughter.

'What's going on, Officer?' asked Lady Hennessey in her most aristocratic voice. The Sergeant almost curtseyed; Lady Hennessey was a formidable woman and a JP to boot.

'They are disturbing the peace, Your Ladyship,' he explained deferentially. 'Troublemakers and layabouts. But don't worry, we've got it all under control.'

'Oh good,' said Lady Hennessey as she parked her bike against a tree and then heaved herself up onto a very low branch. 'Carry on, Officer,' she said. The Sergeant looked as if he might be about to burst into tears.

A reporter and photographer from the *Tarminster Echo* arrived and took a lot of pictures and interviewed the Foreman and the Sergeant. 'Disgusting behaviour,' said the Foreman. 'They ought to be at home taking care of their families. Women like this are ruining the country.'

DON'T LET THEM MURDER OUR COUNTRYSIDE cried the headline in the *Echo* that night. WOMEN TAKE TO THE TREES: THE BIRDS DEFY THE FELLERS added a bright spark of a sub-editor. Miss Bugle bought the late edition on her way home after school and read the story over high tea on a tray.

'Magnificent,' she said out loud to her boiled egg. 'Ye cannot serve God and Mammon,' she continued, slicing the top off excitedly. 'Good gracious me.' She had come to a new paragraph. *'The leaders of the campaign to save Swain's Chard Woods and Hill are three former Tarminster High School girls, Jennifer Cornwood, Ann Dangerfield and Philippa Foster. Jennifer, until recently a kitchen-worker at the Three Bells in Tarminster, said, "This is about something more important than money. This is about the human spirit."* 'Splendid, splendid,' said Miss Bugle, spilling egg-yolk down her cardigan.

By the time Miss Bugle reached the entrance to the woods, it was seven o'clock in the evening and the felling party had given up for the day and gone home. They would be back again tomorrow, they had promised. Most of the women had gone too, to cook supper for their families and to put their children to bed, but the tents were still there and so were Ann and Philippa and Jenny and Marge. So was Lady Hennessey and poor PC Coles who had been left on guard. Joan had taken Jane home to bath her and Alice and Phyllis had brought up supplies of food and drink. 'Cup of tea, Harold?' they had said, but PC Coles, who was quite weak from hunger and thirst and confusion, thought he had better refuse.

Miss Bugle climbed out of the Austin Seven. 'I had to come and see you, girls,' she panted, and her glasses glittered in the evening sun. 'I think it's magnificent, perfectly magnificent, what you are doing. Man simply *cannot* live by bread alone...' They offered her a hunk of bread and cheese and she accepted it with alacrity. As night fell and the women settled into their tents for the second night, Miss Bugle drove back to her cottage to prepare her next morning's Assembly and Lady Hennessey mounted her bike to return to the Manor.

'I'll be back in the morning,' she promised the women. 'Oh dear, Mr Coles,' she added. 'You can't possibly stay out here all night, you'll catch pneumonia. We're still getting frosts, even if it is May.'

PC Coles looked distraught. He was not as young as he used to be and he dreaded pneumonia.

'Look here,' said Lady Hennessey. 'You know and I know that these gels won't do any harm. You go off home to bed and we won't say anything.'

He looked at her in speechless gratitude. After all, she was the Lady of the Manor and a Justice of the Peace. He mounted his bike and wobbled home to climb thankfully into bed beside Mrs Coles. What a good thing he had married her instead of Phyllis, he thought. That Phyllis had turned into quite a wildcat. She would never have done for a policeman's wife...

At four o'clock in the morning, two vanloads of women arrived at the entrance to the woods.

Chapter Forty-Two

By the time the tree-felling party arrived in its own vans with its chainsaws and helmets next morning, every single marked and climbable tree was inhabited by a wild woman. All through the dawn they had kept on coming, from the villages and farms, on foot, by bicycle, in cars, on horseback. More policemen had been drafted in and now they stood around in awkward groups, gazing up into the branches. 'Bloody hell,' said one of them, 'that's my wife up there.'

The continued presence of Lady Hennessey, who was back in position on her very low branch, was a great embarrassment to the Authorities who did not like to be rude to her. And so they stood around muttering to each other, occasionally calling to the roosting women through loudhailers while they breathed in the scent of the earth and the bluebells and the moss and the ferns.

It was time for Morning Assembly. The girls of Tarminster High filed into the hall, class by class and sang the opening hymn; 'Morning has broken, Like the first morning.' Miss Bugle moved to the lectern, opened the Bible and read, '"No man can serve two masters, for either he will love the one and hate the other, or else he will hold to the one and despise the other. Ye cannot serve God and Mammon".'

'What's Mammon?' whispered someone in 4A to her neighbour. 'I thought it was a joint of bacon,' the neighbour whispered back and they both shook with suppressed giggles.

'"Ye cannot serve God and Mammon,"' repeated Miss Bugle. 'Mammon is the god of greed, the god of money, the god of materialism and profit who leads us to pursue material wealth at the cost of everything else. Mammon is the god who despises the things of the spirit. No, ye cannot serve God and Mammon. You must choose.' She gazed at them with her glittering eye.

'Cod or gammon, you must choose,' whispered the 4A wit and a whole row of High School girls shook with silent laughter.

Miss Bugle moved on. '"It is easier for a camel to pass through the needle's eye than for a rich man to enter the Kingdom of Heaven."' She smiled at her girls and hitched her shoulder strap. 'It is easy to recognise Mammon,' she said, 'but it is not always easy to recognise God. I saw Him once, when I was fourteen, in a row of cabbages. And I saw Him again, yesterday, when a flock of wild women climbed some trees and defied the god called Mammon.'

'Batty as hell, poor old thing,' said 4A as Miss Freeman played the opening bars of *Hills of the North, Rejoice*, for the end of Assembly.

At half-past nine, as the High School settled into its first lesson, Mr Crawford arrived at the entrance to Swain's Chard Woods. He borrowed a loudhailer from one of the policemen and addressed his workers angrily. 'If you do not come down immediately and return to work, you can all collect your cards tomorrow morning.'

There was a frightened fluttering in the branches and some cries of distress. Then Marlene Wheeler called down, 'You can't scare us, Mr Crawford. You don't own us or our lives any more. If you sack us, your factory's finished. There's not a woman in Tarminster would work for you if you did that.'

The morning wore on. Blackbirds and thrushes sang and the sun grew stronger. It warmed a secret hollow out on the open hillside and the bee orchid felt its touch and swelled cautiously into flower. The women kept on coming to the woods, busloads of them, so that whenever anybody had to leave her tree to go to the shops or to peel the vegetables for the evening meal, there was always someone else to take her place.

Yvonne Pratt put the *Closed* sign up on the Espresso bar door and caught the Swain's Chard bus. Mary Cornwood and

278

her new baby climbed aboard and sat behind her. Swain's Chard grandmothers suddenly remembered how they used to climb trees fifty years before, and took it in turns to walk to the woods with sandwiches and flasks of tea; reporters and television cameras and men with tape recorders and fluffy microphones arrived and so did the Managing Director of the Contracting Company. He had had to leave an urgent meeting in Basingstoke and he was not happy.

'This is outrageous. You must do something,' he snapped at the Sergeant. 'This delay is costing us thousands.'

'And the thousands you would make will cost us our heritage, my good man,' said Lady Hennessey from her tree in her most magisterial voice.

'Do something,' squawked the Managing Director again. 'Get that silly old bat out of that tree. She's only just off the ground.' He advanced upon Lady Hennessey but was restrained by the Sergeant.

'I can't do that, sir,' whispered the Sergeant, going very red indeed. 'That's Lady Hennessey. She's the Lady of the Manor. She's the local Magistrate.'

A heavy cloud lumbered across the sun and a sudden rain shower fell upon them all. 'That'll fetch 'em down,' said Mr Crawford, but the women laughed as the rain drenched their hair and ran down their faces.

'Heel-toe, heel-toe, gallop gallop gallop gallop,' cried Tit Willow as the rain kept 4A in from rounders and put the *Dashing White Sergeant* onto the record player. When the lesson was over and the girls had draped their damp towels over the pipes in the steaming Towel Room, Miss Willow walked down the corridor towards the staffroom. Little Mr Whittaker came tripping along towards her, carrying his violin case. He blushed when he saw her.

'Ah, Miss Willow,' he said, and stopped.

'Yes?' said Miss Willow, encouragingly.

'I was wondering whether you might care to take tea with me this afternoon?' It had come at last, the invitation for which she had waited for so many years.

'I'm terribly sorry, Mr Whittaker, but I'm afraid that I can't. There's something very important that I've got to do.' He looked so disappointed that she felt she owed him an explanation. 'I'm climbing a tree in Swain's Chard Wood after school this afternoon,' she said, and walked into the staffroom.

Madge Foster had been ringing Joan's telephone number for two days now without getting any answer. At half-past ten on the second day of what was now being called in the Press THE REVOLUTION OF THE ROOSTERS, Norman parked angrily in the driveway. 'I need a cup of coffee,' he said curtly and Madge put the percolator on. She knew what the matter was. 'I'm absolutely furious with Philippa,' he had exclaimed the night before. 'She's nothing but a rabble-rouser. I'm ashamed of her.'

Madge had never seen him so angry before and it was a relief that Philippa was sleeping in the tent. Madge herself had not slept since the Revolution had begun; her family was breaking up in front of her and she felt helpless. She was very worried about Norman's blood pressure too. What on earth would they do if he had a stroke or a heart attack or something and was unable to work any more?

She looked at him, all red-faced and pop-eyed and shining with rage and anxiety, and suddenly she thought, Is it worth it? A phrase came into her head as the water boiled and bubbled through the percolator; she must have heard it a hundred times in church without taking any particular notice of it. 'Consider the lilies of the field,' it said quietly, 'Consider the lilies of the field, how they grow; they toil not, neither do they spin.'

She wanted very much to say it to Norman, but she was afraid that he would become apoplectic if she did, so she poured him a cup of coffee instead and tried not to listen to him being angry with someone on the phone in the hall. The words would not go out of her head. '*Consider the lilies of the field*,' they kept on whispering until, in the end, she had to go out of the house and up the lane to consider them.

Little, bright, forget-me-not-blue butterflies scurried and trembled in the air around her head as she walked. She saw a black and red moth clinging damply to a plantain stem, drying out from its hatching, waiting for the sun to stiffen its wings until they were strong enough to fly. A wren shouted at her with its huge and tinny voice from a hawthorn bush and there were still cowslips along the sides of the lane. Vetch and convolvulus and dog roses tangled together over the hawthorns.

Madge walked on until she came to the corner where the lane joined the main road to Tarminster. She turned right towards the entrance to the woods and she saw the tents and heard the laughter and the voices. She thought of poor Norman, rushing and spluttering and worried and important, and she saw Joan and Lady Hennessey and Phyllis Cornwood drinking tea out of plastic cups. She saw other men like Norman; Mr Crawford and the Managing Director of the Contracting Company, rich, important, successful, angry men waving loudhailers and talking to reporters. A forget-me-not-blue butterfly perched briefly on the bald head of one of them.

Then Madge Foster saw very clearly what she wanted to do and she walked towards the trees and hitched her summer skirt into her pants. Joan did not see her at first because her attention had been caught by a funeral procession winding its slow way down towards the village and the church. Joan smiled at the coffin and thought, I've done it, my splendid thing – the thing I can be really proud of. And when my coffin rides down through the village, they'll say, 'There she goes, old Joan Dangerfield – you know, one of the ones who helped to save the woods,' and she began to climb her tree. Phyllis Cornwood, waving to her from four trees away heard, for the first time in thirty-seven years, the first line of a poem wriggle sideways into the corner of her mind.

Thirty feet above them and still the best climber in the village, Jenny Cornwood swung her legs and smiled at the sky. It's all right, she said to herself, over and over again. It's all right, it's all right, it's all right. The sun shone brightly as ever it had done, the sound of the wind in the leaves sang in her head again and the touch of the rough bark welcomed her back.

At half-past four, an old Austin Seven, a green MG and a very battered bicycle climbed the hill out of Tarminster and parked against the drystone wall near the gates of the wood. Miss Bugle, Miss Freeman and Miss Cameron got out and Miss Willow dismounted and they all advanced upon the trees. Miss Cameron had long, thin arms and legs and she clung to a tall tree like some exotic lizard. Miss Freeman and Miss

Willow surprised themselves by reaching branches at least five feet above ground level. Miss Bugle, being of mature years and build and with a certain puffiness about the ankles, stayed lower than the others. She kept one foot firmly on the ground and hooked the other into a forked notch a little way above it.

Out on the hill, the bee orchid plumped its body up into the sun.

The ghost of God, lightly disguised as a Cabbage White Butterfly, fluttered around Miss Bugle's head and rested for a moment on the rim of her glasses. She recognised Him at once and grinned and hitched her shoulder strap.

The Cabbage White flew on and out into the sunlight of the hill.

Epilogue

April, 1997

Friday Night

Ann Dangerfield, aged fifty-four, free woman and singer-song-writer of some note within a thirty-mile radius of Tarminster, kicked off her ridiculously high-heeled shoes, poured herself a whisky and flopped into an armchair in front of the hotel telly. Tonight she was the singer with the band at a middle-aged wedding party. She had done her first spot and now it was half-time. She pressed the zapper for the *Ten O'clock News*.

A dozen or so flimsy tents crouched in the wind and the rain on a bare hillside while young men and women in woolly hats and oilskins clung to trees below the hill. The television cameras pointed down hurriedly-dug tunnels to barricaded doors and then moved up into the treetops where the hatted children had lashed themselves with ropes and handcuffs to trunks and branches.

Ann stared, listening to the excited chatter of the television reporter and the stern voice of a man in a metal hat who spoke through a megaphone, ordering the protestors to stop protesting and behave in a responsible manner.

The Assistant Manager of the hotel stuck his head through the door. 'Five minutes, please, Miss Dangerfield.' A police-man climbed a tree and began to untie the ropes that held a young man to its trunk. The camera came in for a close-up of the young man's face.

Ann drank her whisky and slid her feet into the impossible shoes. It was time to go back and perform.

283

The wedding party applauded enthusiastically as the Sensational Ann Dangerfield appeared, wearing a tight black dress that was not so very different from the one she had worn that first night in the Three Bells. Her voice was better now, she knew. It was richer, deeper, stronger, more flexible than it had been in its twenties. 'The first time ever I saw your face...' she sang, and in her mind's eye, Ann saw the face of the young man as the policeman climbed the tree towards him.

Later that night, she drove home along the link road that now joined Swain's Chard to Tarminster and Honeyford. The telephone began to ring as she let herself in through her front door. It was Jane, calling from London.

'Hello, Mum. Have you been out singing?'

'Yes.'

'I guessed you were. I've been trying to get you all evening.'

'Is anything the matter?'

Jane laughed. 'No, everything's brilliant. That's why I'm ringing. I'm with this fantastic new man and I really want to show you to each other. Can I bring him home tomorrow?'

Ann opened her mouth to say, 'Yes, of course – how wonderful! What's his name? What does he do?' when the picture of the tents in the rain and the young men and women tying themselves to the trees flew back into her head again.

'Oh darling, I'm really sorry. Not this weekend. Any other weekend... I'm terribly sorry, really sorry. But there's something I've got to do. Please don't be hurt. I'll meet him soon, I promise. But there's something I've got to do.'

Friday afternoon

Dr Jennifer Cornwood Ph.D, aged fifty-three, smiled at 4A and told them to put away their pencils and rulers. Chattering, 4A did as they were told and pushed the Biology lab stools back under the benches. 'Good afternoon, 4A,' said Jenny. 'See you on Monday. Have a nice weekend.'

'Same to you, Miss Cornwood,' said 4A.

'She's a dear old thing, isn't she?' said a girl called Emily to her friend Charlotte. 'I bet she used to be pretty when she was young.'

'I wonder why she never got married?' whispered Charlotte.

Dr Jenny Cornwood drove home to her cottage said hello to

her horse and made herself a cup of tea. She cut two slices of her mother's fruit cake and gave one to the horse, who had followed her into the kitchen. Thank goodness it was Friday and she need not mark the books tonight. She smiled luxuriously, sat down and stretched her legs out in front of her. She would boil an egg later and eat it in front of the *Six O'clock News*.

A dozen or so flimsy tents crouched in the wind and the rain on a bare hillside. Jenny Cornwood put down her tray and turned the sound up. 'It is time to stop this nonsense and behave in a responsible manner,' said the man in the metal hat through his megaphone.

Jenny frowned.

Saturday night

Mrs Jeremy Carruthers, aka and née Philippa Foster, walked off the stage at the end of the play to loud applause. She sat in her dressing room, wiping off her make-up and listening to the delighted chatter coming from the corridor. Somebody knocked on the door and then came into the room.

'Hello, Philippa,' said Vivian Day and kissed her. 'Well. Many, many congratulations, my dearest Philippa. You were magnificent.'

Philippa laughed. 'Thank you, Vivian. And thank you again for taking the risk with me after all these years.'

Vivian Day shook his head. 'It was never a risk. I knew from the first minute I auditioned you – where on earth was it?'

'The Theatre Royal, Hamilton.'

Vivian Day clutched his head in mock despair. 'Dear God, how could I possibly forget? And speaking of God, I suppose you'll be scurrying back to the Vicarage now it's all over?'

'Too right I will.' Philippa smeared another dollop of cleansing cream over her face. 'But I do mean it, Vivian. It was wonderful to get the chance to come back and do this season with you. To know I still belong, that I'm not past it.'

'You'll never be past it. But doesn't he mind – your Vicar?'

Philippa smiled. 'Jeremy? He's delighted. He's been up to see the play three times.'

She caught the train back home that night and Jeremy was waiting to meet her at the station. They watched the late-night news together.

A dozen or so flimsy tents crouched in the wind and the rain on a bare hillside. The camera focused on a young man who had handcuffed himself to a tree at the bottom of the hill. Then it swung round to pick up two middle-aged women protestors. One, despite her fifty-three years, had climbed to the top of an oak and was sitting astride a branch, swinging her legs and laughing at a young policeman who was trying to persuade her to come down. The other clung like a stick insect to the trunk of a beech tree.

'Good Lord,' said Mrs Jeremy Carruthers. 'Jeremy darling, don't be hurt, but I've got to go away again tomorrow morning. There's something absolutely vital I've got to do.'

Sunday morning
Jenny Cornwood swung her legs from her high branch and grinned down at Ann Dangerfield, who still clung to her beech tree. Philippa Foster shoved her boot into a low fork and began to climb.

The rain stopped and a cabbage-white butterfly flew out into the sunshine on the hillside.

BONDED
Chrissa Mills

The sixties didn't swing for everybody...

Shy, sweet-natured Roberta opts for husband, home and child, and is content to let the brash decade pass her by.

Julia is a true child of her times: a beautiful, adventurous free spirit, totally confident of her power over the opposite sex.

While Roberta settles into domesticity in Suffolk, Julia, a talented designer, makes a success of her boutique on the ultra-fashionable King's Road. But achieving your dreams isn't always enough, and both sisters come to envy what the other has. Growing up at odds with each other, neither girl places much reliance on the family tie, or thinks of turning to her sister for comfort. But life can take some strange twists, and time can forge bonds stronger than steel ...

BUMPS

The bestselling novel by

Zoë Barnes

Bump number one… Just when Taz Norton's life is on a smooth upward glide – youngest sales manager at a flagship department store, own flat, cat and vintage motorbike – her lover leaves her for her ex-best friend.

Bump number two… is finding out she is pregnant the same day she is asked to handle the biggest store promotion in the company's history.

Bump number three… is the one in front of her. Goodbye toes and glamour, hello heartburn, morning sickness and support tights.

Typically, Taz decides to be Superwoman. No one is going to tell her she can't get to the top and be a single mum as well. But no one told her it was going to be so damned hard…

Fresh, funny and deadly accurate – *Bumps* is the essential career girl's guide to babies!

"A brilliant sense of comic timing; the ability to create believable characters and a touching sense of the trickiness of family relationships ... an enjoyable and moving read"   *Daily Mail*

"An entertaining and light-hearted story of parenthood"

Observer

HITCHED

The bestselling new novel by
Zoë Barnes

Hitch number one ... A quick jaunt to the registry office and off to the pub with a few friends to celebrate. That's all Gemma wants for her wedding to Rory. But then the parents hear the news.

Hitch number two ... Suddenly her little wedding is hijacked and turned into a Hollywood-style extravaganza. Before she knows what's hit her, Gemma is stampeded into yards of frothing tulle, fork buffets for five hundred, kilted page boys and an all-inclusive honeymoon in the Maldives ...

Hitch number three ... And while the dress may be a perfect fit, Gemma and Rory's relationship is coming apart at the seams ...

An irresistible look at wedding fever from the bestselling author of *Bumps*.

"An enjoyable and moving read ... funny and likeable novel"
Maeve Haran, Daily Mail

"Funny and eye-opening"   *Sunday Post*

"An entertaining and light-hearted story"   *The Observer*

THE COUNT

A Modern Fairytale

Helena Dela

Once upon a time...

...a young widow called Ella agreed to marry a handsome German Count and provide him with an heir. In return, she would live in a fabulous castle, have access to his enormous wealth and almost certainly – under the terms of the family curse – die within a year.

It couldn't happen today though, could it? Not to a modern girl at the end of our century. Because stuff like that is for fairytales – like ghosts, and curses. And falling in love ...

THE COUNT is Helena Dela's fabulously funny debut novel – a must for closet romantics everywhere!

"Young, fresh, compulsive, original and fun..."

The Bookseller

THE LONG MIDNIGHT OF BARNEY THOMSON

The hilariously funny debut novel by

Douglas Lindsay

Black humour. Bloody murder. And no kissing.

Barney has never had the knack of talking drivel to complete strangers, and it irks him. Certainly, he can talk about the weather with the best of them, but when it comes to uncompromising, asinine bollocks, he just doesn't have it ...

Barney Thomson's success as a barber is limited. It's not just that he's crap at cutting hair (and he is); it's because he has no blather. He hates football for one thing. He hates most people. He hates his colleagues most of all, and the glib confidence with which they can discuss Florence Nightingale's sexuality or the ongoing plight of Partick Thistle.

But a serial killer is spreading terror throughout the city. The police are baffled. And for one sad little Glasgow barber, life is about to get seriously strange ...

"All good fun, with a surprising twist"   *The Bookseller*

SCHRÖDINGER'S BABY
H.R. McGregor

Billy the lad, nihilistic Petruchio, hippy Chris, rational Juliet, Kerry the drama queen. A typical student house in Glasgow: cigarettes and alcohol, soft drugs, carefully casual sex and showing off. Until Juliet finds a dead body at their digs. And then it disappears.

The quantum theory of Schrödinger's Cat has always appealed to Juliet's scientific mind. Polar opposites can co-exist simultaneously - life and death, black and white, good and evil. And as Juliet gets more deeply involved in Kerry's fantasies, another division begins to obsess her - that between lies and truth. Because Kerry inhabits a world of lies, and rational, logical Juliet has to question the evidence of her senses, not to mention her sanity ... and quantum theory ...

"frighteningly confident first novel"   *Daily Telegraph*

"A gripping mystery and a sharp, ironic look at student life."
                                                Publishing News

"A very funny book that has helped me along the road to understanding the intricacies of quantum theory more than any text book I have read. A fabulous novel that may or may not actually exist until you open the cover"

                                                New Insight